The Best of
K^{The}enyon Review

The Best of
K̶e̶n̶y̶o̶n̶ ̶R̶e̶v̶i̶e̶w̶
The Kenyon Review

editor David H. Lynn

introduction by Joyce Carol Oates

SOURCEBOOKS LANDMARK™
AN IMPRINT OF SOURCEBOOKS, INC.®
NAPERVILLE, ILLINOIS

Published by Sourcebooks, Inc.
P.O. Box 4410, Naperville, Illinois 60567-4410
(630) 961-3900
FAX: (630) 961-2168
www.sourcebooks.com

Library of Congress Cataloging-in-Publication Data

The best of the Kenyon review : poetry, stories, and essays / edited by David
   Lynn.
p. cm.
ISBN 1-4022-0035-8 (alk. paper)
1. American literature—20th century. I. Lynn, David (David H.) II. Kenyon
review (Gambier, Ohio : 1939)
PS535.5.B498 2003
810.8'005—dc21

2003004791

Printed and bound in the United States of America
BG 10 9 8 7 6 5 4 3 2 1

Acknowledgments

Without the leadership and energy of Matthew Winkler, editor in chief of Bloomberg News and chair of the Kenyon Review Board of Trustees, this book would never have come about. The hard work, loyalty, and excellence of the editors and staff of *The Kenyon Review* are its greatest strength. My thanks, therefore, to David Baker, John Kinsella, and Nancy Zafris; to Doris Jean Dilts, Meg Galipault, Jenny Hedden, Ellen Sheffield, and Cy Wainscott. And special thanks to Andy Grace who authored the biographies in this volume and to Jen Underwood for editing them.

Table of Contents

Preface

An Anthology That Embraces
the Past and Looks to the Future

by David H. Lynn

Assembling a book such as this is an exciting and, for an editor of a thriving magazine, a rather daunting project. The stories, poems, and essays contained here, drawn from across more than sixty years, set a high standard. But it's the very striving to meet or even exceed that standard that's such a challenge, that's such fun. And as Joyce Carol Oates will so generously point out in her introduction, while the ultimate standard of literary excellence has remained constant across the decades, each generation articulates itself in remarkably different ways. Our job today remains to seek out, to nurture, to bring into print those authors who will be setting standards for decades to come.

I am often asked what precisely I am looking for as I forage through the thousands upon thousands of unsolicited submissions that arrive every year in deep mail buckets for *The Kenyon Review*. What glint of gold does my hand snatch up in exultation? Ah, if only it were a matter of carats or a straightforward recipe. A flip answer, which contains a truth as well, is that like the judge defining pornography, I know a great poem, short story, or essay when I see it.

A more serious response, however, involves the continuing mission of *The Kenyon Review* as well as a personal philosophy about the nature of art. KR embraces the eclectic. We are not bound by current fashion or the aesthetic ideology of any one school or agenda. We are neither formalists nor anti-, neither bound solely to minimalism, realism, nor experimentalism. Simply put, we are in perpetual quest of superb writing.

Our mission also includes the publishing of new voices—of talented younger writers, as well as those from many communities across the nation and around the world—along with those award-winning authors whom we have published for years.

Discovering the extraordinary compels us to read each and every unsolicited submission that arrives in those mail tubs. No small challenge for our staff and a handful of dedicated volunteers at a liberal arts college. It's hard. It's often mind-numbing work. But what an incredible joy to read a first paragraph or a stanza and feel the rush of excitement: this, this manuscript in my hands, it's the real thing!

But doesn't that beg the question? What's the real thing? First, I believe that all successful art must contain two essential elements: surprise and delight. If, for example, a reader can anticipate each move the author will make, then why keep reading? There's no suspense, merely the conventional or stale. Indeed, one of the most remarkable elements of truly great art is the perpetual sense of surprise one experiences with each reading or re-reading of a superb poem. How exhilarating to discover, time after time, something new in a story we know so well and perhaps even something new about ourselves.

Delight is a delightfully capacious category. Whether we experience deep and sober insight, or hilarious recognition, or a breathless amazement at what an author accomplishes before us and with us, our emotional being as well as our intellect will be engaged, at least in the art that interests me and that I publish.

I am also, always, searching for mastery of the craft. Truly, it's the sine quo non of literary excellence. With each word and phrase, with each image or sound, writers must demonstrate authority. That is, they must be in total control of the language they employ. Although older authors who have honed their skills for many years may be capable of sophisticated as well as subtle strategies, young virtuosi surprise and delight us all the time with their control, their energy and insight. Often, on the other hand, a misstep in the first paragraph or stanza, a poorly chosen metaphor, a sloppy or ragged sentence, is enough to tell me that this piece won't be right for our pages. Is that unduly harsh? Perhaps. But I can't imagine any other standard.

The Best of The Kenyon Review is but a snapshot. It contains only a small sample of the many wonders our archives hold. It also demonstrates the vitality of this ongoing project. Each issue of *The Kenyon Review* boasts new stories, poems, and essays that may belong in the next version of this anthology.

The Kenyon Review has also become more than a print magazine. We now offer two fine summer writing programs, one for high school students and one for adults. Our Student Associate program offers marvelous opportunities at Kenyon College.

Individuals who believe in the importance of *KR* to the nation's literary culture now serve on our distinguished Board of Trustees. They have created an endowment fund to ensure the financial stability of *The Kenyon Review*, and they also now present the Kenyon Review Award for Literary Achievement annually at a gala dinner in New York.

As you enjoy this extraordinary anthology, I hope you will drop me a note or an email message to share your thoughts. And I invite you to visit kenyonreview.org to learn more about the nation's most honored literary magazine.

—David H. Lynn, Editor

Introduction

by Joyce Carol Oates

Founded in 1939 at Kenyon College in Gambier, Ohio, by the poet-critic John Crowe Ransom, *The Kenyon Review* was initially known as a "little magazine" associated with the Southern Agrarians (Allen Tate, John Crowe Ransom) and with the formalist New Criticism at its rigorous close-readings of literary texts detached from historical and biographical contexts. Within a few years, however, under Ransom's ambitious editorship, *The Kenyon Review* emerged as a major literary journal publishing the very best and newest—what we now call "cutting-edge"—fiction and poetry, as well as literary criticism by W.H. Auden, Cleanth Brooks, William Empson, Northrup Frye, and F.O. Matthiessen among others. By the 1950s, *The Kenyon Review* had defined itself as a worthy successor to such legendary American "little magazines" as the Dial (1920–29) and *The Little Review* (1914–21); only *Poetry: A Magazine of Verse* (founded in 1912) survives from that era of literary adventure and experimentation. In the 1940s and 1950s, *The Kenyon Review* was perhaps the most revered and influential literary magazine in America, along with the aggressively polemical *Partisan Review*, founded in the 1930s with an initially Marxist-revolutionary agenda. And over the decades, only *Paris Review*, *Antaeus*, and the more recent *Conjunctions* bear comparison with *The Kenyon Review* as "little magazines" of historic distinction.

The Kenyon Review was temporarily discontinued in 1969, to be vigorously revived in 1979 under the co-editorship of Ronald Sharp and Frederick Turner, of the English faculty at Kenyon College. Since that time, editors have included the poets T.R. Hummer (1988–89) and Marilyn

Hacker (1990–94); the current editor, David H. Lynn, has overseen the development of *The Kenyon Review* as a publication of international scope, while continuing to publish imaginative and critical work of high merit. What is perhaps the most exciting about *The Kenyon Review*, from a reader's perspective, is its unpredictability: in its stylishly designed pages you will find "traditional" and "innovative" writing—fiction, poetry, essays, criticism unencumbered by political or aesthetic bias.

Given the history of the review, assembling *The Best of The Kenyon Review* could not have been an easy task. This splendidly multifarious gathering of fiction, poetry, and essays contains work by numerous contributors whom one might expect, among them Peter Taylor, Flannery O'Connor, Robert Lowell, Randall Jarrell, Delmore Schwartz, James Dickey, Marianne Moore, and yet a nearly equal number of surprises: Samuel Beckett? Sylvia Plath? Italo Calvino? F. Scott Fitzgerald? Vladimir Nabokov? Julio Cortázar? Thomas Pynchon? Woody Allen? Though no obvious common thread links contributors to *The Best of The Kenyon Review*, editor David H. Lynn has chosen with taste and an eye for the exemplary. Within *The Best of The Kenyon Review* covers we move from the formally elegant, vatic poetry of early Robert Lowell and Randall Jarrell to the edgy contemporary voices of Philip Levine, Yusef Komunyakaa, and the Irish poet Eavan Boland ("Write us out of the poem. Make us human / in cadences of change and mortal pain / and words we can grow old and die in"); perhaps most dramatically, we move from the voice of W.H. Auden at his most oracular, in the classic essay "Yeats as an Example" ("The duty of the present is neither to copy nor to deny the past but to resurrect it") to the provocative contemporary voice of the cultural critic Gerald Early in "The Black Intellectual and the Sport of Prizefighting" with its frank analysis of race and culture and its bold pronouncements ("One could argue that the three most important black figures in twentieth-century American culture were prizefighters: Jack Johnson, Joe Louis, and Muhammad Ali"). No criticism is intended of *The Kenyon Review's* distinguished founding editor by suggesting that an essay like Gerald Early's, in which gradations of blackness in iconic black boxers are studied with the scrupulosity of a New Critic dissecting a poem by John Donne, would not have been likely to be published in the review's early years.

Among the splendid gathering of short stories are such classics of the genre as Flannery O'Connor's "The Life You Save May Be Your Own," with its elaborate allegorical Christian symbolism bizarrely adjoined to a rural

Georgia variant of the traveling salesman joke; one of Peter Taylor's finest and most characteristic stories, "Venus, Cupid, Folly, and Time," itself an inspired tall tale of an old, inbred genteel mid-South on the verge of cultural extinction; and Thomas Pynchon's "Entropy," a hippie-American variant of Samuel Beckett's cosmic pessimism ("He found himself, in short, restated Gibbs's prediction in social terms, and envisioned a heat-death for his culture in which ideas, like heat-energy, would no longer be transferred, since each point in it would ultimately have the same quantity of energy; and intellectual motion would, accordingly, cease"). The poems range from vintage Beckett in "A Piece of Monologue" ("At suck first fiasco. With the first totters. From mammy to nanny and back. All the way. Bandied back and forth. So ghastly grinning on. From funeral to funeral. To now") to vintage Sylvia Plath in the mournful, eloquent dirge "The Beekeeper's Daughter" ("Father, bridegroom, in this Easter egg / Under the coronal of sugar roses / The queen bee marries the winter of your year"). There is quintessential Dylan Thomas in "Poem" ("If my bunched monkey coming is cruel / Rage me back to the making house"), and there is William Carlos Williams in an atypical mode. There is Wallace Stevens's famous "The Auroras of Autumn" with its reiterated refrain "Farewell to an idea..." and there is one of James Wright's most powerful poems, "All the Beautiful are Blameless," with its elegiac final lines:

> But the dead have no names, they lie so still,
> And all the beautiful are blameless now.

The Best of The Kenyon Review is a remarkable gathering of twentieth-century literary riches.

—Joyce Carol Oates

Randall Jarrell

Randall Jarrell was born in Nashville, Tennessee, in 1914. He moved with his parents to Los Angeles soon after, then returned to Nashville with his mother after his parents divorced. Jarrell earned both his B.A. and M.A. from Vanderbilt University, where he found a mentor in *The Kenyon Review*–founder John Crowe Ransom. When Ransom accepted a position at Kenyon College, Jarrell joined him as an assistant, teaching in the English department. At Kenyon, Jarrell met Robert Lowell and Peter Taylor, with whom he would hold longstanding friendships. His first book of poems, *Blood for a Stranger*, came out in 1942, the same year Jarrell entered the U.S. Air Force. His military experience provided him material for his next two books, *Little Friend, Little Friend* (1945) and *Losses* (1948). Jarrell's reputation as a poet was only exceeded by his reputation as a brilliant, engaging, and sometimes biting critic. In 1952, he took a position at the University of North Carolina at Greensboro, where he would remain for the rest of his life. After completing *The Lost World*, which won him the National Book Award in 1965, Jarrell became mentally ill, eventually leading to an attempted suicide. While recovering at a hospital, he went walking at dusk on a nearby highway and was struck by a car and killed immediately. The coroner's verdict was accidental death, although the circumstances will never be entirely clear. What is clear is that Jarrell remains a highly respected poet and is regarded as the pre-eminent critic of his generation.

The Winter's Tale *(1939)*

by Randall Jarrell

The storm rehearses through the bewildered fields
Its general logic; the contorted or dispassionate
Faces work out their incredulity, or stammer
The mistaking sentences. Night falls. In the lit
Schoolroom the hothouse guests are crammed
With their elaborate ignorance, repeat
The glib and estranged responses of the dead
To the professor's nod. The urgent galleries
Converge in anticipation on the halls
Where at announced hours the beauty,
Able, and Laughable commence patiently
The permanent recital of their aptitudes:
The song of the world. To the wicked and furred,
The naked and curious, the instruments proffer
Their partial and excessive knowledge; here in the suites,
Among the grains, the contraceptives and textiles,
Or inside the board cave lined with newspapers
Where in one thoroughly used room are initiated,
Persevered in, and annihilated, the forbidding ranges
Of the bewildered and extravagant responses of the cell;
Among all the inexhaustible variations—of milieu,
Of compensation and excess—the waltz-theme shudders,
Frivolous, inexorable, the inadequate and conclusive
Sentence of our genius.
Along the advertisements the blisses flicker,
Partial as morphine, the terminal moraine
Of sheeted continents, a calendar of woe.

We who have possessed the world
As efficiently as a new virus; who classified the races,
Species, and cultures of the world as scrub
To be cleared, stupidity to be liquidated, matter
To be assimilated into the system of our destruction;
Are finding how quickly the resistance of our hosts
Is built up—can think, "Tomorrow we may be remembered

As a technologist's nightmare, the megalomaniacs
Who presented to posterity as their justification
The best armies that the world ever saw."
Who made virtue and poetry and understanding
The prohibited reserves of the expert, of workers
Specialized as the ant-soldier; and who turned from their difficult
Versions to the degenerate myth, the cruelties
So incredible and habitual they seemed escapes.

Yet, through our night, just as before,
The discharged thief stumbles, nevertheless
Weeps at its crystals, feels at the winter's
Tale the familiar and powerful delight;
The child owns the snow-man; the skier
Hesitant along the stormy crest, or wrenching
His turn from the bluff's crust, to glide
Down the stony hillside past the robbers' hut
To the house of the typhoid-carrier; the understanding
Imperturbable in their neglect, concentrating
In obscure lodgings the impatient genius
That informs all the breasts; the few who keep
By lack or obstinacy scraps of the romantic
And immediately adequate world of the past—the
Strangers with a stranger's inflections, the broken
And unlovely English of the unborn world:

All, all, this winter night
Are weak, are emptying fast. Tomorrow puffs
From its iron centers into the moonlight, men move masked
Through streets abrupt with excavations, the explosive triumphs
Of a new architecture: the twelve-floor dumps
Of smashed stone starred with limbs, the monumental
Tombs of a whole age. A whole economy;
The fiascoes of the metaphysician, a theology's disasters,
The substitutes of the geometer for existence, the observation
Of peas and galaxies—the impatient fictions
Of the interminable and euphuist's metaphor exploding
Into use, into breath, into terror; the millennia

Of patience, of skills, of understanding, the centuries
Of terms crystallizing into weapons, the privative
And endless means, the catastrophic
Magnificence of paranoia; are elaborated into
A few bodies in the torn-up street.
The survivor poking in the ruins with a stick
Finds only portions of his friends. In this universe
Of discourse the shameless and witless facility
Of such a conclusion is normal, and no one thinks:
"What came before this was worse. Expected so long,
Arrived at last, tomorrow is death."

From the disintegrating bomber, the mercenary
Who has sown without hatred or understanding
The shells of the absolute world that flowers
In the confused air of the dying city
Plunges for his instant of incandescence, acquiesces
In our death and his own, and welcomes
The fall of the western hegemonies.

Federico Garcia Lorca

Federico Garcia Lorca was born in 1898, in Fuente Vaqueros, a village near Granada, in Andalusia, Spain. His family moved to Granada in 1908, and, after secondary school, he attended Sacred Heart University where he took up law. His first book of prose, *Impresiones y Viajes,* was published in 1919. That same year Garcia Lorca left the university and moved to Madrid, where he would spend the next fifteen years. In 1921, *Libro de Poemas,* Garcia Lorca's first book of poetry, was published, but his real breakthrough as a poet came with the release of *Romancero Gitano (The Gypsy Ballads),* which brought him far-reaching renown. In 1929, Garcia Lorca famously visited New York and fell in love with Harlem. He returned to Spain in 1930 and was appointed artistic director of "La Barraca," a traveling theater company, getting several of his own plays produced. In 1936, civil war broke out in Spain. Toward the end of July, he was arrested by Franquist soldiers. A few days later he was executed on the roadside outside Viznar. His books were burned in Granada's Plaza del Carmen and were soon banned from Franco's Spain. No one knows the exact location of Garcia Lorca's grave. He posthumously published *Lament for the Death of a Bullfighter and Other Poems, Poet in New York,* and *Selected Poems.* His poem "The Interrupted Concert" was also published posthumously in *The Kenyon Review* in 1939. Garcia Lorca is remembered as possibly the most important Spanish poet and dramatist of the twentieth century.

The Interrupted Concert *(1939)*

by Federico Garcia Lorca

The sleepy frozen caldron
Of the half moon
Broke the harmony
Of the deep night.

The ditches, musty with sedge,
Protest in silence,
And the frogs, muezzins of shadow,
Keep very still.

In the old village inn
The sad music failed,
And the most antique of the stars
Muted its strings.

The wind has come to rest
In the dark mountain caves;
A single poplar tree,
Pythagoras of the pure plain,
Raises an aged hand
To strike the moon in the face.

John Berryman

John Berryman was born in 1914 in MacAlester, Oklahoma. His family moved frequently, settling in Tampa, Florida, where his father committed suicide in 1926. His family relocated to New York City, and John enrolled in Columbia University, publishing poems at an early age; at only twenty-six his first collected poems appeared in *Five Young American Poets* (1940), the same year his poem "Letter to His Brother" appeared in *The Kenyon Review*. After studying two years at Cambridge, Berryman took a position at Wayne State University, going on to teach at Harvard and Princeton. Berryman married Eileen Mulligan in 1942, and the next year he published *Poems*, his first full volume. *The Dispossessed* was released in 1948, and in 1953, he published "Homage to Mistress Bradstreet" in the *Partisan Review*, a poem that was hailed as "the poem of his generation." That same year his marriage fell apart. Two years later Berryman took a position at the University of Minnesota, where he would stay for the rest of his life. Over the next several years, Berryman's mental state became increasingly unstable; he was repeatedly hospitalized for exhaustion and alcoholism and was divorced and remarried several times. In 1964, Berryman published his most critically acclaimed work to date, *The Dream Songs*, which earned him the Pulitzer Prize and the National Book Award. Tragically, his success did not end his depression; Berryman jumped off of a bridge in Minneapolis in 1972. He was fifty-eight years old.

Letter to His Brother *(1940)*

by John Berryman

The night is on these hills, and some can sleep.
Some stare into the dark, some walk.
Only the sound of glasses and of talk,
Of cracking logs, and of a few who weep,
Comes on the night wind to my waking ears.
Your enemies and mine are still,
None works upon us either good or ill:
Mint by the stream, tree-frogs, are travellers.

What shall I say for anniversary?
At Dachau many blows forbid
And Becket's brains upon the pavement spread
Forbid my trust, my hopeful prophecy.
Prediction if I make, I violate
The just expectancy of youth.
And yet you know as well as I the tooth
Sunk in our heels, the latest guise of fate.

When Patrick Barton chased the murderer
He heard behind him in the wood
Pursuit, and suddenly he knew he fled:
He was the murderer, the others were
His vigilance. But when he crouched behind
A tree, the tree moved off and left
Him naked while the chase came on; he laughed
And like a hound he leapt out of his mind.

I wish for you—the moon was full, is gone—
Whatever comfort can be got
From the violent world our fathers bought,
For which we pay with fantasy at dawn,
Dismay at noon, fatigue, horror by night.
May love, or its image in work,
Bring you that dignity to know the dark
And so to gain responsible delight.

Dylan Thomas

Dylan Thomas was born in 1914 in Swansea, Glamorganshire (Wales). A sickly child, Thomas dropped out of school at age sixteen. From 1931 to 1932, he worked as a reporter for *The South Wales Daily Post* in Swansea before the publication of his first book, *18 Poems,* in 1934, when he was just twenty years old. His second book, *25 Poems,* was released in 1936, and the following year he married Caitlin Macnamara, with whom he would have three children. In the early 1940s, Thomas began to focus on writing prose, with such works as *Portrait of the Artist as a Young Dog*, *Adventures in the Skin Trade*, and *Quite Early One Morning.* He had wanted to serve in World War II, but was rejected, so he worked with a documentary film unit during the war. Thomas, who eventually split his time between London and Wales, first visited America in 1950, launching into his first of several famous reading tours. He gained a reputation as a brilliant reader of his work and did much to popularize the poetry reading as a new public medium for the art. He became a legend nearly as much for his heavy drinking and flamboyant behavior as for his poetic genius. He went on to write some of the most loved poems of the English language in such books as *The World I Breathe, The Map of Love, Deaths and Entrances,* and *In Country Sleep, And Other Poems.* Thomas died of alcohol poisoning New York City in 1953 at the age of thirty-nine. "Poem" appeared in *The Kenyon Review* in 1940.

Poem *(1940)*
by Dylan Thomas

"If my head hurt a hair's foot
Pack back the downed bone. If the unpricked ball of my breath
Bump on a spout let the bubbles jump out.
Sooner drop with the worm of the ropes round my throat
Than bully ill love in the clouted scene.

"All game phrases fit your ring of a cockfight:
I'll comb the snared woods with a glove on a lamp,
Peck, sprint, dance on fountains and duck time
Before I rush in a crouch the ghost with a hammer, air,
Strike light, and bloody a loud room.

"If my bunched, monkey coming is cruel
Rage me back to the making house. My hand unravel
When you sew the deep door. The bed is a cross place.
Bend, if my journey ache, direction like an arc or make
A limp and riderless shape to leap nine thinning months."

"No. Not for Christ's dazzling bed
Or a nacreous sleep among soft particles and charms
My dear would I change my tears or your iron head.
Thrust, my daughter or son, to escape, there is none, none, none,
Nor when all ponderous heaven's host of waters breaks.

"Now to awake husked of gestures and my joy like a cave
To the anguish and carrion, to the infant forever unfree,
O my lost love bounced from a good home;
The grain that hurries this way from the rim of the grave
Has a voice and a house, and there and here you must couch
                                        and cry.
"Rest beyond choice in the dust-appointed grain,
At the breast stored with seas. No return
Through the waves of the fat streets nor the skeleton's thin ways.
The grave and my calm body are shut to your corning as stone,
And the endless beginning of prodigies suffers open."

Allen Tate

Allen Tate was born in 1899 near Winchester, Kentucky. The marriage between his parents failed by 1911, and he entered into "perpetual motion" with his mother and two brothers. Tate went to Vanderbilt University, where he met professor John Crowe Ransom, founding editor of *The Kenyon Review*, and Robert Penn Warren, with whom Tate would form The Fugitives, a group of Southern writers who defended formal technique and the traditional values of the agrarian South. Tate moved to New York City, where he married Caroline Gordon and published his first book of poems, *Mr. Pope and Other Poems* in 1928. After a brief stint in Europe, Tate settled in Tennessee and fully embraced agrarian life. In the 1930s, Tate published his first *Selected Poems* and *The Fathers*, a Civil War novel, both of which cemented his position as a distinguished American man of letters. In the 1940s, Tate spent time at Princeton, New York University, as consultant in poetry at the Library of Congress, and also as editor of the *Sewanee Review*. In 1951, Tate took a teaching position at the University of Minnesota, where he would remain until his retirement. Tate continued to publish books including *The Forlorn Demon: Didactic and Critical Essays* and *The Swimmers and Other Selected Poems* until his death in 1979. Tate remained closely connected to *The Kenyon Review*, publishing a poem in the first-ever issue in 1939. "The Trout Map" is from the fourth issue of *The Kenyon Review*.

The Trout Map *(1940)*

by Allen Tate

The Management Area of Cherokee
National Forest, interested in fish,
Has mapped Tellico and Bald Rivers
And North River, with the tributaries
Brookshire Branch and Sugar Cove Creek:
A fishy map for facile fishery.

Now consider it: nicely drawn in two
Colors, blue and red; blue for the hue
Of Europe (Tennessee water is green),
Red lines by blue streams to warn
The fancy-fishmen from protected fish;
Black borders hold the Area in a cracked dish.

Other black lines, the dots and dashes, wire
The fisher's will through classic laurel
Over boar tracks to foamy pot-holes lying
Under Bald falls that thump the buying
Trout: we sold Professor, Brown Hackle, Worms.
Tom Bagley and I were dotted and dashed wills.

Up Green Cove Gap from Preacher Milisaps' cabin
We walked an hour confident of victory,
Went to the west down a trail that led us
To Bald River-here map and scene were one
In scene-identity. Eight trout is the story
In three miles. We came to a rock bridge

On which the road went left around a hill,
The river, right, tumbled into a cove;
But the map dashed the road along the stream
And we dotted man's fishiest enthymeme
With jellied feet upon deductive love
Of what eyes see not, that nourishes the will:

We were fishers, weren't we? And tried to fish
The egoed belly's dry cartograph—
Which made the government fish lie down and laugh;
Tommy and I listened, we heard them shake
Mountains and cove because the map was fake.
After eighteen miles our feet were clownish;

Then darkness took us into wheezing straits
Where coarse Magellan, idling with his fates,
Ran with the gulls for map around the Horn,
Or wheresoever the mind with tidy scorn
Revisits the world to hear an eagle scream
Vertigo! Mapless, the mountains were a dream.

Marianne Moore

Marianne Moore was born in 1887, in Kirkwood, Missouri, near St. Louis, and was raised largely by her mother. Moore graduated from Bryn Mawr in 1909 and in 1914 moved with her mother to Greenwich Village in New York and began to publish her poetry. Moore's first book, *Observations*, was actually issued without her knowledge by the Egoist Press in 1921, but was officially released in 1924. In 1925, she became editor of *The Dial*, a major international magazine of the arts, remaining at that position until 1929, significantly advancing the standing of Avant Garde arts in the U.S. Also in 1929, she moved from Greenwich Village to Brooklyn, where she would remain until 1966. Moore permanently made her mark on the world of poetry with her *Selected Poems* in 1935, which went on to win every major American award for literature, including the Bollingen Prize, the National Book Award, and the Pulitzer Prize. In the following decades, Moore's fame spread, and she became a nationally known figure, always sporting her trademark tricorn hats and capes on the cover of magazines like *Esquire* and *Vogue*. She is also remembered as a great fan of professional baseball and an admirer of Muhammad Ali, for whom she wrote the liner notes to his record, *I Am the Greatest!*. Moore's *Complete Poems* was published near her eightieth birthday in 1967. She died in 1972 at the age of eighty-five in her New York home. Her poem "Four Quartz Crystal Clocks" appeared in *The Kenyon Review* in 1940.

Four Quartz Crystal Clocks *(1940)*

by Marianne Moore

There are four vibrators, the world's exactest clocks;
    and these quartz time-pieces that tell
time intervals to other clocks,
    these worksless clocks work well;
and all four, independently the
    same are there, in the cool Bell
        Laboratory time

vault. Checked by a comparator with Arlington,
    they punctualize the "radio,
cinema, and press,"—a group the
    Giraudoux truth-bureau
of hoped-for accuracy has termed
    "instruments of truth." We know—
        as Jean Giraudoux says

certain Arabs have not heard—that Napoleon
    is dead; that a quartz prism when
the temperature changes, feels
    the change and that the then
electrified alternate edges
    oppositely charged, threaten
        careful timing; so that

this water-clear "crystal" as the Greeks used to say,
    this "clear ice" must be kept at the
same coolness. Repetition, with
    the scientist, should be
synonymous with accuracy.
    The lemur-student can see
        that an aye-aye is not

an angwan-tíbo, potto, or loris. The sea-
    side burden should not embarrass
the bell-boy with the buoy-ball

endeavoring to pass
hotel patronesses; nor could a
        practiced ear confuse the glass
                eyes for taxidermists

with eye-glasses from the optometrist. And as
        Meridian 7 one-two
one-two gives, each fifteenth second
        in the same voice, the new
data—"The time will be" so and so—
        you realize that "when you
                hear the signal," you'll be

hearing Jupiter or jour pater, the day god—
        the salvaged son of Father Time—
telling the cannibal Chronos
        (eater of his proxime,
newborn progeny) that punctual-
        ity is not now a crime.

F.O. Matthiessen

F.O. Matthiessen was born Francis Otto Matthiessen in 1902 in California, but was raised in Illinois, Pennsylvania, and New York. Educated both in the United States and abroad, he started teaching in 1927, first at Yale and then at Harvard, where he would become a prominent figure as Professor of History and Literature for the next several decades. He would establish himself as a one of the leading critics of literature with his highly influential book *American Renaissance—Art and Expression in the Age of Emerson and Whitman*, published in 1941. As a leftist scholar and homosexual, Matthiessen was repeatedly targeted by the FBI as a suspected communist. Beginning in the early 1920s, he shared a relationship with Russell Cheney; correspondence between the two have been collected by Kenyon College professor Lewis Hyde in the book *The Rat and the Devil*. Matthiessen was a Senior Fellow of the Kenyon School of English and in 1950, his important anthology *The Oxford Book of English Verse* was released. Tragically, that same year, "feeling oppressed by the present conditions," Matthiessen committed suicide by jumping from the twelfth floor of a Boston hotel. *James and the Plastic Arts*, written about Henry James, first appeared in *The Kenyon Review* in 1943.

James and the Plastic Arts *(1943)*

by F. O. Matthiessen

At the outset of recapturing his memories in *A Small Boy and Others,* James declared that the only terms in which life had treated him to experience were "in the vivid image and the very scene." The nature of what he was conditioned to see and the very process of his intensely visual imagination may be reconstructed through those terms. No one was ever more the percipient observer. No son of a transcendental philosopher could have emulated more closely Emerson's desire of becoming "a transparent eyeball." No passive younger brother could have followed more admiringly the example of his activist elder, whom Henry recalled, from his earliest days, as "drawing, always drawing…under the lamplight of the Fourteenth Street back parlor." When his biography has been adequately written, we shall probably have the most complete instance in American annals of a life determined by a father's highly selective environing. Already we can read the headings of the main chapters of Henry's response to his father's decision—unique pioneering in the year '49 to give his boys "a better sensuous education than they are likely to get here."

Even before he was taken to Europe a few years after that decision he had begun to experiment with his first form, with what he was to call in his reminiscenses "dramatic, accompanied by pictorial composition," short scenes, each followed by its illustration. It was no accident that the language in which he was to discuss his novels half a century later combined the terms of the stage with those of the studio. The absorbed spectator of any drama, the experience of his adolescence came to him through the plastic arts and especially through painting. According to his own reckoning, one of the most significant events of his first initiation into Europe was the day when he "crossed the bridge over to Style" in the Galerie d'Apollon in the Louvre, and inhaled "a general sense of glory." That preceded by only a couple of years William's decision to study painting, and the family's return to America in line with their father's belief that the best teacher would be Hunt—another unique act of pioneering, if you consider the rival resources of Paris and of Newport in 1860. Henry, with as yet no defined bent of his own, lurked in the corners of the studio, shyly sketching without talent, and feeling himself "at the threshold of a world." An even more important contact for him than Hunt was LaFarge who, then in his mid-twenties, thrilled Henry with the richness of his culture, introduced him to Balzac, urged him to translate a story of Mérimée's, and brought home to him his first realization that "the arts were after all essentially one." When he at last found the art in which he himself was to work, "it was to feel, with reassurance, that the picture was still after all in essence one's aim."

It is not my concern here to detail James's enduring interest in painting, although a glance at his many reviews of exhibitions would reveal one mode by which he disciplined his own seeing.[1] Another, even more important mode was through his long series of "portraits of places" wherein he followed the lead of Gautier and other Frenchmen who were bringing literature closer to the art of the Impressionists. When we turn to his novels we must recognize that his critical use of such words as "composition," "relations," and "values," is not a loose analogy. By seeing life in pictures, he found his organic form. If we pursue the various implications that he elaborated from that fact, we may have a fresh source of appreciation of some of his finest effects.

Quite apart from any knowledge of painting was one of the many devices Hawthorne had taught him: the use of a portrait to bring out character, as Holgrave's daguerreotype pries beneath judge Pyncheon's smooth appearance and shows his real kinship to his hard and grasping ancestor. James was to borrow this device in stories at both the beginning and the end of his career: the pathetic hero of *The Passionate Pilgrim* insists on his title to the English estate on the grounds of his resemblance to the ancestral portrait by Reynolds; the most eerie moment in *The Sense of the Past* is when Ralph Pendrel so identifies himself with the figure in his ancestral portrait that the two exchange places. But one ground of James's dissatisfaction with Hawthorne was that in his hands such devices remained naked allegories. When the author of *The Ambassadors* remarked that "art deals with what we see, it must first contribute full-handed that ingredient," he could make it sound an easy matter. But thirty years before, in *The Madonna of the Future,* he had been very close in his own background to the disaster resulting from the failure to represent. What gives that story of the old American painter its poignancy is that his is the case of the transcendental genius without the disciplined talent to bring his ideals to concretion. Many such cases had haunted the America of James's youth. In fact the utter inability of James's father to condense his ballooning ideas into readable

---

1) James collected, in Pictures and Text (1893), his critical studies of Edwin Abbey, Alfred Parsons, Sargent, Daumier, and others. For the most part these essays, like that on DuMaurier, discuss subject matter and points of view rather than technique. The essay on Sargent is the most illuminating, since James could discern the dangers in store for this artist who offered "the slightly 'uncanny' spectacle of a talent which on the very threshold of its career has nothing more to learn."

shape must have been one of the strongest warnings that impelled his son's unflagging pursuit of form.

One of the ways in which he tried to escape Hawthorne's bareness was through the use, again and again, of a painter as the narrator of his stories. He hit upon this in *A Landscape Painter* (1866)—the second story that he printed—and although the suit there is hardly above the general run of New England local color sketches, what James was feeling his way towards was a density of impression that might best be given unity if seen through a painter's eyes. He was soon to experiment with more complex effects. *Travelling Companions* (1870) is virtually a guide book to his first excited immersion in Italian art. It bears out what he had written William from Rome the year before: "for the first time I know what the picturesque is." As a story it is as unexceptional as its opening sentence: "The most strictly impressive picture in Italy is incontestably the Last Supper of Leonardo at Milan." Such a sentence can remind us that James was a genius not born but made, that for years his stories were not much more alive than the magazine fiction of his day. But what marks *Travelling Companions* with some distinction is James's way of staging its initial scene. The narrator, not a painter but an American tourist with his Murray, on coming to see the great fresco, finds three other figures before it: a copyist, an elderly gentleman watching the copy rather than the original, and a girl lost in beholding the picture itself. Here, at a stroke, James has hit upon the possibility of developing multiple points of view, and has caught each of his three principals at a characterizing compositional angle: the American father not caring for the Last Supper any more than Mark Twain did, his daughter reverent before it, and the conscious narrator absorbing and "framing" the whole scene.

The scenes that James would be most eager to "frame" would naturally compose themselves around the accumulated treasures of Europe. *Roderick Hudson,* his second attempt at a novel and his first success, made an earnest effort to present the life of the American art colony in Rome. It was the era of the sculptor Story whom Hawthorne had known and whom James was to commemorate with a biography in the crowded year between *The Wings of the Dove* and *The Golden Bowl.* The discussions in Roderick's studio on the conflict between the ideal and the real in art, between spirit and form, seem very amateurish until we remember that the vagueness of *The Marble Faun* was hardly fifteen years behind. The more closely we look at James, the more signs we find of Hawthorne everywhere. If, for instance, we follow Roderick's career through his characteristic productions, we realize that we have been presented with an allegory of the life of an artist. We recall that what struck Rowland Mallet with Roderick's genius was his figurine of Thirst, and that when Rowland, in his enthusiasm, made the proposal of taking Roderick to Rome, the young sculptor smashed his portrait bust of the Yankee lawyer Barnaby Stryker, as a symbolic gesture of his release. In Rome he produces first a colossal idealized Adam and then an Eve before he is deflected by the dangerous charms of Christina Light. It is at this point that the sophisticated sculptor Gloriani congratulates Roderick on having come down from his goddesses among the clouds—much as Mephistopheles might have congratulated Faust. Thereafter Roderick is only outraged when Mr. Leavenworth, a rich mine-owner from the Middle West, wants to commission a statue "in pure white marble, of the idea of Intellectual Refinement." As the story advances, Roderick's undisciplined temperament hurtles him rapidly to self-destruction, in such a foreshortened time-scheme, as James later recognized, as "just fails to wreck" the book.

James was to construct only one other novel wholly around the life of art, and it is significant that what gives *The Tragic Muse* a greater aesthetic maturity than *Roderick Hudson* is not any less external handling of Nick Dormer's problems as a painter, but rather James's accruingly intimate knowledge of an art he had observed even more intently, that of the theatre, especially at the Comédie Française. The point thus emphasized is that what James learned from his assiduous attendance at the Salons was not the art of painting but the necessity to master all the secrets of composition in his own art. He was repeatedly stimulated to set his scenes in art galleries, since these challenged him to suggest long vistas and perspectives of his own. He delighted in opening *The American* in the Salon Carré, and in introducing us to Newman, on the verge of his initiation into Europe, lounging in front of Murillo's Madonna. His particular relish of elegance would cause him to center a whole *nouvelle* on "the felt beauty" of "the old Things" at Poynton. But such enumerations still leave us on the surface of the subject. It is not too much to say that James grew from allegory to his own peculiarly rich kind of symbolism by way of what his imagination had absorbed of plastic skills.

He did not confuse one art with another. He knew from the start that Balzac "does not *paint,* does not copy, objects; his chosen instrument being a pen, he is content to *write* them. He is literally real; he presents objects as they are." But James's own enormous growth in the ability so to present objects depended on the increasing vividness with which he came to see them in his mind's eye. In the preface to *Roderick Hudson* he spoke of his revisions for the collected edition in terms of the painter's freshening sponge and varnish bottle. But if we turn to any of the three novels that he re-worked most—*Roderick Hudson, The American,* or *The Portrait of a Lady*—we can see that the process amounted to far more than that. Revision meant for him literally *re-seeing,* as a few instances from *The Portrait* may amply attest. He was determined that no abstractions should lie inertly on his pages. Where he had formerly spoken of Mr. Touchett's hope that Ralph might "carry on the bank in a pure American spirit," he now wrote: "carry on the grey old bank in the white American light." Ideas became images, with special effectiveness when James wanted to bring out the quality of one of his characters. The whole distance travelled by the apprentice in becoming the master could be measured in this changed description of Ralph: "His face wore its pleasant perpetual smile, which perhaps suggested wit rather than achieved it" became "Blighted and battered, but still responsive and still ironic, his face was like a lighted lantern patched with paper and unsteadily held." Such transformations brought James's style to the point where it seems fitting to describe him, as Eliot once did, as "a metaphysical novelist." The mature James had grown to possess the quality with which he endowed Merton Densher, whose most living thoughts "at the moment of their coming to him had thrilled him almost like adventures."

The most subtle fusions of thought and feeling in the revised *Portrait* occur when James was impelled to heighten an entire pictorial effect. On the day when Isabel pays her first visit to Osmond, James wants her to be impressed with the rare distinction of the collector's surroundings. The footboy is made deliberately picturesque: instead of remaining merely "the shabby footboy," he becomes "tarnished as to livery and quaint as to type," and, with a fine added flourish, James tells us that he might "have issued from some stray sketch of old-time manners, been 'put in' by the brush of a Longhi or a Goya." Through such accruing details it is made even more natural that Isabel should take a romantic view of Osmond. In the first edition she reflects after this visit that his care for beauty "had been the main occupation of a lifetime of which the arid places were watered with the sweet sense of a quaint, half-anxious, halfhelpless fatherhood." In the revision these thoughts rise from her impression of how she had seen him: his preoccupation with beauty made his life "stretch beneath it in the disposed vistas and with the ranges of steps and terraces and fountains of a formal Italian garden—allowing only for arid places freshened by the natural dews," and so on. Dozens of comparable citations could be made, but we need only one more to attest to the wholeness of James's imagination. When Osmond first reflected about Miss Archer, he thought her "sometimes too eager, too pronounced. It was a pity she had that fault; because if she had not had it she would really have had none; she would have been as bright and soft as an April cloud." That concluding image was visual enough, but it did not satisfy James, it was not in keeping with the collector's world he was drawing, and so it became: "she would have been as smooth to his general need of her as handled ivory to the palm."

James came to the height of his plastic resources, as of all his other technical developments, in the three crowning works which signalized his return to the long novel following the lapse of a dozen years after *The Tragic Muse*. "Seeing" is, of course, the theme of *The Ambassadors*; the whole meaning of the book is determined by Strether's vision. At first the accumulating images of Paris are almost more than he can handle. As he says to Littie Bilham: "You've all of you here so much visual sense that you've somehow all 'run' to it. There are moments when it strikes one that you haven't any other." But Strether keeps his own balance. On the morning of this hero's first stroll through the streets, James created the passage which was probably the touchstone of his attraction for a whole generation of Americans in the nineteen-tens and -twenties for whom Paris was the symbol of liberation. The "vast bright Babylon" into which Strether sets forth to investigate how Chad is living, strikes him, in one of James's most famous elaborate images, as a hard brilliant jewel, bewilderingly iridescent, since "what seemed all surface one moment seemed all depth the next." That sets the tone for Strether's initial discovery in the Boulevard Malesherbes; for when he looks up at the third-floor apartment which he knows to be Chad's, he recognizes at a flash, in the essence of Jamesian revelation, "that wherever one paused in Paris the imagination reacted before one could stop it." All Woollett's prejudices about Chad's scandalous doings fall away. Strether can discern something quite other from the very look of the house, "its cold fair grey, warmed a little by life." James makes such a magnificently functional use of his architectural details that his hero can tell—and thousands of his countrymen have had the same yearning belief—that the life which goes on behind those windows and that balcony must also be characterized by tact and taste, "by measure and balance, the fine relation of part to part and space to space."

The virtuosity with which James makes artistic impressions now work as part of his organic effect may be instanced by a touch that he alone would have given. Strether calls at Sarah Pocock's hotel, only to find her out. While he is standing in her empty salon, he suddenly notices in the window, open onto the balcony, the reflection of a woman's dress. No other novelist until Proust would have taken the trouble to introduce Strether's brief talk with Mamie in that fashion; but this device serves to carry our attention out of the room to "the faint murmur" of the city, and keeps alive for us, as James is at pains to do throughout this book, some sense of "the huge collective life" beyond his circle. Such a scene also delights our eyes as it did Strether's. Another such delight is when he encounters Madame de Vionnet in Notre Dame—cathedrals rank with art-galleries as favorite Jamesian settings. And when Strether throws to the winds all scruples as to what Mrs. Newsome would think, and invites Madame de Vionette to lunch, James presents us with an impressionistic canvas:

How could he wish it to be lucid for others, for any one, that he, for the hour, saw reasons enough in the mere way the bright clean ordered water-side life came in at the open window?—the mere way Madame de Vionnet, opposite him over their intensely white tablelinen, their *omelette aux tomates,* their bottle of strawcolored Chablis, thanked him for everything almost with the smile of a child, while her grey eyes moved in and out of their talk, back to the quarter of the warm spring air, in which early summer had already begun to throb, and then back again to his face and their human questions.

Whether or not even James was wholly conscious of how much the new painting had taught him, he could scarcely have come nearer to Renoir's effects, in the wonderful sense of open air; in the sensuous relish of all the surfaces, with exactly the right central spot of color in that *omelette aux tomates*; in the exquisite play of light around his figures. And when James added a further accent, it made for the very kind of charm by which the Impressionists declared their art a release from stuffy manners as well as from stale techniques: Madame de Vionnet "was a woman who, between courses, could be graceful with her elbows on the table. It was a posture unknown to Mrs. Newsome…"

James's incredibly disciplined eye was to demonstrate, at the climax of this novel, how deeply he had meditated on what can be accomplished by the "framing" effect of art. Art puts a frame around experience in the sense of selecting a significant design, and, by thus concentrating upon it, enabling us to share in the essence without being distracted by irrelevant details. For James's sensibility, part of the fun would lie in a highly developed, wholly unexpected illustration of this aesthetic truth. When Strether decides on a day in the country, what leads him there is his far off memory "of a certain small Lambinet that had charmed him, long years before, at a Boston dealer's." It is interesting to recall that this nearly forgotten painter of scenes along the Seine was of the era of Rousseau and Daubigny, all of whom James noted as having been first shown to him in the early days by Hunt. On one level, Strether's being drawn by art to nature to verify an old impression shows the curious reversal of order in the moden sensibility. On another level, as he dwells on how much that canvas, not expensive but far beyond his purse, had meant to him in the Tremont Street gallery, we have a sharp contrast between Strether's New England actuality and his long smothered French ideal. But James doesn't leave it at that. Strether's entire day progresses as though he had "not once overstepped the oblong gilt frame." The whole scene was there, the clustered houses and the poplars and the willows: "it was Tremont Street, it was France, it was Lambinet." In the later afternoon, as he sits at a village cafe overlooking a reach of the river, his landscape takes on a further interest. It becomes a Landscape with Figures, as a boat appears around the bend, a man rowing, a lady with a pink parasol. There, in an instant, was "the lie in the charming affair." The skill with which James has held our eyes within his frame has so heightened the significance of every slight detail that this recognition scene leaps out with the intensity of the strongest drama.

The Wings of the Dove presents us with the opulence of Venice in the same free-handed experienced connoisseur's fashion as *The Ambassadors* gave us the sense of Paris. But James was not repeating his themes at this stage of his development. Here, as his preface tells us, was his supreme effort to portray the heiress of all the ages. If Isabel Archer, through Mr. Touchett's legacy, was made able to meet Europe on her own terms, Milly Theale has swum far out of any restricted sphere as a millionairess in her own right. More than that, James wants explicitly to endow her with all the glamour of a princess. He does everything he can to build up a realm of fairy-tale enchantment for her, and, characteristically, he again finds that he can do this best through a renewed use of pictorial devices. Milly's swift intimacy with Kate Croy, which gives the full accent to her bewilderingly rapid acceptance by social London, is symbolized as though the handsome English girl "had been as a figure in a picture stepping by magic out of its frame." An ingenious reversal of this device, which underlines for the reader how little Kate is to be a good fairy, comes on the day when Milly has gone alone to the National Gallery. Overhearing an American lady comment on something "in the English style," she turns and sees, not a painting, but Kate together with Densher.

A recrudescence of Hawthorne's profound influence is to be read throughout James's late work, to a far greater degree than in his deliberately "realistic" middle period. In *The Sacred Fount* he squeezed every possible implication out of the likeness between some of his characters and the portrait of the pale young man in black, with a mask in his hand. Was it a Mask of Death or a Mask of Life? Couldn't one see Mrs. Server's face in it? And wasn't the exhausted young man poor Briss? But there are too many conflicting implications for the reader to handle, as is the case throughout this overwrought *nouvelle*, an exhausting end-product of Poe's detective tales of ratiocination, almost an unconscious parody of James's own novels of intelligence. The use of a Renaissance picture in *The Wings of the Dove* is much simpler and more stirring. When Milly is escorted by Lord Mark to see the wonderful Bronzino that looks so like her, we have one of the most poignant moments in all James's fiction. By virtue of insisting on this likeness, James has fulfilled his wish of making his heroine the equivalent of a Renaissance princess. He has let her feel that already she has entered "the mystic circle": "things melted together—the beauty and the history and the facility and the splendid midsummer glow: it was a sort of magnificent maximum, the pink dawn of an apotheosis coming so curiously soon." The poignance lies in the sense that none of this will last. Even as Milly looks, she realizes that the joyless lady on the canvas is "dead, dead, dead"; and the words reverberate for us as an omen of her own future.

This scene before the Bronzino operates almost like a musical theme:[2] it strikes the first note of the shift to Venice, where Milly plays out her make-believe role in the gorgeous rented palace which increases the ironic contrast "between her fortune and her fear." There her setting becomes explicitly a Veronese, and Susan Stringham, to whom this comparison occurs, deems all the sumptuous magnificence to be only fitting, since Milly's is "one of the courts of heaven, the court of a reigning seraph, a sort of vicequeen of an angel." At such an elevation does Milly make her final public appearance, and when James changes her dress for the only time in the book from black to white and heightens her red-haired pallor with lace and pearls, he gives us the

---

2) James, however, possessed none of the technical knowledge of music exhibited by Proust and Mann.

heart-rending mildness of his "dove" at the same time that he avails himself in the whole scene of resources of light and color and intricate perspective to rival even Veronese's.

Shortly after that evening reception Lord Mark turns up with his brutal news, and James underscores his with a Shakespearean use of storm: for in the Venice of dark skies and lashing rain, "all of evil" has broken out. Equally symbolically, when Sir Luke Strett arrives for his final visit, the storm is superseded by "autumn sunshine," and the renewed beauty of the city is "like a hanging-out of vivid stuffs, a laying-down of fine carpets." In such terms to the end are symbolized the fruits of civilization for which Milly has just reached out her hands, and which she hates so terribly to relinquish in death.

In *The Golden Bowl* James's attraction to the life of art has become obsessive. The bowl itself operates as his most consummately complex symbol. In some lights it represents the Prince himself, who, bought at immense expense, is to constitute the prize of Mr. Verver's collection, "a pure and perfect crystal." But in the scene when Charlotte and the Prince first come upon the bowl in the antique shop, it stands most for their relationship—significantly the Prince detects at once the crack beneath the gilt surface, whereas Charlotte is blind to it. When Maggie, in search of a present for her father, learns from the antique dealer of the others' visit to the shop, the bowl means to her the sign of their hidden intimacy. When Fanny Assingham dashes it to the floor, it splits into three pieces, and the urgent question for Maggie then is what can be salvaged from this triangle. What she wants, as she says, "is the golden bowl—as it *was* to have been." It thus becomes the token of her possible happiness with the Prince, and what must finally be proved is whether or not he has a flaw. The expertness with which James handles all the connotations latent in the bowl prevents this symbol from ever becoming schematized. In each conversation involving it every possible play of association is kept shiftingly alive, and James has thus succeeded in making an *objet d'art* the cohesive center of his own intricate creation.

But here his virtuosity betrays him. Everything tends to become a collector's item in Adam Verver's highly special world. The book shines throughout with innumerable other images of gold. In two of James's most breathtakingly elaborate images the Prince is at one time a Palladian church, at another a dazzling pagoda. As though challenged by the works of art that he has conjured up, James devotes every effort to make his structure architectural in its rigorous symmetry. The climactic scene in Maggie's dilemma is again put in a frame: as she paces the terrace in her unhappiness, she keeps glancing through the window at the others in the great room. And, at the close, when Maggie and her father are commenting on the fineness of one of his early Italian sacred subjects, they are really exchanging views on the resolution of their own situation. So many heaped up artistic analogies and effects finally become stifling. There is not enough discrimination between Mr. Verver's property and his human acquisitions. It would be one thing if he was portrayed as a Midas, whose touch finally turned gold to horror. But, instead, an enormously heightened value is attributed to his role as a collector, ranking him almost with the great creators. His boyish innocence is continually stressed, though that quality seems hardly the most natural product of his background as a shrewd money-maker in the post–Civil War West. James has concentrated here so excessively on a few personal relations that he has almost lost the connections between his enchanted realm and the real world. He has furnished verification for Veblen's *Theory of the Leisure Class,* apparently without understanding his own implications.

He was generally by no means blind to the economic foundations of his art-stuffed interiors. Through Densher's glimpse of Mrs. Lowder's "treasures" he wrote, for instance, an incisive critique of the curiously mixed state of mind we now call Victorian:

> It was only manifest they were splendid and were furthermore conclusively British. They constituted an order and abounded in rare material—precious woods, metals, stuffs, stones....He had never dreamed of so much gilt and glass, so much satin and plush, so much rosewood and marble and malachite. But it was above all the solid forms, the wasted finish, the misguided cost, the general attestation of morality and money, a good conscience and a big balance.

Such a description might have sprung from Veblen's own analysis. But the trouble with *The Golden Bowl* is that James was bent on making a final affirmation of his international theme, of the superior ethical refinement of his kind of Americans.

He needed to break the web of enchantment by fresh knowledge of the sources of their wealth. He gained this in the very next year by his painstaking observations from the White Mountains to Palm Beach, and from New York to Los Angeles. The resulting *American Scene* is one of the curiosities of our literature. It reads as though James had explicitly decided to be the "transparent eyeball" and nothing else, as though the rules of the game prohibited him from going beyond what he had seen for himself. The effect is as though a camera was clicking nervously over every surface it encountered; and we have to piece together for ourselves the meaning of scenes both in and out of historical focus. One of the most grotesque instances of the latter was James's impression of the Country Club which, being so unlike European exclusiveness, struck him as "one of the great garden-lamps in which the flame of Democracy burns whitest and steadiest." Such a notion was hardly to be verified by Sinclair Lewis, or by those deeply moving passages in *An American Tragedy* where the Country Club becomes a symbol of all the brittle glamour from which Clyde Griffiths feels himself excluded.

But James saw the object as it really was in 1905 whenever his trained eye alone could serve him, especially whenever he was confronted with American works of art. Despite his admiration for Saint-Gaudens' Sherman, he confessed his uneasiness at the Destroyer's horse being led by "a beautiful American girl." His taste thus landed him at the center of a social judgment: he was sharply suspicious "of all attempts, however glittering and golden, to confound destroyers with benefactors." He also saw things in New York architecture that only our Chicago pioneers of the modern movement were then aware of. He reflected that "nowhere else does pecuniary power so beat its wings in the void" as in New York; and he read "the whole costly up-town demonstration" of its imitative chateaux "as a record, in the last analysis, of individual loneliness." And although an inheritor of the age of the individual, the very sight of the conflicting crudities of the unplanned blocks of Riverside Heights struck him as "the vividest of lectures on the subject of individualism." In a passage where his eye carried him much farther than his amorphous social philosophy could have followed, he was led to ask: "Why should conformity and subordination, that acceptance of control and assent to collectivism in the name of which our age has seen such dreary things done, become on a given occasion the one not vulgar way of meeting a problem?"

Such issues were to beat more insistently upon his consciousness in his draft of *The Ivory Tower*, which again was to have found its central symbol in an *objet d'art*. If James had lived to bring his ambitious scheme to completion, this book would have ranked with his very greatest. What still remains vague in his notes are the positive values that Graham Fielder was finally to affirm in withdrawing from the Newport scene. But what is not left in the least uncertain are the predatory bases of that scene. On the page before he broke off James gave us a final image from his response to art. Fielder has gone out on the lawn of the vast empty house he has inherited, and circling around it, looks at it "more critically than had hitherto seemed relevant." He is suddenly overwhelmed by its "unabashed ugliness." Its "senseless architectural ornament" makes it seem an oppressive monument to waste. Then—using an analogy which reminds us that James had seen only the clumsy first attempts of a new age—Fielder is seized with a sense of terror, eying his house "very much as he might have eyed some monstrous modern machine, one of those his generation was going to be expected to master, to fly in, to fight in, to take the terrible women of the future out for airings in…."

Fielder was the last of James's leisurely observers, whose satisfactions in life came mostly by holding it off at a distance and viewing it in perspective. The characteristic design of a Jamesian canvas thus groups its figures at the ends of long alleys and formal gardens, in the receding polished corridors of great mansions. Emerson had delighted in the eye as the least sensual of the senses, and though James had travelled far from the disembodied seer, his endlessly curious spectators tended to prefer their "Platonic" vision of events to direct participation in them. A painter like Little Bilham had taken in so much of the beautiful surface of Paris that even though his productive power had faltered before it, he was happy with what he had seen. The case was different with James's most trapped spectator, who, significantly, was his one revolutionary hero. Hyacinth Robinson's image of the art and architecture of Paris was overwhelming in its weight. For he could not escape from the knowledge that "the most brilliant city in the world was also the most bloodstained." His awareness that civilization was as cruel as it was magnificent ended by making him a hopelessly split personality. He came to reverence the fruits of the older order at the same time as he recognized the necessity of its destruction.

Since Hyacinth Robinson's suicide, the victim of his own aesthetic sensibility, the heroes of our fiction and their creators have possessed more dynamic conceptions of social forces than James ever glimpsed. Our artists have looked with far less reverence upon the Big House, and have known, as Hyacinth Robinson did not, that the flourishing of the arts is not dependent upon its survival. They have been no longer satisfied to regard Europe from the connoisseur's point of view. If they have looked at Venice, they have been aware of the rats beneath the decaying piles of a gone society. But they have also felt themselves more implicated. Few today would fail to be restive under Henry James Senior's chief educational principle, that his sons should learn *to be* rather than *to do*. But no one in American literature has made anything like so much out of the role of the multiple observer as his novelist son did. He saw both with and through his eye; and the abundance of his images and scenes gave his art compositional permanence.

Bertolt Brecht

Bertolt Brecht, a poet first and foremost, but also known for his important contributions to the theatre, was born in 1898 in Augsburg, Germany. He remained in Bavaria until 1924, having studied medicine (Munich, 1917–21), served in an army hospital (1918), and written his first two plays and one volume of verse. During this period he also developed a violently antibourgeois attitude that reflected his generation's deep disappointment in civilization at the end of World War I. From there Brecht moved to Berlin, where he became a Marxist. He went into exile in 1933, first in Scandinavia, then in America (1941–47), where he did some film work in Hollywood. It was during this time that *The Kenyon Review* ran his "Poems of Exile" (1945). In 1949, Brecht published *A Little Organum for the Theatre*, his most important theoretical work. Brecht was determined to destroy theatrical illusion, that is, he wanted his audiences to be clear that the theatre is *fake*, in order for them to be able to think critically about the issues being raised in a play, instead of just emotionally identifying with the characters. Among his theatrical works are *Mother Courage and Her Children*, *The Good Person of Szechwan,* and *The Caucasian Chalk Circle*. He died in 1956.

Poems of Exile *(1945)*

by Bertolt Brecht

(Translated by H. R. Hays)

I.

Having taken refuge under the Danish straw roof, friends,
I follow your struggle. Herewith I send you
A few words as if they were flushed out, here and there,
By bloody faces from the foliage and over the sound.
Handle those that reach you with care!
Yellowed books, crumbling reports
Are what I depend on. If we meet once more,
I shall gladly begin all over again.

II. Thoughts Concerning the Duration of Exile

1

Don't drive a nail into the wall,
Throw your coat on a chair!
Why bother about four days?
Tomorrow you'll go back!

Let the little tree go unwatered!
Why plant a tree at all?
Before it's as high as a stair tread
You'll be happily leaving this place!

Pull your cap over your eyes when you pass people!
Why turn the pages of a strange grammar?
The news that calls you home
Is written in a familiar language.

As the calsomime peels from a column
(Do nothing to stop it!)
So the fence of force will crumble
That has been reared up on the border
Against justice.

2

See the nail in the wall, the nail you hammered into it!
When do you think you'll be going back?
Do you want to know what you really believe in your heart?

Day after day
You work for the liberation
Sitting in your room writing,
Do you want to know what you really think of your work?
Look at the little chestnut tree in the corner of the courtyard
That you carry your canful of water to.

III. Exiled with Good Reason

I grew up as the son
Of well-to-do people. My parents buttoned
A collar around my neck and they trained me
In the habit of being served
And schooled me in the art of giving orders. But
When I grew up and looked around me
The people of my class did not please me
Nor did giving orders and being served
And so I left my class and consorted
With lowly people.

Thus
They bred up a traitor, schooled him
In their arts and he
Betrayed them to the enemy.

Yes, I blurt out their secrets. Among the people
I stand up and explain
How they betray them and prophesy what will happen for I
Am initiated into their schemes.
The Latin of their corrupt preachers
I translate word for word into the vulgar tongue whereby
It is revealed as humbug. Their scales of justice
I take down and point out

The false weight. And their informers tell them,
When they betray the uprising, that I take my stand
With the plundered.

They warned me and took from me
What I had earned from my work. And as I did not reform
They hunted me down but
In my house
They found nothing but manuscripts that revealed
Their assault on the people. And so
They issued a warrant and sent it after me
That charged me with low sentiments which means
The sentiments of the lowly.

In the place I came to I was thus branded
For all the haves but the havenots
Read the warrant and
Slipped weapons to me. You, I heard them say,
They have exiled with
Good reason.

IV.

My young son asks me: shall I study mathematics?
I might well say to him, why? That two pieces of bread are more than one
You can tell already.
My young son asks me: shall I study English?
I might well say to him, why? This country is on the downgrade. Just
Rub your belly with the flat of your hand and groan
And people will understand you.
My young son asks me: shall I study history
I might well say to him, why? Learn to stick your head in the ground
And you'll have a chance of survival.

Yes, study mathematics, I say,
Study English, study history!

V.

In flight from my own people
I have now reached Finland. Friends,
Whom yesterday I did not know, put up a couple of beds
In a clean room. On the radio
I hear the scum of the earth announcing victories. Curiously
I scan the map of the world. High up in Lapland
I see there is still one small door.

VI. Landscape of Exile

But even I, on the last boat,
Saw the gaiety of dawn in the rigging
And the greyish bodies of dolphins emerge
From the Japanese sea.

The little horsecarts with gilt decorations
And the pink bracelets of the matrons
In the alleys of doomed Manila
The refugee also beheld with joy.

The oil derricks and the thirsty gardens of Los Angeles,
The ravines of California at evening and the fruit markets
Also did not leave the messenger of misfortune
Unmoved.

VII. California Autumn

1

In my garden
There are only evergreen plants. If I wish to see autumn
I go to my friend's country house in the hills. There
I can stand for five minutes and look at a tree
Robbed of its leaves and leaves robbed of their trunk.

2

I saw a large autumn leaf which the wind
Was driving down the street and I thought: difficult
To figure out which way a leaf will next be going!

John Crowe Ransom

John Crowe Ransom was born in Pulaski, Tennessee, in 1888. After graduating from Vanderbilt University, Ransom went on to study at Oxford in
1910. He returned several years later and began teaching at his alma mater.
Ransom remained at Vanderbilt, except for a period of service as an artillery
officer in France during World War I, until his departure for Kenyon College
in 1937. By this time, Ransom had established himself as a prominent poet,
after publishing such books as *Poems about God*, *Chills and Fever,* and *Two
Gentlemen in Bonds*. All of these works reflected the values of The
Fugitives, a group of writers centered in Nashville who believed in writing
formal verse that praised agrarian traditions. By 1927, he claimed he had
"exhausted" his poetic output and began to concentrate on criticism and
editing. Ransom founded *The Kenyon Review* in 1939 and acted as its editor until 1959, establishing its reputation as one of the finest literary journals in America. While regarded as a conservative critic, Ransom often
published writers whose values and aesthetics were very different from his
own. While at Kenyon, he also founded the Kenyon School of English,
designed to gather distinguished critics and students together to develop a
more critical approach to studying literature along the lines of his "New
Criticism," which claimed that in most scholarly consideration of poetry too
little attention was being paid to the actual words of poems as opposed to
when and where the poet wrote them. His criticism was highly influential,
and books like *The New Criticism* and *Poetic Sense: A Study of Problems in
Defining Poetry by Content* made him one of the century's most renowned
critics. Ransom remained active in the academic world until his death in his
sleep at his Kenyon home in 1974.

Art and the Human Economy *(1945)*

by John Crowe Ransom

The two preceding papers were furnished independently, and there is some editorial presumption in having collated them, and now in commenting them together. Special disservice is done to Mr. Southard, whose essay in the first place is a literary appreciation of Robert Penn Warren's poetry, and of a quality permitting us to think the poet is lucky in having found his exegete so soon. But Mr. Southard in the course of his exegesis, and Mr. Adorno immediately, embark upon the same topic, and it is one that has a great urgency for us: the unhappy human condition that has risen under the modern economy, and the question of whether religion and art can do anything about it. It is true that the writers do not have quite the same diagnosis of this condition, but it will be noticed that they make cross-references to each other unknowingly.

Mr. Adorno is evidently for collectivism in politics, but not with all the potential ferocity of a partisan, i.e., fanatically. His social ideal has no room for religion yet provides a special asylum for art. But art is curiously close to religion in his very original and engaging description of it, as a concrete monad representing the universal concretion itself; that is to say, as a construction from which the experient receives cosmic or ontological vision. What else is it for? It is not attached to the practical life which falls under the over-all survey of the political economy. It is not attached, it is free, and Mr. Adorno awards to it an *imperium in imperio*. That is a handsome concession which many collectivists have not made.

The marvelous concretions of Proust's novel are principally of human beings in relations too tangled ever to be resolved intellectually. The element of external nature—the scene or the natural object—is never excluded, for Proust has the sensibility of a poet as well as that of a modern novelist, but for our attention it is certainly not dominant. Proust does not follow the lead of Wordsworth, returning to external nature to find God, returning there also to find—by an indirection that Wordsworth scarcely succeeded in making clear—man himself. It would seem to be a bad logical error, and I do not know that Mr. Adorno commits it, to think that God is a term of discourse which referred to the mystery of nature as long as nature was mysterious, but for the moderns who have "conquered" nature can have no particular exigency. But it would be a form of the same error, and Mr. Adorno distinctly is free of this one, to think that art deals with the "magic" of external nature but that there is nothing equally magical in a human concretion, which therefore only needs to be understood and disposed of by political science. There is mystery everywhere, as we hear it said in pious quarters; and let us say that there is mystery for the intellect in every concretion, and no possibility of thinking it out of existence.

Has art then no effect upon action, and does it not modify in any way one's commitment to action? I am inclined to think that it is in more or less ironic reaction from the fury of the practical life, and might be called "pietistic" in its mildly disparaging effect upon agents. Mr. Adorno seems to think that religion was repressive upon one or another developing form of practice, but I wonder if art does not register a disaffection with all practice. If it does not oppose something in advance, it seems at any rate to record the transaction afterwards in the strangest manner. It takes us back into the concretion from which action has already delivered us.

At any picnic we have the politeness to remark for the host's benefit the local concretions of nature to which he has conducted us, but it may be that we will regard our fellow picnickers as simple and understandable creatures. The history of that might go back a long way, and even to the famous division of labor of which Mr. Adorno speaks. The division of labor made action effective by limiting sharply the apparent concreteness of the natural materials which the laborer manipulated. It is true that modern life must come to terms either here or there with the whole of nature, and indeed modern life confronts a denser nature than the ancients could possibly know. But the divided laborer does not entertain this vision, nor does he know nature professionally as other than the humble if stubborn set of materials assigned him. (It might be said that the productive society at large confronts the whole concretion of nature, but so far as this purpose is concerned society is principally a fiction.) Now his own labor is not sufficient to maintain his life, but has to be integrated with all the other labors which likewise are divided and dependent. He is in daily or even hourly relation with the other laborers if he cares to live. But the explicitude of these relations tends to limit the depth of his acquaintance, and to induce the feeling that the laborer in the other field has merely a kind of functional existence, or is in fact principally the other "party" to a contract. It was at the stage of the loose agrarian society, where the laborer dealt individually with his local microcosm, and did not need to relate himself incessantly to the other laborers, that acquaintance was more spontaneous and went deeper. The basis of relations then might be the curious reciprocal exploration of their human concretions, on personal or aesthetic grounds. Friendship or brotherly love, in Aristotle's account, ripens between economically independent and fully rounded men. And, even now, it is not Proust the machine-tender or Proust the draper who can dwell so long on a human history without exhausting it, but Proust the free citizen, the man of means and leisure, and even the voluptuary of human relations. He knows the human heart because his own vision, his own experience, is complete. And it is because there will be in any society men strong enough to complete their experience eventually, and no society able to repress them permanently, that we say art has an eternal vitality.

But when we say there will be men strong enough for art, we are conscious that we are saying also, men weak enough, that is, men backward enough; engaged upon the progressive division of labor yet given to hideous lapses of zeal and faith; going to the length of art by way of looking back. Is not there a kind of weakness in all this Remembrance of Things Past? I wonder that we have not heard about the "failure of nerve" on the part of artists as such, and not merely of particular writers. When I was a boy we used to say that somebody had "gone back on" somebody else. We were describing a kind of renegade, who couldn't after all go through with his pledge, and the novel individuation demanded. But in art we do not go back with any such finality.

Now we come to the terms of Mr. Southard's argument. We are far gone in our habit of specialized labor, whether we work with our heads or our hands; it has become our second nature and nearly the only human nature that we can have, in a responsible public sense. We have fallen, as Mr. Southard would say, and henceforth a condition we might properly call "decadence" is our portion; guilt and repentance, guilt followed by such salvation as can be achieved. In the forms which this salvation takes, we do go back into our original innocence, but vicariously or symbolically, not really. We cannot actually go back, and if we try it the old estate becomes insupportable; a little trial will show that. It was the estate of good animals opposing nature with little benefit of rational discourse, therefore of abstraction (the splitting off of the concept from the total image) and special effectiveness. We would not like it now. So we manage as we are with the help of salvation, an excellent thing though only for a guilty species. Salvation simple as picnics, or games, it may be; but for superior sinners it must take a higher form, such as individual works of art, or religious exercises which are works of art institutionalized and rehearsed in ritual. All these are compensatory concretions—they return to primitive experience but only formally; by no means do they propose to abandon the forward economy.

I find myself in the fullest sympathy with Mr. Southard's argument—up to the unexpected jump he makes at the end. It seemed that we had taken our constitutional and predestined development, and our progress was irreversible; but suddenly Mr. Southard proposes to found an agrarian community within which innocence may be recovered. I can reproach him for his phantasy with the better conscience inasmuch as I have entertained it too, as one of the Southern agrarians. And it seems to be in order to offer a brief notice about that, though I will not pretend to be representing Mr. Warren, or Mr. Tate, or others of the group.

Mr. Southard taxes the Southern agrarians for not having practiced what they preached, and that is a hit in a place where they have been hit before, though rarely by critics of his philosophical calibre. But I am struck by a slight dampness of spirit in his abjuration of the world. He says the young would seem to have made sacrifices enough in these days, as if that would be almost the greatest one yet. And it would be; it is a sacrifice which I hope he would not make. For without consenting to division of labor, and hence modern society, we should have not only no effective science, invention, and scholarship, but nothing to speak of in art, e.g., Reviews and contributions to Reviews, fine poems and their exegesis, and on both sides of the line he has already given achievement. The pure though always divided knowledges, and the physical gadgets and commodities, constitute our science, and are the guilty fruits; but the former are triumphs of muscular intellect, and the latter at best are clean and wholly at our service. The arts are the expiations, but they are beautiful. Together they comprise the detail of human history. They seem worth the vile welter through which homeless spirits must wade between times, with sensibilities subject to ravage as they are. On these terms the generic human economy can operate, and they are the only terms practicable now. So the Southern agrarians did not go back to the farm, with exceptions which I think were not thoroughgoing. And presently it seemed to them that they could not invite other moderns, their business friends for example, to do what they were not doing themselves. Nor could they even try to bring it about that practicing agrarians, such as there might still be in the Old South, should be insulated from the division of labor and confined securely in their garden of innocence. An educator or a writer cannot abandon the presuppositions behind his whole vocation, nor imagine that they have less than a universal validity for the region, and ought to be kept out of the general circulation as beyond the common attainment. I find an irony at my expense in remarking that the judgment just delivered by the Declaration of Potsdam against the German people is that they shall return to an agrarian economy. Once I should have thought there could have been no greater happiness for a people, but now I have no difficulty in seeing it for what it is meant to be: a heavy punishment. Technically it might be said to be an inhuman punishment, in the case where the people in the natural course of things have left the garden far behind.

But I think the agrarian nostalgia was very valuable to the participants, a mode of repentance not itself to be repented. It matured their understanding of the forward-and-backward rhythm of the human economy. And now, for example, whatever may be the politics of the agrarians, I believe it may be observed that they are defending the freedom of the arts, whose function they understand. Not so much can be said for some intemperate exponents of the economic "progress."

As a formal definition of the art-work I have nothing to offer that would compete with Mr. Adorno's adaptation of the Leibnizian monad. But as a natural history of the event, giving a sense of its background and its participation in the total human economy, it leaves something to be desired, and in conclusion I will try to sketch this area of meaning as it might be revealed upon a public occasion. It will be a historic occasion, but I am improvising the detail, since I do not know my facts. Let us say that it is time to unveil the statue of an eminent public man, and let it be Bismarck. His program has been notably strenuous, and it has succeeded. His very physiognomy and carriage when rendered by the faithful sculptor will betoken the audacity of his conceptions, his persistence with them, and even the habit of success. The citizens do not let their rites wait upon his death, and it is to be emphasized that these are not death rites, and in no sense exult in his mortality but in the grandeur of his career at its prime. It is only 1879, but everybody now can see his greatness, and he is already in history, a firm instance of those uncompromising human spirits who travel far from their origins and make their mark.

But there is an ambiguity in the event. In the act of turning him to stone and planting him immovably in the earth, there is a question of what these people really mean to celebrate by their festal occasion. It is as if they were not honoring the efficacious Bismarck any more than they are honoring the Nature to whom they now commit him, like a truant returned to the parental bosom. In the mound and in the pedestal upon the mound that support the stone Bismarck the earth seems to rise a little way, but still with an inscrutable dignity, to welcome him; as if his wilful alienation had always been conceded, had in no wise been mortal for her, and now, if he liked, was over. The golden Rhine flows past evenly, as if he did not mind having upon his bank a thing even so sternly individuated as a Bismarck. By the art of the statue Bismarck himself is invested with a beauty whose conditions he would not and could not have fulfilled in his own person. And all who are present understand these things, perhaps without knowing it. Let us say, Those who are supposed to commemorate action are commemorating reaction; they are pledged to the Enlightenment but, even in Its name, they clutter It with natural piety.

Muriel Rukeyser

Muriel Rukeyser was born in 1913 in New York City. She studied for two years at Vassar before graduating from Columbia University in 1932. Three years later her first book of poems, *Theory of Flight,* largely influenced by her time as a student at Roosevelt Aviation School, was published as a part of the Yale Younger Poets Series. By this time in her life, Rukeyser was heavily involved in the political issues to which she would remain committed for the rest of her life. Working for the International Labor Defense, she traveled to Alabama during the 1930s to cover the Scottsboro case, which involved nine black youths who were wrongly accused of raping two white women. She also wrote for the *Daily Worker*, which sent her to Spain when the Spanish Civil War broke out. Rukeyser famously traveled to West Virginia to investigate for herself a rash of silicosis cases among miners. Her experiences would form the basis of many of the poems in *U.S. 1,* which appeared in 1938. Over the following decades, Rukeyser continued her social efforts, protesting the Vietnam War, speaking out for feminist issues, and amassing a 118-page FBI file. She also continued her career as a poet, publishing such books as *A Turning Wind, Beast in View, The Green Wave, The Speed of Darkness, Breaking Open,* and *The Life of Poetry*. While she was attacked on many sides by critics, her poetry was a major influence on a generation of younger writers. She died in New York City in 1980. "The Dream-Singing Elegy" appeared in *The Kenyon Review* in 1946.

The Dream-Singing Elegy[1] *(1946)*
by Muriel Rukeyser

Darkness, giving us dream's black unity.
Images in procession start to flow
among the river-currents down the years of judgment
and past the cities to another world.

There are flat places. After the waterfall
arched like the torso of love, after the voice
singing behind the waterfall, after the water
lying like a lover on the heart,
there is defeat.

And moving through our spirit in the night
memories of these places.
Not ritual, not nostalgia, but our cries,
the axe at the heart, continual rebirth,
the crying of our raw desire,
young. O many-memoried America!

In defeat there are no prophets and no magicians,
only the look in the loved and tortured eyes
when every fantasy restores, and day denies.
The act of war debased to an act of treason

in an age of treason. We were strong at the first.
We resisted. We did not plan enough. We killed.
But the enemy came like thunder in the wood,
a storm over the treetops like a horse's head

---

1) After 1870, the American Indians of the West faced their defeat. As among many deprived groups,
their reaction to defeat took the form of fantasy and religious revival. This movement was expressed
in the Ghost Dance, dream singing, and other expressions of ritual symbolism. I have used some of
the Indian material in this poem, and especially a paper by Philleo Nash, "Revivalism on Klamath
Reservation," included in *Social Organization of North American Tribes*. This material appears to me
to have certain connections with expression in the over-run countries of our own time. *Author's Note.*

reared to a great galloping, and war
trampled us down. We lost our young men in the fighting,
we lost our homeland, our crops went under the frost,
our children under the hunger. Now we stand
around this fire, our black hills far behind us,
black water far ahead, a glitter of time on the sea,
glitter of fire on our faces, the still faces—
stillness waiting for dreams
and only the shadows moving,
shadows and revelations.

In the spring of the year, this new fighting broke out.
No, when the fields were blond. No, the leaves crimson.
When the old fighting was over, we knew what we were
seeing as if for a first time our dark hills masked with green,
our blond fields with the trees flame-shaped and black
in burning darkness on the unconsumed.
Seeing for a first time the body of our love,
our wish and our love for each other.
Then word came from a runner, a stranger:
"They are dancing to bring the dead back, in the mountains."

We danced at an autumn fire, we danced the old hate and change,
the coming again of our leaders. But they did not come.
Our singers lifted their arms, and a singer cried,
"You must sing like me and believe, or be turned to rock!"

The winter came, but the dead did not come back.
News came on the frost, "The dead are on the march!"
We danced in prison to a winter music,
many we loved began to dream of the dead.
They made no promises, we never dreamed a threat.
And the dreams spread.

But there were no armies, and the dead were dead,
there was only ourselves, the strong and symbol self
dreaming among defeat, our torture and our flesh.
We made the most private image and religion,

stripped to the last resistance of the wish,
remembering the fighting and the lava beds,
the ground that opened, the red wounds opening,
remembering the triumph in the night,
the big triumph and the little triumph—
wide singing and the battle-flash—
assassination and whisper.

In the summer, dreaming was common to all of us,
the drumbeat hope, the bursting heart of wish,
music to bind us as the visions streamed
and midnight brightened to belief.
In the morning we told our dreams.
They all were the same dream.

Dreamers wake in the night and sing their songs.
In the flame-brilliant midnight, promises
arrive, singing to each of us with tongues of flame:
"We are hopes, you should have hoped us,
"We are dreams, you should have dreamed us."
Calling our name.

When we began to fight, we sang hatred and death.
The new songs say, "Soon all people on earth
will live together." We resist and bless
and we begin to travel from defeat.
Now, as you sing your dream, you ask the dancers,
in the night, in the still night, in the night,
"Do you believe what I say?"
And all the dancers answer "Yes."

To the farthest west, the sea and the striped country
and deep in the camps among the wounded cities
half-world over, the waking dreams of night
outrange the horrors. Past fierce and tossing skies
the rare desires shine in constellation.

I hear your cries, you little voices of children
swaying wild, night lost, in black fields calling.
I hear you as the seething dreams arrive
over the sea and past the flaming mountains.

Now the great human dream as great as birth or death,
only that we are not given to remember birth,
only that we are not given to hand down death,
this we hand down and remember.

Brothers in dream, naked-standing friend
rising over the night, crying aloud,
beaten and beaten and rising from defeat,
crying as we cry: We are the world together.
Here is the place in hope, on time's hillside,
where hope, in one's image, wavers for the last time
and moves out of one's body up the slope.
That place in love, where one's self, as the body of love,
moves out of the old lifetime towards the beloved.
Singing.

We look at the many colors of the world
knowing the peace of the spaces and the eyes of love,
who resists beyond suffering, travels beyond dream,
knowing the promise of the night-flowering worlds
sees in a clear day love and child and brother
living, resisting, and the world one world
dreaming together.

William Carlos Williams

William Carlos Williams was born in Rutherford, New Jersey, in 1883. He graduated from a New York high school in 1902 and attended the University of Pennsylvania, entering the medical school. It was here that Williams befriended Ezra Pound and H.D. (Hilda Doolittle), and all three would become major modern poets. After traveling abroad, Williams opened a private practice in his hometown and married Florence "Flossie" Herman in 1912. By 1913, Williams had two books of poetry published, *Poems* and *The Tempers*, and a third, *Al Que Quiere!,* was published in 1917, but his full talent as a poet did not appear until more experimental works like *Kora in Hell: Improvisations* and *Spring and All*. In the late 1920s, Williams and his wife spent time in Europe, meeting many expatriate writers, spurring his desire to achieve literary success by focusing on his *American* experiences and trying to capture *American* speech. World War II and Williams's busy practice with civilian patients nearly brought his writing career to a halt. He did manage to publish the first part of *Paterson*, an epic poem about Paterson, New Jersey, in 1946, the same year his poem "A Place (Any Place) to Transcend All Places" appeared in *The Kenyon Review.* In 1950, Williams was given the National Book Award for his *Selected Poems*. In 1951, he suffered a stroke, forcing him to retire from medical practice, but he continued to publish steadily. He died in 1963 at the age of eighty in Rutherford, being posthumously awarded the Pulitzer Prize for his collection *Pictures from Brueghel and Other Poems* that same year.

A Place (Any Place) to Transcend All Places *(1946)*
by William Carlos Williams

In New York, it is said,
they *do* meet (if that is
what is wanted, talk) but
nothing is exchanged
unless that guff
can be retranslated: as
to say, that is not
the end, there are channels
above that, draining
places from which New York
is dignified, created (the
deaf are not tuned in).

A church in New Hampshire
built by its pastor
from his own wood-lot. One
black (of course, red)
rose; a fat old woman backing
through a screen door. Two,
from the armpits
down, contrasting in bed,
breathless; a letter from
a ship; leaves filling,
making, a tree (but
wait) not just leaves,
leaves of one design that
make a certain design,
no two alike, not like
the locust either, next in line,
nor the rose of Sharon, in
the pod stage, near it—a
tree! Imagine it! Pears
philosophically hard. Nor
thought that is from
branches on a root, from
an acid soil, with scant

grass about the bole
where it breaks through.

New York is built of
such grass and weeds; a modern
tuberculous-tested herd
white-faced behind a
white fence, patient and
uniform; a museum of looks
across a breakfast
table; subways of dreams;
towers of divisions
from thin pay envelopes.
What else is it? And what
else can it be? Sweat-shops
and railroad yards at dusk
(puffed up by fantasy
to seem real) what else
can they be budded on
to live a little longer?
The eyes by this
far quicker than the mind.

   —and we have
southern writers, foreign
writers, hugging a
distinction, while perspectived
behind them following
the crisis (at home)
peasant loyalties inspire
the *avant-garde*. Abstractly?
No. That was for something
else. "Le futur!" grimly.
New York? That hodge-podge?
The international city
(from the Bosphorus). Poor
Hobokezi. Poor sad
Eliot. Poor memory.

—and we have
—the memory of Elsa
von Freytag Loringhofen,
a fixation from the street
door of a Berlin
playhouse; all who "wear
their manner too obviously,"
the adopted English (white)
and many others.

—and we have
—the script writer advising
"every line to be like
a ten word telegram" but
neglecting to add, "to a
child of twelve," obscene
beyond belief.

Obscene and
abstract as excrement—
that no one wants to own
except the coolie
with a garden of which
the lettuce particularly
depends on it—if you
like lettuce, but
very, very specially, heaped
about the roots for nourishment.

Robert Lowell

Robert Lowell was born in Boston, Massachusetts, in 1917. Educated at Harvard for two years, Lowell decided to transfer to Kenyon College to study under John Crowe Ransom. While at Kenyon, Lowell befriended Randall Jarrell and Peter Taylor, all of whom would become major literary figures. Shortly after graduating in 1940, Lowell married writer Jean Stafford and went on to study at Louisiana State University. In 1943, Lowell spent several months in jail as a conscientious objector to WWII. His first book, *Land of Unlikeness,* was later revised and published as *Lord Weary's Castle* in 1946, earning him the Pulitzer Prize at the age of thirty. In 1948, Lowell and Stafford divorced and in 1949 Lowell married Elizabeth Hardwick. During the next few years, Lowell began to suffer from bouts of manic depression, a condition for which he would be hospitalized throughout his life. He began writing autobiographical poems about his mental state and surroundings, culminating with the watershed collection *Life Studies* (1959), spearheading the "confessional" movement. During the 1960s, Lowell remained politically and artistically active, befriending Robert and Jacqueline Kennedy and protesting the Vietnam War while producing such acclaimed works as *For the Union Dead* and *Near the Ocean.* He won his second Pulitzer Prize for *The Dolphin,* after his third marriage to Caroline Blackwood in 1972. He died of a heart attack in 1977 at the age of sixty. In November 1998, *The Kenyon Review* held a celebration for the sixty-year anniversary of Lowell's arrival at Kenyon, where writers from all over the country came to read from and discuss the work of perhaps the most influential poet of the post-WWII period.

Winter in Dunbarton *(1946)*

by Robert Lowell

Time smiling on this sundial of a world
Corrupted the snow-monster and the worm,
Ransacker of shard statues and the peers
Of Europe; but our cat is cold, is curled
For rigor mortis: she no longer smears
Her catnip mouse from Christmas; the germ,
Mindless and ice, a world against our world,
Hurtles her round of brains into her ears;

This winter only snowmen turn to stone:
And, sick of the long hurly-burly, rise
Like butterflies into Jehovah's eyes
And shift until their crystals must atone

To water; but the days are short and rot
The holly on our Father's mound. All day
The wastes of snow about our house stare in
Through idle windows at the brainless cat;
The coke-barrel in the corner whimpers. May
The snow recede and red clay furrows set
In the grim grin of their erosion, in
The fusion of uprooted fallow, fat

With muck and winter dropsy, where the tall
Snow-monster wipes the coke fumes from his eyes
And scatters his corruption and it lies
Gaping until the fungus-eyeballs fall
Into this eldest of the seasons. Cold
Cracks the bronze toes and fingers of the Christ
Our Father fetched from Florence, and the dead
Narrow to nothing in the thankless ground
Grandfather wrenched from Charlie Stark and sold
To the selectmen of Dunbarton. Head
And shoulders narrow: Father's stone is crowned
With snowflakes and the bronze-age shards of Christ.

Wallace Stevens

Wallace Stevens was born in Reading, Pennsylvania, on October 2, 1879, and died at the age of seventy-six in Hartford, Connecticut, on August 2, 1955. He was a student at Harvard before eventually graduating from New York Law School in 1903. Wallace was admitted to the U.S. Bar in 1904 and spent several years working for New York law firms before settling at the home office of the Hartford Accident and Indemnity in Hartford, Connecticut, where he would spend the rest of his life. Stevens published his first book, *Harmonium*, in 1923, but was disappointed with his reviews, so he published nothing for the remainder of the '20s. In the following decades, Stevens published with renewed vigor, releasing such books as *Ideas of Order* (1935), *Owl's Clover* (1937), *The Man with the Blue Guitar* (1937), *Parts of a World* (1942), *Notes toward a Supreme Fiction* (1942), and *Auroras of Autumn* (1951), the title poem of which was originally printed in 1948 in *The Kenyon Review*, and for which he received the National Book Award. These books established Stevens as one of the greatest poets of the twentieth century, a rare talent that continued to develop into his seventies. His poems–exuberant, vivid, and philosophical–are widely read and taught today.

The Auroras of Autumn *(1948)*
by Wallace Stevens

I
This is where the serpent lives, the bodiless.
His head is air. Beneath his tip at night
Eyes open and fix on us in every sky.

Or is this another wriggling out of the egg,
Another image at the end of the cave,
Another bodiless for the body's slough?

This is where the serpent lives. This is his nest,
These fields, these hills, these tinted distances,
And the pines above and along and beside the sea.

This is form gulping after formlessness,
Skin flashing to wished-for disappearances
And the serpent body flashing without the skin.

This is the height emerging and its base…
These lights may finally attain a pole
In the midmost midnight and find the serpent there,

In another nest, the master of the maze
Of body and air and forms and images,
Relentlessly in possession of happiness.

This is his poison: that we should disbelieve
Even that. His meditations in the ferns,
When he moved so slightly to make sure of sun,

Made us no less as sure. We saw in his head,
Black beaded on the rock, the flecked animal,
The moving grass, the Indian in his glade.

II
Farewell to an idea... A cabin stands,
Deserted, on a beach. It is white,
As by a custom or according to

An ancestral theme or as a consequence
Of an infinite course. The flowers against the wall
Are white, a little dried, a kind of mark

Reminding, trying to remind, of a white
That was different, something else, last year
Or before, not the white of an aging afternoon,

Whether fresher or duller, whether of winter cloud
Or of winter sky, from horizon to horizon.
The wind is blowing the sand across the floor.

Here, being visible is being white,
Is being of the solid of white, the accomplishment
Of an extremist in an exercise...

The season changes. A cold wind chills the beach.
The long lines of it grow longer, emptier,
A darkness gathers though it does not fall

And the whiteness grows less vivid on the wall.
The man who is walking turns blankly on the sand.
He observes how the north is always enlarging the change,

With its frigid brilliances, its blue-red sweeps
And gusts of great enkindlings, its polar green,
The color of ice and fire and solitude.

III
Farewell to an idea... The mother's face,
The purpose of the poem, fills the room.
They are together, here, and it is warm,

With none of the prescience of oncoming dreams.
It is evening. The house is evening, half dissolved.
Only the half they can never possess remains,

Still-starred. It is the mother they possess,
Who gives transparence to their present peace.
She makes that gentler that can gentle be.

And yet she too is dissolved, she is destroyed.
She gives transparence. But she has grown old.
The necklace is a carving not a kiss.

The soft hands are a motion not a touch.
The house will crumble and the books will burn.
They are at ease in a shelter of the mind

And the house is of the mind and they and time,
Together, all together. Boreal night
Will look like frost as it approaches them

And to the mother as she falls asleep
And as they say good-night, good-night. Upstairs
The windows will be lighted, not the rooms.

A wind will spread its windy grandeurs round
And knock like a rifle-butt against the door.
The wind will command them with invincible sound.

IV
Farewell to an idea... The cancellings,
The negations, are never final. The father sits
In space, wherever he sits, of bleak regard,

As one that is strong in the bushes of his eyes.
He says no to no and yes to yes. He says yes
To no; and in saying yes he says farewell.

He measures the velocities of change.
He leaps from heaven to heaven more rapidly
Than bad angels leap from heaven to hell in flames.

But now he sits in quiet and green-a-day.
He assumes the great speeds of space and flutters them
From cloud to cloudless, cloudless to keen clear

In flights of eye and ear, the highest eye
And the lowest ear, the deep ear that discerns,
At evening, things that attend it until it hears

The supernatural preludes of its own,
At the moment when the angelic eye defines
Its actors approaching, in company, in their masks.

Master O master seated by the fire
And yet in space and motionless and yet
Of motion the ever-brightening origin,

Profound, and yet the king and yet the crown,
Look at this present throne. What company,
In masks, can choir it with the naked wind?

V
The mother invites humanity to her house
And table. The father fetches tellers of tales
And musicians who mute much, muse much, on the tales.

The father fetches negresses to dance,
Among the children, like curious ripenesses
Of pattern in the dance's ripening.

For these the musicians make insidious tones,
Clawing the sing-song of their instruments.
The children laugh and jangle a tinny time.

The father fetches pageants out of air,
Scenes of the theatre, vistas and blocks of woods
And curtains like a naive pretense of sleep.

Among these the musicians strike the instinctive poem.
The father fetches his unherded herds,
Of barbarous tongue, slavered and panting halves

Of breath, obedient to his trumpet's touch.
This then is Chatillon or as you please.
We stand in the tumult of a festival.

What festival? This loud, disordered mooch?
These hospitaliers? These brute-like guests?
These musicians dubbing at a tragedy,

A-dub, a-dub, which is made up of this:
That there are no lines to speak? There is no play.
Or, the persons act one merely by being here.

VI
It is a theatre floating through the clouds,
Itself a cloud, although of misted rock
And mountains running like water, wave on wave,

Through waves of light. It is of cloud transformed
To cloud transformed again, idly, the way
A season changes color to no end,

Except the lavishing of itself in change,
As light changes yellow into gold and gold
To its opal elements and fire's delight,

Splashed wide-wise because it likes magnificence
And the solemn pleasures of magnificent space.
The cloud drifts idly through half thought of forms.

The theatre is filled with flying birds,
Wild wedges, as of a volcano's smoke, palm-eyed
And vanishing, a web in a corridor

Or massive portico. A capitol,
It may be, is emerging or has just
Collapsed. The denouement has to be postponed.

This is nothing until in a single man contained,
Nothing until this named thing nameless is
And is destroyed. He opens the door of his house

On flames. The scholar of one candle sees
Arctic effulgence flaring on the frame
Of everything he is. And he feels afraid.

VII
Is there an imagination that sits enthroned
As grim as it is benevolent, the just
And the unjust, which in the midst of summer stops

To imagine winter? When the leaves are dead,
Does it take its place in the north and enfold itself,
Goat-leaper, crystalled and luminous, sitting

In highest night? And do these heavens adorn
And proclaim it, the white creator of black, jetted
By extinguishings, even of planets as may be,

Even of earth, even of sight, in snow,
Except as needed by way of majesty,
In the sky, as crown and diamond cabala?

It leaps through us, through all our heavens leaps,
Extinguishing our planets, one by one,
Leaving, of where we were and looked, of where

We knew each other and of each other thought,
A shivering residue, chilled and foregone,
Except for that crown and mystical cabala.

But it dare not leap by chance in its own dark.
It must change from destiny to slight caprice.
And thus its jetted tragedy, its stele

And shape and mournful making move to find
What must unmake it and, at last, what can,
Say, a flippant communication under the moon.

VIII
There may be always a time of innocence.
There is never a place. Or if there is no time,
If it is not a thing of time, nor of place,

Existing in the idea of it, alone,
In the sense against calamity, it is not
Less real. For the oldest and coldest philosopher,

There is or may be a time of innocence
As pure principle. Its nature is its end,
That it should be, and yet not be, a thing

That pinches the pity of the pitiful man,
Like a book at evening beautiful but untrue,
Like a book on rising beautiful and true.

It is like a thing of ether that exists
Almost as predicate. But it exists,
It exists, it is visible, it is, it is.

So, then, these lights are not a spell of light,
A saying out of a cloud, but innocence.
An innocence of the earth and no false sign

Or symbol of malice. That we partake thereof,
Lie down like children in this holiness,
As if, awake, we lay in the quiet of sleep,

As if the innocent mother sang in the dark
Of the room and on an accordion, half-heard,
Created the time and place in which we breathed.

IX
And of each other thought—in the idiom
Of the work, in the idiom of an innocent earth,
Not of the enigma of the guilty dream.

We were as Danes in Denmark all day long
And knew each other well, hale-hearted landsmen,
For whom the outlandish was another day

Of the week, queerer than Sunday. We thought alike
And that made brothers of us in a home
In which we fed on being brothers, fed

And fattened as on a decorous honey-comb.
This drama that we live—We lay sticky with sleep.
This sense of the activity of fate—

The rendezvous, when she came alone,
By her coming became a freedom of the two,
An isolation which only the two could share.

Shall we be found hanging in the trees next spring?
Of what disaster in this the imminence:
Bare limbs, bare trees and a wind as sharp as salt?

The stars are putting on their glittering belts.
They throw around their shoulders cloaks that flash
Like a great shadow's last embellishment.

It may come to-morrow in the simplest word,
Almost as part of innocence, almost,
Almost as the tenderest and the truest part.

X
An unhappy people in a happy world—
Read, rabbi, the phases of this difference.
An unhappy people in an unhappy world—

Here are too many mirrors for misery.
A happy people in an unhappy world—
It cannot be. There's nothing there to roll

On the expressive tongue, the finding fang.
A happy people in a happy world—
Buffo! A ball, an opera, a bar.

Turn back to where we were when we began:
An unhappy people in a happy world.
Now, solemnize the secretive syllables.

Read to the congregation, for to-day
And for to-morrow, this extremity,
This contrivance of the spectre of the spheres,

Contriving balance to contrive a whole,
The vital, the never-failing genius,
Fulfilling his meditations, great and small.

In these unhappy he meditates a whole,
The full of fortune and the full of fate,
As if he lived all lives, that he might know,

In hall harridan, not hushful paradise,
To a haggling of wind and weather, by these lights
Like a blaze of summer straw, in winter's nick.

Robert Lowell

Robert Lowell was born in Boston, Massachusetts, in 1917. Educated at Harvard for two years, Lowell decided to transfer to Kenyon College to study under John Crowe Ransom. While at Kenyon, Lowell befriended Randall Jarrell and Peter Taylor, all of whom would become major literary figures. Shortly after graduating in 1940, Lowell married writer Jean Stafford and went on to study at Louisiana State University. In 1943, Lowell spent several months in jail as a conscientious objector to WWII. His first book, *Land of Unlikeness,* was later revised and published as *Lord Weary's Castle* in 1946, earning him the Pulitzer Prize at the age of thirty. In 1948, Lowell and Stafford divorced and in 1949 Lowell married Elizabeth Hardwick. During the next few years, Lowell began to suffer from bouts of manic depression, a condition for which he would be hospitalized throughout his life. He began writing autobiographical poems about his mental state and surroundings, culminating with the watershed collection *Life Studies* (1959), spearheading the "confessional" movement. During the 1960s, Lowell remained politically and artistically active, befriending Robert and Jacqueline Kennedy, and protesting the Vietnam War while producing such acclaimed works as *For the Union Dead* and *Near the Ocean.* He won his second Pulitzer Prize for *The Dolphin,* after his third marriage to Caroline Blackwood in 1972. He died of a heart attack in 1977 at the age of sixty. In November 1998, *The Kenyon Review* held a celebration for the sixty-year anniversary of Lowell's arrival at Kenyon, where writers from all over the country came to read from and discuss the work of perhaps the most influential poet of the post-WWII period

Falling Asleep over the Aeneid[1] *(1948)*
by Robert Lowell

An old man in Concord forgets to go to Morning Service. He falls asleep,
while reading Virgil, and dreams that he is Aeneas at the funeral of Pallas,
an Italian prince.

The sun is blue and scarlet on my page,
And *yuck-a, yuck-a, yuck-a, yuck-a,* rage
The yellowhammers mating. Yellow fire
Blankets the captives dancing on their pyre,
And the scorched lictor screams and drops his rod.
Trojans are singing to their drunken God,
Ares. Their helmets catch on fire. Their files
Clank by the body of my comrade—miles
Of filings! Now the scythe-wheeled chariot rolls
Before their lances long as vaulting poles,
And I stand up and heil the thousand men,
Who carry Pallas to the bird-priest. Then
The bird-priest groans, and as his birds foretold,
I greet the body, lip to lip. I hold
The sword that Dido used. It tries to speak,
A bird with Dido's sworded breast. Its beak
Clangs and ejaculates the Punic word
I hear the bird-priest chirping like a bird.
I groan a little. "Who am I, and why?"
It asks, a boy's face, though its arrow-eye
Is working from its socket. "Brother, try,
O Child of Aphrodite, try to die:
To die is life." His harlots hang his bed
With feathers of his long-tailed birds. His head
Is yawning like a person. The plumes blow;
The beard and eyebrows ruffle. Face of snow,
You are the flower that country girls have caught,
A wild bee-pillaged honeysuckle brought

---

1) This paper was read at the Conference on the Heritage of the English-Speaking Peoples and Their
   Responsibilities, September 27, 1947, at Kenyon College.

To the returning bridegroom—the design
Has not yet left it, and the petals shine;
The earth, its mother, has, at last, no help:
It is itself. The broken-winded yelp
Of my Phoenician hounds, that fills the brush
With snapping twigs and flying, cannot flush
The ghost of Pallas. But I take his pall,
Stiff with its gold and purple, and recall
How Dido hugged it to her, while she toiled,
Laughing—her golden threads, a serpent coiled
In cypress. Now I lay it like a sheet;
It clinks and settles down upon his feet,
The careless golden hair that seemed to burn
Beforehand. Left foot, right foot—as they turn,
More pyres are rising: armored horses, bronze,
And gagged Italians, who must pass by ones
Across the bitter river, when my thumb
Tightens into their wind-pipes. The beaks drum;
Their headman's cow-horned death's head bites its tongue,
And stiffens, as it eyes the hero slung
Inside his feathered hammock on the crossed
Staves of the eagles that we winged. Our cost
Is nothing to the lovers, whoring Mars
And Venus, father's lover. Now the car's
Plumage is ready, and my marshals fetch
His squire, Acoetes, white with age, to hitch
Aethon, the hero's charger, and its ears
Prick, and it steps and steps, and stately tears
Lather its teeth; and then the harlots bring
The hero's charms and baton—but the King,
Vain-glorious Turnus, carried off the rest.
"I was myself, but Ares thought it best
The way it happened." At the end of time,
He sets his spear, as my descendants climb
The knees of Father Time, his beard of scalps,
His scythe, the arc of steel that crowns the Alps.
The elephants of Carthage hold those snows,
Terms of Numidian horse unsung their bows,

The flaming turkey-feathered arrows swarm
Beyond the Alps. "Pallas," I raise my arm
And shout, "Brother, eternal health. Farewell
Forever." Church is over, and its bell
Frightens the yellowhammers, as I wake,
And watch the whitecaps wrinkle up the lake.
Mother's great aunt, who died when I was eight,
Stands by the parlor sabre. "Boy, it's late.
Virgil must keep the Sabbath." Forty years!
It all comes back. My Uncle Charles appears,
Blue-capped and bird-like. Phillips Brooks and Grant
Are frowning at his coffin, and my aunt,
Hearing his colored volunteers parade
Through Concord, laughs, and tells her English maid
To clip his yellow nostril hairs, and fold
His colors on him. It is I. I hold
His sword to keep from falling, for the dust
On the stuffed birds is breathless, for the bust
Of young Augustus weighs on Virgil's shelf:
It scowls into my glasses at itself.

W.H. Auden

W.H. Auden, born Wystan Hugh Auden, was born in York, England, in 1907. He moved to Birmingham during his childhood and was educated at Christ's Church, Oxford. After college he spent time in Berlin and later went to Spain to contribute on the republican side of the Civil War. His early poetic work, *Poems* (1930), *The Orators* (1932), *The Dance of Death* (1933), and *Look, Stranger!* (1936) made his reputation as a witty and technically accomplished writer. In 1939, Auden traveled to America and settled in New York, where he met lifelong partner Chester Kallman. He spent the rest of his life primarily in the U.S. teaching at various universities. Auden went through several major ideological shifts in his life that were reflected in his writing, from Marxism to Christianity–he revised his early work to reflect his interest in Christianity. Auden is responsible for some of the finest poems written in the English language, including "Musee Des Beaux Arts" and "In Memory of W.B. Yeats," and such books as *The Age of Anxiety, The Shield of Achilles*, and *The Dyer's Hand and Other Essays*. In 1972, Auden returned to Oxford. He died in his sleep during a trip to Austria the following year at the age of sixty-five. His essay "Yeats as an Example" appeared in *The Kenyon Review* in 1948.

Yeats as an Example *(1948)*
by W.H. Auden

One drawback, and not the least, of practicing any art is that it becomes very difficult to enjoy the works of one's fellow artists, living or dead, simply for their own sakes.

When a poet, for instance, reads a poem written by another, he is apt to be less concerned with what the latter actually accomplished by his poem than with the suggestions it throws out upon how he, the reader, may solve the poetic problems which confront him now. His judgments of poetry, therefore, are rarely purely aesthetic; he will often prefer an inferior poem from which he can learn something at the moment to a better poem from which he can learn nothing. This gap between his evaluations and those of the pure critic is all the wider in the case of his immediate predecessors. All generations overlap, and the young poet naturally looks for and finds the greatest help in the work of those whose poetic problems are similar to his because they have experiences in common. He begins, therefore, with an excessive admiration for one or more of the mature poets of his time. But, as he grows older, he becomes more and more conscious of belonging to a different generation faced with problems that his heroes cannot help him to solve, and his former hero-worship, as in other spheres of life, is all too apt to turn into an equally excessive hostility and contempt. Those of us who, like myself, have learned, as we think, all we can, and that is a good deal, from Yeats, are tempted to be more conscious and more critical of those elements in his poems with which we are not in sympathy than we ought to be.

Our criticisms may sometimes be objectively correct, but the subjective resentment with which we make them is always unjust. Further, as long as we harbor such a resentment, it will be a dangerous hindrance to our own poetic development, for, in poetry as in life, to lead one's own life means to relive the lives of one's parents and, through them, of all one's ancestors; the duty of the present is neither to copy nor to deny the past but to resurrect it.

I shall not attempt, therefore, in this paper, to answer such questions as, "How good a poet is Yeats? Which are his best poems and why"—that is the job of better critics than I and of posterity—but rather to consider him as a predecessor whose importance no one will or can deny, to raise, that is to say, such questions as, "What were the problems which faced Yeats as a poet as compared with ours? How far do they overlap? How far are they different? In so far as they are different, what can we learn from the way in which Yeats dealt with his world, about how to deal with our own?"

Let me begin with the element in his work which seems most foreign to us, his cosmology, his concern with the occult. Here, I think, is a curious fact. In most cases, when a major writer influences a beginner, that influence extends to his matter, to his opinions as well as to his manner—think of Hardy, or Eliot, or D.H. Lawrence; yet, though there is scarcely a lyric written today in which the influence of his style and rhythm is not detectable, one whole side of Yeats, the side summed up in the *Vision*, has left virtually no trace.

However diverse our fundamental beliefs may be, the reaction of most of us to all that occult is, I fancy, the same: how on earth, we wonder, could a man of Yeats's gifts take such nonsense seriously? I have a further bewilderment, which may be due to my English upbringing, one of snobbery. How *could* Yeats, with his great aesthetic appreciation of aristocracy, ancestral houses, ceremonious tradition, take up something so essentially lower-middle class—or should I say Southern Californian—so ineluctably associated with suburban villas and clearly unattractive faces? A.E. Housman's pessimistic stoicism seems to me nonsense too, but at least it is a kind of nonsense that can be believed by a gentleman—but mediums, spells, the Mysterious Orient—*how* embarrassing. In fact, of course, it is to Yeats's credit, and an example to me, that he ignored such considerations, nor, granted that his Weltanschauung was false, can we claim credit for rejecting what we have no temptation to accept, nor deny that the poetry he wrote involving it is very good. What we should consider, then, is firstly, why Celtic mythology in his earlier phases, and occult symbolism in his later, should have attracted Yeats when they fail to attract us; secondly, what are the comparable kinds of beliefs to which we are drawn and why; thirdly, what is the relation between myth, belief, and poetry?

Yeats's generation grew up in a world where the great conflict was between the Religion of Reason and the Religion of Imagination, objective truth and subjective truth, the Universal and the Individual.

Further, Reason, Science, the general, seemed to be winning and Imagination, Art, and the individual on the defensive. Now in all conflicts it is the side which takes the offensive that defines the issues which their opponents have to defend, so that when scientists said, "Science is knowledge of reality, Art is a fairyland," the artists were driven to reply, "Very well, but fairies are fun, science is dull." When the former said, "Art has no relation to life," the latter retorted, "Thank God." To the assertion that "every mind can recognize the absolute truths of science, but the values of art are purely relative, an arbitrary affair of individual taste," came back the counterclaim, "Only the exceptional individual matters."

Thus, if we find Yeats adopting a cosmology apparently on purely aesthetic grounds, i.e., not because it is true but because it is interesting; or Joyce attempting to convert the whole of existence into words; or even a dialectician like Shaw, after the most brilliant and devastating criticism of the pretensions of scientists, spoiling his case by being a crank and espousing Lamarckism, we must see their reactions, I think, if we are to understand them, in terms of a polemical situation in which they accepted—they probably could do nothing else—the antithesis between reason and imagination which the natural sciences of their time forced upon them, only reversing, with the excessive violence of men defending a narrow place against superior numbers, the value signs on each side.

Our situation is somewhat different. The true natural sciences like physics and chemistry no longer claim to explain the meaning of life (that presumption has passed to the so-called Social Sciences) nor—at least since the Atom Bomb—would any one believe them if they did. The division of which we are aware is not between Reason and Imagination but between the good and evil will, not between objectivity and subjectivity but between the integration of thought and feeling and their dissociation, not between the individual and the masses but between the social person and the impersonal state.

Consequently the dangers that beset us are different. We are unlikely to believe something because it would be fun to believe it; but we are very likely to do one of two things, either to say that everything is relative, that there is no absolute truth, or that those who do not hold what we believe to be absolute reject it out of malice.

When two people today engage in an argument, each tends to spend half of his time and energy not in producing evidence to support his point of view but in looking for the hidden motives which are causing his opponent to hold his. If they lose their tempers, instead of saying, "You are a fool," they say, "You are a wicked man."

No one now asserts that art ought not to describe immoral persons or acts; but many assert that it must show those on the right side as perfectly moral and those on the wrong as completely immoral. An artist today is less likely than his predecessors to claim that his profession is supremely important but he is much more likely to sacrifice his artistic integrity for economic or political reward.

No private citizen today thinks seriously, "Here is superior me and there are all those other people"; but "Here are we, all in the same boat, and there is It, the Government." We are not likely to become snobs—the great houses have become state institutions anyway—but we can all too easily become anarchists who, by passively refusing to take any part in political life, or by acting blindly in terms of our own advantage alone, promote the loss of that very individual liberty we would like to keep.

To return from life to poetry: any poet today, even if he deny the importance of dogma to life, can see how useful myths are to poetry—how much, for instance, they helped Yeats to make his private experiences public and his vision of public events personal. He knows, too, that in poetry all dogmas become myths; that the aesthetic value of the poem is the same whether the poet and/or the reader actively believe what it says or not. He is apt then to look around for some myth—any myth, he thinks, will do—to serve the same purpose for himself. What he overlooks is that the only kind of myth which will do for him must have one thing in common with believed dogma, namely, that the relation of the former to the poet, as of the latter to the soul, must be a personal one. The Celtic legends Yeats used were woven into his childhood—he really went to seances, he seriously studied all those absurd books. You cannot use a Weltanschauung like Psychoanalysis or Marxism or Christianity as a poetic myth unless it involves your emotions profoundly, and, if you have not inherited it, your emotions will never become involved unless you take it more seriously than as a mere myth.

Yeats, like us, was faced with the modern problem, i.e., of living in a society in which men are no longer supported by tradition without being aware of it, and in which, therefore, every individual who wishes to bring order and coherence into the stream of sensations, emotions, and ideas entering his consciousness, from without and within, is forced to do deliberately for himself what in previous ages had been done for him by family, custom, church, and state, namely the choice of the principles and presuppositions in terms of which he can make sense of his experience. There are, of course, always authorities in each field, but which expert he is to consult and which he is to believe are matters on which he is obliged to exercise his own free choice. This is very annoying for the artist as it takes up much time which he would greatly prefer to spend on his proper work, where he is a professional and not an amateur.

Because Yeats accepted the fact that we have lost the old nonchalance of the hand, being critics who but half create,

Timid, entangled, empty and abashed
Lacking the countenance of our friends,

accepted it as a working condition and faced its consequences, he is an
example to all who come after him. That is one reason why he may be called
a major poet. There are others.

The difference between major and minor poetry has nothing to do with
the difference between better and worse poetry. Indeed it is frequently the
case that a minor poet produces more single poems which seem flawless
than a major one, because it is one of the distinguishing marks of a major
poet that he continues to develop, that the moment he has learnt how to write
one kind of poem, he goes on to attempt something else, new subjects, new
ways of treatment or both, an attempt in which he may quite possibly fail.
He invariably feels, as Yeats puts it, "the fascination of what's difficult"; or,
in another poem,

I made my song a coat
Covered with embroideries
Out of old mythologies
From heel to throat;
But the fools caught it,
Wore it in the world's eyes
As though they'd wrought it.
Song, let them take it,
For there's more enterprise
In walking naked.

Further, the major poet not only attempts to solve new problems, but the
problems he attacks are central to the tradition, and the lines along which he
attacks them, while they are his own, are not idiosyncratic, but produce
results which are available to his successors. Much as I admire his work, I
consider Hopkins a minor poet, and one of my reasons for thinking so is that
his attempt to develop a rhetoric to replace the Tennysonian rhetoric is too
eccentric, the proof of which is that he cannot influence later poets in any
fruitful way; they can only imitate him. Yeats on the other hand has effected
changes which are of use to every poet. His contributions are not, I think, to
new subject matter, nor to the ways in which poetic material can be organized—where Eliot for instance has made it possible for English poetry to

deal with all the properties of modern city life, and to write poems in which the structure is musical rather than logical. Yeats sticks to the conventional romantic properties and the traditional step-by-step structure of stanzaic verse. His main legacies to us are two. First, he transformed a certain kind of poem, the occasional poem, from being either an official performance of impersonal virtuosity or a trivial *vers de société* into a serious reflective poem of at once personal and public interest.

A poem such as *In Memory of Major Robert Gregory* is something new and important in the history of English poetry. It never loses the personal note of a man speaking about his personal friends in a particular setting—in *Adonais,* for instance, both Shelley and Keats disappear as people—and at the same time the occasion and the characters acquire a symbolic public significance.

Secondly, Yeats released regular stanzaic poetry, whether reflective or lyrical, from iambic monotony; the Elizabethans did this originally for dramatic verse, but not for lyric or elegiac. Thus:

> What youthful mother, a shape upon her lap
> Honey of generation had betrayed,
> And that must sleep, shriek, struggle to escape
> As recollection or the drug decide,
> Would think her son, did she but see that shape
> With sixty or more winters on its head,
> A compensation for the pang of his birth,
> Or the uncertainty of his setting forth?

Or take this:

> Acquaintance; companion;
> One dear brilliant woman;
> The best endowed, the elect
> All by their youth undone,
> All, all, by that inhuman
> Bitter glory wrecked.

> But I have straightened out
> Ruin, wreck and wrack;
> I toiled long years and at length

Came to so deep a thought
I can summon back
All their wholesome strength.

What images are these
That turn dull-eyed away,
Or shift Time's filthy load,
Straighten aged knees,
Hesitate or stay?
What heads shake or nod?

In spite of all the rhythmical variations and the half-rhymes which provide freedom for the most natural and lucid speech, the formal base, i.e., the prosodic rhythms of iambic pentameter in the first, and iambic trimeter in the second, and the rhyme patterns which supply coherent dignity and music, these remain audible.

The magazine *Vogue* is preparing, I believe, to run two series of photographs, one called Contemporary Great, the other Contemporary Influences, a project which is calculated to cause considerable ill-feeling. Does a man feel prouder of what he achieves himself or of the effect he has on the achievements of posterity? Which epitaph upon a poet's grave would please him more: "I wrote some of the most beautiful poetry of my time" or "I rescued English lyric from the dead hand of Campion and Tom Moore"? I suspect that more poets would prefer the second than their readers would ever guess, particularly when, like Yeats, they are comfortably aware that the first is also true.

F. Scott Fitzgerald

F. Scott Fitzgerald was born in St. Paul, Minnesota, in 1896. Fitzgerald attended Princeton University until 1917, when, on academic probation and unlikely to graduate, he joined the army. While stationed at Camp Sheridan, Alabama, Fitzgerald met Zelda Sayre, with whom he would embark on a tumultuous and famous marriage. Upon the publication of his first novel, *This Side of Paradise,* in 1920, Fitzgerald was famous virtually overnight. Mainly earning his living by writing short stories for *The Saturday Evening Post*, Fitzgerald went on to write *The Beautiful and Damned* and, during one of his many periods in France, *The Great Gatsby*. While now widely considered as the defining American novel, *The Great Gatsby* was not an immediate commercial success. Fitzgerald made little progress on his fourth novel, a study of American expatriates in France provisionally titled *The World's Fair*. (The story of the same title originally appearing posthumously in *The Kenyon Review* in 1948). The 1930s brought further turmoil for Fitzgerald, his wife suffering several breakdowns and his finances in ruin. He published his fifth novel, *Tender Is the Night,* and had written half of a working draft of *The Last Tycoon* before he died of a heart attack in 1940, forty-four years old and estranged from his beloved Zelda. Fitzgerald's life and fiction continue to captivate readers worldwide.

The World's Fair *(1948)*

by F. Scott Fitzgerald

All that afternoon Francis knew that part of Dinah wanted to be rid of him, to be swiftly busy with her own affairs. She was short in her speech when he went with her persistently to a milliner's shop and she made him wait outside; he spent the time gazing at a miniature of the battlefields in the window of a tourist office. There was dust gathered on the tangle of tiny tree trunks, wrecked toy tanks, broken caissons, and roofless doll houses marked Verdun, Côté 304, Cambrai, and the panorama seemed as old as the war itself; it depressed him as it lay baking and fading in the sun. He grew cross at waiting but as Dinah came out of the shop the middle phase of the day moved past, the sky deepened and they both relaxed a little feeling the better hours ahead. Still she insisted she had things to do but instinct told him that had she entirely wanted to be rid of him she could have easily done so and he took this as a concession.

He tried to get her to go to the Ritz but she wouldn't and they had tea at Sherry's.

"You'll both be tired of me soon," he said. "I hear you get tired of everybody."

"No. It's just that you have quarrels or you go to new places and then you like the people that you see most of—don't you think?"

"Please don't get tired of me."

"I like old friends."

"Am I an old friend?"

"You'll age," she laughed.

"Because you're the two most charming people I've ever met." He knew that neither of them ever got tired of that, and in addition he meant it. The sound of it and the tea excited him and he struck a more decided note. "I'm falling terribly in love with you and I know it's absurd—no, but really."

She drew on her gloves and suddenly time seemed to be getting short, night coming, the end coming. And as time grew shorter so her qualities grew larger inside the reduced dimension. She was kinder and sweeter; the bravery of all her words grew—those words of hers that it seemed brave for her to speak at all, as if she alone knew how presumptuous it was to speak. Her mouth which in youth had been hurt so much, frightened so persistently into silence by a mother or a series of governesses, became now for a moment something that could be hurt again, and when she stood up she was taller, very tall, flowering in a beautiful straight line from her perfect hat.

"I won't go yet," he said, and reluctantly she sat down again; he was not sure what he was going to say but unexpectedly he was saying it, "I know that being in love with you leads nowhere but I can't help it—those things happen. You belong to Seth and I like him better than any man I know, but there you are, I'm in love with you." He paused and then leaned forward, "I love you, Dinah. I love your dear face and your dear self."

"I suppose this was your line to every girl in Hollywood."

"No. There was only one there. And that was different. She was older."

"So am I."

"No, I mean really older—almost—faded. I was crazy about her and then when she liked me she seemed old. And then when I broke it off I was sorry and I used to have a queer painful feeling when I saw her, but I never wanted to go back."

She sat balanced on the edge of her chair, not restless but resistant. She sat that way for half an hour while they drank a port. He knew that she was entirely womanly, that she would not help him or encourage him by so much as a word and he knew that Seth was always with her, was with her now, but he knew too that in different degrees they were both in the grey gentle world of a hangover when the nerves relax in bunches like piano strings and crackle suddenly like wicker chairs. The nerves so raw and tender must surely join other nerves, lips to lips, breast to breast.

In the taxi they clung together and she kissed him really and they stayed close. They stopped thinking with an almost painful relief, stopped seeing; they only breathed and sought each other. Their lips became things interchangeably owned in common but twice she whispered don't in a cool little voice with no doubt in it whatever.

The lift in her apartment house was broken. As she started up the stairs he went beside her and at a touch of his hand she stopped at the first landing. By the dimming light of a window above they embraced breathlessly. Again he went with her—she was careful on the next landing, on the third more careful still. On the next—there were three more—she stopped halfway and kissed him fleetingly good-bye. At his urgency she walked down with him to the one below. Then it was good-bye with their arms stretching to touch hands along the diagonals of the bannister and then the fingers slipping apart. The next floor swallowed her, then the next diminishing; a door opened and closed above.

Across the street Francis lingered a moment, in love now and wildly jealous of her absence watching the last sunlight smolder on the apartment's big front windows. Even as he watched a taxi drove up and Seth got out and went into the house. His step was quick and alert as if he had just come from some great doings and was hurrying on toward others, organizer of gaiety, master of a richly encrusted, esoteric happiness. His hat was a grand hat and he carried a heavy stick and thin yellow gloves. Francis thought what a good time everyone would have who was with him tonight, and the aura of Seth's good taste cooled his blood for a moment.

"Yes," he said to himself, "they're the most attractive people in the world. Absolutely perfect."

He hurried on for he was to meet that girl a little after eight.

When Francis reached the bar where he had arranged to meet Wanda Breasted he found her in the company of three other girls. They were tall slender girls with rather small, well-carried heads, groomed to the preciseness of mannequins' heads, and charming floating faces. They had evidently been in the bar a long time but none of them was tight and when Wanda presented Francis, their heads above their black tailored suits waved gracefully at him like cobras' hoods or long-stemmed flowers in the wind. Francis had an immediate feeling that he had met all three of them somewhere before. Wanda whispered to him that they were all having dinner together—she couldn't avoid it, but he was not to pay for anything for it was Miss Hart's party and there was another young man, now out telephoning, who would join them presently.

Wanda said to the others that he was a friend of Seth Piper's and at once the three women extended themselves toward him expressing surprise and interest that the Pipers were in Paris. The girl whose mouth twisted kindly under a hooked nose said:

"Not that I should be concerned—after their being so obviously fed up with me."

Then the tallest and handsomest girl said bitterly, "I must say I prefer people whose lives have more corrugated surfaces. Seth might be all right if she'd give him a chance."

Miss Hart, a boyish, jaunty girl who might have been anything between twenty-five and thirty-five, spoke in a hearty voice.

"After all, darling, what's so extraordinary about them. I've met them here and there and after expecting at least St. Louis and Joan of Arc I haven't been able to get really excited about them."

"Seth's the extraordinary one," said the girl the Pipers were fed up with. "Dinah's just a very loyal, frank person."

"A loyal frank person," repeated the other bitterly. "Yes—she's going to be that if she has to bitch everybody in the world to do it."

Francis was furious but he was somewhat intimidated by their height and sleekness and by the attentive and finely critical look they bent upon him whenever he opened his mouth to speak. Feeling himself slipping here and there among changing indignations he gave up and told himself how hard and superficial everyone was after Seth and Dinah. They were in any case not talking to him, but to each other. Again they reminded him of something and again it slipped away.

"I don't really think she likes all this changing around of friends," insisted Miss Taube. "Of course my private opinion is that Seth made her up."

"But why the entirely liquid Mr. Grant?" asked Miss Hart.

"That's Mrs. Grant—Seth will stand a lot from anyone capable of telling him in new ways how charming he is."

"My God!" muttered Francis—they all threw him a flinching glance and Miss Taube said conciliatingly:

"After all, I'm only sorry Seth doesn't like me anymore–and some day it might be his whim to honor me once again with a moment or so of his attentions, and hand me my self-respect, my justification on a platter as he has a way of doing."

The handsomest head swayed forward eagerly like a cobra's hood.

"Once I tried to paint him. I know how his face goes but I always had one eye left over. The answer was that his eyes are too close together."

"My God," said Francis again.

"So are mine, dearest. Seth's great quality is in that politeness of his that seems to extend right out of the ordinary world of courtesy. One advantage of politeness like that in a man is to be able to deal with women on our own grounds—please or torture them as it may prove necessary. And not fire random shots from his own camp many miles away. Like Big Bertha you know, accidentally slaying whole congregations."

"What struck me is their self-satisfaction, their positive admiration for their own things—"

"—Which you must admit are usually the best things."

"Oh, they give a good show—I'd be the last one to ever deny that. I remember that famous houseboat party. And I'm willing to admit that Seth is quite amusing—but so Irish—his face begins to move before he says anything in that Irish way. And those phrases he uses over and over: 'Oldest inhabitant gnawed by rodents'—how many times have you heard him say that? And that one way of imitating everything, whether it's an Englishman or a billy goat—he widens his nostrils, waves his head from side to side and talks through his nose."

"Everybody has only one way of imitating that they use for everything."

Sometime during this conversation they were joined by the young man who had been telephoning. To Francis's disgust he was One of the Boys, and Francis searched vainly for any way he might extricate himself from the situation. He looked reproachfully at Wanda who smiled back encouragingly—and again his desire for her was renewed. She was a special red and white type that always aroused him and certainly the pressure of her hand the other day had been in a sense a promise, of how much he couldn't say.

Through dinner he felt his mind wandering off the company—things were so dead after the Pipers and he wondered what they were doing tonight. They had saved tonight for something, perhaps he thought with a sudden sense of being shut out—perhaps to be alone.

He drank a lot of champagne at dinner but was taciturn and had the feeling that the three girls didn't like him any more than he liked them. First he felt this only casually but later it deepened and dancing afterwards at the Boeuf sur le Toit he saw they were inclined to be cold with him.

"I'm getting tight and cross," he thought, "I'd better go home. What a rotten evening. What bum people." He asked Wanda if they couldn't go.

"Yes, but wait," she answered. "They'll be furious if I take you off."

"Well, who are they? Why should you care?"

"I don't, but wait."

They were dancing close together and suddenly he told her he wanted her. Surely her smile as she bent back and looked up at him was consent, yet she said:

"Isn't this enough?"

"Of course not."

"Don't you think this is enough?"

He got nothing more than that from her but his next glass of champagne made him genial at last; he even consented to move on to another place but Miss Carmichael was in the taxi with Wanda and himself and he could do no more than press her hand.

He knew they were girls of some distinction—he did not make the mistake of lumping them as bluestockings or Lesbians. They were three tall rich

American girls and that was the principal thing about them. To be a tall rich American girl is a form of hereditary achievement whether or not progress does eventually culminate in her insouciant promenade along the steel girder of our prosperity. Nevertheless it was increasingly clear to him that Miss Taube had more immediate concerns—there was a flick of the lip somewhere, a bending of the smile toward some indirection, a momentary lifting and dropping of the curtain over a hidden passage. An hour later he came out of somewhere to a taxi whither they had preceded him and found Wanda limp and drunk in Miss Taube's arms.

"What's the idea?" he demanded furiously.

Miss Taube smiled at him. Wanda opened her eyes sleepily and said: "Hello."

"What's all this business?" he repeated.

"I love Wanda," said Miss Taube.

"Vivian is a nice girl," said Wanda. "Come sit back here with us."

"Why can't you get out of the taxicab and go home with your friends," said Francis harshly to Miss Taube. "You know you have no business to do this. She's tight."

"I love Wanda," repeated Miss Taube good-naturedly.

"I don't care. Please get out."

In answer Wanda drew the girl close to her again, whereupon in a spasm of fury Francis opened the door, took her by the arm and before the girl understood his purpose deposited her in a sitting position on the curb.

"This is perfectly outrageous!" she cried.

"I should say it is!" he agreed, his voice trembling. A chasseur and several by-standers hurried up; Francis spoke to the driver and got into the cab quickly. The incident had wakened Wanda.

"Why did you do that?" she demanded. "I'll have to go back."

"Do you realize what she was doing?"

"Vivian's a nice girl."

"Vivian's a—"

"I don't feel good."

"What's your address?"

She told him, and he sat back robbed and glowering. The sight of this almost legendary aberration in action had spoiled some great series of human facts for him, as it had when he had first become aware of its other face some years before. Better Hollywood's bizarre variations on the normal, with George Collins on the phone ordering twelve beautiful girls for dinner, none over nineteen. He wanted to go back and kill that girl.

The cab stopped in front of a cluster of murky brown doors so alike that to be identified it seemed that hers must be counted off from the abutting blackness of an alley.

"Can you get in alone?"

"Maybe." But getting from the cab she wobbled helplessly and he helped her to the door and up an ancient circular stairway to her apartment where he fumbled in her bag for the key.

It was one room in listless disorder, opening off a bathroom with a tin tub. The day bed was covered with a length of blue felt on which reversed letters of ravelled thread spelled out "Bryn Mawr—1924." Wanda went into the bathroom without speaking and Francis opened a window which looked on a narrow and tubular court, grey as rats, but echoing at the moment to a plaintive and peculiar music. It was two men chanting in an unfamiliar language full of K's and L's—he leaned out but he could not see them; there was obviously a religious significance in the sounds, and tired and emotionless he let them pray for him too, but what for, save that he should never lose himself in the darkness of his own mind, he did not know. He felt no passion, only a lowering of his faculties—but they tightened with a nervous wrench of his heart at the sound of a pistol shot from the bathroom.

"Ah, my!" he gasped.

In a second he opened the door of the bathroom. Wanda faced him weakly with a small pistol wobbling in her hand. It was an old pistol for as he took it away from her a slice of pearl came off the handle and fell on the floor.

"What do you want to do?" he asked imperatively.

"I don't know, I was just shooting it."

She sat down on the water closet with a coquettish smile. Her eyes, glazed a few minutes since, were full of an impish malice.

"What's the trouble? Are you in any trouble?"

"Nobody's in trouble. Nothing's trouble. Everybody is responsible for what they do."

"You're not, you're tight."

Any minute he expected a knocking at the door but perhaps from fear or indifference, nothing stirred in the house—even the singing in the areaway continued, sad as a flute, and moment by moment they were more alone in the flat.

"You'd better go to bed," he said.

She laughed scornfully.

"Go to bed and lie there? What for?"

"Well—" he said, after considering unsuccessfully, "I don't like to go away and leave you like this. Are you all right now?"

"Oh, get out!" she said unpleasantly. "Leave me my pistol."

He took out the little shells and handed the gun to her, but at the look of childish craftiness in her eyes he took it back quickly.

"You've got more shells. Look here, you're behaving like an idiot. What's the matter—are you broke?"

She shook her head.

"Just lousy with money."

"Is it something about that girl?"

Her eyes narrowed defiantly.

"She's a very nice girl. She's been very good to me."

"She wasn't behaving very well tonight."

"She's very nice." Suddenly she seemed to remember. "You were the one. You pulled her out of the cab into the public gutter. She'll never forgive that," she shook her head solemnly, "never—never. Got a cigarette?"

She leaned back comfortably against the waterpipe, as one enjoying the moment at leisure. Francis lit her a cigarette impatiently and waited. He was very tired but he was afraid to leave her alone, as much for himself as for her. At the moment he didn't give a damn whether she killed herself or not because he was so tired, but her friends knew that he had taken her home and there was a concierge below.

"I'm pretty tired," he said—unfortunately, because this gave her an advantage; she wasn't tired; although her mind moved in a tedious half time like a slow moving picture her nerves were crowded with feverish traffic. She tried to think of some mischief.

"You were after me," she said accusingly.

"What of it?"

She laughed sneeringly.

"I'll go home—if you'll tell me where the rest of the shells are and then hop into bed and get some sleep."

"Oh, s...!" she cried, "You'll tuck the baby in will you—you God damn old fool—you meig me sick to my stomach."

Half an hour passed. When he was silent she took her ease refusing to leave the bathroom. When he made a motion to go she woke like a watchdog, and held him there. He looked in the bureau for shells 'til she cried: "Let my things alone." He thought of calling the concierge but that would be to arouse the house surely; dawn was filtering into the bedroom now, the singing had long ago ceased.

He hated her for entangling him in this sordidness—it was unbelievable that he had ever desired her, a hysterical Lesbian, keeping him there as if she had any possible right. He would have liked to hit her—but at the thought of her bruised in all this trouble of hers a complete revulsion of feeling went over him; he went and knelt beside her and put his arm about her shoulder.

"Poor little girl—what is it? Tell me. Are you busted or something, or have you gotten mixed up with those Lesbians?"

She broke down suddenly.

"Oh, no," she cried, "I wanted to see if I could—sleep with you—I—"

Then as suddenly she was herself again.

"You can go now," she said after a moment coldly.

"What are you going to do?"

"Going to sleep, what do you think I'm going to do—set myself on fire? Take the pistol if you want."

She began taking off her dress.

Without looking at him she turned on the hot water in the wash basin, and looked at herself in the mirror.

"Good-bye."

"Bye."

Outside it was morning; he stopped at a workman's bistro for a cup of coffee. "Good God, this is getting to be a hell of a world," he thought. Now he remembered stories he had heard in California. It was all very depressing and it frightened him, as if someone he knew were being operated on. He wanted to see Seth and Dinah and he made up his mind on a savage impulse to tell the story to his mother. "God damn these women!" he thought.

Sean O'Faolain

Sean O'Faolain was born in Cork, Ireland, in 1900. He attended University College, Cork, but soon left to join the revolutionary movement as a volunteer in the Irish Republican Army. After two years, O'Faolain returned to Cork and received his B.A. While earning his M.A., he received a fellowship that allowed him to study at Harvard, where he met and married Eileen Gould, also a native of Cork. The two returned to Ireland in 1933, and O'Faolain began his battle with the Irish Censorship Board who, in response to its restrictive moral code, banned his first two novels, *Midnight Summer Madness* (1932) and *Bird Alone* (1936). In the 1940s he edited the journal *The Bell*, ushering in a generation of Irish writers opposed to the conservative establishment. He was also publishing widely, releasing such books as *Come Back to Erin* and *The Man Who Invented Sin and Other Stories*. The 1950s brought many travels abroad, including time in Italy and America, where he lectured at Princeton. O'Faolain continued to publish, gaining notoriety for works like *The Vanishing Hero* and *I Remember! I Remember!*. He exhibited rare longevity for a writer, still producing major works into his seventies and eighties. He died in 1991 in Dublin. O'Faolain is remembered as one of Ireland's finest writers of fiction. His story "Persecution Mania" appeared in *The Kenyon Review* in 1949.

Persecution Mania *(1949)*

by Sean O'Faolain

There are two types of Irishman whom I cannot stand. The first is always trying to behave the way he thinks the English behave. The second is always behaving the way he thinks the Irish behave. That sort is a roaring bore. Ike Dignam is like that. He has a notion that the Irish have a gift for fantasy, so he is constantly talking fey. He also has a notion that the Irish have a magnificent gift for malice, mixed up with another idea of the Irish as great realists, so that he loves to abuse everybody for not having more common sense. But as he also believes that the Irish are the most kind and charitable people in the world he ends up every tirade with an "Ah, sure, God help us, maybe the poor fellow is good at heart." The result is that you do not know, from one moment to the next, whom you are talking to—Ike the fey, or Ike the realist, Ike the vicious, or Ike the kind.

I am sure he has no clear idea of himself. He is a political journalist. I have seen him tear the vitals out of a man, and then, over a beer, say, with a shocked guffaw,

"I'm after doin' a terrible thing. Do you know what I said in my column this morning about Harry Lombard? I said, 'There is no subject under the sun on which the eloquence does not pour from his lips with all the thin fluidity of asses' milk.' Honest to God, we're a terrible race. Of course, the man will never talk to me again."

All as if Right Hand had no responsibility for Left Hand. But the exasperating thing is that his victims do talk to him again, and in the most friendly way, though how they do it I do not know, considering some of the things he says and writes about them. He is the man, for instance, who said of a certain woman who is in the habit of writing letters to the press in defense of the Department of Roads and Railways: "Ah, sure, she wrote that with the Minister's tongue in her cheek." Yet the Minister for Roads and Railways is one of his best friends: he says, "Ike Dignam? He's all right. The poor divil is good at heart." And the cursed thing is that Ike is good at heart. I have long since given up trying to understand what that means: something vaguely connected with hope and consolation and the endless mercy of God.

Ike naturally has as many enemies as friends, and this is something that *he* cannot understand. If one is mentioned somebody present may say,

"But you're forgetting, Ike, what you said about him last year. You said every time he sings *Galway Bay* he turns it into a street puddle."

Ike will laugh delightedly,

"That was only a bit o' fun. Who'd mind that?"

"How would you like to have things like that said about yourself?"

He will reply, valiantly,

"I wouldn't mind one bit. Not one bit in the world. I'd know 'twas all part of the game. I'd know the poor fellow was really good at heart."

A few weeks ago he had a taste of his own medicine, and he did not like it. He committed the folly of granting to his rivals the ancient wish of all rivals, "Oh! That mine enemy would write a book." The subject of his book—it was more of a pamphlet than a book—was *The Irish Horse in Irish History,* and it had been savagely disembowelled in an anonymous review in one of the popular weeklies. Not that it was difficult to cut it up, for what little Ike knew about horses had been culled from the works of other journalists who had known just as little as himself before they, in turn, culled their information, adding a few further inaccuracies as they did so, from generations of hacks before them.

That very afternoon I met him in Mooney's on the quay. He was staring into the boghole deeps of a pint of porter. Seeing me he turned such a morose eye on me that I could tell he had been badly hit.

"You saw what the *Sun* said about my book?" he asked, and when I nodded: "That's a low paper. A dirty, low rag. A vicious-minded rag, that's what it is. Full of venom and hate and the lust for power. And," he added, slapping the counter, "destruction!"

"Somebody getting his own back, I suppose?"

Ike stared at me in astonishment.

"What did I ever do to anybody? Only a bit of give and take. What's done every day of the week in journalism. Surely to Gawd nobody takes me as seriously as all that!"

"Well, that's more or less all your reviewer implied about your book?"

Again the indignant palm slapped the mahogany.

"That's exactly what I dislike about that review. The mean implication. The dirty innuendo. Why couldn't he come out and say it in the open like a man? It's the anonymity of the thing that's so despicable." Here he fixed me with a cunning eye. "Who do ye think wrote it?"

I spread my hands.

"I think," he said sourly, "that it was Mulvaney wrote it. I made a hare of him one time in my column. But I'm not sure. That's the curse of it. He hasn't enough brains to write it." He gazed at me for a moment through his eyelashes. "You didn't write it yourself by any chance?"

I laughed and told him I hadn't read his book. I'd bought it, of course (which I had not), and had every intention of reading it (which was also untrue). "Or it could be that drunk Cassidy," he said. "That fellow has it in for me ever since I said that he spoke in the Dail with the greatest sobriety." He laughed feebly. "Everyone knew what I meant. Unfortunately! Do you think it might be Cassidy?"

"Ikey, it might be a dozen people."

"It could be anybody," he snarled. "Anybody! Damn it all if I ever say a thing I say it straight out from the shoulder. Why can't they come into the open?" He leaned nearer and dropped to a whisper. "I was thinking it might be that redheaded bastard from the All Souls Club. That fellow thinks I'm anti-clerical. And," he guffawed, "I'm not, that's the joke of it, I'm not!"

"What in the name of all that's holy," I asked crossly, "has anti-clericalism got to do with horses?"

He scratched his head fiercely and moaned and shook it,

"Ye never know. The people in this country have as much sense when it comes to religion…Tell me, did ye ever hear of a thing called Discovery of Documents?"

It was only then I fully realized how badly he had been hit.

"You're not being such an idiot as to be thinking of taking this thing to law?"

"Look't! I don't give one tinker's curse about what anybody says against me, but the one…thing…I…*must*…knowiswhowroteit! If I don't find out who wrote it I'll be suspecting my best friends for the rest of my born days."

"Well," I said, finishing my drink and leaving him, "happy hunting to you."

A couple of days later I saw him coming towards me along O'Connell Street glowing like a sunrise.

"I'm on the track of that," he shouted at me from fifteen yards off. "I'm on the right scent," he babbled, and I had time to remember what he was talking about while he explained how he had worked up a friendship with a girl in the office of the *Sun*. "'Tis none of the people I suspected at all. Do you know who I think wrote it now?"

"God knows maybe you wrote it yourself?"

He shook with laughter.

"'Twould be great publicity if I could say I did it." Then he glowered.

"They're entirely capable of saying I did it. If they thought anybody would believe 'em. No!" he gripped my arm. "'Twas a woman did it. I should have guessed it from the word Go."

"Who is she?"

"I don't know," he said, sadly.

"Then why did you say…?"

"I had a dream about it. Didn't I see the long, lean, bony hand holding the pen, coming out like a snake from behind a red curtain! Didn't I see the gold bangle on the wrist and all?"

"Did you pull the curtain to see who it was?"

"I pulled and I pulled," Ikey assured me enthusiastically. "Dear Gawd I was all the night pullin'!"

"And," I suggested bitterly, "I suppose the curtain was made of iron? You know, Ikey, you'll go crackers if you go on like this."

With his two hands he dragged his hat down on his head as if he wanted to extinguish himself.

"I will!" he cried, so loudly that passers-by turned to look at the pair of us. "I'll go stark, staring, roaring mad if I don't find out who wrote that thing about me."

"Look," I pleaded, "What on earth does it all matter? The whole thing is gone completely out of everybody's head but your own. It's all over and done with. And even supposing you did find out who wrote it, what could you do then?"

He folded his arms and gazed down O'Connell Street like Napoleon looking over the Atlantic from Saint Helena.

"I'd write a lampoon on him. I'd *shrivel* him. Begod, I wouldn't leave a peck on his bones. As a matter of fact," cocking an eye on me, "I've done it already. Or I think I have. I wrote ten lampoons the other night on ten different people who might have written that review. I'm thinking of publishing the whole lot of 'em, and if the cap fits they can wear it."

"And that'll be ten enemies you'll make instead of one. Come in here and let me talk to you like a father."

We went across to Mooney's and we talked for half an hour. I told him we had all been through this sort of thing. I told him that no man who cannot grow an epidermis against malice should try to live in small countries like ours. I said that all that matters is a man's work. I assured him, Heaven forgive me, that he had written a masterly record of *The Irish Horse in Irish History* and that was the main thing. I developed this soundly into the theory that everything is grist to a writer's mill, and that instead of worrying about this silly review he should go home and write a comic piece about it, which, indeed, he could do very well. I built him up as Dignam, the lone artist, *solus contra mundum.* He agreed to every word of it. We parted cordially. He was in the happiest temper.

Three days later he came striding towards me, beaming. From afar he hailed my passing ship.

"I found out the bastard. It *was* Mulvaney. A friend of mine charged him with it and he didn't deny it."

"Good. You're satisfied now."

"I am. I don't give a damn about it now. Sure that fellow's brains are all in his behind. Who'd mind anything he'd say?"

"The whole thing is of no importance."

"None what-so-ever."

"Splendid. It's all over now."

"Finished. And done with."

"Grand."

"I sent him a hell of a postcard."

"No!"

"I did," he chortled, "I did. All I wrote on it was what I said to yourself. *Your brains are all in your behind.* An open postcard. It was a terrible thing to do," he beamed. "Oh, shocking!" His laughter gusted.

"And you put your name to that?"

"I did not. What a fool I'd be. That'll keep him guessing for a while. 'Twill do him no harm in the world. He's not a bad poor gom. The poor divil is good at heart."

Off he went, striding along, as happy as a child. I went into Mooney's. There at the counter was Mulvaney, sucking his empty pipe, staring in front of him, his bushy eyebrows as black as night. I wheeled quickly but he caught the movement and called me. His hand strayed to his breast pocket.

"I'm after receiving a very strange communication," he said sombrely.

I did not hear what else he said. You could do nothing with these people. I realized that the only sensible thing to do was to write a satire on the whole lot of them, and I began to wonder could I get any editor to publish it over a pseudonym.

Randall Jarrell

Randall Jarrell was born in Nashville, Tennessee, in 1914. He moved with his parents to Los Angeles soon after, then returned to Nashville with his mother after his parents divorced. Jarrell earned both his B.A. and M.A. from Vanderbilt University, where he found a mentor in *The Kenyon Review*–founder John Crowe Ransom. When Ransom accepted a position at Kenyon College, Jarrell joined him as an assistant, teaching in the English department. At Kenyon, Jarrell met Robert Lowell and Peter Taylor, with whom he would hold longstanding friendships. His first book of poems, *Blood for a Stranger*, came out in 1942, the same year Jarrell entered the U.S. Air Force. His military experience provided him material for his next two books, *Little Friend, Little Friend* (1945) and *Losses* (1948). Jarrell's reputation as a poet was only exceeded by his reputation as a brilliant, engaging, and sometimes biting critic. In 1952, he took a position at the University of North Carolina at Greensboro, where he would remain for the rest of his life. After completing *The Lost World*, which won him the National Book Award in 1965, Jarrell became mentally ill, eventually leading to an attempted suicide. While recovering at a hospital, he went walking at dusk on a nearby highway and was struck by a car and killed immediately. The coroner's verdict was accidental death, although the circumstances will never be entirely clear. What is clear is that Jarrell remains a highly respected poet and is regarded as the pre-eminent critic of his generation.

Walt Whitman: He Had His Nerve *(1953)*

by Randall Jarrell

Whitman, Dickinson, and Melville seem to me the best poets of the nineteeth century here in America. Melville's poetry has been grotesquely underestimated, but of course it is only in the last four or five years that it has been much read; in the long run, in spite of the awkwardness and amateurishness of so much of it, it will surely be thought well of. (In the short run it will probably be thought entirely too well of. Melville is a great poet only in the prose of *Moby Dick*.) Dickinson's poetry has been thoroughly read, and well though undifferentiatingly loved—after a few decades or centuries almost everybody will be able to see through Dickinson to her poems. But something odd has happened to the living changing part of Whitman's reputation: nowadays it is people who are not particularly interested in poetry, people who say that they read a poem for what it says, not for how it says it, who admire Whitman most. Whitman is often written about, either approvingly or disapprovingly, as if he were the Thomas Wolfe of nineteenth-century democracy, the hero of a de Mille movie about Walt Whitman. (People even talk about a war in which Walt Whitman and Henry James chose up sides, to begin with, and in which you and I will go on fighting 'til the day we die.) All this sort of thing, and all the bad poetry that there of course is in Whitman—for any poet has written enough bad poetry to scare away anybody—has helped to scare away from Whitman most "serious readers of modern poetry." They do not talk of his poems, as a rule, with any real liking or knowledge. Serious readers, people who are ashamed of not knowing all Hopkins by heart, are not at all ashamed to say, "I don't really know Whitman very well." This may harm Whitman in your eyes, they know, but that is a chance that poets have to take. Yet "their" Hopkins, that good critic and great poet, wrote about Whitman, after seeing five or six of his poems in a newspaper review: "I may as well say what I should not otherwise have said, that I always knew in my heart Walt Whitman's mind to be more like my own than any other man's living. As he is a very great scoundrel this is not a very pleasant confession." And Henry James, the leader of "their" side in that awful imaginary war of which I spoke, once read Whitman to Edith Wharton (much as Mozart used to imitate, on the piano, the organ) with such power and solemnity that both sat shaken and silent; it was after this reading that James expressed his regret at Whitman's "too extensive acquaintance with the foreign languages." Almost all the

most "original and advanced" poets and critics and readers of the last part
of the nineteenth century thought Whitman as original and advanced as
themselves, in manner as well as in matter. Can Whitman really be a sort of
Thomas Wolfe or Carl Sandburg or Robinson Jeffers or Henry Miller—or a
sort of Balzac of poetry, whose every part is crude but whose whole is somehow good? He is not, nor could he be; a poem, like Pope's spider, "lives
along the line," and all the dead lines in the world will not make one live
poem. As Blake says, "all sublimity is founded on minute discrimination,"
and it is in these "minute particulars" of Blake's that any poem has its primary existence.

To show Whitman for what he is one does not need to praise or explain or
argue, one needs simply to quote. He himself said, "I and mine do not convince by arguments, similes, rhymes, / We convince by our presence." Even
a few of his phrases are enough to show us that Whitman was no sweeping
rhetorician, but a poet of the greatest and oddest delicacy and originality and
sensitivity, so far as words are concerned. This is, after all, the poet who said,
"Blind loving wrestling touch, sheath'd hooded sharp-tooth'd touch"; who
said, "Smartly attired, countenance smiling, form upright, death under the
breast-bones, hell under the skull-bones"; who said, "Agonies are one of my
changes of garments"; who saw grass as the "flag of my disposition," saw
"the sharp-peak'd farmhouse, with its scallop'd scum and slender shoots from
the gutters," heard a plane's "wild ascending lisp," and saw and heard how at
the amputation "what is removed drops horribly in a pail." This is the poet for
whom the sea was "howler and scooper of storms," reaching out to us with
"crooked inviting fingers"; who went "leaping chasms with a pike-pointed
staff, clinging to topples of brittle and blue"; who, a runaway slave, saw how
"my gore dribs, thinn'd with the ooze of my skin"; who went "lithographing
Kronos...buying drafts of Osiris"; who stared out at the "little plentiful mannequins skipping around in collars and tail'd coats, / I am aware who they are,
(they are positively not worms or fleas)." For he is, at his best, beautifully
witty: he says gravely, "I find I incorporate gneiss, coals, long-threaded
moss, fruits, grain, esculent roots, / And am stucco'd with quadrupeds and
birds all over"; and of these quadrupeds and birds "not one is respectable or
unhappy over the whole earth." He calls advice: "Unscrew the locks from the
doors! Unscrew the doors from their jambs!" He publishes the results of
research: "Having pried through the strata, analyz'd to a hair, counsel'd with
doctors and calculated close, / I find no sweeter fat than sticks to my own
bones." Everybody remembers how he told the Muse to "cross out please

those immensely overpaid accounts, / That matter of Troy and Achilles' wrath, and Aeneas', Odysseus' wanderings," but his account of the arrival of the "illustrious emigré" here in the New World is even better: "Bluff'd not a bit by drainpipe, gasometer, artificial fertilizers, / Smiling and pleas'd with palpable intent to stay, / She's here, install'd amid the kitchenware." Or he sees, like another Breughel, "the mechanic's wife with the babe at her nipple interceding for every person born, / Three scythes at harvest whizzing in a row from three lusty angels with shirts bagg'd out at their waists, / The snag-toothed hostler with red hair redeeming sins past and to come"—the passage has enough wit not only (in Johnson's phrase) to keep it sweet, but enough to make it believable. He says:

> I project my hat, sit shame-faced, and beg.
> Enough! Enough! Enough!
> Somehow I have been stunn'd. Stand back!
> Give me a little time beyond my cuff'd head, slumbers,
> > dreams, gaping,
> I discover myself on the verge of a usual mistake.

There is in such changes of tone as these the essence of wit. And Whitman is even more far-fetched than he is witty; he can say about Doubters, in the most improbable and explosive of juxtapositions: "I know every one of you, I know the sea of torment, doubt, despair and unbelief. / How the flukes splash! How they contort rapid as lightning, with splashes and spouts of blood!" Who else would have said about God: "As the hugging and loving bed-fellow sleeps at my side through the night, and withdraws at the break of day with stealthy tread, / Leaving me baskets cover'd with white towels, swelling the house with their plenty"?—the Psalmist himself, his cup running over, would have looked at Whitman with dazzled eyes. (Whitman was persuaded by friends to hide the fact that it was God he was talking about.) He says, "Flaunt of the sunshine I need not your bask—lie over!" This unusual employment of verbs is usual enough in participle-loving Whitman, who also asks you to "look in my face while I snuff the sidle of evening," or tells you, "I effuse my flesh in eddies, and drift it in lacy jags." Here are some typical beginnings of poems: "City of orgies, walks, and joys...Not heaving from my ribb'd breast only...O take my hand Walt Whitman! Such gliding wonders! Such sights and sounds! Such join'd unended links...." He says to the objects of the world, "You have waited, you always wait, you dumb, beautiful ministers"; sees "the sun and stars that float in the open air, / The apple-shaped earth"; says, "O suns— O grass of graves— O perpetual transfers and promotions, / If you do not say anything how can I say anything?" Not many poets have written better, in queerer and more convincing and more individual language, about the world's *gliding wonders:* the phrase seems particularly right for Whitman. He speaks of those "circling rivers the breath," of the "savage old mother incessantly crying, / To the boy's soul's questions sullenly timing, some drown'd secret hissing"—ends a poem, once, "We have voided all but freedom and our own joy." How can one quote enough? If the reader thinks that all this is like Thomas Wolfe he *is* Thomas Wolfe; nothing else could explain it. Poetry like this is as far as possible from the work of any ordinary rhetorician, whose phrases cascade over us like suds of the oldest and most-advertised detergent.

The interesting thing about Whitman's worst language (for, just as few poets have ever written better, few poets have ever written worse) is how unusually absurd, how really ingeniously bad, such language is. I will quote none of the most famous examples; but even a line like *O culpable! I acknowledge. I exposé!* is not anything that you and I could do—only a man with the most extraordinary feel for language, or none whatsoever, could have cooked up Whitman's worst messes. For instance: what other man in all the history of this planet would have said, "I am a habitan of Vienna"? (One has an immediate vision of him as a sort of French-Canadian halfbreed to whom the Viennese are offering, with trepidation, through the bars of a zoological garden, little mounds of whipped cream.) And *enclaircise*—why, it's as bad as *explicate!* We are right to resent his having made up his own horrors, instead of sticking to the ones that we ourselves employ. But when Whitman says, "I dote on myself, there is that lot of me and all so luscious," we should realize that we are not the only ones who are amused. And the queerly bad and the merely queer and the queerly good will often change into one another without warning: "Hefts of the moving world, at innocent gambols silently rising, freshly exuding, / Scooting obliquely high and low"—not good, but *queer!*—suddenly becomes, "Something I cannot see puts up libidinous prongs, / Seas of bright juice suffuse heaven," and it is sunrise.

But it is not in individual lines and phrases, but in passages of some length, that Whitman is at his best. In the following quotation Whitman has something difficult to express, something that there are many formulas, all bad, for expressing; he expresses it with complete success, in language of the most dazzling originality:

The orchestra whirls me wider than Uranus flies,
It wrenches such ardors from me I did not know I
    possess'd them,
It sails me, I dab with bare feet, they are lick'd by the
    indolent waves,
I am cut by bitter and angry hail, I lose my breath,
Steep'd amid honey'd morphine, my windpipe throttled
    in fakes of death,
At length let up again to feel the puzzle of puzzles,
And that we call Being.

One hardly knows what to point at—everything works. But *wrenches* and *did not know I possess'd them*; the incredible *it sails me, I dab with bare feet; lick'd by the indolent; steep'd amid honey'd morphine; my windpipe throttled in fakes of death*—no wonder Crane admired Whitman! This originality, as absolute in its way as that of Berlioz's orchestration, is often at Whitman's command:

I am a dance—play up there! the fit is whirling me fast!

I am the ever-laughing—it is new moon and twilight,
I see the hiding of douceurs, I see nimble ghosts whichever way I look,
Cache and cache again deep in the ground and sea, and where it is
    neither ground nor sea.
Well do they do their jobs those journeymen divine,
Only from me can they hide nothing, and would not if
    they could,
I reckon I am their boss and they make me a pet besides,
And surround me and lead me and run ahead when I walk,
To lift their sunning covers to signify me with stretch'd arms, and
    resume the way;
Onward we move, a gay gang of blackguards! with mirth-shouting
    music and wild-flapping pennants of joy!

If you did not believe Hopkins's remark about Whitman, that *gay gang of blackguards* ought to shake you. Whitman shares Hopkins's passion for "dappled" effects, but he slides in and out of them with ambiguous swiftness. And he has at his command a language of the calmest and most prosaic reality, one that seems to do no more than present:

The little one sleeps in its cradle.
I lift the gauze and look a long time, and silently brush away flies
    with my hand.

The youngster and the red-faced girl turn aside up the bushy hill, I
    peeringly view them from the top.

The suicide sprawls on the bloody floor of the bedroom.
    I witness the corpse with its dabbled hair, I note where the pistol
    has fallen.

It is like magic: that is, something has been done to us without our knowing how it was done; but if we look at the lines again we see the *gauze, silently, youngster, red-faced, bushy, peeringly, dabbled*—not that this is all we see. "Present! present!" said James; these are presented, put down side by side to form a little "view of life," from the cradle to the last bloody floor of the bedroom. Very often the things presented form nothing but a list:

The pure contralto sings in the organ loft,
The carpenter dresses his plank, the tongue of his
    foreplane whistles its wild ascending lisp,
The married and unmarried children ride home to their
    Thanksgiving dinner,
The pilot seizes the king-pin, he heaves down with a
    strong arm,
The mate stands braced in the whale-boat, lance and
    harpoon are ready,
The duck-shooter walks by silent and cautious stretches,
The deacons are ordained with cross'd hands at the altar,
The spinning-girl retreats and advances to the hum of the big wheel,
The farmer stops by the bars as he walks on a First-day loafe and
    looks at the oats and rye.
The lunatic is carried at last to the asylum a confirm'd case,
(He will never sleep any more as he did in the cot in his mother's
    bed-room;)
The jour printer with gray head and gaunt jaws works at his case,
He turns his quid of tobacco while his eyes blur with the
    manuscript,

The malform'd limbs are tied to the surgeon's table,
What is removed drops horribly in a pail....

It is only a list—but what a list! And how delicately, in what different ways—likeness and opposition and continuation and climax and anticlimax—the transitions are managed, whenever Whitman wants to manage them. Notice them in the next quotation, another "mere list":

The bride unrumples her white dress, the minute-hand of the clock
    moves slowly,
The opium-eater reclines with rigid head and just-open'd lips,
The prostitute draggles her shawl, her bonnet bobs on her tipsy and
    pimpled neck....

The first line is joined to the third by *unrumples* and *draggles, white dress* and *shawl*; the second to the third by *rigid head, bobs, tipsy, neck;* the first to the second by *slowly, just-open'd*, and the slowing-down of time in both states. And occasionally one of these lists is metamorphosed into something we have no name for; the man who would call the next quotation a mere list—anybody will feel this—would boil his babies up for soap:

Ever the hard unsunk ground,
Ever the eaters and drinkers, ever the upward and
    downward sun,
Ever myself and my neighbors, refreshing, wicked, real,
Ever the old inexplicable query, ever that thorned thumb, that breath
    of itches and thirsts,
Ever the vexer's hoot! hoot! till we find where the sly one hides and
    bring him forth,
Ever the sobbing liquid of life,
Ever the bandage under the chin, ever the trestles of death.

Sometimes Whitman will take what would generally be considered an unpromising subject (in this case, a woman peeping at men in bathing naked) and treat it with such tenderness and subtlety and understanding that we are ashamed of ourselves for having thought it unpromising, and murmur that Chekhov himself couldn't have treated it better:

Twenty-eight young men bathe by the shore,
Twenty-eight young men and all so friendly,
Twenty-eight years of womanly life and all so lonesome.

She owns the fine house by the rise of the bank,
She hides handsome and richly drest aft the blinds of the window.

Which of the young men does she like the best?
Ah the homeliest of them is beautiful to her.

Where are you off to, lady? for I see you,
You splash in the water there, yet stay stock still in your room.

Dancing and laughing along the beach came the
    twenty-ninth bather,
The rest did not see her, but she saw them and loved them.

The beards of the young men glistened with wet, it ran from their
    long hair,
Little streams pass'd all over their bodies.

An unseen hand also pass'd over their bodies,
It descended tremblingly from their temples and ribs.

The young men float on their backs, their white bellies bulge to the
    sun, they do not ask who seizes fast to them,
They do not know who puffs and declines with pendant and bending
    arch,
They do not know whom they souse with spray.

And in the same poem (that "Song of Myself" in which one finds half his best work) the writer can say of a sea-fight:

Stretched and still lies the midnight,
Two great hulls motionless on the breast of the darkness,
Our vessel riddled and slowly sinking, preparations to pass to the
    one we have conquer'd,
The captain on the quarter-deck coldly giving his orders through a
    countenance white as a sheet,

Near by the corpse of the child that serv'd in the cabin,
The dead face of an old salt with long white hair and
 carefully curl'd whiskers,
The flames spite of all that can be done flickering aloft
 and below,
The husky voices of the two or three officers yet fit for duty,
Formless stacks of bodies and bodies by themselves,
 dabs of flesh upon the masts and spars,
Cut of cordage, dangle of rigging, slight shock of the soothe of
 waves,
Black and impassive guns, litter of powder-parcels, strong scent,
A few large stars overhead, silent and mournful shining,
Delicate snuffs of sea-breeze, smells of sedgy grass and fields by
 the shore, death-messages given in charge to survivors,
The hiss of the surgeon's knife, the gnawing teeth of his saw,
Wheeze, cluck, swash of falling blood, short wild scream, and long,
 dull, tapering groan,
These, so, these irretrievable.

There are faults in this passage, and they *do not matter:* the serious truth, the complete realization of these last lines make us remember that few poets have shown more of the tears of things, and the joy of things, and of the reality beneath either tears or joy. Even Whitman's most general or political statements often are good: everybody knows his "When liberty goes out of a place it is not the first to go, nor the second or third to go, / It waits for all the rest to go, it is the last"; these sentences about the United States just before the Civil War may be less familiar:

Are those really Congressmen? are those the great judges? is that
 the President?
Then I will sleep awhile yet, for I see that these States sleep,
 for reasons;
(With gathering murk, with muttering thunder and lambent shoots
 we all duly awake,
South, North, East, West, inland and seaboard, we will surely
 awake.)

How well, with what firmness and dignity and command, Whitman does such passages! And Whitman's doubts that he has done them or anything else well—ah, there is nothing he does better:

> The best I had done seemed to me blank and suspicious,
> My great thoughts as I supposed them, were they not in reality
>   meagre?
> I am he who knew what it was to be evil,
> I too knitted the old knot of contrariety...
> Saw many I loved in the street or ferry-boat or public assembly, yet
>   never told them a word,
> Lived the same life with the rest, the same old laughing, gnawing,
>   sleeping,
> Played the part that still looks back on the actor and actress,
> The same old role, the role that is what we make it...

Whitman says once that the "look of the bay mare shames silliness out of me." This is true—sometimes it is true; but more often the silliness and affectation and cant and exaggeration are there shamelessly, the Old Adam that was in Whitman from the beginning and the awful new one that he created to keep it company. But as he says, "I know perfectly well my own egotism, / Know my omnivorous lines and must not write any less." He says over and over that there are in him good and bad, wise and foolish, anything at all and its antonym, and he is telling the truth; there is in him almost everything in the world, so that one responds to him, willingly or unwillingly, almost as one does to the world, that world which makes the hairs of one's flesh stand up, which seems both evil beyond any rejection and wonderful beyond any acceptance. We cannot help seeing that there is something absurd about any judgment we make of its whole—for there is no "point of view" at which we can stand to make the judgment, and the moral categories that mean most to us seem no more to apply to its whole than our spatial or temporal or causal categories seem to apply to its beginning or its end. (But we need no arguments to make our judgments seem absurd—we feel their absurdity without argument.) In some like sense Whitman is a world, a waste with, here and there, systems blazing at random out of the darkness. Only an innocent and rigidly methodical mind will reject it for this disorganization, particularly since there are in it, here and there, little systems as beautifully and astonishingly organized as the rings and satellites of Saturn:

I understand the large hearts of heroes,
The courage of present times and all times,
How the skipper saw the crowded and rudderless wreck of the
    steam-ship, and Death chasing it up and down the storm,
How he knuckled tight and gave not back an inch, and was faithful
    of days and faithful of nights,
And chalked in large letters on a board, Be of good cheer, we will
    not desert you;
How he follow'd with them and tack'd with them three days and
    would not give it up,
How he saved the drifting company at last,
How the lank loose-gown'd women looked when boated from the
    side of their prepared graves,
How the silent old-faced infants and the lifted sick, and the sharp-
    lipp'd unshaved men;
All this I swallow, it tastes good, I like it well, it becomes mine,
I am the man, I suffered, I was there.

In the last lines of this quotation Whitman has reached—as great writers always reach—a point at which criticism seems not only unnecessary but absurd: these lines are so good that even admiration feels like insolence, and one is ashamed of anything that one can find to say about them. How anyone can dismiss or accept patronizingly the man who wrote them, I do not understand.

The enormous and apparent advantage of form, of omission and selection, of the highest degree of organization, are accompanied by important disadvantages—and there are far greater works than *Leaves of Grass* to make us realize this. But if we compare Whitman with that very beautiful poet Alfred Tennyson, the most skillful of all Whitman's contemporaries, we are at once aware of how limiting Tennyson's forms have been, of how much Tennyson has had to leave out, even in those discursive poems where he is trying to put everything in. Whitman's poems *represent* his world and himself much more satisfactorily than Tennyson's do his. In the past a few poets have both formed and represented, each in the highest degree; but in modern times what controlling, organizing, selecting poet has created a world with as much in it as Whitman's, a world that so plainly is the world? Of all modern poets he has, quantitatively speaking, "the most comprehensive soul"—and, qualitatively, a most comprehensive and comprehending one, with charities and concessions and qualifications that are rare in any time.

"Do I contradict myself? Very well then I contradict myself," wrote Whitman, as everybody remembers, and this is not naïve, or something he got from Emerson, or a complacent pose.

When you organize one of the contradictory elements out of your work of art, you are getting rid not just of it, but of the contradiction of which it was a part; and it is the contradictions in works of art which make them able to represent to us—as logical and methodical generalizations cannot—our world and our selves, which are also full of contradictions. In Whitman we do not get the controlled, compressed, seemingly concordant contradictions of the great lyric poets, of a poem like, say, Hardy's *During Wind and Rain;* Whitman's contradictions are sometimes announced openly, but are more often scattered at random throughout the poems. For instance: Whitman specializes in ways of saying that there is in some sense (a very Hegelian one, generally) no evil—he says a hundred times that evil is not Real; but he also specializes in making lists of the evil of the world, lists of an unarguable reality. After his minister has recounted "the rounded catalogue divine complete," Whitman comes home and puts down what has been left out: "the countless (nineteen-twentieths) low and evil, crude and savage...the barren soil, the evil men, the slag and hideous rot." He ends another such catalogue with the plain unexcusing "All these—all meanness and agony without end I sitting look out upon, / See, hear, and am silent." Whitman offered himself to everybody, and said brilliantly and at length what a good thing he was offering:

> Sure as the most certain sure, plumb in the uprights, well entreatied,
>   braced in the beams,
> Stout as a horse, affectionate, haughty, electrical,
> I and this mystery here we stand.

Just for oddness, characteristicalness, differentness, what more could you ask in a letter of recommendation? (Whitman sounds as if he were recommending a house—haunted, but what foundations!) But after a few pages he is oddly different:

> Apart from the pulling and hauling stands what I am,
> Stands amused, complacent, compassionating, idle, unitary,
> Looks down, is erect, or bends an arm on an impalpable certain rest
> Looking with side curved head curious what will come next,
> Both in and out of the game and watching and wondering at it.

Tamburlaine is already beginning to sound like Hamlet: the employer feels uneasily, *Why, I might as well hire myself...*And, a few pages later, Whitman puts down in ordinary-sized type, in the middle of the page, this warning to any *new person drawn toward me:*

Do you think I am trusty and faithful?
Do you see no further than this façade, this smooth and tolerant
   manner of me?
Do you suppose yourself advancing on real ground toward a real
   heroic man?
Have you no thought O dreamer that it may be all maya, illusion?

Having wonderful dreams, telling wonderful lies, was a temptation Whitman could never resist; but telling the truth was a temptation he could never resist, either. When you buy him you know what you are buying. And only an innocent and solemn and systematic mind will condemn him for his contradictions: Whitman's catalogues of evils represent realities, and his denials of their reality represent other realities, of feeling and intuition and desire. If he is faithless to logic, to Reality As It Is—whatever that is—he is faithful to the feel of things, to reality as it seems; this is all that a poet has to be faithful to, and philosophers even have been known to leave logic and Reality for it.

Whitman is more coordinate and parallel than anybody, is *the* poet of parallel present participles, of twenty verbs joined by a single subject: all this helps to give his work its feeling of raw hypnotic reality, of being that world which also streams over us joined only by *ands,* until we supply the subordinating conjunctions; and since as children we see the *ands* and not the *becauses,* this method helps to give Whitman some of the freshness of childhood. How inexhaustibly *interesting* the world is in Whitman! Arnold all his life kept wishing that we could see the world "with a plainness as near, as flashing" as that with which Moses and Rebekah and the Argonauts saw it. He asked with elegiac nostalgia, "Who can see the green earth any more / As she was by the sources of Time?"—and all the time there was somebody alive who saw it so, as plain and near and flashing, and with a kind of calm, pastoral, biblical dignity and elegance as well, sometimes. The *thereness* and *suchness* of the world are incarnate in Whitman as they are in few other writers.

They might have put on his tombstone WALT WHITMAN: HE HAD HIS NERVE. He is the rashest, the most inexplicable and unlikely—the most impossible, one wants to say—of poets. He somehow is in a class by himself, so that one compares him with other poets about as readily as one compares *Alice* with other books. (Even his free verse has a completely different effect from anybody else's.) Who would think of comparing him with Tennyson or Browning or Arnold or Baudelaire?—it is Homer, or the sagas, or something far away and long ago, that comes to one's mind only to be dismissed; for sometimes Whitman is epic, just as *Moby Dick* is, and it surprises us to be able to use truthfully this word that we have misused so many times. Whitman is grand, and elevated, and comprehensive, and real with an astonishing reality, and many other things—the critic points at his qualities in despair and wonder, all method failing, and simply calls them by their names. And the range of these qualities is the most extraordinary thing of all. We can surely say about him, "He was a man, take him for all in all. I shall not look upon his like again"—and wish that people had seen this and not tried to be his like: one Whitman is miracle enough, and when he comes again it will be the end of the world.

I have said so little about Whitman's faults because they are so plain: baby critics who have barely learned to complain of the lack of ambiguity in *Peter Rabbit* can tell you all that is wrong with *Leaves of Grass*. But a good many of my readers must have felt that it is ridiculous to write an essay about the obvious fact that Whitman is a great poet. It is ridiculous—just as, in 1851, it would have been ridiculous for anyone to write an essay about the obvious fact that Pope was no "classic of our prose" but a great poet. Critics have to spend half their time reiterating whatever ridiculously obvious things their age or the critics of their age have found it necessary to forget: they say despairingly, at parties, that Wordsworth is a great poet, and *won't* bore you, and tell Mr. Leavis that Milton is a great poet whose deposition *hasn't* been accomplished with astonishing ease by a few words from Eliot and Pound.... There is something essentially ridiculous about critics, anyway: what is good is good without our saying so, and beneath all our majesty we know this.

Let me finish by mentioning another quality of Whitman's—a quality, delightful to me, that I have said nothing of. If some day a tourist notices, among the ruins of New York City, a copy of *Leaves of Grass*, and stops and picks it up and reads some lines in it, she will be able to say to herself: "How very American! If he and his country had not existed, it would have been impossible to imagine them."

James Wright

James Wright was born in 1927 in Martins Ferry, Ohio. After being drafted to the army in 1946, Wright attended Kenyon College on the G.I. Bill, studying under *The Kenyon Review*–founder John Crowe Ransom. After spending a year in Vienna on a Fulbright Scholarship, he entered graduate school at the University of Washington. While at Washington, Wright's first book, *The Green Wall*, was selected for publication by W.H. Auden in the *Yale Younger Poets* Series in 1957. He joined the faculty at the University of Minnesota, and his second collection, *Saint Judas*, was released. In 1962, Wright's marriage with Liberty Kardules, with whom he had been married since in 1953, ended. The next year, *The Branch Shall Not Break* was released, which, with its experimental free verse and strong social consciousness, would become one of the most influential volumes of the 1960s. By this time, Wright had taken a teaching position at Hunter College, and, in 1967, he married Edith Anne Crunk, the "Annie" of several of his later poems. He continued to publish such books as *Shall We Gather at the River*, *Collected Poems* (which earned Wright the Pulitzer Prize), *Two Citizens*, and *Moments of an Italian Summer*. In 1979, a chronic sore throat was diagnosed as cancer of the tongue. Wright died on March 25, 1980, the manuscript of *This Journey*, his final book, just completed.

Robert Sitting in My Hands *(1953)*
by James Wright

The time I lifted Robert overhead
His age was five long years. His little head
Shone gold as any god's whom Ovid would
Approve as lovelier than bone and blood,
Yet with the same good warmth. His eyes
Looked down. I held him like a sacrifice
In my two hands so that his buttocks were
Lighter than cobweb swimming on the air
Through shadow cast as by a parasol
Threaded and silk and small.

Yet he remained the god. He would not be
Animal on an airy altar. He
Ran through the vines his fingers. Gnarled tapes
Of green extended nets surrounded grapes
He sought for us, so we could go and eat
Them rich beneath a tree out of the heat
That afternoon retained against the gray
Ghost of a snow coming from far away
Beyond the hills that soon would wear
Snow blooms like garlands tossed on tousled hair.

A deity this Robert was
Over the lawns of grass.
Luminosity of planet myriads
Showed him the shapes of clusters in the shades
Left from the afternoon as twilight sank
Into the eastern cellars of the dank
Darkness. Loftier were the genuine
Stars reappearing than the grapes whose wine
Hung sealed in skins brown, green. I was not sure
That someone called us from the kitchen door;

But I forebore, told him to make an end,
Lowered my hands and let Robert descend

Out of the suns and dappled leaves in fire
As green as ocean at whose edge a choir
Of girls sang purely, murmurous, of the lost
Luminary ghost.
Lorelei in the rocks. Robert, come down,
Return, I said, the grapes are gone in brown
Shadows, and all the vines are lame;
And dragging down the drifting sky in flame,
The moon. Come get your glass of milk. He came.

Flannery O'Connor

Flannery O'Connor was born in Savannah, Georgia, in 1925. Her family moved to Atlanta in 1938, but O'Connor and her mother moved to Milledgeville, Georgia, shortly thereafter. Her father died of lupus when O'Connor was fifteen, leaving her and her mother to fend for themselves. She entered the Georgia State College for Women where she studied sociology. O'Connor then was admitted to the Iowa Writers' Workshop, where she would receive her M.F.A. She taught at Iowa for a year before accepting an invitation to Yadoo, an artist colony in upstate New York. She began publishing chapters of what would become her first novel, *Wise Blood*, which was released in 1952. A year before the appearance of the novel, O'Connor was diagnosed with lupus. She moved back to Georgia so her mother could care for her, and the two moved to a farm on the outskirts of Milledgeville. O'Connor continued to write, raising peacocks as a hobby. In 1953, she was awarded a Kenyon Review Fellowship in fiction and continued to publish a story in *The Kenyon Review* every year from 1953 to 1956. Her first collection of stories, *A Good Man Is Hard to Find,* was released in 1955. A second novel, *The Violent Bear It Away,* was published in 1960. O'Connor lived three years past what doctors predicted, but died on August 3, 1964. She created a relatively small body of work (two novels, thirty-one short stories), but she is considered one of the finest fiction writers of the twentieth century.

The Life You Save May Be Your Own *(1953)*

by Flannery O'Connor

The old woman and her daughter were sitting on their porch when Mr. Shiftlet came up their road for the first time. The old woman slid to the edge of her chair and leaned forward, shading her eyes from the piercing sunset with her hand. The daughter could not see far in front of her and continued to play with her fingers. Although the old woman lived in this desolate spot with only her daughter and she had never seen Mr. Shiftlet before, she could tell, even from a distance, that he was a tramp and no one to be afraid of. His left coat sleeve was folded up to show there was only half an arm in it and his gaunt figure listed slightly to the side as if the breeze were pushing him. He had on a black town suit and a brown felt hat that was turned up in the front and down in the back and he carried a tin tool box by a handle. He came on, at an amble, up her road, his face turned toward the sun which appeared to be balancing itself on the peak of a small mountain.

The old woman didn't change her position until he was almost into her yard; then she rose with one hand fisted on her hip. The daughter, a large girl in a short blue organdy dress, saw him all at once and jumped up and began to stamp and point and make excited speechless sounds.

Mr. Shiftlet stopped just inside the yard and set his box on the ground and tipped his hat at her as if she were not in the least afflicted; then he turned toward the old woman and swung the hat all the way off. He had long black slick hair that hung flat from a part in the middle to beyond the tips of his ears on either side. His face descended in forehead for more than half its length and ended suddenly with his features just balanced over a jutting steel-trap jaw. He seemed to be a young man but he had a look of composed dissatisfaction as if he understood life thoroughly.

"Good evening," the old woman said. She was about the size of a cedar fence post and she had a man's grey hat pulled down low over her head.

The tramp stood looking at her and didn't answer. He turned his back and faced the sunset. He swung both his whole and his short arm up slowly so that they indicated an expanse of sky and his figure formed a crooked cross. The old woman watched him with her arms folded across her chest as if she were the owner of the sun, and the daughter watched, her head thrust forward and her fat helpless hands hanging at the wrists. She had long pink-gold hair and eyes as blue as a peacock's neck.

He held the pose for almost fifty seconds and then he picked up his box and came on to the porch and dropped down on the bottom step. "Lady," he said in a firm nasal voice, "I'd give a fortune to live where I could see me a sun do that every evening."

"Does it every evening," the old woman said and sat back down. The daughter sat down too and watched him with a cautious sly look as if he were a bird that had come up very close. He leaned to one side, rooting in his pants pocket, and in a second he brought out a package of chewing gum and offered her a piece. She took it and unpeeled it and began to chew without taking her eyes off him. He offered the old woman a piece but she only raised her upper lip to indicate she had no teeth.

Mr. Shiftlet's pale sharp glance had already passed over everything in the yard—the pump near the corner of the house and the big fig tree that three or four chickens were preparing to roost in—and had moved to a shed where he saw the square rusted back of an automobile. "You ladies drive?" he asked.

"That car ain't run in fifteen year," the old woman said. "The day my husband died, it quit running."

"Nothing is like it used to be, Lady," he said. "The world is almost rotten."

"That's right," the old woman said. "You from around here?"

"Name Tom T. Shiftlet," he murmured, looking at the tires.

"I'm pleased to meet you," the old woman said. "Name Lucynell Crater and daughter Lucynell Crater. What you doing around here, Mr. Shiftlet?"

He judged the car to be about a 1928 or '29 Ford. "Lady," he said, and turned and gave her his full attention, "lemme tell you something. There's one of these doctors in Atlanta that's taken a knife and cut the human heart—the human heart," he repeated, leaning forward, "out of a man's chest and held it in his hand," and he held his hand out, palm up, as if it were slightly weighted with the human heart, "and studied it like it was a day-old chicken, and Lady," he said, allowing a long significant pause in which his head slid forward and his clay-colored eyes brightened, "he don't know no more about it than you or me."

"That's right," the old woman said.

"Why, if he was to take that knife and cut into every corner of it, he still wouldn't know no more than you or me. What you want to bet?"

"Nothing," the old woman said wisely. "Where you come from, Mr. Shiftlet?"

He didn't answer. He reached into his pocket and brought out a sack of tobacco and a package of cigarette papers and rolled himself a cigarette, expertly with one hand, and attached it in a hanging position to his upper lip. Then he took a box of wooden matches from his pocket and struck one on his shoe. He held the burning match as if he were studying the mystery of flame while it traveled dangerously toward his skin. The daughter began to make loud noises and to point to his hand and shake her finger at him, but when the flame was just before touching him, he leaned down with his hand cupped over it as if he were going to set fire to his nose and lit the cigarette.

He flipped away the dead match and blew a stream of grey into the evening. A sly look came over his face. "Lady," he said, "nowadays, people'll do anything anyways. I can tell you my name is Tom T. Shiftlet and I come from Tarwater, Tennessee, but you never have seen me before: how you know I ain't lying? How you know my name ain't Aaron Sparks, Lady, and I come from Singleberry, Georgia, or how you know it's not George Speeds and I come from Lucy, Alabama, or how you know I ain't Thompson Bright from Toolafalls, Mississippi?"

"I don't know nothing about you," the old woman muttered, irked.

"Lady," he said, "people don't care how they lie. Maybe the best I can tell you is, I'm a man, but listen, Lady," he said and paused and made his tone more ominous still, "what is a man?"

The old woman began to gum a seed. "What you carry in that tin box, Mr. Shiftlet?" she asked.

"Tools," he said, put back. "I'm a carpenter."

"Well, if you come out here to work, I'll be able to feed you and give you a place to sleep but I can't pay. I'll tell you that before you begin," she said.

There was no answer at once and no particular expression on his face. He leaned back against the two-by-four that helped support the porch roof. "Lady," he said slowly, "there's some men that some things mean more to them than money." The old woman rocked without comment and the daughter watched the trigger that moved up and down in his neck. He told the old woman then that all most people were interested in was money, but he asked what a man was made for. He asked her if a man was made for money, or what. He asked her what she thought she was made for but she didn't answer, she only sat rocking and wondered if a one-armed man could put a new roof on her garden house. He asked a lot of questions that she didn't answer. He told her that he was twenty-eight years old and had lived a varied life. He had been a gospel singer, a foreman on the railroad, an assistant in an undertaking parlor, and he had come over the radio for three months with Uncle Roy and his Red Creek Wranglers. He said he had fought and bled in the Arm Service of his country and visited every foreign land and that everywhere he had seen people that didn't care if they did a thing one way or another. He said he hadn't been raised thataway.

A fat yellow moon appeared in the branches of the fig tree as if it were going to roost there with the chickens. He said that a man had to escape to the country to see the world whole and that he wished he lived in a desolate place like this where he could see the sun go down every evening like God made it to do.

"Are you married or are you single?" the old woman asked.

There was a long silence. "Lady," he asked finally, "where would you find you an innocent woman today? I wouldn't have any of this trash I could just pick up."

The daughter was leaning very far down, hanging her head almost between her knees, watching him through a triangular door she had made in her over-turned hair; and she suddenly fell in a heap on the floor and began to whimper. Mr. Shiftlet straightened her out and helped her get back in the chair.

"Is she your baby girl?" he asked.

"My only," the old woman said, "and she's the sweetest girl in the world. I wouldn't give her up for nothing on earth. She's smart too. She can sweep the floor, cook, wash, feed the chickens, and hoe. I wouldn't give her up for a casket of jewels."

"No," he said kindly, "don't ever let any man take her away from you."

"Any man come after her," the old woman said, "'ll have to stay around the place."

Mr. Shiftlet's eye in the darkness was focussed on a part of the automobile bumper that glittered in the distance. "Lady," he said, jerking his short arm up as if he could point with it to her house and yard and pump, "there ain't a broken thing on this plantation that I couldn't fix for you, one-arm jackleg or not. I'm a man," he said with a sullen dignity, "even if I ain't a whole one. I got," he said, tapping his knuckles on the floor to emphasize the immensity of what he was going to say, "a moral intelligence!" and his face pierced out of the darkness into a shaft of doorlight and he stared at her as if he were astonished himself at this impossible truth.

The old woman was not impressed with the phrase. "I told you you could hang around and work for food," she said, "if you don't mind sleeping in that car yonder."

"Why listen, Lady," he said with a grin of delight, "the monks of old slept in their coffins!"

"They wasn't as advanced as we are," the old woman said.

The next morning he began on the roof of the garden house while Lucynell, the daughter, sat on a rock and watched him work. He had not been around a week before the change he had made in the place was apparent. He had patched the front and back steps, built a new hog pen, restored a fence, and taught Lucynell who was completely deaf, and had never said a word in her life, to say the word "bird." The big rosy-faced girl followed him everywhere, saying "Burrttddt ddbirrrttdt," and clapping her hands. The old woman watched from a distance, secretly pleased. She was ravenous for a son-in-law.

Mr. Shiftlet slept on the hard narrow back seat of the car with his feet out the side window. He had his razor and a can of water on a crate that served him as a bedside table and he put up a piece of mirror against the back glass and kept his coat neatly on a hanger that he hung over one of the windows.

In the evenings he sat on the steps and talked while the old woman and Lucynell rocked violently in their chairs on either side of him. The old woman's three mountains were black against the dark blue sky and were visited off and on by various planets and by the moon after it had left the chickens. Mr. Shiftlet pointed out that the reason he had improved this plantation was because he had taken a personal interest in it. He said he was even going to make the automobile run.

He had raised the hood and studied the mechanism and he said he could tell that the car had been built in the days when cars were really built. You take now, he said, one man puts in one bolt and another man puts in another bolt and another man puts in another bolt so that it's a man for a bolt. That's why you have to pay so much for a car: you're paying all those men. Now if you didn't have to pay but one man, you could get you a cheaper car and one that had had a personal interest taken in it, and it would be a better car. The old woman agreed with him that this was so.

Mr. Shiftlet said that the trouble with the world was that nobody cared, or stopped and took any trouble. He said he never would have been able to teach Lucynell to say a word if he hadn't cared and stopped long enough.

"Teach her to say something else," the old woman said.

"What you want her to say next?" Mr. Shiftlet asked.

The old woman's smile was broad and toothless and suggestive. "Teach her to say 'sugarpie,'" she said.

Mr. Shiftlet already knew what was on her mind.

The next day he began to tinker with the automobile and that evening he told her that if she would buy a fan belt, he would be able to make the car run.

The old woman said she would give him the money. "You see that girl yonder?" she asked, pointing to Lucynell who was sitting on the floor a foot away, watching him, her eyes blue even in the dark. "If it was ever a man wanted to take her away, I would say, 'No man on earth is going to take that sweet girl of mine away from me!' but if he was to say, 'Lady, I don't want to take her away, I want her right here,' I would say, 'Mister, I don't blame you none. I wouldn't pass up a chance to live in a permanent place and get the sweetest girl in the world myself. You ain't no fool,' I would say."

"How old is she?" Mr. Shiftlet asked casually.

"Fifteen, sixteen," the old woman said. The girl was nearly thirty but because of her innocence it was impossible to guess.

"It would be a good idea to paint it too," Mr. Shiftlet remarked. "You don't want it to rust out."

"We'll see about that later," the old woman said.

The next day he walked into town and returned with the parts he needed and a can of gasoline. Late in the afternoon, terrible noises issued from the shed and the old woman rushed out of the house, thinking Lucynell was somewhere having a fit. Lucynell was sitting on a chicken crate, stamping her feet and screaming, "Burrddttt! bddurrddtttt!" but her fuss was drowned out by the car. With a volley of blasts it emerged from the shed, moving in a fierce and stately way. Mr. Shiftlet was in the driver's seat, sitting very erect. He had an expression of serious modesty on his face as if he had just raised the dead.

That night, rocking on the porch, the old woman began her business at once. "You want you an innocent woman, don't you?" she asked sympathetically. "You don't want none of this trash."

"No'm, I don't," Mr. Shiftlet said.

"One that can't talk," she continued, "can't sass you back or use foul language. That's the kind for you to have. Right there," and she pointed to Lucynell sitting cross-legged in her chair, holding both feet in her hands.

"That's right," he admitted. "She wouldn't give me any trouble."

"Saturday," the old woman said, "you and her and me can drive into town and get married."

Mr. Shiftlet eased his position on the steps.

"I can't get married right now," he said. "Everything you want to do takes money and I ain't got any."

"What you need with money?" she asked.

"It takes money," he said. "Some people'll do anything anyhow these days, but the way I think, I wouldn't marry no woman that I couldn't take on a trip like she was somebody. I mean take her to a hotel and treat her. I wouldn't marry the Duchesser Windsor," he said firmly, "unless I could take her to a hotel and give her something good to eat.

"I was raised thataway and there ain't a thing I can do about it. My old mother taught me how to do."

"Lucynell don't even know what a hotel is," the old woman muttered. "Listen here, Mr. Shiftlet," she said sliding forward in her chair, "you'd be getting a permanent house and a deep well and the most innocent girl in the world. You don't need no money. Lemme tell you something: there ain't any place in the world for a poor disabled friendless drifting man."

The ugly words settled in Mr. Shiftlet's head like a group of buzzards in the top of a tree. He didn't answer at once. He rolled himself a cigarette and lit it and then he said in an even voice, "Lady, a man is divided into two parts, body and spirit."

The old woman clamped her gums together.

"A body and a spirit," he repeated. "The body, Lady, is like a house: it don't go anywhere; but the spirit, Lady, is like a automobile: always on the move, always...."

"Listen, Mr. Shiftlet," she said, "my well never goes dry and my house is always warm in the winter and there's no mortgage on a thing about this place. You can go to the court house and see for yourself. And yonder under that shed is a fine automobile." She laid the bait carefully. "You can have it painted by Saturday. I'll pay for the paint."

In the darkness, Mr. Shiftlet's smile stretched like a weary snake waking up by a fire. "Yes'm," he said softly.

After a second he recalled himself and said, "I'm only saying a man's spirit means more to him than anything else. I would have to take my wife off for the weekend without no regards at all for cost. I got to follow where my spirit says to go."

"I'll give you fifteen dollars for a weekend trip," the old woman said in a crabbed voice. "That's the best I can do."

"That wouldn't hardly pay for more than the gas and the hotel," he said. "It wouldn't feed her."

"Seventeen-fifty," the old woman said. "That's all I got so it isn't any use you trying to milk me. You can take a lunch."

Mr. Shiftlet was deeply hurt by the word "milk." He didn't doubt that she had more money sewed up in her mattress but he had already told her he was not interested in her money. "I'll make that do," he said and rose and walked off without treating with her further.

On Saturday the three of them drove into town in the car that the paint had barely dried on and Mr. Shiftlet and Lucynell were married in the Ordinary's office while the old woman witnessed. As they came out of the courthouse, Mr. Shiftlet began twisting his neck in his collar. He looked morose and bitter as if he had been insulted while someone held him. "That didn't satisfy me none," he said. "That was just something a woman in an office did, nothing but paper work and blood tests. What do they know about my blood? If they was to take my heart and cut it out," he said, "they wouldn't know a thing about me. It didn't satisfy me at all."

"It satisfied the law," the old woman said sharply.

"The law," Mr. Shiftlet said and spit. "It's the law that don't satisfy me."

He had painted the car dark green with a yellow band around it just under the windows. The three of them climbed in the front seat and the old woman said, "Don't Lucynell look pretty? Looks like a baby doll." Lucynell was dressed up in a white dress that her mother had uprooted from a trunk and there was a panama hat on her head with a bunch of red wooden cherries on the brim. Every now and then her placid expression was changed by a sly isolated little thought like a shoot of green in the desert. "You got a prize!" the old woman said.

Mr. Shiftlet didn't even look at her.

They drove back to the house to let the old woman off and pick up the lunch. When they were ready to leave, she stood staring in the window of the car, with her fingers clenched around the glass. Tears began to seep sideways out of her eyes and run along the dirty creases in her face. "I ain't ever been parted with her for two days before," she said.

Mr. Shiftlet started the motor.

"And I wouldn't let no man have her but you because I seen you would do right. Good-bye, Sugarbaby," she said, clutching at the sleeve of the white dress. Lucynell looked straight at her and didn't seem to see her there at all. Mr. Shiftlet eased the car forward so that she had to move her hands.

The early afternoon was clear and open and surrounded by pale blue sky. The hills flattened under the car one after another and the climb and dip and swerve went entirely to Mr. Shiftlet's head so that he forgot his morning bitterness. He had always wanted an automobile but he had never been able to afford one before. He drove very fast because he wanted to make Mobile by nightfall.

Occasionally he stopped his thoughts long enough to look at Lucynell in the seat beside him. She had eaten the lunch as soon as they were out of the yard and now she was pulling the cherries off the hat one by one and throwing them out the window. He became depressed in spite of the car. He had driven about a hundred miles when he decided that she must be hungry again and at the next small town they came to, he stopped in front of an aluminum-painted eating place called The Hot Spot and took her in and ordered her a plate of ham and grits. The ride had made her sleepy and as soon as she got up on the stool, she rested her head on the counter and shut her eyes. There was no one in The Hot Spot but Mr. Shiftlet and the boy behind the counter, a pale youth with a greasy rag hung over his shoulder. Before he could dish up the food, she was snoring gently.

"Give it to her when she wakes up," Mr. Shiftlet said. "I'll pay for it now."

The boy bent over her and stared at the long pink-gold hair and the half-shut sleeping eyes. Then he looked up and stared at Mr. Shiftlet. "She looks like an angel of Gawd," he murmured.

"Hitch-hiker," Mr. Shiftlet explained. "I can't wait. I got to make Tuscaloosa."

The boy bent over again and very carefully touched his finger to a strand of the golden hair and Mr. Shiftlet left.

He was more depressed than ever as he drove on by himself. The late afternoon had grown hot and sultry and the country had flattened out. Deep in the sky a storm was preparing very slowly and without thunder as if it meant to drain every drop of air from the earth before it broke. There were times when Mr. Shiftlet preferred not to be alone. He felt too that a man with a car had a responsibility to others and he kept his eye out for a hitch-hiker. Occasionally he saw a sign that warned: "Drive carefully. The life you save may be your own."

The narrow road dropped off on either side into dry fields and here and there a shack or a filling station stood in a clearing. The sun began to set directly in front of the automobile. It was a reddening ball that through his windshield was slightly flat on the bottom and top. He saw a boy in overalls and a grey hat, standing on the edge of the road and he slowed the car down and stopped in front of him. The boy didn't have his hand raised to thumb the ride, he was only standing there, but he had a small cardboard suitcase and his hat was set on his head in a way to indicate that he had left some-where for good. "Son," Mr. Shiftlet said, "I see you want a ride."

The boy didn't say he did or he didn't but he opened the door of the car and got in, and Mr. Shiftlet started driving again. The child held the suitcase on his lap and folded his arms on top of it. He turned his head and looked out the window away from Mr. Shiftlet. Mr. Shiftlet felt oppressed. "Son," he said after a minute, "I got the best old mother in the world so I reckon you only got the second best."

The boy gave him a quick dark glance and then turned his face back out the window.

"It's nothing so sweet," Mr. Shiftlet continued, "as a boy's mother. She taught him his first prayers at her knee, she give him love when no other would, she told him what was right and what wasn't, and she seen that he done the right thing. Son," he said, "I never rued a day in my life like the one I rued when I left that old mother of mine."

The boy shifted in his seat but he didn't look at Mr. Shiftlet. He unfolded his arms and put one hand on the door handle.

"My mother was a angel of Gawd," Mr. Shiftlet said in a very strained voice. "He took her from heaven and giver to me and I left her." His eyes were instantly clouded over with a mist of tears.

The boy turned angrily in the seat. "You go to the devil!" he cried. "My old woman is a flea bag and your's is a stinking pole cat!" and with that he flung the door open and jumped out with his suitcase into the ditch.

Mr. Shiftlet was so shocked that for about a hundred feet he drove along slowly with the door still open like his mouth. Then he reached over and shut both. A cloud, the exact color of the boy's hat and shaped like a turnip, had descended over the sun, and another, worse looking, crouched behind the car. Mr. Shiftlet felt that the rottenness of the world was about to engulf him. He raised his arm and let it fall again to his breast. "Oh Lord!" he prayed, "break forth and wash the slime from this earth!"

The turnip continued slowly to descend. After a few minutes there was a guffawing peal of thunder from behind and fantastic raindrops, like tin can tops, crashed over the rear of Mr. Shiftlet's car. Very quickly he pushed in his clutch and stepped on the gas and, with his stump sticking out the win-dow, he raced the galloping shower into Mobile.

Konstantinos Kavaphes

Konstantinos Kavaphes was born in Alexandria, Egypt, in 1863, the ninth and last child of Constantinopolitan parents. At the age of nine, after the death of his father, Kavaphes moved with his family to London for seven years, where his eldest brothers struggled to keep alive the family business, an export-import firm dealing in Egyptian cotton and Manchester textiles. It was during this period that Kavaphes's poetic sensibility began to develop. He returned to Alexandria from London, then moved with his mother to her native Constantinople. This was a time of poverty and discomfort for him, but also saw the production of his first poems. After returning once again to Alexandria in 1885, Kavaphes took up an appointment as special clerk in the Irrigation Service (Third Circle) of the Ministry of Public Works. He held this appointment for the next thirty years, yet much of his ambitions centered around his poetic life. Writing mainly in Greek, Kavaphes remained in relative obscurity during his lifetime. While his poetry was not in the fashion of his day, since the publication of his first book of collected poems in 1935, Kavaphes has been established as one of the enduring poets of the Western World. This version of "Waiting for the Barbarians" was translated by renowned translator Richmond Lattimore, originally appearing in 1955. Kavaphes died in 1933.

Waiting for the Barbarians *(1955)*

by Konstantinos Kavaphes

(Translated by Richmond Lattimore)

Why are we all assembled and waiting in the market place?

It is the barbarians; they will be here today.

Why is there nothing being done in the senate house?
Why are the senators in session but are not passing laws?

Because the barbarians are coming today.
Why should the senators make laws any more?
The barbarians will make the laws when they get here.

Why has our emperor got up so early
and sits there at the biggest gate of the city
high on his throne, in state, and with his crown on?

Because the barbarians are coming today
and the emperor is waiting to receive them
and their general. And he has even made ready
a parchment to present them, and thereon
he has written many names and many titles.

Why have our two consuls and our praetors
come out today in their red embroidered togas?
Why have they put on their bracelets with all those amethysts
and rings shining with the glitter of emeralds?
Why will they carry their precious staves today
which are decorated with figures of gold and silver?

Because the barbarians are coming today
and things like that impress the barbarians.

Why do our good orators not put in any appearance
and make public speeches, and do what they generally do?

Because the barbarians are coming today
and they get bored with eloquent public speeches.

Why is everybody beginning to be so uneasy?
Why so disordered? (See how grave all the faces have
become!) Why do the streets and the squares empty so quickly,
and they are all anxiously going home to their houses?

Because it is night, and the barbarians have not got here,
and some people have come in from the frontier
and say that there aren't any more barbarians.

What are we going to do now without the barbarians?
In a way, those people were a solution.

Ruth Stone

Ruth Stone was born in 1915 in Roanoke, Virginia, but moved as a child to Indianapolis, Indiana. At age nineteen, Stone moved to Illinois with her first husband. While there, she met and married the poet and novelist Walter Stone. The couple had three daughters, and the family moved to Vassar College in 1952. Ruth Stone first published poetry in *The Kenyon Review* in 1953. Tragically, while spending time in England in 1959, Walter Stone committed suicide. It was in this same year that Stone's first book of poems, *In an Iridescent Time*, was published. Soon thereafter she was awarded a Kenyon Review Fellowship in Poetry, and with the prize money, Stone bought a house in Vermont, a place she has returned to during the summers between teaching jobs for decades. Stone is famous for her prowess as a teacher of poetry and has taught at a multitude of colleges and universities, including Harvard, Indiana University, the University of California at Davis, New York University, and, most recently, Harpur College. Her poems often deal with death and loss, but point out the humor and beauty that occurs in the midst of tragedy. She is the author of such books as *Cheap, Second-Hand Coat,* and *Who Is the Widow's Muse* and has won numerous awards, including the Delmore Schwartz Award (1983), the Whiting Writer's Award (1986), and the Paterson Poetry Prize (1988). In 2000, she won the National Book Critics Circle Award for her collection *Ordinary Words*. In 2002, at the age of eighty-seven, she was awarded the National Book Award for her eighth collection, *In the Next Galaxy*. Stone retired from teaching as Bartle Professor of English at Harpur College last December. The poems reprinted here span nearly half a century. "Memoir" appeared in *The Kenyon Review* in 1956; "The Word *Though* As a Coupler" and "This Space" appeared in 1999.

Memoir *(1956)*

by Ruth Stone

Out of the shadows from the lamp at night we'd see
The lines of Braque on the walls,
Or where the shadow cut across the books, the free
Formality of a pink Matisse;
My eye recalls the moustache of Rousseau
Above any lover's smile,
The light delineates them so,
Each innocent of style,
Plaiting my hair the room would be at peace.

I recall him now, my lover of the academy;
How the page of my darling's ever changing choice
Would be open to some unraveled evanescent verse,
As he grumbled on, a man alone with his voice.
Oh, not one word in an ordinary way
To tell us meanings reverse,
That the back of the hand is stranger
To the palm of the hand. Just the unmindful voice
Taking its single journey divorced from danger.
Out of the shadows of the street by day I see
The rain at the gutted curb,
Or where the fountains play in the circular masonry,
A verve without release,
The spew of a stone cherub.
My heart searches for some ingenuous grace,
And rages outside the room where all things cease.

Peter Taylor

Peter Taylor was born in Trenton, a small town in western Tennessee, in 1917. Soon the Taylor family moved to the city—first to Nashville, then to St. Louis and Memphis. Taylor has a rich history with *The Kenyon Review*, beginning in his college years. After stints at Southwestern (now Rhodes College) in Memphis and Vanderbilt University, Taylor settled in at Kenyon College to study under John Crowe Ransom, founding editor of *The Kenyon Review*. There he found a group of life-long literary friends, which included the poets Robert Lowell and Randall Jarrell. In 1940, Taylor was drafted into the army, serving until 1945. In the decades following WWII, Taylor was among those writers that established American ascendancy in the short story. He taught at various colleges, including Kenyon, Harvard, Ohio State, and Virginia and wrote such masterful novels and collections of short fiction as *A Long Fourth and Other Stories*, *The Old Forest and Other Stories,* and *A Summons to Memphis*, which earned him a Pulitzer Prize in 1986. Although Taylor's fiction concentrates on the South's upper middle class, he was not primarily interested in capturing regional texture, but in how, universally, human character survived in the environment in which it found itself. He died in 1994.

Venus, Cupid, Folly and Time *(1958)*

by Peter Taylor

Their house alone would not have made you think there was anything so awfully wrong with Mr. Dorset or his old maid sister. But certain things about the way both of them dressed had, for a long time, annoyed and disturbed everyone. We used to see them together at the grocery store, for instance, or even in one of the big department stores downtown, wearing their bedroom slippers. Looking more closely we would sometimes see the cuff of a pyjama top or the hem of a hitched up nightgown showing from underneath their ordinary daytime clothes. Such slovenliness in one's neighbors is so unpleasant that even husbands and wives in West Vesey Place, which was the street where the Dorsets lived, had got so they didn't like to joke about it with each other. Were the Dorsets, poor old things, losing their minds? If so, what was to be done about it? Some neighbors got so they would not even admit to themselves what they saw. And a child coming home with an ugly report on the Dorsets was apt to be told that it was time he learned to curb his imagination.

Mr. Dorset wore tweed caps and sleeveless sweaters. Usually he had his sweater stuffed down inside his trousers with his shirt tails. To the women and young girls in West Vesey Place this was extremely distasteful. It made them feel as though Mr. Dorset had just come from the bathroom and had got his sweater inside his trousers by mistake. There was, in fact, nothing about Mr. Dorset that was not offensive to the women. Even the old touring car he drove was regarded by most of them as a disgrace to the neighborhood. Parked out in front of his house, as it usually was, it seemed a worse violation of West Vesey's zoning than the house itself. And worst of all was seeing Mr. Dorset wash the car.

Mr. Dorset washed his own car! He washed it not back in the alley or in his driveway but out there in the street of West Vesey Place. This would usually be on the day of one of the parties which he and his sister liked to give for young people or on a day when they were going to make deliveries of the paper flowers or the home grown figs which they sold to their friends. Mr. Dorset would appear in the street carrying two buckets of warm water and wearing a pair of skin-tight coveralls. The skin-tight coveralls, of khaki material but faded almost to flesh color, were still more offensive to the women and young girls than his way of wearing his sweaters. With sponges and chamois cloths and a large scrub brush (for use on the canvas top) the old fellow would fall to and scrub away, gently at first on the canvas top and more vigorously as he progressed to the hood and body, just as though the car were something alive. Neighbor children felt that he went after the head-lights exactly as if he were scrubbing the poor car's ears. There was an ele-ment of brutality in the way he did it and yet an element of tenderness too. An old lady visiting in the neighborhood once said that it was like the cleansing of a sacrificial animal. I suppose it was some such feeling as this that made all women want to turn away their eyes whenever the spectacle of Mr. Dorset washing his car presented itself.

As for Mr. Dorset's sister, her behavior was in its way just as offensive as his. To the men and boys in the neighborhood it was she who seemed quite beyond the pale. She would come out on her front terrace at mid-day clad in a faded flannel bathrobe and with her dyed black hair all undone and hang-ing down her back like the hair of an Indian squaw. To us whose wives and mothers did not even come downstairs in their negligees, this was very unsettling. It was hard to excuse it even on the grounds that the Dorsets were too old and lonely and hard-pressed to care about appearances anymore.

Moreover, there was a boy who had gone to Miss Dorset's house one morning in the early fall to collect for his paper route and saw this very Miss Louisa Dorset pushing a carpet sweeper about one of the downstairs rooms without a stitch of clothes on. He saw her through one of the little lancet windows that opened on the front loggia of the house, and he watched her for quite a long while. She was cleaning the house in preparation for a party they were giving for young people that night, and the boy said that when she finally got hot and tired she dropped down in an easy chair and crossed her spindly, blue-veined, old legs and sat there completely naked, with her legs crossed and shaking one scrawny little foot, just as unconcerned as if she didn't care that somebody was likely to walk in on her at any moment. After a little bit the boy saw her get up again and go and lean across a table to arrange some paper flowers in a vase. Fortunately he was a nice boy, though he lived only on the edge of the West Vesey Place neighborhood, and he went away without ringing the doorbell or collecting for his paper that week. But he could not resist telling his friends about what he had seen. He said it was a sight he would never forget! And she an old lady more than sixty years old who, had she not been so foolish and self-willed, might have had a house full of servants to push that carpet sweeper for her!

This foolish pair of old people had given up almost everything in life for each other's sake. And it was not at all necessary. When they were young they could have come into a decent inheritance, or now that they were old they might have been provided for by a host of rich relatives. It was only a matter of their being a little tolerant—or even civil—toward their kins-people. But this was something that old Mr. Dorset and his sister could never consent to do. Almost all their lives they had spoken of their father's kin as "Mama's in-laws" and of their mother's kin as "Papa's in-laws." Their family name was Dorset, not on one side but on both sides. Their parents had been distant cousins. As a matter of fact, the Dorset family in the city of Mero had once been so large and was so long established there that it would have been hard to estimate how distant the kinship might be. But still it was something that the old couple never liked to have mentioned. Most of their mother's close kin had, by the time I am speaking of, moved off to California, and most of their father's people lived somewhere up East. But Miss Dorset and her old bachelor brother found any contact, correspon-dence, even an exchange of Christmas cards with these in-laws intolerable. It was a case, so they said, of the in-laws respecting the value of the dollar above all else, whereas they, Miss Louisa and Mr. Alfred Dorset, placed importance on other things.

They lived in a dilapidated and curiously mutilated house on a street which, except for their own house, was the most splendid street in the entire city. Their house was one that you or I would have been ashamed to live in—even in the lean years of the early thirties. In order to reduce taxes the Dorsets had had the third story of the house torn away, leaving an ugly, flat-topped effect without any trim or ornamentation. Also they had had the south wing pulled down and had sealed the scars not with matching brick but with a speckled stucco that looked raw and naked. All this the old cou-ple did in violation of the strict zoning laws of West Vesey Place, and for doing so they would most certainly have been prosecuted except that they were the Dorsets and except that this was during the depression when zon-ing laws weren't easy to enforce in a city like Mero.

To the young people whom she and her brother entertained at their house once each year Miss Louisa Dorset liked to say: "We have given up every-thing for each other. Our only income is from our paper flowers and our figs." The old lady, though without showing any great skill or talent for it, made paper flowers. During the winter months her brother took her in that fifteen-year-old touring car of theirs, with its steering wheel on the wrong side and with isinglass side-curtains that were never taken down, to deliver these flowers to her customers. The flowers looked more like sprays of tinted potato-chips than like any real flowers. Nobody could possibly have wanted to buy them except that she charged next to nothing for them and except that to people with children it seemed important to be on the Dorsets' list of worthwhile people. Nobody could really have wanted Mr. Dorset's figs either. He cultivated a dozen little bushes along the back wall of their house, covering them in the wintertime with some odd looking boxes which he had constructed for the purpose. The bushes were very productive, but the figs they produced were dried up little things without much taste. During the summer months he and his sister went about in their car, with the side-curtains still up, delivering the figs to the same customers who bought the paper flowers. The money they made could hardly have paid for the gas it took to run the car. It was a great waste and it was very foolish of them.

And yet, despite everything, this foolish pair of old people, this same Miss Louisa and Mr. Alfred Dorset, had become social arbiters of a kind in our city. They had attained this position entirely through their fondness for giving an annual dancing party for young people. To *young* people—to *very* young people the Dorsets' hearts went out. I don't mean to suggest that their hearts went out to orphans or to the children of the poor, for they were not foolish in that way. The guests at their little dancing parties were the thirteen- and fourteen-year-olds from families like the one they had long ago set themselves against, young people from the very houses to which, in season, they delivered their figs and their paper flowers. And when the night of one of their parties came round, it was in fact the custom for Mr. Alfred to go in the same old car and fetch all the invited guests to his house. His sister might explain to reluctant parents that this saved the children the embarrassment of being taken to their first dance by mommy and daddy. But the parents knew well enough that for twenty years the Dorsets had permitted no adult person, besides themselves, to put foot inside their house.

At those little dancing parties which the Dorsets gave, peculiar things went on—unsettling things to the boys and girls who had been fetched round in the old car. Sensible parents wished to keep their children away. Yet what could they do? For a Mero girl to have to explain, a few years later, why she never went to a party at the Dorsets' was like having to explain why she had never been a debutante. For a boy it was like having to explain why he had not gone up East to school or even why his father hadn't belonged to the Mero Raquet Club. If when you were thirteen or fourteen you got invited to the Dorsets' house, you went; it was the way of letting people know from the outset who you were. In a busy, modern city like Mero you cannot afford to let people forget who you are—not for a moment, not at any age. Even the Dorsets knew that.

Many a little girl, after one of those evenings at the Dorsets', was heard to cry out in her sleep. When waked, or half waked, her only explanation might be: "It was just the fragrance from the paper flowers." Or: "I dreamed I could really smell the paper flowers." Many a boy was observed by his parents to seem "different" afterward. He became "secretive." The parents of the generation that had to attend those parties never pretended to understand what went on at the Dorsets' house. And even to those of us who were in that unlucky generation it seemed we were half a lifetime learning what really took place during our one evening under the Dorsets' roof. Before our turn to go ever came round we had for years been hearing about what it was like from older boys and girls. Afterward, we continued to hear about it from those who followed us. And, looking back on it, nothing about the one evening when you were actually there ever seemed quite so real as the glimpses and snatches which you got from those people before and after you—the second-hand impressions of the Dorsets' behavior, of things they said, of looks that passed between them.

Since Miss Dorset kept no servants she always opened her own door. I suspect that for the guests at her parties the sight of her opening her door, in her astonishing attire, came as the most violent shock of the whole evening. On these occasions she and her brother got themselves up as we had never seen them before and never would again. The old lady invariably wore a modish white evening gown, a garment perfectly fitted to her spare and scrawny figure and cut in such high fashion that it must necessarily have been new that year. And never to be worn but that one night! Her hair, long and thick and newly dyed for the occasion, would be swept upward and forward in a billowy mass which was topped by a corsage of yellow and coral paper flowers. Her cheeks and lips would be darkly rouged. On her long bony arms and her bare shoulders she would have applied some kind of suntan powder. Whatever else you had been led to expect of the evening, no one had ever warned you sufficiently about the radical change to be noted in her appearance—or in that of her brother, either. By the end of the party Miss Louisa might look as dowdy as ever, and Mr. Alfred a little worse than usual. But at the outset, when the party was assembling in their drawing room, even Mr. Alfred appeared resplendent in a nattily tailored tuxedo, with exactly the shirt, the collar, and the tie which fashion prescribed that year.

His grey hair was nicely trimmed, his puffy old face freshly shaven. He was powdered with the same dark powder that his sister used. One felt even that his cheeks had been lightly touched with rouge.

A strange perfume pervaded the atmosphere of the house. The moment you set foot inside, this awful fragrance engulfed you. It was like a mixture of spicy incense and sweet attar of roses. And always, too, there was the profusion of paper flowers. The flowers were everywhere—on every cabinet and console, every inlaid table and carved chest, on every high, marble mantel piece, on the bookshelves. In the entrance hall special tiers must have been set up to hold the flowers, because they were there in overpowering masses. They were in such abundance that it seemed hardly possible that Miss Dorset could have made them all. She must have spent weeks and weeks preparing them, even months, perhaps even the whole year between parties. When she went about delivering them to her customers, in the months following, they were apt to be somewhat faded and dusty; but on the night of the party the colors of the flowers seemed even more impressive and more unlikely than their number. They were fuchsia, they were chartreuse, they were coral, aqua-marine, brown, they were even black.

Everywhere in the Dorsets' house too were certain curious illuminations and lighting effects. The source of the light was usually hidden and its purpose was never obvious at once. The lighting was a subtler element than either the perfume or the paper flowers, and ultimately it was more disconcerting. A shaft of lavender light would catch a young visitor's eye and lead it, seemingly without purpose, in among the flowers. Then just beyond the point where the strength of the light would begin to diminish, the eye would discover something. In a small aperture in the mass of flowers, or sometimes in a larger grotto-like opening, there would be a piece of sculpture—in the hall a plaster replica of Rodin's *The Kiss*, in the library an antique plaque of Leda and the Swan. Or just above the flowers would be hung a picture, usually a black and white print but sometimes a reproduction in color. On the landing of the stairway leading down to the basement ballroom was the only picture that one was likely to learn the title of at the time. It was a tiny color print of Bronzino's *Venus, Cupid, Folly and Time*. This picture was not even framed. It was simply tacked on the wall, and it had obviously been torn—rather carelessly, perhaps hurriedly—from a book or magazine. The title and the name of the painter were printed in the white margin underneath.

About these works of art most of us had been warned by older boys and girls; and we stood in painful dread of that moment when Miss Dorset or her brother might catch us staring at any one of their pictures or sculptures. We had been warned, time and again, that during the course of the evening moments would come when she or he would reach out and touch the other's elbow and indicate, with a nod or just the trace of a smile, some guest whose glance had strayed among the flowers.

To some extent the dread which all of us felt of that evening at the Dorsets' cast a shadow over the whole of our childhood. Yet for nearly twenty years the Dorsets continued to give their annual party. And even the most sensible of parents were not willing to keep their children away.

But a thing happened finally which could almost have been predicted. Young people, even in West Vesey Place, will not submit forever to the prudent counsel of their parents. Or some of them won't. There was a boy named Ned Meriwether and his sister Emily Meriwether, who lived with their parents in West Vesey Place just one block away from the Dorsets' house. In November Ned and Emily were invited to the Dorsets' party, and because they dreaded it they decided to play a trick on everyone concerned—even on themselves, as it turned out…They got up a plan for smuggling an uninvited guest into the Dorsets' party.

The parents of this Emily and Ned sensed that their children were concealing something from them and suspected that the two were up to mischief of some kind. But they managed to deceive themselves with the thought that it was only natural for young people—"mere children"—to be nervous about going to the Dorsets' house. And so instead of questioning them during the last hour before they left for the party, these sensible parents tried to do everything in their power to calm their two children. The boy and the girl, seeing that this was the case, took advantage of it.

"You must not go down to the front door with us when we leave," the daughter insisted to her mother. And she persuaded both Mr. and Mrs. Meriwether that after she and her brother were dressed for the party they should all wait together in the upstairs sitting room until Mr. Dorset came to fetch the two young people in his car.

When, at eight o'clock, the lights of the automobile appeared in the street below, the brother and sister were still upstairs—watching from the bay window of the family sitting room. They kissed Mother and Daddy good-bye and then they flew down the stairs and across the wide, carpeted entrance hall to a certain dark recess where a boy named Tom Bascomb was hidden. This boy was the uninvited guest whom Ned and Emily were going to smuggle into the party. They had left the front door unlatched for Tom, and from the upstairs window just a few minutes ago they had watched him come across their front lawn. Now in the little recess of the hall there was a quick exchange of overcoats and hats between Ned Meriwether and Tom Bascomb; for it was a feature of the plan that Tom should attend the party as Ned and that Ned should go as the uninvited guest.

In the darkness of the recess Ned fidgeted and dropped Tom Bascomb's coat on the floor. But the boy, Tom Bascomb, did not fidget. He stepped out into the light of the hall and began methodically getting into the overcoat which he would wear tonight. He was not a boy who lived in the West Vesey Place neighborhood (he was in fact the very boy who had once watched Miss Dorset cleaning house without any clothes on), and he did not share Emily's and Ned's nervous excitement about the evening. The sound of Mr. Dorset's footsteps outside did not disturb him. When both Ned and Emily stood frozen by that sound, he continued buttoning the unfamiliar coat and even amused himself by stretching forth one arm to observe how high the sleeve came on his wrist.

The doorbell rang, and from his dark corner Ned Meriwether whispered to his sister and to Tom: "Don't worry. I'll be at the Dorsets' in plenty of time."

Tom Bascomb only shrugged his shoulders at this reassurance. Presently when he looked at Emily's flushed face and saw her batting her eyes like a nervous monkey, a crooked smile played upon his lips. Then, at a sign from Emily, Tom followed her to the entrance door and permitted her to introduce him to old Mr. Dorset as her brother.

From the window of the upstairs sitting room the Meriwether parents watched Mr. Dorset and this boy and this girl walking across the lawn toward Mr. Dorset's peculiar looking car. A light shone bravely and protectively from above the entrance of the house, and in its rays the parents were able to detect the strange angle at which Brother was carrying his head tonight and how his new fedora already seemed too small for him. They even noticed that he seemed a bit taller tonight.

"I hope it's all right," said the mother.

"What do you mean 'all right'?" the father asked petulantly.

"I mean—," the mother began, and then she hesitated. She did not want to mention that the boy out there did not look like their own Ned. It would have seemed to give away her feelings too much. "I mean that I wonder if I should have put Sister in that long dress at this age and let her wear my cape.

I'm afraid the cape is really inappropriate. She's still young for that sort of thing."

"Oh," said the father, "I thought you meant something else."

"Whatever else did you think I meant, Edwin?" the mother said, suddenly breathless.

"I thought you meant the business we've discussed before," he said although this was of course not what he had thought she meant. He had thought she meant that the boy out there did not look like their Ned. To him it had seemed even that the boy's step was different from Ned's. "The Dorsets' parties," he said, "are not very nice affairs to be sending your children off to, Muriel. That's all I thought you meant."

"But we can't keep them away," the mother said defensively.

"Oh, it's just that they are growing up faster than we realize," said the father, glancing at his wife out of the corner of his eye.

By this time Mr. Dorset's car had pulled out of sight, and from downstairs Muriel Meriwether thought she heard another door closing. "What was that?" she said, putting one hand on her husband's.

"Don't be so jumpy," her husband said irritably, snatching away his hand. "It's the servants closing up in the kitchen."

Both of them knew that the servants had closed up in the kitchen long before this. Both of them had heard quite distinctly the sound of the side door closing as Ned went out. But they went on talking and deceiving themselves in this fashion during most of that evening.

Even before she opened the door to Mr. Dorset, little Emily Meriwether had known that there would be no difficulty about passing Tom Bascomb off as her brother. In the first place, she knew that without his spectacles Mr. Dorset could hardly see his hand before his face and knew that due to some silly pride he had he never put on his spectacles except when he was behind the wheel of his automobile. This much was common knowledge. In the second place, Emily knew from experience that neither he or his sister ever made any real pretense of knowing one child in their general acquaintance from another. And so, standing in the doorway and speaking almost in a whisper, Emily had merely to introduce first herself and then her pretended brother to Mr. Dorset. After that the three of them walked in silence from her father's house to the waiting car.

Emily was wearing her mother's second best evening wrap, a white lapin cape which, on Emily, swept the ground. As she walked between the boy and the man, the touch of the cape's soft silk lining on her bare arms and on her shoulders spoke to her silently of a strange girl she had seen in her looking glass upstairs tonight. And with her every step toward the car the skirt of her long taffeta gown whispered her own name to her: *Emily...Emily.* She heard it distinctly, and yet the name sounded unfamiliar. Once during this unreal walk from house to car she glanced at the mysterious boy, Tom Bascomb, longing to ask him—if only with her eyes—for some reassurance that she was really she. But Tom Bascomb was absorbed in his own irrelevant observations. With his head tilted back he was gazing upward at the nondescript winter sky where, among drifting clouds, a few pale stars were shedding their dull light alike on West Vesey Place and on the rest of the world. Emily drew her wrap tightly about her, and when presently Mr. Dorset held open the door to the back seat of his car she shut her eyes and plunged into the pitch-blackness of the car's interior.

Tom Bascomb was a year older than Ned Meriwether and he was nearly two years older than Emily. He had been Ned's friend first. He and Ned had played baseball together on Saturdays before Emily ever set eyes on him. Yet according to Tom Bascomb himself, with whom several of us older boys talked just a few weeks after the night he went to the Dorsets, Emily always insisted that it was she who had known him first. On what she based this false claim Tom could not say. And on the two or three other occasions when we got Tom to talk about that night, he kept saying that he didn't understand what it was that had made Emily and Ned quarrel over which of them knew him first and knew him better.

We could have told him what it was, I think. But we didn't. It would have been too hard to say to him that at one time or another all of us in West Vesey had had our Tom Bascombs. Tom lived with his parents in an apartment house on a wide thoroughfare known as Division Boulevard, and his only real connection with West Vesey Place was that that street was included in his paper route. During the early morning hours he rode his bicycle along West Vesey and along other quiet streets like it, carefully aiming a neatly rolled paper at the dark loggia, at the colonnaded porch, or at the ornamented doorway of each of the palazzos and chateaux and manor houses that glowered at him in the dawn. He was well thought of as a paper boy. If by mistake one of his papers went astray and lit on an upstairs balcony or on the roof of a porch, Tom would always take more careful aim and throw another. Even if the paper only went into the shrubbery, Tom got off his bicycle and fished it out. He wasn't the kind of boy to whom it would have occurred that the old fogies and the rich kids in West Vesey could very well get out and scramble for their own papers.

Actually a party at the Dorsets' house was more a grand tour of the house than a real party. There was a half hour spent over very light refreshments (fruit jello, English tea biscuits, lime punch). There was another half hour ostensibly given to general dancing in the basement ballroom (to the accompaniment of victrola music). But mainly there was the tour. As the party passed through the house, stopping sometimes to sit down in the principal rooms, the host and hostess provided entertainment in the form of an almost continuous dialogue between themselves. This dialogue was famous and was full of interest, being all about how much the Dorsets had given up for each other's sake and about how much higher the tone of Mero society used to be than it was nowadays. They would invariably speak of their parents, who had died within a year of each other when Miss Louisa and Mr. Alfred were still in their teens; they even spoke of their wicked in-laws. When their parents died, the wicked in-laws had first tried to make them sell the house, then had tried to separate them and send them away to boarding schools, and had ended by trying to marry them off to "just anyone." Their two grandfathers had still been alive in those days and each had had a hand in the machinations, after the failure of which each grandfather had disinherited them. Mr. Alfred and Miss Louisa spoke also of how, a few years later, a procession of "young nobodies" had come of their own accord trying to steal the two of them away from each other. Both he and she would scowl at the very recollection of those "just anybodies" and those "nobodies," those "would-be suitors" who always turned out to be misguided fortune-hunters and had to be driven away.

The Dorsets' dialogue usually began in the living room the moment Mr. Dorset returned with his last collection of guests. (He sometimes had to make five or six trips in the car.) There, as in other rooms afterward, they were likely to begin with a reference to the room itself or perhaps to some piece of furniture in the room. For instance, the extraordinary length of the drawing room—or reception room, as the Dorsets called it—would lead them to speak of an even longer room which they had had torn away from the house. "It grieved us, we wept," Miss Dorset would say, "to have Mama's French drawing room torn away from us."

"But we tore it away from ourselves," her brother would add, "as we tore away our in-laws—because we could not afford them." Both of them spoke in a fine declamatory style, but they frequently interrupted themselves with a sad little laugh which expressed something quite different from what they were saying and which seemed to serve them as an aside not meant for our ears.

"That was one of our greatest sacrifices," Miss Dorset would say, referring still to her mother's French drawing room.

And her brother would say: "But we knew the day had passed in Mero for entertainments worthy of that room."

"It was the room which Mama and Papa loved best, but we gave it up because we knew, from our upbringing, which things to give up."

From this they might go on to anecdotes about their childhood. Sometimes their parents had left them for months or even a whole year at a time with only the housekeeper or with trusted servants to see after them. "You could trust servants then," they explained. And: "In those days parents could do that sort of thing, because in those days there was a responsible body of people within which your young people could always find proper companionship."

In the library, to which the party always moved from the drawing room, Mr. Dorset was fond of exhibiting snapshots of the house taken before the south wing was pulled down. As the pictures were passed around, the dialogue continued. It was often there that they told the story of how the in-laws had tried to force them to sell the house. "For the sake of economy!" Mr. Dorset would exclaim, adding an ironic, "Ha ha!"

His sister would repeat the exclamation, "For the sake of economy!" and also the ironic, "Ha ha!"

"As though money—" he would begin.

"As though money ever took the place," his sister would come in, "of living with your own kind."

"Or of being well born," said Mr. Dorset.

After the billiard room, where everyone who wanted it was permitted one turn with the only cue that there seemed to be in the house, and after the dining room, where it was promised refreshments would be served later, the guests would be taken down to the ball room—purportedly for dancing. Instead of everyone's being urged to dance, however, once they were assembled in the ballroom, Miss Dorset would announce that she and her brother understood the timidity which young people felt about dancing and that all that she and he intended to do was to set the party a good example...It was only Miss Louisa and Mr. Alfred who danced. For perhaps thirty minutes, in a room without light excepting that from a few weak bulbs concealed among the flowers, the old couple danced; and they danced with such grace and there was such perfect harmony in all their movements that the guests stood about in stunned silence, as if hypnotized. The Dorsets waltzed, they two-stepped, they even fox-trotted, stopping only long enough between dances for Mr. Dorset, amid general applause, to change the victrola record.

But it was when their dance was ended that all the effects of the Dorsets' careful grooming that night would have vanished. And, alas, they made no effort to restore themselves. During the remainder of the evening Mr. Dorset went about with his bow tie hanging limply on his damp shirtfront, a gold collar button shining above it. A strand of grey hair, which normally covered his bald spot on top, now would have fallen on the wrong side of his part and hung like fringe about his ear. On his face and neck the thick layer of powder was streaked with perspiration. Miss Dorset was usually in an even more dishevelled state, depending somewhat upon the fashion of her dress that year. But always her powder was streaked, her lipstick entirely gone, her hair falling down on all sides, and her corsage dangling somewhere about the nape of her neck. In this condition they led the party upstairs again, not stopping until they had reached the second floor of the house.

On the second floor we—the guests—were shown the rooms which the Dorsets' parents had once occupied (The Dorsets' own rooms were never shown). We saw, in glass museum cases along the hallway, the dresses and suits and hats and even the shoes which Miss Louisa and Mr. Alfred had worn to parties when they were very young. And now the dialogue, which had been left off while the Dorsets danced, was resumed. "Ah, the happy time," one of them would say, "was when we were *your* age!"

And then, exhorting us to be happy and gay while we were still safe in the bosom of our own kind and before the world came crowding in on us with its ugly demands, the Dorsets would recall the happiness they had known when they were very young. This was their *pièce de résistance*. With many a wink and blush and giggle and shake of the forefinger—and of course standing before the whole party—they each would remind the other of his or her naughty behavior in some old-fashioned parlor game or of certain silly little flirtations which they had long ago caught each other in.

They were on their way downstairs again now, and by the time they had finished with this favorite subject they would be downstairs. They would be in the dark, flower bedecked downstairs hall and just before entering the dining room for the promised refreshments: the fruit jello, the English tea biscuits, the lime punch.

And now for a moment Mr. Dorset bars the way to the dining room and prevents his sister from opening the closed door. "Now, my good friends," he says, "let us eat, drink, and be merry!"

"For the night is yet young," says his sister.

"Tonight you must be gay and carefree," Mr. Dorset enjoins.

"Because in this house we are all friends," Miss Dorset says. "We are all young, we all love one another."

"And love can make us all young forever," her brother says.

"Remember!"

"Remember this evening always, sweet young people!"

"Remember!"

"Remember what our life is like here!"

And now Miss Dorset, with one hand on the knob of the great door which she is about to throw open, leans a little toward the guests and whispers hoarsely: "This is what it is like to be young forever!"

Ned Meriwether was waiting behind a big japonica shrub near the sidewalk when, about twenty minutes after he had last seen Emily, the queer old touring car drew up in front of the Dorsets' house. During the interval, the car had gone from the Meriwether house to gather a number of other guests, and so it was not only Emily and Tom who alighted on the sidewalk before the Dorsets' house. The group was just large enough to make it easy for Ned to slip out from his dark hiding place and join them without being noticed by Mr. Dorset. And now the group was escorted rather unceremoniously up to the door of the house, and Mr. Dorset departed to fetch more guests.

They were received at the door by Miss Dorset. Her eyesight was no doubt better than her brother's, but still there was really no danger of her detecting an uninvited guest. Those of us who had gone to that house in the years just before Ned and Emily came along, could remember that during a whole evening, when their house was full of young people, the Dorsets made no introductions and made no effort to distinguish which of their guests was which. They did not even make a count of heads. Perhaps they did vaguely recognize some of the faces, because sometimes when they had come delivering figs or paper flowers to a house they had of necessity encountered a young child there, and always they smiled sweetly at it, asked its age, and calculated on their old fingers how many years must pass before the child would be eligible for an invitation. Yet at those moments something in the way they had held up their fingers and in the way they had gazed *at* the little face instead of into it had revealed their lack of interest in the individual child. And later when the child was finally old enough to receive their invitation he found it was still no different with the Dorsets. Even in their own house it was evidently to the young people as a group that the Dorsets' hearts went out; while they had the boys and girls under their roof they herded them about like so many little thoroughbred calves. Even when Miss Dorset opened the front door she did so exactly as though she were opening a gate. She pulled it open very slowly, standing half behind it to keep out of harm's way. And the children, all huddled together, surged in.

How meticulously this Ned and Emily Meriwether must have laid their plans for that evening! And the whole business might have come out all right if only they could have foreseen the effect which one part of their plan—rather a last minute embellishment of it—would produce upon Ned himself. Barely ten minutes after they entered the house Ned was watching Tom as he took his seat on the piano bench beside Emily. Ned probably watched Tom closely, because certainly he knew what the next move was going to be. The moment Miss Louisa Dorset's back was turned Tom Bascomb slipped his arm gently about Emily's little waist and commenced kissing her all over her pretty face. It was almost as if he were kissing away tears.

This spectacle on the piano bench, and others like it which followed, had been an inspiration of the last day or so before the party. Or so Ned and Emily maintained afterward when defending themselves to their parents. But no matter when it was conceived, a part of their plan it was, and Ned must have believed himself fully prepared for it. Probably he expected to join in the round of giggling which it produced from the other guests. But now that the time had come—it is easy to imagine—the boy Ned Meriwether found himself not quite able to join in the fun. He watched with the others, but he was not quite infected by their laughter. He stood a little apart, and possibly he was hoping that Emily and Tom would not notice his failure to appreciate the success of their comedy. He was no doubt baffled by his own feelings, by the failure of his own enthusiasm, and by a growing desire to withdraw himself from the plot and from the party itself.

It is easy to imagine Ned's uneasiness and confusion that night. And I believe the account which I have given of Emily's impressions and her delicate little sensations while on the way to the party has the ring of truth about it, though actually the account was supplied by girls who knew her only slightly, who were not at the party, who could not possibly have seen her afterward. It may, after all, represent only what other girls imagined she would have felt. As for the account of how Mr. and Mrs. Meriwether spent the evening, it is their very own. And they did not hesitate to give it to any-one who would listen.

It was a long time, though, before many of us had a clear picture of the main events of the evening. We heard very soon that the parties for young people were to be no more, that there had been a wild scramble and chase through the Dorsets' house, and that it had ended by the Dorsets locking some boy—whether Ned or Tom was not easy to determine at first—in a queer sort of bathroom in which the plumbing had been disconnected, and even the fixtures removed, I believe. (Later I learned that there was nothing literally sinister about the bathroom itself. By having the pipes disconnected to this, and perhaps other bathrooms, the Dorsets had obtained further reductions in their taxes.) But a clear picture of the whole evening wasn't to be had—not without considerable searching. For one thing, the Meriwether parents immediately, within a week after the party, packed their son and daughter off to boarding schools. Accounts from the other children were contradictory and vague—perversely so, it seemed. Parents reported to each other that the little girls had nightmares which were worse even than those which their older sisters had had. And the boys were secretive and elusive, even with us older boys when we questioned them about what had gone on.

One sketchy account of events leading up to the chase, however, did go the rounds almost at once. Ned must have written it back to some older boy in a letter, because it contained information which no one but Ned could have had. The account went like this: When Mr. Dorset returned from his last round-up of guests, he came hurrying into the drawing room where the others were waiting and said in a voice trembling with excitement: "Now, let us all be seated, my young friends, and let us warm ourselves with some good talk."

At that moment everyone who was not already seated made a dash for a place on one of the divans or love seats or even in one of the broad window seats. (There were no individual chairs in the room.) Everyone made a dash, that is, except Ned. Ned did not move. He remained standing beside a little table rubbing his fingers over its polished surface. And from this moment he was clearly an object of suspicion in the eyes of his host and hostess. Soon the party moved from the drawing room to the library, but in whatever room they stopped Ned managed to isolate himself from the rest. He would sit or stand looking down at his hands until once again an explosion of giggles filled the room. Then he would look up just in time to see Tom Bascomb's cheek against Emily's or his arm about her waist.

For nearly two hours Ned didn't speak a word to anyone. He endured the Dorsets' dialogue, the paper flowers, the perfumed air, the works of art. Whenever a burst of giggling forced him to raise his eyes he would look up at Tom and Emily and then turn his eyes away. Before looking down at his hands again he would let his eyes travel slowly about the room until they came to rest on the figures of the two Dorsets. That, it seems, was how he happened to discover that the Dorsets understood, or thought they understood, what the giggles meant. In the great mirror mounted over the library mantel he saw them exchanging half-suppressed smiles. Their smiles lasted precisely as long as the giggling continued, and then, in the mirror, Ned saw their faces change and grow solemn when their eyes—their identical, tiny, dull, amber colored eyes—focussed upon himself.

From the library the party continued on the regular tour of the house. At last when they had been to the ballroom and watched the Dorsets dance, had been upstairs to gaze upon the faded party clothes in the museum cases, they descended into the downstairs hall and were just before being turned into the dining room. The guests had already heard the Dorsets teasing each other about the silly little flirtations and about their naughtiness in parlor games when they were young and had listened to their exhortations to be gay and happy and carefree. Then just when Miss Dorset leaned toward them and whispered, "This is what it is like to be young forever," there rose a chorus of laughter, breathless and shrill, yet loud and intensely penetrating.

Ned Meriwether, standing on the bottom step of the stairway, lifted his eyes and looked over the heads of the party to see Tom and Emily half hidden in a bower of paper flowers and caught directly in a ray of mauve light. The two had squeezed themselves into a little niche there and stood squarely in front of the Rodin statuary. Tom had one arm placed about Emily's shoulders and he was kissing her lightly first on the lobe of one ear and then on the tip of her nose. Emily stood as rigid and pale as the plaster sculpture behind her and with just the faintest smile on her lips. Ned looked at the two of them and then turned his glance at once on the Dorsets.

He found Miss Louisa and Mr. Alfred gazing quite openly at Tom and Emily and frankly grinning at the spectacle. It was more than Ned could endure. "Don't you *know?*" he fairly wailed, as if in great physical pain. "Can't you *tell?* Can't you see who they *are*? They're *brother* and *sister!*"

From the other guests came one concerted gasp. And then an instant later, mistaking Ned's outcry to be something he had planned all along and probably intended—as they imagined—for the very cream of the jest, the whole company burst once again into laughter—not a chorus of laughter this time but a volley of loud guffaws from the boys, and from the girls a cacophony of separately articulated shrieks and trills.

None of the guests present that night could—or would—give a satisfactory account of what happened next. Everyone insisted that he had not even looked at the Dorsets, that he, or she, didn't know how Miss Louisa and Mr. Alfred reacted at first. Yet this was precisely what those of us who had gone there in the past *had* to know. And when finally we did manage to get an account of it, we knew that it was a very truthful and accurate one. Because we got it, of course, from Tom Bascomb.

Since Ned's outburst came after the dancing exhibition, the Dorsets were in their most dishevelled state. Miss Louisa's hair was fallen half over her face, and that long, limp strand of Mr. Alfred's was dangling about his left ear. Like that, they stood at the doorway to the dining room grinning at Tom Bascomb's antics. And when Tom Bascomb, hearing Ned's wail, whirled about, the grins were still on the Dorsets' faces even though the guffaws and the shrieks of laughter were now silenced. Tom said that for several moments they continued to wear their grins like masks and that you couldn't really tell how they were taking it all until presently Miss Louisa's face, still wearing the grin, began turning all the queer colors of her paper flowers. Then the grin vanished from her lips and her mouth fell open and every bit of color went out of her face. She took a step backward and leaned against the doorjamb with her mouth still open and her eyes closed. If she hadn't been on her feet, Tom said he would have thought she was dead. Her brother didn't look at her, but his own grin had vanished just as hers did, and his face, all drawn and wrinkled, momentarily turned a dull copperish green.

Presently, though, he too went white, not white in faintness but in anger. His little brown eyes now shone like rosin. And he took several steps toward Ned Meriwether. "What we know is that you are not one of us," he croaked. "We have perceived that from the beginning! We don't know how you got here or who you are. But the important question is, What are you doing here among these nice children?"

The question seemed to restore life to Miss Louisa. Her amber eyes popped wide open. She stepped away from the door and began pinning up her hair which had fallen down on her shoulders, and at the same time addressing the guests who were huddled together in the center of the hall. "Who is he, children? He is an intruder, that we know. If you know who he is, you must tell us."

"Who *am* I? Why, I am Tom Bascomb!" shouted Ned, still from the bottom step of the stairway. "I am Tom Bascomb, your paper boy!"

Then he turned and fled up the stairs toward the second floor. In a moment Mr. Dorset was after him.

To the real Tom Bascomb it had seemed that Ned honestly believed what he had been saying; and his own first impulse was to shout a denial. But being a level-headed boy and seeing how bad things were, Tom went instead to Miss Dorset and whispered to her that Tom Bascomb was a pretty tough guy and that she had better let *him* call the police for her. She told him where the telephone was in the side hall, and he started away.

But Miss Dorset changed her mind. She ran after Tom telling him not to call. Some of the guests mistook this for the beginning of another chase. Before the old lady could overtake Tom, however, Ned himself had appeared in the doorway toward which she and Tom were moving. He had come down the back stairway and he was calling out to Emily, "We're going home, Sis!"

A cheer went up from the whole party. Maybe it was this that caused Ned to lose his head, or maybe it was simply the sight of Miss Dorset rushing at him that did it. At any rate, the next moment he was running up the front stairs again, this time with Miss Dorset in pursuit.

When Tom returned from the telephone, all was quiet in the hall. The guests—everybody except Emily—had moved to the foot of the stairs and they were looking up and listening. From upstairs Tom could hear Ned saying, "All right. All right. All right." The old couple had cornered him.

Emily was still standing in the little niche among the flowers. And it is the image of Emily Meriwether standing among the paper flowers that tantalizes me whenever I think or hear someone speak of that evening. That, more than anything else, can make me wish that I had been there. I shall never cease to wonder what kind of thoughts were in her head to make her seem so oblivious to all that was going on while she stood there, and, for that matter, what had been in her mind all evening while she endured Tom Bascomb's caresses. When, in years since, I have had reason to wonder what some girl or woman is thinking—some Emily grown older—my mind nearly always returns to the image of that girl among the paper flowers. Tom said that when he returned from the telephone she looked very solemn and pale still but that her mind didn't seem to be on any of the present excitement. Immediately he went to her and said, "Your dad is on his way over, Emily." For it was the Meriwether parents he had telephoned, of course, and not the police.

It seemed to Tom that so far as he was concerned the party was now over. There was nothing more he could do. Mr. Dorset was upstairs guarding the door to the strange little room in which Ned was locked up. Miss Dorset was serving lime punch to the other guests in the dining room, all the while listening with one ear for the arrival of the police whom Tom pretended he had called. When the doorbell finally rang and Miss Dorset hurried to answer it, Tom slipped quietly out through the pantry and through the kitchen and left the house by the back door as the Meriwether parents entered by the first.

There was no difficulty in getting Edwin and Muriel Meriwether, the children's parents, to talk about what happened after they arrived that night. Both of them were sensible and clearheaded people, and they were not so conservative as some of our other neighbors in West Vesey. Being fond of gossip of any kind and fond of reasonably funny stories on themselves, they told how their children had deceived them earlier in the evening and how they had deceived themselves later. They tended to blame themselves more than the children for what had happened. They tried to protect the children from any harm or embarrassment that might result from it by sending them off to boarding school. In their talk they never referred directly to Tom's reprehensible conduct or to the possible motives that the children might have had for getting up their plan. They tried to spare their children and they tried to spare Tom, but fortunately it didn't occur to them to try to spare the poor old Dorsets.

When Miss Louisa opened the door, Mr. Meriwether said, "I'm Edwin Meriwether, Miss Dorset. I've come for my son, Ned."

"And for your daughter Emily, I hope," his wife whispered to him.

"And for my daughter Emily."

Before Miss Dorset could answer him Edwin Meriwether spied Mr. Dorset descending the stairs. With his wife, Muriel, sticking close to his side Edwin now strode over to the foot of the stairs. "Mr. Dorset," he began, "my son Ned—"

From behind them, Edwin and Muriel now heard Miss Dorset saying, "All the invited guests are gathered in the dining room." From where they were standing the two parents could see into the dining room. Suddenly they turned and hurried in there. Mr. Dorset and his sister of course followed them.

Muriel Meriwether went directly to Emily who was standing in a group of girls. "Emily, where is your brother?"

Emily said nothing, but one of the boys answered: "I think they've got him locked up upstairs somewhere."

"Oh, no!" said Miss Louisa, a hairpin in her mouth—for she was still rather absent-mindedly working at her hair. "It is an intruder that my brother has upstairs."

Mr. Dorset began speaking in a confidential tone to Edwin. "My dear neighbor," he said, "our paper boy saw fit to intrude himself upon our company tonight. But we recognized him as an outsider from the start."

Muriel Meriwether asked: "Where is the paper boy? Where is the paper boy, Emily?"

Again one of the boys volunteered: "He went out through the back door, Mrs. Meriwether."

The eyes of Mr. Alfred and Miss Louisa searched the room for Tom. Finally their eyes met and they smiled coyly. "*All* the children are being mischievous tonight," said Miss Louisa, and it was quite as though she had said, "all *we* children." Then, still smiling, she said, "Your tie has come undone, Brother. Mr. and Mrs. Meriwether will hardly know what to think."

Mr. Alfred fumbled for a moment with his tie but soon gave it up. Now with a bashful glance at the Meriwether parents, and giving a nod in the direction of the children, he actually said, "I'm afraid we've all decided to play a trick on Mr. and Mrs. Meriwether."

Miss Louisa said to Emily: "We've hidden our brother somewhere, haven't we?"

Emily's mother said firmly: "Emily, tell me where Ned is."

"He's upstairs, Mother," said Emily in a whisper.

Emily's father said: "I wish you to take me to the boy upstairs, Mr. Dorset."

The coy, bashful expressions vanished from the two Dorsets' faces. Their eyes were little dark pools of incredulity, growing narrower by the second. And both of them were now trying to put their hair in order. "Why, *we* know nice children when we see them," Miss Louisa said peevishly. There was a pleading quality in her voice, too. "We knew from the beginning that that boy upstairs didn't belong amongst us," she said. "Dear neighbors, it isn't just the money, you know." All at once she sounded like a little girl about to burst into tears.

"It isn't just the money?" Edwin Meriwether repeated.

"Miss Dorset," said Muriel with new gentleness in her tone, as though she had just sensed that she was talking to a little girl, "there has been some kind of mistake—a misunderstanding."

Mr. Alfred Dorset said: "Oh, we wouldn't make a mistake of that kind! People *are* different. It isn't something you can put your finger on, but it isn't the money."

"I don't know what you're talking about," Edwin said, exasperated. "But I'm going upstairs and find that boy." He left the room with Mr. Dorset following him with quick little steps—steps like those of a small boy trying to keep up with a man.

Miss Louisa now sat down in one of the high-backed dining chairs which were lined up along the oak wainscot. She was trembling, and Muriel came and stood beside her. Neither of them spoke, and in almost no time Edwin Meriwether came downstairs again with Ned. Miss Louisa looked at Ned, and tears came into her eyes. "Where is my brother?" she asked accusingly, as though she thought possibly Ned and his father had locked Mr. Dorset in the bathroom.

"I believe he has retired," said Edwin. "He left us and disappeared into one of the rooms upstairs."

"Then I must go up to him," said Miss Louisa. For a moment she seemed unable to rise. At last she pushed herself up from the chair and walked from the room with the slow, steady gait of a somnambulist. Muriel Meriwether followed her into the hall and as she watched the old woman ascending the steps, leaning heavily on the rail, her impulse was to go and offer to assist her. But something made her turn back into the dining room. Perhaps she imagined that her daughter, Emily, might need her now.

The Dorsets did not reappear that night. After Miss Louisa went upstairs, Muriel promptly got on the telephone and called the parents of some of the other boys and girls. Within a quarter of an hour half a dozen parents had arrived. It was the first time in many years that any adult had set foot inside the Dorset house. It was the first time that any parent had ever inhaled the perfumed air or seen the masses of paper flowers and the illuminations and the statuary. In the guise of holding consultations over whether or not they should put out the lights and lock up the house the parents lingered much longer than was necessary before taking the young people home. Some of them even tasted the lime punch. But in the presence of their children they made no comment on what had happened and gave no indication of what their own impressions were—not even their impressions of the punch. At last it was decided that two of the men should see to putting out the lights everywhere on the first floor and down in the ballroom. They were a long time in finding the switches for the indirect lighting. In most cases they simply resorted to unscrewing the bulbs. Meanwhile the children went to the large cloak closet behind the stairway and got their wraps. When Ned and Emily Meriwether rejoined their parents at the front door to leave the house, Ned was wearing his own overcoat and held his own fedora in his hand.

Miss Louisa and Mr. Alfred Dorset lived on for nearly ten years after that night, but they gave up selling their figs and paper flowers and of course they never entertained young people again. I often wonder if growing up in Mero can ever have seemed quite the same since. Some of the terror must have gone out of it. Half the dread of coming of age must have vanished with the dread of the Dorsets' parties.

After that night, their old car would sometimes be observed creeping about town, but it was never parked in front of their house anymore. It stood usually at the side entrance where the Dorsets could climb in and out of it without being seen. They began keeping a servant too—mainly to run their errands for them, I imagine. Sometimes it would be a man, sometimes a woman, never the same one for more than a few months at a time. Both of the Dorsets died during the Second World War while many of us who had gone to their parties were away from Mero. But the story went round—and I am inclined to believe it—that after they were dead and the house was sold, Tom Bascomb's coat and hat were found still hanging in the cloak closet behind the stairs.

Tom himself was a pilot in the War and was a considerable hero. He was such a success and made such a name for himself that he never came back to Mero to live. He found bigger opportunities elsewhere I suppose, and I don't suppose he ever felt the ties to Mero that people with Ned's kind of upbringing do. Ned was in the War too, of course. He was in the navy and after the War he did return to Mero to live, though actually it was not until then that he had spent much time here since his parents bundled him off to boarding school. Emily came home and made her debut just two or three years before the War, but she was already engaged to some boy in the East; she never comes back anymore except to bring her children to see their grandparents for a few days during Christmas or at Easter.

I understand that Emily and Ned are pretty indifferent to each other's existence nowadays. I have been told this by Ned Meriwether's own wife.

Ned's wife maintains that the night Ned and Emily went to the Dorsets' party marked the beginning of this indifference, that it marked the end of their childhood intimacy and the beginning of a shyness, a reserve, even an animosity between them that was destined to be a sorrow forever to the two sensible parents who had sat in the upstairs sitting room that night waiting until the telephone call came from Tom Bascomb.

Ned's wife is a girl he met while he was in the navy. She was a Wave, and her background isn't the same as his. Apparently she isn't too happy with life in what she refers to as "Mero proper." She and Ned have recently moved out into a suburban development, which she doesn't like either and which she refers to as "greater Mero." She asked me at a party one night how Mero ever got its absurd name, and when I told her that it was named for the last Spanish governor of Louisiana she burst out laughing. I don't know why exactly. But what interests me most about her is that after a few drinks she likes to talk about Ned and Emily and Tom Bascomb and the Dorsets. Tom Bascomb has become a kind of hero—and I don't mean a wartime hero—in her eyes, though of course not having grown up in Mero she has never seen him in her life. But she is a clever girl, and there are times when she will say to me, "Tell me about Mero. Tell me about the Dorsets." And I try to tell her. I tell her to remember that Mero looks upon itself as a rather old city. I tell her to remember that it was one of the first English-speaking settlements west of the Alleghenies and that by the end of the American Revolution, when veterans began pouring westward over the Wilderness Road or down the Ohio River, Mero was often referred to as a thriving village. Then she tells me that I am being dull, because it is hard for her to concentrate on any aspect of the story that doesn't center around Tom Bascomb and that night at the Dorsets'.

But I make her listen. Or at least one time I did. The Dorset family, I insisted on saying, was in Mero even in those earliest times right after the Revolution, but they had come here under somewhat different circumstances from those of the other early settlers. How could that really matter, Ned's wife asked, after a hundred and fifty years? How could distinctions between the first settlers matter after the Irish had come to Mero, after the Germans, after the Italians? Well, in West Vesey Place it could matter. It had to. If the distinction was false, it mattered all the more and it was all the more necessary to make it.

But let me interject here that Mero is located in a state about whose history most Mero citizens—not newcomers like Ned's wife, but old timers—

have little interest and less knowledge. Most of us, for instance, are never even quite sure whether during the 1860s our state did secede or didn't secede. As for the city itself, some of us hold that it is geographically Northern and culturally Southern. Others say the reverse is true. We are all apt to want to feel misplaced in Mero, and so we are not content merely to say that it is a border city. How you stand on this important question is apt to depend entirely on whether your family is one of those with a good Southern name or one that had its origin in New England, because those are the two main categories of old society families in Mero.

But truly—I told Ned's wife—the Dorset family was never in either of those categories. The first Dorset had come, with his family and his possessions and even a little capital, direct from a city in the English Midlands to Mero. The Dorsets came not as pioneers, but paying their way all the way. They had not bothered to stop for a generation or two to put down roots in Pennsylvania or Virginia or Massachusetts. And this was the distinction which some people wished always to make. Apparently those early Dorsets had cared no more for putting down roots in the soil of the New World than they had cared for whatever they had left behind in the Old. They were an obscure mercantile family who came to invest in a new western city. Within two generations the business—no, the industry!—which they established made them rich beyond any dreams they could have had in the beginning. For half a century they were looked upon, if any family ever was, as our first family.

And then the Dorsets left Mero—practically all of them except the one old bachelor and the one old maid—left it just as they had come, not caring much about what they were leaving or where they were going. They were city people, and they were Americans. They knew that what they had in Mero they could buy more of in other places. For them Mero was an investment that had paid off. They went to live in Santa Barbara and Laguna Beach, in Newport and on Long Island. And the truth which it was so hard for the rest of us to admit was that, despite our family memories of Massachusetts and Virginia, we were all more like the Dorsets—those Dorsets who left Mero—than we were unlike them. Their spirit was just a little closer to being the very essence of Mero than ours was. The obvious difference was that we had to stay on here and pretend that our life had a meaning which it did not. And if it was only by a sort of chance that Miss Louisa and Mr. Alfred played the role of social arbiters among the young people for a number of years, still no one could honestly question their divine right to do so.

"It may have been their right," Ned's wife said at this point, "but just think what might have happened."

"It's not a matter of what might have happened," I said. "It is a matter of what did happen. Otherwise, what have you and I been talking about?"

"Otherwise," she said with an irrepressible shudder, "I would not be forever getting you off in a corner at these parties to talk about my husband and my husband's sister and how it is they care so little for each other's company nowadays?"

And I could think of nothing to say to that except that probably we had now pretty well exhausted our subject.

Delmore Schwartz

Delmore Schwartz was born in 1913 in Brooklyn, New York. At age nine his parents separated; he stayed with his mother in New York. He attended the University of Wisconsin at Madison, transferring later to New York University. In 1937, Delmore married Gertrude Buckman. His first book, a collection of short stores and poems titled *In Dreams Begin Responsibilities,* appeared when Schwartz was only twenty-four. He became an instant sensation, earning praise from such literary luminaries as T.S. Eliot and Ezra Pound. Schwartz began a career as a teacher, holding positions at Harvard, Bennington, New York University, and Kenyon College. In 1948, his book of short stories, *The World is a Wedding*, was published. At this time, Schwartz was acting as poetry editor of the *Partisan Review*. That same year, his first marriage ended; a year later he married writer Elizabeth Pollet. Early in the marriage, Schwartz became increasingly consumed by alcoholism, making him delusional and violent, even forcing him to spend time in Bellevue Hospital. He continued to have literary success, becoming the youngest writer to ever win the prestigious Bollingen prize in 1960, but his personal life was in shambles as he drifted through different New York flats. He taught for three years at Syracuse University before his death in 1966 at the age of fifty-two. His later writings include *Vaudeville for a Princess and Other Poems*, *Summer Knowledge,* and *Successful Love and Other Stories.*

Sonnet *(1958)*

by Delmore Schwartz

The world was warm and white when I was born:
Beyond the window pane the world was white,
A glaring whiteness in a leaded frame,
Yet warm as in the hearth and heart of light.
Although the whiteness was almond and was bone
In midnight's still paralysis, nevertheless
The world was warm and hope was infinite
All things would come to me and be my own,
    all things would be enjoyed, fulfilled and known.

How like a summer the years of youth have passed!
—How like the summer of 1914, in all truth!—
Patience, my soul, the truth is never known
Until the future has become the past
And then, only, when the love of truth at last
Becomes the truth of love, when both are one;
When Eden becomes Utopia, and is surpassed:
For then the dream is knowledge and knowledge knows
Motive and joy at once wherever it goes.

James Wright

James Wright was born in 1927 in Martins Ferry, Ohio. After being drafted to the army in 1946, Wright attended Kenyon College on the G.I. Bill, studying under *The Kenyon Review*–founder John Crowe Ransom. After spending a year in Vienna on a Fulbright Scholarship, he entered graduate school at the University of Washington. While at Washington, Wright's first book, *The Green Wall,* was selected for publication by W.H. Auden in the *Yale Younger Poets* Series in 1957. He joined the faculty at the University of Minnesota, and his second collection, *Saint Judas*, was released. In 1962, Wright's marriage with Liberty Kardules, with whom he had been married since in 1953, ended. The next year, *The Branch Shall Not Break* was released, which, with its experimental free verse and strong social consciousness, would become one of the most influential volumes of the 1960s. By this time, Wright had taken a teaching position at Hunter College, and, in 1967, he married Edith Anne Crunk, the "Annie" of several of his later poems. He continued to publish such books as *Shall We Gather at the River*, *Collected Poems* (which earned Wright the Pulitzer Prize), *Two Citizens*, and *Moments of an Italian Summer*. In 1979, a chronic sore throat was diagnosed as cancer of the tongue. Wright died on March 25, 1980, the manuscript of *This Journey,* his final book, just completed.

All the Beautiful Are Blameless *(1958)*

by James Wright

Out of a dark into the dark she leaped
Lightly this day.
Heavy with prey, the evening skiffs are gone,
And drowsy divers lift their helmets off,
Dry on the shore.

Two stupid harly-charlies got her drunk
And took her swimming naked on the lake.
The waters rippled lute-like round the boat,
And far beyond them dipping up and down,
Unmythological sylphs, their names unknown,
Beckoned to sandbars where the evenings fall.

Only another drunk would say she heard
A natural voice
Luring the flesh across the water.
I think of those unmythological
Sylphs of the trees.

Slight but orplidean shoulders weave in dusk
Before my eyes when I walk lonely forward
To kick beer-cans from tracked declivities.
If I, being lightly sane, may carve a mouth
Out of the air to kiss, the drowned girl surely
Listened to lute-song where the sylphs are gone.
The living and the dead glide hand in hand
Under cool waters where the days are gone.
Out of the dark into a dark I stand.
The ugly curse the world and pin my arms
Down by their grinning teeth, sneering a blame.

Closing my eyes, I look for hungry swans
To plunder the lake and bear the girl away,
Back to the larger waters where the sea
Sifts, judges, gathers the body, and subsides.

But here the starved, touristic crowd divides
And offers the dead
Hell for the living body's evil:
The girl flopped in the water like a pig
And drowned dead drunk.

So do the pure defend themselves. But she,
Risen to kiss the sky, her limbs still whole,
Rides on the dark tarpaulin toward the shore;
And the hired saviours turn their painted shell
Along the wharf, to list her human name.
But the dead have no names, they lie so still,
And all the beautiful are blameless now.

Thomas Pynchon

Thomas Pynchon was born in 1937 in Long Island, New York. He attended Cornell University and published his first story, "The Small Rain," in the *Cornell Writer* in 1959. The following year, *The Kenyon Review* published "Entropy," one of Pynchon's first appearances in a major journal. Pynchon is a notorious figure in literature for several reasons–first for his brilliant but difficult novels (he has been quoted as saying "Why should things be easy to understand?"), and second for his extreme privacy. So little is known about his personal life that wild theories about his identity have sprung up, accusing him of being everyone from J.D. Salinger to the Unabomber. What we are clear about is the impressiveness of his oeuvre of fiction, including *V.*, *The Crying of Lot 49*, *Slow Learner*, *Mason & Dixon,* and *Gravity's Rainbow*, which in 1974 momentarily won Pynchon the Pulitzer Prize, until the selection was overruled by the Pulitzer advisory board whose members called it "unreadable," "turgid," "overwritten," and "obscene." No prize was given that year. Pynchon remains one of our most elusive, literarily and personally, writers of fiction.

Entropy *(1960)*
by Thomas Pynchon

> Boris has just given me a summary of his views. He is a weather prophet. The weather will continue bad, he says. There will be more calamities, more death, more despair. Not the slightest indication of a change anywhere...We must get into step, a lockstep toward the prison of death. There is no escape. The weather will not change.

> *—Tropic of Cancer*

Downstairs, Meatball Mulligan's lease-breaking party was moving into its fortieth hour. On the kitchen floor, amid a litter of empty champagne fifths, were Sandor Rojas and three friends, playing spit in the ocean and staying awake on Heidseck and benzedrine pills. In the living room Duke, Vincent, Krinkles, and Paco sat crouched over a fifteen-inch speaker which had been bolted into the top of a wastepaper basket, listening to twenty-seven watts' worth of *The Heroes' Gate at Kiev*. They all wore horn-rimmed sunglasses and rapt expressions, and smoked funny-looking cigarettes which contained not, as you might expect, tobacco, but an adulterated form of *cannabis sativa*. This group was the Duke di Angelis quartet. They recorded for a local label called Tambu and had to their credit one 10" LP entitled *Songs of Outer Space*. From time to time one of them would flick the ashes from his cigarette into the speaker cone to watch them dance around. Meatball himself was sleeping over by the window, holding an empty magnum to his chest as if it were a teddy bear. Several government girls, who worked for people like the State Department and NSA, had passed out on couches, chairs, and in one case the bathroom sink.

This was in early February of '57 and back then there were a lot of American expatriates around Washington, D.C., who would talk, every time they met you, about how someday they were going to go over to Europe for real but right now it seemed they were working for the government. Everyone saw a fine irony in this. They would stage, for instance, polyglot parties where the newcomer was sort of ignored if he couldn't carry on simultaneous conversations in three or four languages. They would haunt Armenian delicatessens for weeks at a stretch and invite you over for bulghour and lamb in tiny kitchens whose walls were covered with bullfight posters. They would have affairs with sultry girls from Andalucía or the

Midi who studied economics at Georgetown. Their Dôme was a collegiate Rathskeller out on Wisconsin Avenue called the Old Heidelberg and they had to settle for cherry blossoms instead of lime trees when spring came, but in its lethargic way their life provided, as they said, kicks.

At the moment, Meatball's party seemed to be gathering its second wind. Outside there was rain. Rain splatted against the tar paper on the roof and was fractured into a fine spray off the noses, eyebrows, and lips of wooden gargoyles under the eaves, and ran like drool down the windowpanes. The day before, it had snowed and the day before that there had been winds of gale force and before that the sun had made the city glitter bright as April, though the calendar read early February. It is a curious season in Washington, this false spring. Somewhere in it are Lincoln's Birthday and the Chinese New Year, and a forlornness in the streets because cherry blossoms are weeks away still and, as Sarah Vaughan has put it, spring will be a little late this year. Generally crowds like the one which would gather in the Old Heidelberg on weekday afternoons to drink Würtzburger and to sing Lili Marlene (not to mention The Sweetheart of Sigma Chi) are inevitably and incorrigibly Romantic. And as every good Romantic knows, the soul (*spiritus, ruach, pneuma*) is nothing, substantially, but air; it is only natural that warpings in the atmosphere should be recapitulated in those who breathe it. So that over and above the public components—holidays, tourist attractions—there are private meanderings, linked to the climate as if this spell were a *stretto* passage in the year's fugue: haphazard weather, aimless loves, unpredicted commitments: months one can easily spend *in* fugue, because oddly enough, later on, winds, rains, passions of February and March are never remembered in that city, it is as if they had never been.

The last bass notes of *The Heroes' Gate* boomed up through the floor and woke Callisto from an uneasy sleep. The first thing he became aware of was a small bird he had been holding gently between his hands, against his body. He turned his head sidewise on the pillow to smile down at it, at its blue hunched-down head and sick, lidded eyes, wondering how many more nights he would have to give it warmth before it was well again. He had been holding the bird like that for three days: it was the only way he knew to restore its health. Next to him the girl stirred and whimpered, her arm thrown across her face. Mingled with the sounds of the rain came the first tentative, querulous morning voices of the other birds, hidden in philodendrons and small fan palms: patches of scarlet, yellow, and blue laced through this Rousseau-like fantasy, this hothouse jungle it had taken him seven years to weave together. Hermetically sealed, it was a tiny enclave of regularity in the city's chaos, alien to the vagaries of the weather, of national politics, of any civil disorder. Through trial-and-error Callisto had perfected its ecological balance, with the help of the girl its artistic harmony, so that the swayings of its plant life, the stirrings of its birds and human inhabitants were all as integral as the rhythms of a perfectly executed mobile. He and the girl could no longer, of course, be omitted from that sanctuary; they had become necessary to its unity. What they needed from outside was delivered. They did not go out.

"Is he all right," she whispered. She lay like a tawny question mark facing him, her eyes suddenly huge and dark and blinking slowly. Callisto ran a finger beneath the feathers at the base of the bird's neck; caressed it gently. "He's going to be well, I think. See: he hears his friends beginning to wake up." The girl had heard the rain and the birds even before she was fully awake. Her name was Aubade: she was part French and part Annamese, and she lived on her own curious and lonely planet, where the clouds and the odor of poincianas, the bitterness of wine, and the accidental fingers at the small of her back or feathery against her breasts came to her reduced inevitably to the terms of sound: of music which emerged at intervals from a howling darkness of discordancy. "Aubade," he said, "go see." Obedient, she arose; padded to the window, pulled aside the drapes, and after a moment said: "It is 37. Still 37." Callisto frowned. "Since Tuesday, then," he said. "No change." Henry Adams, three generations before his own, had stared aghast at Power; Callisto found himself now in much the same state over Thermodynamics, the inner life of that power, realizing like his predecessor that the Virgin and the dynamo stand as much for love as for power; that the two are indeed identical; and that love therefore not only makes the world go 'round but also makes the boccie ball spin, the nebula precess. It was this latter or sidereal element which disturbed him. The cosmologists had predicted an eventual heat-death for the universe (something like Limbo: form and motion abolished, heat-energy identical at every point in it); the meteorologists, day-to-day, staved it off by contradicting with a reassuring array of varied temperatures.

But for three days now, despite the changeful weather, the mercury had stayed at 37 degrees Fahrenheit. Leery at omens of apocalypse, Callisto shifted beneath the covers. His fingers pressed the bird more firmly, as if needing some pulsing or suffering assurance of an early break in the temperature.

It was that last cymbal crash that did it. Meatball was hurled wincing into consciousness as the synchronized wagging of heads over the wastebasket stopped. The final hiss remained for an instant in the room, then melted into the whisper of rain outside. "Aarrgghh," announced Meatball in the silence, looking at the empty magnum. Krinkles, in slow motion, turned, smiled, and held out a cigarette. "Tea time, man," he said. "No, no," said Meatball. "How many times I got to tell you guys. Not at my place. You ought to know, Washington is lousy with Feds." Krinkles looked wistful. "Jeez, Meatball," he said, "you don't want to do nothing no more." "Hair of dog," said Meatball. "Only hope. Any juice left?" He began to crawl toward the kitchen. "No champagne, I don't think," Duke said. "Case of tequila behind the icebox." They put on an Earl Bostic side. Meatball paused at the kitchen door, glowering at Sandor Rojas. "Lemons," he said after some thought. He crawled to the refrigerator and got out three lemons and some cubes, found the tequila, and set about restoring order to his nervous system. He drew blood once cutting the lemons and had to use two hands squeezing them and his foot to crack the ice tray but after about ten minutes he found himself, through some miracle, beaming down into a monster tequila sour. "That looks yummy," Sandor Rojas said. "How about you make me one." Meatball blinked at him. *"Kitchi lofass a shegitbe,"* he replied automatically, and wandered away into the bathroom. "I say," he called out a moment later to no one in particular. "I say, there seems to be a girl or something sleeping in the sink." He took her by the shoulders and shook. "Wha," she said. "You don't look too comfortable," Meatball said. "Well," she agreed. She stumbled to the shower, turned on the cold water, and sat down crosslegged in the spray. "That's better," she smiled.

"Meatball," Sandor Rojas yelled from the kitchen. "Somebody is trying to come in the window. A burglar, I think. A second-story man." "What are you worrying about," Meatball said. "We're on the third floor." He loped back into the kitchen. A shaggy woebegone figure stood out on the fire escape, raking his fingernails down the windowpane. Meatball opened the window. "Saul," he said.

"Sort of wet out," Saul said. He climbed in, dripping. "You heard, I guess."

"Miriam left you," Meatball said, "or something, is all I heard."

There was a sudden flurry of knocking at the front door. "Do come in," Sandor Rojas called. The door opened and there were three coeds from George Washington, all of whom were majoring in philosophy. They were each holding a gallon of Chianti. Sandor leaped up and dashed into the living room. "We heard there was a party," one blonde said. "Young blood," Sandor shouted. He was an ex-Hungarian freedom fighter who had easily the worst chronic case of what certain critics of the middle class have called Don Giovannism in the District of Columbia. *Purche porti la gonnella, voi sapete quel che fa.* Like Pavlov's dog: a contralto voice or a whiff of Arpege and Sandor would begin to salivate. Meatball regarded the trio blearily as they filed into the kitchen; he shrugged. "Put the wine in the icebox," he said "and good morning."

Aubade's neck made a golden bow as she bent over the sheets of foolscap, scribbling away in the green murk of the room. "As a young man at Princeton," Callisto was dictating, nestling the bird against the gray hairs of his chest, "Callisto had learned a mnemonic device for remembering the Laws of Thermodynamics: you can't win, things are going to get worse before they get better, who says they're going to get better. At the age of fifty-four, confronted with Gibbs's notion of the universe, he suddenly realized that undergraduate cant had been oracle, after all. That spindly maze of equations became, for him, a vision of ultimate, cosmic heat-death. He had known all along, of course, that nothing but a theoretical engine or system ever runs at 100 percent efficiency; and about the theorem of Clausius, which states that the entropy of an isolated system always continually increases. It was not, however, until Gibbs and Boltzmann brought to this principle the methods of statistical mechanics that the horrible significance of it all dawned on him: only then did he realize that the isolated system— galaxy, engine, human being, culture, whatever—must evolve spontaneously toward the Condition of the More Probable. He was forced, therefore, in the sad dying fall of middle age, to a radical reevaluation of everything he had learned up to then; all the cities and seasons and casual passions of his days had now to be looked at in a new and elusive light. He did not know if he was equal to the task. He was aware of the dangers of the reductive fallacy and, he hoped, strong enough not to drift into the graceful decadence of an enervated fatalism. His had always been a vigorous, Italian sort of pessimism: like Machiavelli, he allowed the forces of *virtú* and *fortuna* to be about 50/50; but the equations now introduced a random factor which pushed the odds to some unutterable and indeterminate ratio which he found himself afraid to calculate." Around him loomed vague hothouse shapes; the pitifully small heart fluttered against his own. Counterpointed against his words the girl heard the chatter of birds and fitful car honkings scattered along the wet morning and Earl Bostic's alto rising in occasional wild peaks through the floor. The architectonic purity of her world was constantly threatened by such hints of anarchy: gaps and excrescences and skew lines, and a shifting or tilting of planes to which she had continually to readjust lest the whole structure shiver into a disarray of discrete and meaningless signals. Callisto had described the process once as a kind of "feedback": she crawled into dreams each night with a sense of exhaustion, and a desperate resolve never to relax that vigilance. Even in the brief periods when Callisto made love to her, soaring above the bowing of taut nerves in haphazard double-stops would be the one singing string of her determination.

"Nevertheless," continued Callisto, "he found in entropy or the measure of disorganization for a closed system an adequate metaphor to apply to certain phenomena in his own world. He saw, for example, the younger generation responding to Madison Avenue with the same spleen his own had once reserved for Wall Street: and in American 'consumerism' discovered a similar tendency from the least to the most probable, from differentiation to sameness, from ordered individuality to a kind of chaos. He found himself, in short, restating Gibbs's prediction in social terms, and envisioned a heat-death for his culture in which ideas, like heat-energy, would no longer be transferred, since each point in it would ultimately have the same quantity of energy; and intellectual motion would, accordingly, cease." He glanced up suddenly. "Check it now," he said. Again she rose and peered out at the thermometer. "37," she said. "The rain has stopped." He bent his head quickly and held his lips against a quivering wing. "Then it will change soon," he said, trying to keep his voice firm.

Sitting on the stove Saul was like any big rag doll that a kid has been taking out some incomprehensible rage on. "What happened," Meatball said. "If you feel like talking, I mean."

"Of course I feel like talking," Saul said. "One thing I did, I slugged her."

"Discipline must be maintained."

"Ha, ha. I wish you'd been there. Oh Meatball, it was a lovely fight. She ended up throwing a *Handbook of Chemistry and Physics* at me, only it missed and went through the window, and when the glass broke I reckon something in her broke too. She stormed out of the house crying, out in the rain. No raincoat or anything."

"She'll be back."

"No."

"Well." Soon Meatball said: "It was something earth-shattering, no doubt. Like who is better, Sal Mineo or Ricky Nelson."

"What it was about," Saul said, "was communication theory. Which of course makes it very hilarious."

"I don't know anything about communication theory."

"Neither does my wife. Come right down to it, who does? That's the joke."

When Meatball saw the kind of smile Saul had on his face he said: "Maybe you would like tequila or something."

"No. I mean, I'm sorry. It's a field you can go off the deep end in, is all. You get where you're watching all the time for security cops: behind bushes, around corners. MUFFET is top secret."

"Wha."

"Multi-unit factorial field electronic tabulator."

"You were fighting about that."

"Miriam has been reading science-fiction again. That and *Scientific American*. It seems she is, as we say, bugged at this idea of computers acting like people. I made the mistake of saying you can just as well turn that around, and talk about human behavior like a program fed into an IBM machine."

"Why not," Meatball said.

"Indeed, why not. In fact it is sort of crucial to communication, not to mention information theory. Only when I said that she hit the roof. Up went the balloon. And I can't figure out *why*. If anybody should know why, I should. I refuse to believe the government is wasting taxpayers' money on me, when it has so many bigger and better things to waste it on."

Meatball made a moue. "Maybe she thought you were acting like a cold, dehumanized amoral scientist type."

"My god," Saul flung up an arm. "Dehumanized. How much more human can I get? I worry, Meatball, I do. There are Europeans wandering around North Africa these days with their tongues torn out of their heads because those tongues have spoken the wrong words. Only the Europeans thought they were the right words."

"Language barrier," Meatball suggested.

Saul jumped down off the stove. "That," he said, angry, "is a good candidate for sick joke of the year. No, ace, it is *not* a barrier. If it is anything it's a kind of leakage. Tell a girl: 'I love you.' No trouble with two-thirds of that, it's a closed circuit. Just you and she. But that nasty four-letter word in the middle, that's the one you have to look out for. Ambiguity. Redundance. Irrelevance, even. Leakage. All this is noise. Noise screws up your signal, makes for disorganization in the circuit."

Meatball shuffled around. "Well, now, Saul," he muttered, "you're sort of, I don't know, expecting a lot from people. I mean, you know. What it is is, most of the things we say, I guess, are mostly noise."

"Ha! Half of what you just said, for example."

"Well, you do it too."

"I know." Saul smiled grimly. "It's a bitch, ain't it."

"I bet that's what keeps divorce lawyers in business. Whoops."

"Oh I'm not sensitive. Besides," frowning, "you're right. You find I think that most 'successful' marriages—Miriam and me, up to last night—are sort of founded on compromises. You never run at top efficiency, usually all you have is a minimum basis for a workable thing. I believe the phrase is Togetherness."

"Aarrgghh."

"Exactly. You find that one a bit noisy, don't you. But the noise content is different for each of us because you're a bachelor and I'm not. Or wasn't. The hell with it."

"Well sure," Meatball said, trying to be helpful, "you were using different words. By 'human being' you meant something that you can look at like it was a computer. It helps you think better on the job or something. But Miriam meant something entirely—"

"The hell with it."

Meatball fell silent. "I'll take that drink," Saul said after a while.

The card game had been abandoned and Sandor's friends were slowly getting wasted on tequila. On the living room couch, one of the coeds and Krinkles were engaged in amorous conversation. "No," Krinkles was saying, "no, I can't put Dave *down*. In fact I give Dave a lot of credit, man. Especially considering his accident and all." The girl's smile faded. "How terrible," she said. "What accident?" "Hadn't you heard?" Krinkles said. "When Dave was in the army, just a private E-2, they sent him down to Oak Ridge on special duty. Something to do with the Manhattan Project. He was handling hot stuff one day and got an overdose of radiation. So now he's got to wear lead gloves all the time." She shook her head sympathetically. "What an awful break for a piano-player."

Meatball had abandoned Saul to a bottle of tequila and was about to go to sleep in a closet when the front door flew open and the place was invaded by five enlisted personnel of the U.S. Navy, all in varying stages of abomination. "This is the place," shouted a fat, pimply seaman apprentice who had lost his white hat. "This here is the hoorhouse that chief was telling us about." A stringy-looking 3rd class boatswain's mate pushed him aside and cased the living room. "You're right, Slab," he said. "But it don't look like much, even for Stateside. I seen better tail in Naples, Italy." "How much, hey," boomed a large seaman with adenoids, who was holding a Mason jar full of white lightning. "Oh, my god," said Meatball.

Outside the temperature remained constant at 37 degrees Fahrenheit. In the hothouse Aubade stood absently caressing the branches of a young mimosa, hearing a motif of sap-rising, the rough and unresolved anticipatory theme of those fragile pink blossoms which, it is said, insure fertility. That music rose in a tangled tracery: arabesques of order competing fugally with the improvised discords of the party downstairs, which peaked sometimes in cusps and ogees of noise. That precious signal-to-noise ratio, whose delicate balance required every calorie of her strength, seesawed inside the small tenuous skull as she watched Callisto, sheltering the bird. Callisto was trying to confront any idea of the heat-death now, as he nuzzled the feathery lump in his hands. He sought correspondences. Sade, of course. And Temple Drake, gaunt and hopeless in her little park in Paris, at the end of *Sanctuary*. Final equilibrium. *Nightwood*. And the tango. Any tango, but more than any perhaps the sad sick dance in Stravinsky's *L'Histoire du Soldat*. He thought back: what had tango music been for them after the war, what meanings had he missed in all the stately coupled automatons in the *cafés-dansants,* or in the metronomes which had ticked behind the eyes of his own partners? Not even the clean constant winds of Switzerland could cure the *grippe espagnole:* Stravinsky had had it, they all had had it. And now many musicians were left after Passchendaele, after the Marne? It came down in this case to seven: violin, double-bass. Clarinet, bassoon. Cornet, trombone. Tympani. Almost as if any tiny troupe of saltimbanques had set about conveying the same information as a full pit-orchestra. There was hardly a full complement left in Europe. Yet with violin and tympani Stravinsky had managed to communicate in that tango the same exhaustion, the same airlessness one saw in the slicked-down youths who were trying to imitate Vernon Castle, and in their mistresses, who simply did not care. *Ma maitresse.* Celeste. Returning to Nice after the second war he had found that cafe replaced by a perfume shop which catered to American tourists. And no secret vestige of her in the cobblestones or in the old pension next door; no perfume to match her breath heavy with the sweet Spanish wine she always drank. And so instead he had purchased a Henry Miller novel and left for Paris, and read the book on the train so that when he arrived he had been given at least a little forewarning. And saw that Celeste and the others and even Temple Drake were not all that had changed. "Aubade," he said, "my head aches." The sound of his voice generated in the girl an answering scrap of melody. Her movement toward the kitchen, the towel, the cold water, and his eyes following her formed a weird and intricate canon; as she placed the compress on his forehead his sigh of gratitude seemed to signal a new subject, another series of modulations.

"No," Meatball was still saying, "no, I'm afraid not. This is not a house of ill repute. I'm sorry, really I am." Slab was adamant. "But the chief said," he kept repeating. The seaman offered to swap the moonshine for a good piece. Meatball looked around frantically, as if seeking assistance. In the middle of the room, the Duke di Angelis quartet were engaged in a historic moment. Vincent was seated and the others standing: they were going through the motions of a group having a session, only without instruments. "I say," Meatball said. Duke moved his head a few times, smiled faintly, lit a cigarette, and eventually caught sight of Meatball. "Quiet, man," he whispered. Vincent began to fling his arms around, his fists clenched; then, abruptly, was still, then repeated the performance. This went on for a few minutes while Meatball sipped his drink moodily. The navy had withdrawn to the kitchen. Finally at some invisible signal the group stopped tapping their feet and Duke grinned and said, "At least we ended together."

Meatball glared at him. "I say," he said. "I have this new conception, man," Duke said. "You remember your namesake. You remember Gerry."

"No," said Meatball. "I'll remember April, if that's any help."

"As a matter of fact," Duke said, "it was Love for Sale. Which shows how much you know. The point is, it was Mulligan, Chet Baker, and that crew, way back then, out yonder. You dig?"

"Baritone sax," Meatball said. "Something about a baritone sax."

"But no piano, man. No guitar. Or accordion. You know what that means."

"Not exactly," Meatball said.

"Well first let me just say, that I am no Mingus, no John Lewis. Theory was never my strong point. I mean things like reading were always difficult for me and all—"

"I know," Meatball said drily. "You got your card taken away because you changed key on Happy Birthday at a Kiwanis Club picnic."

"Rotarian. But it occurred to me, in one of these flashes of insight, that if that first quartet of Mulligan's had no piano, it could only mean one thing."

"No chords," said Paco, the baby-faced bass.

"What is he trying to say," Duke said, "is no root chords. Nothing to listen to while you blow a horizontal line. What one does in such a case is, one *thinks* the roots."

A horrified awareness was dawning on Meatball. "And the next logical extension," he said.

"Is to think everything," Duke announced with simple dignity. "Roots, line, everything."

Meatball looked at Duke, awed. "But," he said.

"Well," Duke said modestly, "there are a few bugs to work out."

"But," Meatball said.

"Just listen," Duke said. "You'll catch on." And off they went again into orbit, presumably somewhere around the asteroid belt. After a while Krinkles made an embouchure and started moving his fingers and Duke clapped his hand to his forehead. "Oaf!" he roared. "The new head we're using, you remember, I wrote last night?" "Sure," Krinkles said, "the new head. I come in on the bridge. All your heads I come in then." "Right," Duke said. "So why—" "Wha," said Krinkles, "sixteen bars, I wait, I come in—" "sixteen?" Duke said. "No. No, Krinkles. Eight you waited. You want me to sing it? A cigarette that bears a lipstick's traces, an airline ticket to romantic places." Krinkles scratched his head. "These Foolish Things, you mean." "Yes," Duke said, "yes, Krinkles. Bravo." "Not I'll Remember April," Krinkles said. *"Minghe morte,"* said Duke. "I *figured* we were playing it a little slow," Krinkles said. Meatball chuckled. "Back to the old drawing board," he said. "No, man," Duke said, "back to the airless void." And they took off again, only it seemed Paco was playing in G sharp while the rest were in E flat, so they had to start all over.

In the kitchen two of the girls from George Washington and the sailors were singing Let's All Go Down and Piss on the Forrestal. There was a two-handed, bilingual *mura* game on over by the icebox. Saul had filled several paper bags with water and was sitting on the fire escape, dropping them on passersby in the street. A fat government girl in a Bennington sweatshirt, recently engaged to an ensign attached to the Forrestal, came charging into the kitchen, head lowered, and butted Slab in the stomach. Figuring this was as good an excuse for a fight as any, Slab's buddies piled in. The *mura* players were nose-to-nose, screaming *trois, sette* at the tops of their lungs. From the shower the girl Meatball had taken out of the sink announced that she was drowning. She had apparently sat on the drain and the water was now up to her neck. The noise in Meatball's apartment had reached a sustained, ungodly crescendo.

Meatball stood and watched, scratching his stomach lazily. The way he figured, there were only about two ways he could cope: (a) lock himself in the closet and maybe eventually they would all go away, or (b) try to calm everybody down, one by one. (a) was certainly the more attractive alternative. But then he started thinking about that closet. It was dark and stuffy and he would be alone. He did not feature being alone. And then this crew off the good ship Lollipop or whatever it was might take it upon themselves to kick down the closet door, for a lark. And if that happened he would be, at the very least, embarrassed. The other way was more a pain in the neck, but probably better in the long run.

So he decided to try and keep his lease-breaking party from deteriorating into total chaos: he gave wine to the sailors and separated the *mura* players; he introduced the fat government girl to Sandor Rojas, who would keep her out of trouble; he helped the girl in the shower to dry off and get into bed; he had another talk with Saul; he called a repairman for the refrigerator, which someone had discovered was on the blink. This is what he did until nightfall, when most of the revellers had passed out and the party trembled on the threshold of its third day.

Upstairs Callisto, helpless in the past, did not feel the faint rhythm inside the bird begin to slacken and fail. Aubade was by the window, wandering the ashes of her own lovely world; the temperature held steady, the sky had become a uniform darkening gray. Then something from downstairs—a girl's scream, an overturned chair, a glass dropped on the floor, he would never know what exactly—pierced that private time-warp and he became aware of the faltering, the constriction of muscles, the tiny tossings of the bird's head; and his own pulse began to pound more fiercely, as if trying to compensate. "Aubade," he called weakly, "he's dying." The girl, flowing and rapt, crossed the hothouse to gaze down at Callisto's hands. The two remained like that, poised, for one minute, and two, while the heartbeat ticked a graceful diminuendo down at last into stillness. Callisto raised his head slowly. "I held him," he protested, impotent with the wonder of it, "to give him the warmth of my body. Almost as if I were communicating life to him, or a sense of life. What has happened? Has the transfer of heat ceased to work? Is there no more…"

He did not finish.

"I was just at the window," she said. He sank back, terrified. She stood a moment more, irresolute; she had sensed his obsession long ago, realized somehow that that constant 37 was now decisive. Suddenly then, as if seeing the single and unavoidable conclusion to all this she moved swiftly to the window before Callisto could speak; tore away the drapes and smashed out the glass with two exquisite hands which came away bleeding and glistening with splinters; and turned to face the man on the bed and wait with him until the moment of equilibrium was reached, when 37 degrees Fahrenheit should prevail both outside and inside, and forever, and the hovering, curious dominant of their separate lives should resolve into a tonic of darkness and the final absence of all motion.

Sylvia Plath

Sylvia Plath was born in Boston in 1932, the daughter of German immigrant parents. Her father was a professor of biology at Boston University and specialized in bees. A disturbed but brilliant young student, Plath excelled at Smith College before receiving a Fulbright Scholarship to study at Cambridge where she met future husband Ted Hughes. In 1957, Plath returned to the U.S. and began to study poetry with Kenyon College alum Robert Lowell. Plath went on to become loosely associated with the confessionalism movement spearheaded by Lowell and wrote some of the most popular books of poetry of all time, including *Ariel,* and wrote *The Bell Jar,* an autobiographical novel. Arguably, her most celebrated work was written in the final months before her death by suicide on January 7, 1963, at the age of thirty. "The Beekeeper's Daughter," first published by *The Kenyon Review* in August 1960, is not only one of Plath's most recognizable poems, but also is slated to be the title of a major motion picture about Plath and Hughes's relationship under production by the BBC.

The Beekeeper's Daughter *(1960)*
by Sylvia Plath

A garden of mouthings. Purple, scarlet-speckled, black
The great corollas dilate, peeling back their silks.
Their musk encroaches, circle after circle,
A well of scents almost too dense to breathe in.
Hieratical in your frock coat, maestro of the bees,
You move among the many-breasted hives,

My heart under your foot, sister of a stone.

Trumpet-throats open to the beaks of birds.
The Golden Rain Tree drips its powders down.
In these little boudoirs streaked with orange and red
The anthers nod their heads, potent as kings
To father dynasties. The air is rich.
Here is a queenship no mother can contest—

A fruit that's death to taste: dark flesh, dark parings.

In burrows narrow as a finger, solitary bees
Keep house among the grasses. Kneeling down
I set my eye to a hole-mouth and meet an eye
Round, green, disconsolate as a tear.
Father, bridegroom, in this Easter egg
Under the coronal of sugar roses

The queen bee marries the winter of your year.

James Dickey

James Dickey was born in Atlanta, Georgia, in 1923. After high school, Dickey planned to pursue his college education and a college football career at the University of Clemson in Clemson, South Carolina. Attending only one semester, he dropped out in 1942 to enlist in the Army Air Corps to serve in World War II, eventually flying thirty-nine missions in the South Pacific. Upon his return to the U.S., Dickey married Maxine Webster Syerson in Nashville, Tennessee, where he attended Vanderbilt University on the G. I. Bill, earning his B.A. in English. Just as he began a teaching position at Rice University, Dickey was recalled to duty in Korea. After his release, Dickey went back to teaching at Rice and the University of Florida, where a controversy over the attempt to censor his poem "The Father's Body" led him to quit teaching and take a job in advertising back in Atlanta in 1956. Following the release of his first book, *Into the Stone and Other Poems,* in 1960, Dickey returned to teaching, eventually taking a job at the University of South Carolina in 1968, a position he would keep for the rest of his life. Dickey went on to write *Buckdancer's Choice* (winner of the National Book Award), *Drowning with Others*, and *Self Interviews.* His popular and respected poetry and prose, coupled with the Hollywood film of his novel *Deliverance*, brought Dickey fame not normally enjoyed by poets. *The Kenyon Review* was an early supporter of Dickey, publishing "The Change" in 1960. He died in 1997 at the age of seventy-four.

The Change *(1960)*

by James Dickey

Blue, unstirrable, dreaming,
The hammerhead goes by the boat,
Passing me slowly in looking.

He has singled me out from the others;
He has put his blue gaze in my brain.
The strength of creation sees through me:

The world is yet blind as beginning.
The shark's brutal form never changes.
No millions of years shall yet turn him

From himself to a man in love,
Yet I feel that impossible man
Hover near, emerging from darkness,

Like a creature of light from the ocean.
He is what I would make of myself
In ten million years, if I could,

And arise from my brute of a body
To a thing the world never thought of
In a place as apparent as Heaven.

I name the blue shark through the water,
And the heart of my brain has spoken
To me, like an unknown brother,

Gently of ends and beginnings,
Gently of sources and outcomes,
Impossible, brighter than sunlight.

Nadine Gordimer

Nadine Gordimer was born in Springs, Transvaal, outside Johannesburg, South Africa, in 1923. Gordimer was educated in a convent school, and she spent a year at Witwaterstrand University without taking a degree, often kept at home by a mother who imagined she had a weak heart. She gained early acceptance as a writer, publishing her first collection of stories, *Face to Face,* at the age of twenty-six. It was followed by *The Soft Voice of the Serpent* (1952), and a novel, *The Lying Days* (1953). She won international renown as a writer who deals with the consequences of a racially divided society. Gordimer has traveled extensively in Africa, Europe, and North America, but since 1948 has continued to live in Johannesburg. She has continued also to publish such works of fiction as *A World of Strangers, Occasion for Loving,* and *The Late Bourgeois World.* In 1954, she married businessman Reinhold Cassirer. Gordimer has always aspired to live outside the public eye, but the many major awards that resulted from her fourteen novels and twelve collections of short stories, among them the Booker Prize in 1974 for *The Conservationist* and, in 1991, the Nobel Prize for Literature, have made her an international figure. Her story "Message in a Bottle" appeared in *The Kenyon Review* in 1962.

Message in a Bottle *(1962)*

by Nadine Gordimer

There are days when the world pauses, gets stuck, senselessly like one of those machines that ought to give cigarettes or make balls bump round but simply becomes an object that takes kicks, shakes, unyieldingly. You drop out of step with the daily work or habit that carries you along and stare about. Halt, halt! It's fatal. This is not Sunday, with cows beside winter willows and dried-up streams, and white egrets catching up with their own forward-jerking necks. I notice a face in the strip of mirror attached with crystal knobs to the pillar in the coffee shop. An uneven face, looks as if it's been up all night for years: my own. Once I had no face to speak of, only a smile, bright eyes, and powdered cheeks, nicely arranged. I order two coffees, one for myself, one for the child—"Would you like a cup of coffee?": it is a piece of clumsy flattery, a status I confer upon her because she has just been to a doctor and suffered a painful treatment. She accepts it, her token smile knowing its worth.

She shivers a little, from shock, in her dusty school clothes; at this time of the morning, she ought to be doing mental arithmetic. I am in my work clothes too, interrupted by necessity. I do not know what to talk to the child about because she has plumbed cheerful, jollying reassurances over months of pain, and efforts at distraction she takes as a kind of insult. She resents my sympathy because I have not her pain; my solicitously gentle voice is easy enough for me, it does not help her, she has discovered. So we don't talk, and I eat a piece of cheesecake, not so much because I want it, but to show her that life must go on. By such moves and signals do we conduct the battle that is waged between the sick and the well.

I eat the cheesecake and look again at the only other two customers in the place at this time on a Wednesday morning. I half-saw them when we came in, but my awareness was merely of a presence that brought to light my old trousers and cardigan. An oldish man and a blonde girl out of a fashion magazine. She is tall as they always are and she sits not with her knees under the table but with the length of her body from seat to head turned diagonally toward him and supported by her elbow on the table. From the door, without detail, they fell into an image of a girl making up to a man. But she is weeping. Tears fill and refract marvellously the one eye I can see and then run slowly down the pale beige cheek. She stretches the muscles of her face to hold them and puts up the forefinger of a clenched hand to catch them.

One distinctly runs over the finger and drops to the tablecloth. There will be a little splotch there, where it fell.

I look away, but when I look back again the tears are still coming, in slow twos and threes down the matte and perfect cheek. She is talking all the time to the man, not looking at him but talking without a sound that I can hear, directly to his ear with the dark shadow in it that must be a tuft of hair. That tense tendon in her neck may become permanent when she is older; but there is no reason why she will be so unhappy often. It looks like the kind of misery one grows out of.

She is a beautiful girl dressed from head to foot in pale beige that matches her face and hair. He would be ugly if he were a poor man, sucked dry, at his age, and leathery; but his crowded features, thin ridged nose and eyes and line of mouth, are filled out, smoothly built up, deal by deal, as a sculptor adds clay daub by daub, by ease and money-making. He has never been a good-looking young man, never. While she talks he looks out across the room, listening. He does not look at her but at the waiters passing, the door opening, the woman at the cash register ringing up the sale of a packet of cigarettes. It is a face that has put love into making money. Yes, he is ugly, but I do not know whether I imagine that she already has the look of one of those lovely creatures whose beauty—that makes them feel they may have any man—brings them nothing but one of these owners of textile factories; while we others, who are ignored by the many, carry off the particular prizes, the distinguished, the gentle, the passionately attractive, the adventurous. Is she pleading with him not to break off an affair? The one remark I do hear belies this: "…what about that boy friend of yours, doesn't he…" The very tone of his voice, raised plainly above the confidential, is that of the confidant importuned, stonily turning nasty and wanting to give up his privilege to anyone who seems under a more valid obligation to deal with the situation. Yet I don't know. She is still pleading, clearly going over and over what she has said a dozen times before. How beautifully she weeps, without a bloated nose; why should one feel not moved by her just because she is beautiful, why, in spite of everything, is there the obstinate cold resentment that her face is more than she deserves?

The man's eyes (he is obviously keenly long-sighted) follow the passing of someone on the other side of the glass barrier, in the street. As he changes focus we meet, my piece of cheesecake halfway to my mouth. We know each other, this morning, above the heads of the child and the weeping one. I should never have thought it; but you don't always choose the ones you know. The girl has not paused in her desperate monologue and the child, beside me, has her one uncovered eye screwed up, nuzzling toward brightness without seeing, like a mole.

I pay and the child and I walk out just behind the other two. There is a big black car outside the door and a black chauffeur, fat henchman, opens the door for them. One feels the girl likes this, it turns up the fragment of a fairy tale. She steps inside elegantly, with a certain melancholy pleasure, balanced like a brimming glass.

I drive out of the city to an address where the child is to have a culture made from the infected tissues in her eyelids. The doctor has drawn a little map for me; through suburbs, past country clubs and chicken farms, everywhere the sun shines evenly through a bloom of blue smoke that marks the position of the city, from far off, like the spout of a whale. The research institute is spread out pleasantly on a rise; there are gardens, and horses standing in a field. We get out of the car and it's as if a felt-lined door has been shut—the sound of life in the city comes only as a slight vibration under one's feet. I take her by the arm and we cross some grass, city people in the sunlight, and wander from building to building. They are white inside and, although we hear voices through frosted doors, all desks are empty. We see an African in a white coat blocking the light at the end of a corridor. He directs us to another building. He has a kind of trolley full of small cages with dark shapes in them that don't move. Out of the clean buildings, round the goldfish ponds (she is too old to want to linger beside them anymore), we come into a courtyard full of gray monkeys in cages. She forgets about her eye and breaks away from me, finding her way: "Oh aren't they sweet!" They swing from gray tails, they have black masks through which amber eyes shine with questions. They have patches where the fur has been shaved and the skin has been punctured again and again and painted with medicaments; oh why, but why? She pulls back from my arm when I tell her. There are rats, crouched guinea pigs, piles of empty cages in yards. The horses, that were standing so peacefully in the field, have glazed eyes and the hopelessness of working animals who have come out of the shafts for good. On their rumps and necks are the shaved and painted patches. Their stalls are being swilled out and scrubbed by men in rubber boots; it is so clean, all this death and disease.

"Now we're going to try and grow these nasty goggas from your eye, dear, we're going to grow them in an egg and see whether we can make you well." The woman in the white coat talks soothingly as she works on the eye.

While she is out of the laboratory for a moment we listen to a kettle that is singing up to the boil, and I say, "Don't rub it." The child says after a silence, "I wish I could be the one who sits and watches." Pain is taking her innocence, she is getting to know me. But if she indicts, she begins at the same time to take on some of the guilt: "They will grow mine in an egg? Only in an egg?" The sun is high; we do not know what time it is, driving back. She tells time by the school bell, I by the cardboard file growing thinner.

My husband has a story to tell when he comes home in the evening. An acquaintance, who took him out shooting, last weekend, has committed suicide. He does not tell it baldly like this but begins slowly at what led up to the beginning, although we can tell, almost from the beginning, what is coming. "He was in wonderful form. I stood next to him and watched him bring down four birds with five cartridges. Alba worked so well and he asked me whether I couldn't ask Jack Strahan to sell him one from the next litter. He couldn't get over the way Alba worked; he said he'd never seen a dog like it, for range. And he asked when I was going to bring you on a shoot again, when're you going to bring your wife out here with you, he said; he remembered that time last year when we had such a good time in the camp."

The man kissed his wife, dropped his children at their school, telephoned his office to say he would be a little late, and then drove out into the veld. "Shut himself in the boot of the car and shot himself through the head." I scarcely knew the man, met him only that once at the camp, but, at this detail of the manner of his death, I suddenly think of something: "But don't you remember, he used to shut his hunting dogs in the boot? He did it that day, and when I picked him out about it he said it wasn't cruel and they didn't mind being shut up in there!" Nobody knows why he killed himself, he has gone without a word to anyone—except this. The stranger who cannot remember clearly what he looked like is the one into whose hands his last message has fallen. What can I do with it? It's like a message picked up on the beach, that may be a joke, a hoax, or a genuine call of distress—one can't tell, and ends by throwing the bottle back into the sea. If it's genuine, the sender is beyond help already. Or someone else may pick it up and know what it's all about.

If I keep it perhaps I might crack the code one day? If only it were the sort of code that children or spies use, made out of numbers or lines from the Bible. But it is made of what couldn't be equated or spelled out to anyone in the world, that could leave communication only in the awkward movement of his body through the air as he scrambled into the smell of dust and petrol, where the dogs had crouched, and closed the lid over his head.

For no reason at all, my mind begins to construct a dialogue with the girl—that girl. I see her somewhere, years later. She is laughing, she is conscious of her beauty. I say to her quite abruptly, "What happened that morning, anyway?—You know, he has developed hardened arteries and his teeth are giving him trouble. He's on a strict diet—no wine, no red meat—and his old wife cooks for him again. He never goes out."

The child comes in and stands squarely before me. She has put her dark glasses on and I can't see her eyes. "And if the egg should hatch," she says, "if the egg hatches?"

John Crowe Ransom

John Crowe Ransom was born in Pulaski, Tennessee, in 1888. After graduating from Vanderbilt University, Ransom went on to study at Oxford in 1910. He returned several years later and began teaching at his alma mater. Ransom remained at Vanderbilt, except for a period of service as an artillery officer in France during World War I, until his departure for Kenyon College in 1937. By this time, Ransom had established himself as a prominent poet, after publishing such books as *Poems about God*, *Chills and Fever,* and *Two Gentlemen in Bonds*. All of these works reflected the values of The Fugitives, a group of writers centered in Nashville who believed in writing formal verse that praised agrarian traditions. By 1927, he claimed he had "exhausted" his poetic output and began to concentrate on criticism and editing. Ransom founded *The Kenyon Review* in 1939 and acted as its editor until 1959, establishing its reputation as one of the finest literary journals in America. While regarded as a conservative critic, Ransom often published writers whose values and aesthetics were very different from his own. While at Kenyon, he also founded the Kenyon School of English, designed to gather distinguished critics and students together to develop a more critical approach to studying literature along the lines of his "New Criticism," which claimed that in most scholarly consideration of poetry, too little attention was being paid to the actual words of poems as opposed to when and where the poet wrote them. His criticism was highly influential, and books like *The New Criticism* and *Poetic Sense: A Study of Problems in Defining Poetry by Content* made him one of the century's most renowned critics. Ransom remained active in the academic world until his death in his sleep at his Kenyon home in 1974.

Prelude to an Evening:
A Poem Revised and Explicated *(1963)*

by John Crowe Ransom

Do not enforce the tired wolf
Dragging his infected wound homeward
To sit tonight with the warm children
Saying the pretty Kings of France.

The images of the invaded mind
Are monstrous only in the dreams
Of your most brief enchanted headful.
Suppose a miracle of confusion:—

That dreamed and undreamt become each other
And mix the night and day of your soul.
For it never mattered your twice crying
From mouth unbeautied against the pillow

To avert the gun of the same old soldier,
If surely cry, cock-crow or bell
Breaking the improbable black spell
Annihilated the poor phantom.

But now, by our confirmed supposal,
Apparition waits upon sunny mornings;
You in your peignoir dividing the oranges;
But gathering its strength in the shadowed places

Invisible evil, deprived and bold.
The day-long clock will metronome
Your gallant fear; the needles clicking;
The heels detonating the stair's cavern.

Freshening the water in the blue bowls
For the buckberries with not all your love
You shall be listening for a low wind,
And the warning sibilance of pines.

Finally evening. Hear me denouncing
Our equal and conniving Furies;
You making Noes but they lack conviction;
Smoothing the heads of the hungry children.

I would have us magnificent at my coming;
Two souls tight-clasped; and a swamp of horrors.
O you shall be handsome and brave at fearing.
Now my step quickens; and meets a huge No!

Whose No was it? like the hoarse policeman's,
Clopping onstage in the Name of the Law.
That was Me; forbidding tricks at homecoming;
At the moment of coming to its white threshold.

I went to the nations of disorder
To be freed of the memory of good and evil;
There even your image was disfigured;
Then the boulevards rocked; they said, Go back.

I am here; and to balk my ruffian I bite
The tongue devising all that treason;
Then creep in my wounds to the sovereign flare
Of the room where you shine on the good children.

And now for the commentary. "Prelude to an Evening," in twelve stanzas, is
a new version of the original poem by that title, which had eight stanzas and
was published thirty years ago. In the new poem the eight stanzas remain
substantially about what they were before. If some of them have been tin-
kered with, that is according to the luxurious habit of poets who, when an
old poem comes up for republication, like to induce the whole delicious
process of composition over again, and even try to make a few fresh beau-
ties here and there if they can. The big change is the addition of four new
stanzas at the end. They are like the others in form, being quatrains of
unrhymed four-beat lines which mostly are end-stopped. It was my hope that
the new stanzas would be like enough in tempo and style to keep continuity
with the old ones as if by a single act of composition. But I am afraid that

these so new and so few stanzas, which have so much to do in so short a space, may be too brisk to suit with the others. What they must do is nothing less than undo the whole intention of the old poem, and bring it to a very different conclusion.

The Editor has asked me to tell why I changed my poem. The simple fact is that it became disagreeable to my ears as I continued to read it on public occasions now and then. But the story is complicated.

Here is a man returning in the evening from his worldly occupations to his own household. He has had plenty of encounters with the world's evils, and his imagination is immoderate and wayward; it has blown the evils up, 'til now he manages to be attended habitually by a vague but overwhelming impression of metaphysical Powers arrayed against him; he can say even to others (if they are capable of sympathy) that he is a man pursued by Furies. And he cannot but think it an anticlimax, a defeat unworthy of his confrontation of his fate, to spend the evening with children at their lessons. The poem is the man's soliloquy as he approaches his house. He is addressing the mother of his children who awaits him, as if rehearsing the speech he will make in her presence in order to persuade her to share his fearful preoccupations and give him her entire allegiance. He seems to think he will win her over; there is no intimation that it may turn out quite differently. But suppose he succeeds: will not that be a dreary fate for the woman? And what of the children? Those are not his questions. But they came to be mine. By the end of the eighth stanza he pictures her prophetically as rapt in her new terrors, almost to the point of forgetting the children; if they are hungry, she will absentmindedly smooth their heads.

I suppose a poet is excused without having to invoke the Fifth Amendment if he believes in his own poem, at least at the stage of first publication. My liking went quite beyond its merits, and lasted much too long. It had to do with some notion of a workmanlike poetic line carrying forward the argument while the woman was being borne through successive terrors not of her own making, yet still invested in her incorruptible dignity. It was with intense pleasure that I watched her suffering there; she was a heroine almost after the pattern of some diminutive classical tragedy. And if the piece had a hero, it must be the husband and speaker. I had not come to saying that the man was odious, that he was, incontestably, the villain. That was rather strange. As for my ordinary conscience in these matters, I believe I have only one other poem so vindictive as this, and I know some readers to whom it is no secret which it must be. It is the one called "Blue Girls," where the girls in the schoolyard are preening themselves in their beauty (as they should) 'til a man looking on addresses them and forces them to take account of a blear-eyed old woman whom he invents on the spot, and describes, with the threat that to her favor they must come soon.

At any rate. One day last winter, what I had not said was said for me; by a strong-minded young woman writing in a very little magazine devoted to the "explication" of difficult verse, in answer to a subscriber's query. What did the man of my poem mean to do? She replied with a commendable severity: this man was simply a brutal character who meant not to do any baby-sitting even if the babies were his own. At once I conceded the justice of her observation, and with more relief than surprise. All the same, I was soon wondering if I might not somehow patch up the poem and save it; by saving the woman and the children from their distress; and of course by saving the villain too, who so far as the genders go belonged to my party. I rather thought not. If I must administer to him a speedy and radical "conversion" after eight stanzas of villainy—the idea was too forbidding.

But another event brought me back to my project of salvage. Six years ago Charles Coffin, my teaching colleague, died at the Huntington Library in the midst of his studies of the theology of *Paradise Lost.* Now Milton had notoriously been a sort of independent theologian; but I was aware that Doctor Coffin, for all his churchmanship, inclined to be an independent theologian too. Unfortunately his packed notebooks were far from complete. But a faithful pupil rescued one complete section or chapter under the title of "Creation and the Self," which he submitted to *ELH, A Journal of English Literary History*; it was published in March 1962. The essay might have been the key chapter of the book. It deals first with the magnanimous creation of man in the Creator's image, and then with the man's adventurous behaviors as they affected his relations with the Creator. We must remember that the writer was exploring the mind of Milton, and limiting his speculation scrupulously to the theological ideas that were feasible at the date of Milton's poem. Milton's theme, said Doctor Coffin, is the story of the friendly association between Creator and creature; it is broken many times by the creature's misdemeanors, but the Creator always is prepared to extend his grace; may I remark, though it will be something of an anachronism: as if He had allowed for them in advance? If the creature repents, the happy connection is restored.

I have liked this theology so much for its friendly note that now, and from here on, I will refer symbolically to the man in my poem as Adam, and to the woman whom he apostrophizes as Eve; these are the names they must bear in our Great Myth. In this way I shall not be altogether compromising my poem by "explicating" it. A poem is not a moral essay nor a religious tract; it is best if our talk about it falls short of being just that. We are still feeling the scars of a long, confused period in the modern history of literary criticism in which this issue has been fought over, and perhaps fought out. Poetry is still the supremely inclusive speech which escapes, as if unaware of them, the strictures and reductions of the systematic logical understanding. Publicly or tacitly, we probably all have some sort of theology, and its teachings are quite capable of entering into a poem, perhaps without losing any of their compulsion. It is difficult to write the proper poem nowadays, because after many ages of hard prose we have come far from the primitive and natural speech of poetry. But it is still being handsomely done. In a true poem it is as if the religious dogma or the moral maxim had been dropped into the pot as soon as the act of composition began; sinking down out of sight and consciousness, it is as if it became a fluid and was transfused into the bloodstream of the poet now, and would be communicated to the bloodstream of his auditors eventually. The significance of the poem is received by feeling; or, more technically, by immediate unconscious intuition. So let the man of my poem be Adam, let the woman and mother of his children be Eve; if the poem did not name them let the commentary do it. At once we are moving over an old and familiar terrain; bearing these names the figures will be invested for everybody with their moral and religious properties.

I cannot fail to remark that I was partly prepared for this symbolic sense of my characters by an event dated 1961: the publication of *The Rhetoric of Religion* by Kenneth Burke; a book which for the largeness of its perspective and the scruple of its discriminations must rate among the important treatises of philosophy. In his foreword Burke remarks:

> The subject of religion falls under the head of *rhetoric* in the sense that rhetoric is the art of *persuasion,* and religious cosmogonies are designed...as exceptionally thoroughgoing modes of persuasion. To persuade men towards certain acts, religions would form the kinds of attitude which prepare men for such acts. And in order to plead for such attitudes as persuasively as possible, the religious always ground their exhortations (to themselves and others) in statements of the widest and deepest possible scope, concerning the authorship of men's motives.

A less hortatory form of persuasion, yet a powerful and rhetorical one, is poetry; and it has to be said that Burke as a cunning verbalist has an extraordinary sensibility for the varied meanings that go with a word or phrase. And Burke would think, as I do, that it is more faithful to the sense of a serious poem to translate it, if we must translate it, into theology than into morality. A poem starts with a crucial human situation, and from there proceeds usually by some mixture of drama, narrative, and contemplation. But does not the priest himself teach theology to the congregation most effectively by means of Scriptural narratives and ritualistic drama? The secular-seeming ordinary poem plies its rhetoric through common words, but theology pervades them invisibly. So digressive, and regressive, is the significance of old words even though we may not choose to stop and dwell on them.

But Charles Coffin supplied my most immediate cues. Adam, he said, was the noblest of God's creatures because he was created free; he could choose his own actions. But to guide him he had reason, which was akin to his Creator's; and imagination, so that he might be in his degree a creator in his own right. Imagination is a great term in the Scriptures, but I am afraid that its usual employment there is by way of mention of the evil imaginations of the heart. How prodigious are Adam's creations, even since Milton's time; especially since Milton's time. He has created commodities exactly suited to his physical need, and machines too, to which he has delegated their automatic creation; and terrible engines of war; and as I think we all think increasingly, a foolish clutter of little machines and mechanisms which by saving his strength impoverish it, leaving his body soft and his mind aimless as to its proper objects. He has created gods in his own image, but sometimes they are not flattering to his intelligence, and not fit for universal worship. Finally, there are his poems, and other works of art, sometimes famed everywhere and regarded as all but everlasting monuments; and they might always have been beneficent and tonic, but often are only hateful. The fictitious Adam of my eight stanzas has a speech precisely as pretty as his zealous author and patron could find for him, but the ruling imagination is that of a "wicked heart"; for this I regret to think that the real Adam his maker is responsible.

Had we not better say that Adam was created half-free, not wholly free? A theme which is not particularly explored in Scripture, but doubtless is there gratefully taken for granted, is that of the marvelous body created to house Adam's soul; replenishing, conditioning, repairing, preserving itself, almost without Adam's consciousness; a machine not of Adam's manufacture, but the fortress and security of his free enterprise. A tight and physical containment is appointed to the body; much of Adam's vital strength must be expended upon its secret operation, and it is just as well if it has not the freedom of Adam's imagination.

We come to Charles Coffin's account of Eve, and here I am all eyes and ears. ("Now my step quickens," says the Adam of my poem.) It appears that the agency in Eve's creation was Adam's as well as the Creator's. Adam took the initiative; he asked for it. Therefore it was from his body that the Creator took the rib out of which she was to be fashioned. This is not to say that the new creature was not as fully authorized as Adam. But she was a more separate and independent creature, says Doctor Coffin. God talks familiarly with Adam but not with Eve. Raphael talks at great length with Adam, but Eve after serving dinner stays discreetly in the background; and when he takes up the "abstruse" matter of the motions of the celestial universe she steals away to her flowers. Adam will explain all this to her later if she wishes. Clearly there is a deficiency in Eve's composition as compared with Adam's. She is not of the "intellectual" type, and it does not seem likely that she will be in all respects his congenial companion; there may have been some irony in the Creator's mind in complying with Adam's request.

Eve is freer than Adam in some respects, and is so declared by Doctor Coffin; she is more natural, confirmed in her direction already, therefore more spontaneous in her responses; she is less reflective. Her deficiency is in the freedom of those adventurous behaviors which go with rational discourse and the metaphysical imagination. So far as my eight stanzas are concerned, the matter turns on whether she is free to respond to the interests of her spouse as an artist; whose art this time is an extravagant but persistent "supposal" or fantasy, having a theological cast and an evil imagination. Is she capable of being swept off her feet by a work of art?—especially one that invokes a vision of evil? Adam hopes to find her capable. But the answer is in the new stanzas. He concedes that she is not capable; he will not ask of her the impossible. She is less free than Adam. Speaking very roughly, let us say that she is one-quarter free.

I found these considerations somewhat chilling. But I asked myself: what development within Eve's personality was so uniquely important that it must replace the missing quarter of her freedom? The answer was not really difficult, and it could be checked against Scripture and Milton rather explicitly. Eve has a special function within her body, and for exercising it a virtue, a habit not acquired but already built into her unconscious mind. Behind it a quarter of her vital energy (if we have to quantify it) has been committed firmly to its consummation. She bears the children in her own body; then she cares for them, teaches them, defends them to the last extremity, even with her life if necessary. One of the most vivid of my memories comes back whenever I think of Eve's composition. It is the recollection of my first "tutorial" in my Oxford college. When I had read my appointed paper, there came the instant suggestion, from the formidable philosopher who was my tutor, that I possess myself at once of *The Origin and Development of the Moral Ideas,* in two large volumes, published in 1906, by Edward Westermarck, professor of moral philosophy at The University of Finland, professor of sociology at The University of London. Two days later I was reading the chapter in which the "maternal instinct" is described as the origin of all human altruism. For the moral ideas of the male have to do with such motives as power, prestige, and aggressiveness. At once I reflected that no altruism is needed to motivate the conception of offspring; that is so important for family and tribe and history that in the scheme of creation the act was invested for both parties with a bodily pleasure so massive that it must prove more than ample for its occasions. The rearing of the children does not have such a sure sanction; unless it is the sanction of Eve's natural goodness, of the tender mercies which are sealed within her, awaiting confidently their occasions.

This paragraph will carry a slightly rueful self-appraisal. Probably the most of my poems are about familiar and familial situations; domestic and homely things. Eventually I was surprised and rather set back by the sense of what a "bourgeois" poet they had turned me into. The "Prelude" seemed to promise a variation in my performance, but even here it is evident that I have reverted. The change of tune in the four new stanzas, and the abject capitulation of Adam, may cause me to be drummed out of the corps of smart and reputable poets; for surely within the whole circuit of poetic occasions I have descended to the nadir of available themes to occupy myself with—a baby-sitting. My pedestrian and precarious defense could only be the argument that in the degree of their commonplace such situations might be denoting precisely those patterns within the great Familial Configuration which had been ordained in our creation, and were therefore the ones likely to be standard and permanent.

Will my readers speculate and generalize with me a little? Suppose Eve first tempted Adam, whether or not instructed by a kindly Serpent as to the facts of life; for she would need to have a prescience of the sequel. She was successful; and perhaps she despised Adam a little for the innocence and haste with which he yielded. Then came the children. After this it would be Adam soliciting Eve; but if possible it would be on his own lordly conditions. Let her share his professional interests; then she will have his preoccupations, sometimes as evil as they will be good, but she will also have him; he may even mention that less time should be spent with the children. But even before Adam comes into her presence to make his proposition, he is condemned out of his own mouth. The children must occupy her mind now; they have replaced their father in her deepest affections; and if he desires her favors he will have to take them not on his terms but hers, which will stipulate that he must share the responsibility for the children. I am aware that both Israel (which was responsible for the Old Testament) and Milton (who elaborated on its story) took a partisan view of Adam as the lord of the household. There has been much question of Milton's personal success in this role. But it was within the history of Israel, from the beginning to this day, that I could easily imagine that Adam's talent for the familial role had been altogether exceptional.

The ninth stanza continues the eighth, by providing a passage with erotic connotations, in order to display Adam truthfully; that requires its first three lines. The fourth line begins the denouement. Suddenly, as Adam approaches, he comes to his senses and knows that Eve will never accept his invitation; not the open and intellectual part, not the implicit erotic part if that is bound up with the other. He knows better than to say it to her actual person. Probably he will never say it out loud.

The eleventh stanza recalls a truancy of Adam's at some time or other, when he had gone among strangers trying to forget his Eve, whose feelings for him had not been the same after the coming of the children. He went on a journey. But what he found was that Eve was still the only woman for him. The soft reader may pity him a little, but we respect him for the constancy of his fixation.

In the last stanza Adam stands on the threshold of his house, but he stops a moment to fortify his wiser self against his own self-defeating eloquence. The final utterance of his soliloquy, and of the poem, is a two-line homage, half mystical, perhaps half maudlin, to the formidable yet beneficent dignity of her status and that of the children. We imagine that he is going to enjoy her favor, but his immediate motive is under the familial sign. He will sit with the children dutifully and, we will think, proudly. It is not the happiest ending that he could possibly conceive, but it is the best he had the right to expect. Perhaps a kindly reader will wish him many happy returns of his homecoming. Does not the poem presuppose a crucial moment in his history? There will be many interims yet when he will be out in the free world again, busied in his own way professionally. But every time he takes his leave he will have said to them and himself: I shall return.

Doris Lessing

Doris Lessing was born in Persia (now Iran) on October 22, 1919, to British parents. In 1925, the family moved to the British colony in Southern Rhodesia (now Zimbabwe), where her father unsuccessfully attempted to farm. Lessing was sent to an all-girls high school in the capital of Salisbury, from which she soon dropped out at age thirteen, thus ending her formal education. Lessing left home when she was fifteen and took a job as a nurse-maid, not to return to Salisbury until 1937, in the meantime educating herself on books ordered from London. After one failed marriage, she married Gottfried Lessing, and the two moved to London in 1949. In the same year, she published her first novel, *The Grass Is Singing*, and began her career as a professional writer. Lessing's novels over the following two decades, such as the *Children of Violence* Series and *The Golden Notebook*, described the injustices of racial inequality existing in Africa, for which she was declared a prohibited alien in both Southern Rhodesia and South Africa in 1956. Lessing has since expanded into science fiction, nonfiction, autobiography, and poetry, all to high acclaim. Lessing has been nominated for the Nobel Prize for Literature and continues to publish her work (the most recent novel being *The Sweetest Dream* in 2002). Her story "One Off the Short List" originally appeared in *The Kenyon Review* in 1963.

One Off the Short List *(1963)*

by Doris Lessing

When he had first seen Barbara Coles, some years before, he only noticed her because someone said: "That's Johnson's new girl." He certainly had not used of her the private erotic formula: *Yes, that one.* He even wondered what Johnson saw in her. "She won't last long," he remembered thinking, as he watched Johnson, a handsome man, but rather flushed with drink, flirting with some unknown girl while Barbara stood by a wall looking on. He thought she had a sullen expression.

She was a pale girl, and although she wasn't slim, for her frame was generous, her figure could pass as good. Her straight yellow hair was parted on one side in a way that struck him as gauche. He did not notice what she wore. But her eyes were all right, he remembered: large, and solidly green, square-looking because of some trick of the flesh at their corners. Emerald-like eyes in the face of a schoolgirl, or young school mistress who was watching her lover flirt and would later sulk about it.

Her name sometimes cropped up in the papers. She was a stage decorator, a designer, something on those lines.

Then a Sunday newspaper had a competition for stage design and she won it. Barbara Coles became one of the "names" in the theatre, and her photograph was seen about. It was always serious. He remembered having thought her sullen.

One night he saw her across the room at a party. She was talking with a well-known actor. Her yellow hair was still done on one side, but now it looked sophisticated. She wore an emerald ring on her right hand that seemed deliberately to invite comparison with her eyes. He walked over and said: "We have met before. Graham Spence." He noted, with discomfort, that he sounded abrupt. "I'm sorry, I don't remember, but how do you do?" she said, smiling. And continued her conversation.

He hung around a bit, but soon she went off with a group of people she was inviting to her home for a drink. She did not invite Graham. There was about her an assurance, a carelessness, that he recognized as the signature of success. It was then, watching her laugh as she went off with her friends, that he used the formula: *Yes, that one.* And he went home to his wife with enjoyable expectation, as if his date with Barbara Coles were already arranged.

His marriage was twenty years old. At first it had been stormy, painful, tragic—full of partings, betrayals, and sweet reconciliations. It had taken him at least a decade to realize that there was nothing remarkable about this marriage that he had lived through with such surprise of the mind and the senses. On the contrary, the marriages of most of the people he knew, whether they were first, second, or third attempts, were just the same. His had run true to form even to the serious love affair with the young girl for whose sake he had *almost* divorced his wife—yet at the last moment had changed his mind, letting the girl down so that he would have her for always (not unpleasurably) on his conscience. It was with humiliation that he had understood that this drama was not at all the unique thing he had imagined. It was nothing more than the experience of everyone in his circle. And presumably in everybody else's circle, too?

Anyway, round about the tenth year of his marriage he had seen a good many things clearly, a certain kind of emotional adventure went from his life, and the marriage itself changed.

His wife had married a poor youth with a great future as a writer. Sacrifices had been made, chiefly by her, for that future. He was neither unaware of them nor ungrateful; in fact, he felt permanently guilty about them. He at last published a decently successful book, then a second which now, thank God, no one remembered. He had drifted into radio, television, book reviewing.

He understood he was not going to make it; that he had become not a hack—no one could call him that—but a member of that army of people who live by their wits on the fringes of the arts. The moment of realization was when he was in a pub one lunchtime near the B.B.C. where he often dropped in to meet others like himself: he understood that was why he went there—they *were* like him. Just as that melodramatic marriage had turned out to be like everyone else's, except that it had been shared with one woman instead of with two or three, so it had turned out that his unique talent, his struggles as a writer, had led him here, to this pub and the half-dozen pubs like it, where all the men in sight had the same history. They all had their novel, their play, their book of poems, a moment of fame to their credit. Yet here they were, running television programs about which they were cynical (to each other or to their wives) or writing reviews about other people's books. Yes, that's what he had become, an impresario of other people's talent. These two moments of clarity, about his marriage and about his talent, had roughly coincided; and (perhaps not by chance) had coincided with his wife's decision to leave him for a man younger than himself who had a future, she said, as a playwright. Well, he had talked her out of it. For her part she had to understand he was not going to be the new T. S. Eliot or Graham Greene—but, after all, how many were? She must finally understand this, for he could no longer bear her awful bitterness. For his part he must stop coming home drunk at 5:00 in the morning, and starting a new romantic affair every six months which he took so seriously that he had to make her miserable because of her implied deficiencies. In short he was to be a good husband. (He had always been a dutiful father.) And she a good wife. And so it was: the marriage became stable, as they say.

The formula—*Yes, that one*—no longer necessarily implied a sexual relationship. In its more mature form, it was far from being something he was ashamed of. On the contrary, it expressed a humorous respect for what he was and for his real talents and flair. These had turned out to be not artistic after all; they had to do instead with emotional life, hard-earned experience. The formula expressed also an ironical dignity, a proving to himself not only: I can be honest about myself, but also: I have earned the best in *that* field whenever I want it.

He watched the field for the women who were well-known in the arts, or in politics; looked out for photographs, listened for bits of gossip. He made a point of going to see them act, or dance, or orate. He built up a not unshrewd picture of them. He would either quietly pull strings to meet one of them or, more often—for there was a gambler's pleasure in waiting—bide his time until he met her in the natural course of events, which was bound to happen sooner or later. He would be seen out with her a few times in public, which was in order, since his work meant he had to entertain well-known people. His wife always knew; he told her. He might have a brief affair with this woman, but more often than not it was the appearance of an affair. Not that he didn't get pleasure from other people envying him—he would make a point, for instance, of taking this woman into the pubs where his male colleagues went. It was that his real pleasure came when he saw her surprise at how well she was understood by him. He enjoyed the atmosphere he was so well able to set up between an intelligent woman and himself: a humorous complicity which had in it much that was unspoken, and which almost made sex irrelevant.

On to the list of women with whom he planned to have this relationship went Barbara Coles. There was no hurry. Next week, next month, next year, they would meet at a party. The world of well-known people in London is a small one. Big and little fishes, they drift around, nose each other, flirt their fins, wriggle off again. When he bumped into Barbara Coles, it would be time to decide whether or not to sleep with her.

Meanwhile he listened. But he didn't discover much. She had a husband and children, but the husband seemed to be in the background. The children were charming and well-brought-up, like everyone else's children. She had affairs, they said; several men he met sounded familiar with her, but it was hard to determine whether they had slept with her, because none directly boasted of her. She was spoken of in terms of her friends, her work, her house, a party she had given, a job she had found someone. She was liked, she was respected, and Graham Spence's self-esteem was flattered because he had chosen her. He looked forward to saying in just the same tone: "Barbara Coles asked me what I thought about the set and I told her quite frankly..."

Then, by chance, he met a young man who did boast about Barbara Coles; he claimed to have had the great love affair with her, and recently at that; and he spoke of it as something generally known. Graham realized how much he had already become involved with her in his imagination because of how perturbed he was now, on account of the character of this youth, Dick Mannheim. He had recently become successful as a magazine editor—one of those young men who are successful from sheer impertinence, effrontery. Without much talent or taste, yet he had the charm of his effrontery. "Yes, I'm going to succeed, because I've decided to; yes, I may be stupid, but not so stupid that I don't know my deficiencies. Yes, I'm going to be successful because you people with integrity etc. etc. etc. simply don't believe in the possibility of people like me. You are too cowardly to stop me. Yes, I've taken your measure and I'm going to succeed because I've got the courage not only to be unscrupulous but to be quite frank about it. And, besides, you admire me; you must, or you'd stop me."

Well, that was young Dick Mannheim, and he shocked Graham. He was a tall, languishing young man, handsome in a dark melting way, and, it was quite clear, he was either a-sexual or homosexual. And this youth boasted of the favors of Barbara Coles; boasted, indeed, of her love. Either she was a raving neurotic with a taste for neurotics, or Dick Mannheim was a most accomplished liar—or she slept with anyone. Graham was intrigued. He took Dick Mannheim out to dinner in order to hear him talk about Barbara Coles. There was no doubt the two were pretty close: all those dinners, theatres, weekends in the country. Graham Spence felt he had put his finger on the secret pulse of Barbara Coles; and it was intolerable that he must wait to meet her; he decided to arrange it.

It became unnecessary. She was in the news again, with a run of luck. She had done a successful historical play, and immediately afterward a modern play, and then a hit musical. In all three, the sets were remarked on. Graham saw some interviews in newspapers and on television. These all centered around the theme of her being able to deal easily with so many different styles of theatre; but the real point was, of course, that she was a woman. And now Graham Spence was asked to do a half-hour radio interview with her. He planned the questions he would ask her with care, drawing on what people had said of her but above all on his instinct and experience with women. The interview was to be at 9:30 at night; he was to pick her up at 6:00 at the theatre where she was currently at work, so that there would be time, as the letter from the B.B.C. had put, it, "for you and Miss Coles to get to know each other."

At 6:00 he was at the stage door, but a message from Miss Coles said she was not quite ready. Could he wait a little? He hung about, then went to the pub opposite for a quick one, but still no Miss Coles. So he made his way backstage, directed by voices, hammering, laughter. It was badly lighted, and the group of people at work did not see him. The director, James Poynter, had his arm around Barbara's shoulders. He was newly well-known, a carelessly good-looking young man reputed to be very intelligent. Barbara Coles wore a dark blue overall, and her flat hair fell over her face so that she kept pushing it back with the hand that had the emerald on it. They were looking at sketches and drawing spread out on a trestle. Three young men, stagehands, were on other side of the trestle. Barbara said, in a voice warm with energy: "Well, so I thought if we did *this*—do you see, James? What do you think, Steven?" "Well, love," said the young man she called Steven, "I see your idea, but I wonder if…" "I think you're right, Babs," said the director. "Look," said Barbara, holding one of the sketches toward Steven, "look; let me show you." They all leaned forward, the five of them, absorbed in the business.

Suddenly, Graham couldn't stand it. He understood he was shaken to his depths. He went offstage and stood with his back against a wall in the dingy passage that led to the dressing rooms. His eyes were filled with tears. He was seeing what a long way he had come from the crude, uncompromising, admirable young egomaniac he had been when he was twenty. That group of people there, working, joking, arguing: yes, that's what he hadn't known for years. What bound them was the democracy of respect for each other's work, a confidence in themselves and in each other. They looked like people banded together against a world which they…no, not despised—which they measured, understood, would fight to the death, out of respect for what they stood for, for what it stood for. It was a long time since he had felt part of that balance. And he understood that he had seen Barbara Coles when she was most herself. It was then, with the tears drying on his eyelids, which felt old and ironic, that he decided he would sleep with her. It was a necessity for him. He went back through the door onto the stage, burning with this single determination.

The five were still together. Barbara had a length of blue gleaming stuff which she was draping over the shoulder of Steven, the stagehand. He was showing it off, and the others watched. "What do you think, James?" she asked the director. "We've got that sort of dirty green, and I thought..." "Well," said James, not sure at all; "well, Babs..."

Graham went forward and stood beside Barbara. He said: "I'm Graham Spence. We've met before." For the second time she smiled socially and said: "Oh, I'm sorry, I don't remember." Graham nodded at James, whom he had known, or at least had met off and on, for years. But it was obvious James didn't remember him, either.

"From the B.B.C.," said Graham to Barbara, again sounding abrupt, against his will. "Oh, I'm sorry; I'm so sorry. I forgot all about it. I've got to be interviewed," she said to the group. "Mr. Spence is a journalist." Graham allowed himself a small ironical smile at the word journalist, but she was not looking at him. She was going on with her work. "We should decide tonight," she said. "Steven's right." "Yes, I am right," said the stagehand. "She's right, James; we need that blue with that sludge-green everywhere." "James," said Barbara, "James, what's wrong with it?" She moved forward to James, passing Graham. Remembering him again, she became contrite. "I'm sorry," she said. "We can none of us agree. Well, look..." She turned to Graham. "You advise us. We've got so involved with it that..." At which James laughed, and so did the stagehands. "No, Babs," said James, "of course Mr. Spence can't advise. He's just this moment come in. We've got to decide. I'll give you 'til tomorrow morning. Time to go home; it must be 6:00 by now."

"It's nearly 7:00," said Graham, taking command.

"It isn't!" said Barbara, dramatic. "My God, how terrible, how appalling! How could I have done such a thing?" She was laughing at herself. "Well, you'll have to forgive me, Mr. Spence, because you haven't got any alternative."

They began laughing again: this was clearly a group joke.

And now Graham took his chance. He said firmly, as if he were her director, in fact copying James Poynter's manner with her: "No, Miss Coles, I won't forgive you. I've been kicking my heels for nearly an hour." She grimaced, then laughed and accepted it. James said: "There, Babs, that's how you ought to be treated. We spoil you." He kissed her on the cheek, she kissed him on both of his, the stagehands moved off. "Have a good evening, Babs," said James, going, and nodding to Graham. Who stood concealing his pleasure with difficulty. He knew, because he had had the courage to be firm, indeed, peremptory, with Barbara, that he had saved himself hours of maneuvering. Several drinks, a dinner—perhaps two or three evenings of drinks and dinners had been saved because he was now on this footing with Barbara Coles, a man who could say: "No, I won't forgive you; you've kept me waiting."

She said: "I've just got to…" and went ahead of him. In the passage she hung her overall on a peg. She was thinking, it seemed, of something else; but, seeing him watching her, she smiled at him, companionably. He realized with triumph that it was the sort of smile she would offer one of the stagehands, or even James. She said again: "Just one second…" and went to the stage door office. She and the stage doorman conferred. There was some problem. Graham said, taking another chance: "What's the trouble; can I help?"—as if he could help, as if he expected to be able to. "Well…" she said, frowning. Then, to the man: "No, it'll be all right. Goodnight." She came to Graham. "We've got ourselves into a bit of a fuss because half the set's in Liverpool and half's here and…But it will sort itself out." She stood, at ease, chatting to him, one colleague to another. All this was admirable, he felt; but there would be a bad moment when they emerged from the special atmosphere of the theatre into the street. He took another decision, grasped her arm firmly, and said: "We're going to have a drink before we do anything at all. It's a terrible evening out." Her arm felt resistant, but remained within his. It was raining outside, luckily. He directed her, authoritative: "No, not that pub. There's a nicer one around the corner." "But I like this pub," said Barbara. "We always use it."

"Of course you do," he said to himself. But in that pub there would be the stagehands, and probably James, and he'd lose contact with her. He'd become a *journalist* again. He took her firmly out of danger around two corners, into a pub he picked at random. A quick look around—no, they weren't there. At least, if there were people from the theatre, she showed no sign. She asked for a beer. He ordered her a double Scotch, which she accepted. Then, having won a dozen preliminary rounds already, he took time to think. Something was bothering him—what? It was what he had observed backstage, Barbara and James Poynter. Was she having an affair with him? Because, if so, it would all be much more difficult. He made himself see the two of them together, and thought with a jealousy surprisingly strong: *Yes, that's it.* Meantime, he sat looking at her, seeing himself look at her, *a man gazing in calm appreciation at a woman:* waiting for her to feel it and respond. She was examining the pub. Her white woollen suit was belted, and had a not unprovocative suggestion of being a uniform. Her flat yellow hair, hastily pushed back after work, was untidy. Her clear white skin, without any color, made her look tired. Not very exciting, at the moment, thought Graham, but he maintained his appreciative pose for when she would turn and see it. He knew what she would see: he was relying not only on the "warm, kindly" beam of his gaze, for this was merely a reinforcement of the impression he knew he made. He had black hair, a little grayed. His clothes were loose and bulky—masculine. His eyes were humorous and apprecia-tive. He was not, never had been, concerned to lessen the impression of being settled, married, dependable: the husband and father. On the contrary, he knew women found it reassuring.

When she at last turned she said, almost apologetic: "Would you mind if we sat down? I've been lugging great things around all day." She had spot-ted two empty chairs in a corner. So had he, and then rejected them because there were other people at the table. "But, my dear, of course!" They took the chairs, and then Barbara said: "If you'll excuse me a moment." She had remembered she needed makeup. He watched her go off, annoyed with him-self. She was tired; and he could have understood, protected, sheltered. He realized that in the other pub, with the people she had worked with all day, she would not have thought: "I must make myself up; I must be on show." That was for outsiders. She had not, until now, considered Graham an out-sider, because of his taking his chance to seem one of the working group in the theatre; but now he had thrown this opportunity away. She returned armored. Her hair was sleek, no longer defenseless. And she had made up her eyes. Her eyebrows were untouched, pale gold streaks above the brilliant green eyes whose lashes were blackened. Rather good, he thought, the con-trast. Yes, but the moment had gone when he could say: did you know you had a smudge on your cheek? Or: my dear girl—pushing her hair back with the edge of a brotherly hand. In fact, unless he was careful, he'd be back at starting point.

He remarked: "That emerald is very cunning"—smiling into her eyes.

She smiled politely, and said: "It's not cunning; it's an accident. It was my grandmother's." She flirted her hand lightly by her face, though, smiling. But that was something she had done before, to a compliment she had had before, and often. It was all social; she had become social entirely. She remarked: "Didn't you say it was half-past 9:00 we had to record?"

"My dear Barbara, we've got two hours. We'll have another drink or two, then I'll ask you a couple of questions, then we'll drop down to the studio and get it over, and then we'll have a comfortable supper."

"I'd rather eat now, if you don't mind. I had no lunch, and I'm really hungry."

"But, my dear, of course." He was angry. Just as he had been surprised by his real jealousy over James, so now he was thrown off balance by his anger: he had been counting on the long quiet dinner afterward to establish intimacy. "Finish your drink and I'll take you to Nott's." Nott's was expensive. He glanced at her assessingly as he mentioned it. She said: "I wonder if you know Butler's? It's good and it's rather close." Butler's was good, and it was cheap, and he gave her a good mark for liking it. But Nott's it was going to be. "My dear, we'll get into a taxi and be at Nott's in a moment. Don't worry."

She obediently got to her feet: the way she did it made him understand how badly he had slipped. She was saying to herself: very well, he's like that; all right, I'll do what he wants and get it over with...

He took her arm in the pub doorway. It was polite within his. Outside, it drizzled. No taxi. He was having bad luck now. They walked in silence to the end of the street. There Barbara glanced into a side street where a sign said Butler's. Not to remind him of it; on the contrary, she concealed the glance. And here she was, entirely at his disposal; they might never have shared the comradely moment in the theatre.

They walked half a mile to Nott's. No taxis. She made conversation: this was, he saw, to cover any embarrassment he might feel because of a half-mile walk through rain when she was tired. She was talking about some theory to do with the theatre, with designs for theatre construction. He heard himself saying repeatedly: yes, yes, yes. He thought about Nott's, how to get things right when they reached Nott's. There he took the headwaiter aside, gave him a pound, and instructions. They were put in a corner. Large Scotches appeared. The menus were spread. "And now, my dear," he said, "I apologize for dragging you here, but I hope you'll think it's worth it."

"Oh, it's charming. I've always liked it. It's just that..." She stopped herself saying: it's such a long way. She smiled at him, raising her glass, and said: "It's one of my very favorite places, and I'm glad you dragged me here." Her voice was flat with tiredness. All this was appalling; he knew it;

and he sat thinking how to retrieve his position. Meanwhile, she fingered the menu. The headwaiter took the order, but Graham made a gesture which said: wait a moment. He wanted the Scotch to take effect before she ate. But she saw his silent order; and, without annoyance or reproach, leaned forward to say, sounding patient: "Graham, please, I've got to eat. You don't want me drunk when you interview me, do you?"

"They are bringing it as fast as they can," he said, making it sound as if she were greedy. He looked neither at the headwaiter nor at Barbara. He noted in himself, as he slipped further and further away from contact with her, a cold determination growing in him, one apart from, apparently, any conscious act of will. Come what may, if it took all night, he'd be in her bed before morning. And now, seeing the small pale face with the enormous green eyes, it was for the first time that he imagined her in his arms. It struck him as strange that although he had said *Yes, that one* weeks ago, it was only now that he imagined her as a sensual experience. Now he did, so strongly that he could only glance at her, and then away toward the waiters who were bringing food.

"Thank the Lord," said Barbara, and all at once her voice was gay and intimate. "Thank heavens. Thank every power that is…" She was making fun of her own exaggeration; and, as he saw, because she wanted to put him at his ease after his boorishness over delaying the food. (She hadn't been taken in, he saw, humiliated, disliking her.) "Thank all the Gods of Nott's," she went on, "because if I hadn't eaten inside five minutes I'd have died, I tell you." With which she picked up her knife and fork and began on her steak. He poured wine, smiling with her, thinking that *this* moment of closeness he would not throw away. He watched her frank hunger as she ate, and thought: sensual—it's strange I hadn't wondered whether she would be or not.

"Now," she said finally, sitting back, having taken the edge off her hunger. "Let's get to work."

He said: "I've thought it over very carefully—how to present you. We must get away from that old chestnut: Miss Coles, how extraordinary for a woman to be so versatile in her work…I hope you agree?" This was his trump. He had noted, when he saw her on television, her polite smile when this note was struck. (The smile he had seen so often tonight.) This smile said: all right, if you *have* to be stupid, what can I do?

Now she laughed and said: "What a relief. I was afraid you were going to do the same thing."

"Good. Now you eat and I'll talk."

In his carefully prepared monologue he spoke of the different styles of theatre she had shown herself mistress of, but not directly: he was flattering her on the breadth of her experience; the complexity of her character, as shown in her work. She ate steadily, her face showing nothing. At last she asked: "And how did you plan to introduce this?"

He had meant to spring that on her as a surprise, something like: Miss Coles, a surprisingly young woman for what she has accomplished (she was thirty? thirty-two?) and a very attractive one...Perhaps I can give you an idea of what she's like if I say she could be taken for the film star Marie Carletta...The Carletta was a strong earthy blonde, known to be intellectual. He now saw he could not possibly say this: he could imagine her cool look if he did.

She went on: "Do you mind if we get away from all that—my manifold talents and so on?" He felt himself stiffen with annoyance; particularly because this was not an accusation. He saw she did not think him worth one. She had assessed him: this is the kind of man who uses this kind of flattery and therefore...It made him angrier that she did not even trouble to say: why did you do exactly what you promised you wouldn't? She was being invincibly polite, trying to conceal her patience with his stupidity.

"After all," she was saying, "it is a stage designer's job to design what comes up. Would anyone take...let's say Johnnie Cranmore"—another stage-designer—"on to the air or television and say: how very versatile you are because you did that musical about Java last month and a modern play about Irish laborers this?"

He battened down his anger. "My dear Barbara, I'm sorry. I didn't realize that what I said would sound just like the mixture as before. So what shall we talk about?"

"What I was saying as we walked to the restaurant: can we get away from the personal stuff?"

Now he almost panicked. Then, thank God, he laughed from nervousness, for she laughed too and said: "You didn't hear one word I said."

"No, I didn't. I was frightened you were going to be furious because I made you walk so far when you were tired."

They laughed together, back to where they had been in the theatre. He leaned over, took her hand, kissed it. He said: "Tell me again." He thought: damn, now she's going to be earnest and intellectual.

But he understood he had been stupid. He had forgotten himself at twenty—or, for that matter, at thirty; forgotten one could live inside an idea, a set of ideas, with enthusiasm. For in talking about her ideas (also the ideas of the people she worked with) for a new theatre, a new style of theatre, she was as she had been with her colleagues over the sketches or the blue material. She was easy, informal, almost chattering. This was how, he remembered, one talked about ideas that were a breath of life. The ideas, he thought, were intelligent enough; and he would agree with them, with her, if he believed it mattered a damn one way or another, if any of these enthusiasms mattered a damn. But at least he now had the key; he knew what to do. At the end of not more than half an hour, they were again two professionals, talking about ideas they shared.

At last he said: "My dear Barbara, do you realize the impossible position you're putting me in? Margaret Ruyen, who runs this program, is determined to do you personally. The poor woman hasn't got a serious thought in her head."

Barbara frowned. He put his hand on hers, teasing her for the frown. "No, wait, trust me. We'll circumvent her." She smiled. In fact, Margaret Ruyen had left it all to him, had said nothing about Miss Coles.

"They aren't very bright—the brass," he said. "Well, never mind: we'll work out what we want, do it, and it'll be a *fait accompli*."

"Thank you. What a relief. How lucky I was to be given you to interview me." She was relaxed now, because of the whiskey, the food, the wine, above all because of this new complicity against Margaret Ruyen. It would all be easy. Over coffee, they worked out five or six questions, and then took a taxi through rain to the studios. He noted that the cold necessity to have her, to make her, to beat her down, had left him. He was even seeing himself, as the evening ended, kissing her on the cheek and going home to his wife. This comradeship was extraordinarily pleasant. It was balm to the wound he had not known he carried until that evening, when he had had to accept the justice of the word *journalist*. He felt he could talk forever about the state of the theatre, its finances, the stupidity of the government, the philistinism of…

At the studios he was careful to make a joke so that they walked in on the laugh. He was careful that the interview began at once, without conversation with Margaret Ruyen; and that, from the moment the green light went on, his voice lost its easy familiarity. He made sure that not one personal note was struck during the interview. Afterward, Margaret Ruyen, who was pleased, came forward to say so; but he took her aside to say that Miss Coles was tired and needed to be taken home at once. He knew this must look to Barbara as if he were squaring a producer who had been expecting a different interview. He led Barbara off, her hand held tight in his against his side.

"Well," he said, "we've done it, and I don't think she knows what hit her."

"Thank you," she said. "It really was pleasant to talk about something sensible for once."

He kissed her lightly on the mouth. She returned it, smiling. By now he felt sure that the mood need not slip again.

"There are two things we can do," he said. "You can come to my club and have a drink. Or I can drive you home and you can give me a drink. I have to go past you."

"Where do you live?"

"Wimbledon." He lived, in fact, at Highgate; but she lived in Fulham. He was taking another chance, but by the time she found out they would be in a position to laugh over his ruse.

"Good," she said. "You can drop me home then. I have to get up early." He made no comment. In the taxi he took her hand; it was heavy in his, and he asked: "Does James slave-drive you?"

"I didn't realize you knew him. No, he doesn't."

"I don't know him intimately. What's he like to work with?"

"Wonderful," she said at once. "There's no one I enjoy working with more."

Jealousy spurted in him. He could not help himself: "Are you having an affair with him?"

"No, I'm not."

"He's very attractive," he said, with a chuckle of wordly complicity. She said nothing, and he insisted: "If I were a woman I'd have an affair with James."

It seemed she might very well say nothing. But she remarked: "He's married."

His spirits rose in a swoop. It was the first stupid remark she had made. It was a remark of such staggering stupidity that...He let out a humoring snort of laughter, put his arm around her, kissed her, said: "My dear little Babs."

She said: "Why Babs?"

"Is that the prerogative of James? And"—he could not prevent himself adding—"of the stagehands?"

"I'm only called that at work." She was stiff inside his arm.

"My dear Barbara, then..." He waited for her to enlighten and explain, but she said nothing. Soon she moved out of his arm, on the pretext of lighting a cigarette. He lighted it for her. He noted that his determination to lay her, and at all costs, had come back. They were outside her house. He said, quickly: "And now, Barbara, you can make me a cup of coffee and give me a brandy." She hesitated; but he was out of the taxi, paying, opening the door for her. The house had no lights on, he noted. He said: "We'll be very quiet so as not to wake the children."

She turned her head slowly to look at him. She said, flat, replying to his real question: "My husband is away. As for the children, they're visiting friends tonight." She now went ahead of him to the door of the house. It was a small house, in a terrace of small and not very pretty houses. Inside a little, bright, intimate hall, she said: "I'll go and make some coffee. Then, my friend, you must go home because I'm very tired."

The my *friend* struck him deep, because he had become vulnerable during their comradeship. He said, gabbling: "You're annoyed with me. Please don't be. I'm sorry."

She smiled, from a cool distance. He saw, in the small light from the ceiling, her extraordinary eyes. "Green" eyes are hazel, are brown with green flecks, are even blue. Eyes are checkered, flawed, changing. Hers were solid green; he had never seen anything like them before. They were like very deep water. They were like…emeralds; or the absolute clarity of green in the depths of a tree in summer. And now, as she smiled almost perpendicularly up at him, he saw a darkness come over them. Darkness swallowed the clear green. She said: "I'm not in the least annoyed." It was as if she had yawned with boredom. "And now I'll get the things." She nodded at a white door. "In there," she said, and left him. He went into a long, very tidy white room that had a narrow bed in one corner. There was also a table covered with drawings, sketches, pencils. Tacked to the walls with drawing pins were swatches of colored stuffs. Two small chairs stood near a round coffee table: an area of comfort in the working room. He thought: I wouldn't like it if my wife had a room like this. I wonder what Barbara's husband?…He had not thought of her 'til now in relation to her husband, or to her children. Hard to imagine her with a frying pan in her hand or, for that matter, cosy in the double bed.

A noise outside: he hastily arranged himself, leaning with one arm on the mantelpiece. She came in with a small tray that had cups, glasses, brandy, coffeepot. She looked abstracted. Graham was on the whole flattered by this: it probably meant she was at ease in his presence. He realized he was a little tight and rather tired. Of course, she was tired, too; that was why she was vague. He remembered that earlier that evening he had lost a chance by not using her tiredness. Well, now, if he were intelligent…She was about to pour coffee. He firmly took the coffeepot out of her hand, and nodded at a chair.

Smiling, she obeyed him. "That's better," he said. He poured coffee, poured brandy, and pulled the table toward her. She watched him. Then he took her hand, kissed it, patted it, laid it down gently. Yes, he thought, I did that well.

Now, a problem. He wanted to be closer to her, but she was fitted into a damned silly little chair that had arms. If he were to sit by her on the floor?—but no. For him, the big, bulky, reassuring man, there could be no casual gestures, no informal postures. Suppose I scoop her out of the chair onto the bed? He drank his coffee as he plotted. Yes, he'd carry her to the bed; but not yet.

"Graham," she said, setting down her cup. She was, he saw with annoyance, looking tolerant. "Graham, in about half an hour I want to be in bed and asleep."

As she said this, she offered him a smile of amusement at this situation—man and woman maneuvering; the great comic situation. And with part of himself he could have shared it. Almost, he smiled with her, laughed. (Not 'til days later did he exclaim to himself: Lord what a mistake I made, not to share the joke with her then: that was where I went seriously wrong.) But he could not smile. His face was frozen with a stiff pride. Not because she had been watching him plot; the amusement she now offered him took the sting out of that; but because of his revived determination that he was going to have his own way, he was going to have her. He was not going home. But he felt that he held a bunch of keys, and did not know which one to choose.

He lifted the second small chair opposite to Barbara, moving aside the coffee table for this purpose. He sat in this chair, leaned forward, took her two hands, and said: "My dear, don't make me go home yet, don't, I beg you." The trouble was, nothing had happened all evening that could be felt to lead up to these words and his tone—simple, dignified, human being pleading with human being for surcease. He saw himself leaning forward, his big hands swallowing her small ones; he saw his face, warm with the appeal. And he realized he had meant the words he used. They were nothing more than what he felt. He wanted to stay with her because she wanted him to, because he was her colleague, a fellow-worker in the arts. He needed this desperately. But she was examining him, curious rather than surprised, and from a critical distance. He heard himself saying: "If James were here, I wonder what you'd do?" His voice was aggrieved; he saw the sudden dark descend over her eyes, and she said: "Graham, would you like some more coffee before you go?"

He said: "I've been wanting to meet you for years. I know a good many people who know you."

She leaned forward, poured herself a little more brandy, sat back, holding the glass between her two palms on her chest.

An odd gesture: Graham felt that this vessel she was cherishing between her hands was herself. A patient, long-suffering gesture. He thought of various men who had mentioned her. He thought of Dick Mannheim, wavered, panicked, said: "For instance, Dick Mannheim."

And now, at the name, an emotion lighted her eyes. What was it? He went on, deliberately testing this emotion, adding to it: "I had dinner with him last week—oh, quite by chance!—and he was talking about you."

"Was he?"

He remembered he had thought her sullen, all those years ago. Now she seemed defensive, and she frowned. He said: "In fact, he spent most of the evening talking about you."

She said in short, breathless sentences, which he realized were due to anger: "I can very well imagine what he says. But surely you can't think I enjoy being reminded that…" She broke off, resenting him, he saw, because he forced her down onto a level she despised. But it was not his level either: it was all her fault, all hers! He couldn't remember not being in control of a situation with a woman for years. Again he felt like a man teetering on a tightrope. He said, trying to make good use of Dick Mannheim, even at this late hour: "Of course, he's a charming boy, but not a man at all."

She looked at him, silent, guarding her brandy glass against her breasts.

"Unless appearances are totally deceptive, of course." He could not resist probing, even though he knew it was fatal.

She said nothing.

"Do you know, you're supposed to have had the great affair with Dick Mannheim?" he exclaimed, making this an amused expostulation against the fools who could believe it.

"So I am told." She set down her glass. "And now," she said, standing up, dismissing him. He lost his head, took a step forward, grabbed her in his arms, and groaned: "Barbara!"

She turned her face this way and that under his kisses. He snatched a diagnostic look at her expression—it was still patient. He placed his lips against her neck, groaned "Barbara" again, and waited. She would have to do something. Fight free, respond, something. She did nothing at all. At last she said: "For the Lord's sake, Graham!" She sounded amused: he was again being offered amusement. If he shared it with her, it would be the end of this chance to have her. He clamped his mouth over hers, silencing her. She did not fight him off so much as blow him off. Her mouth treated his attacking mouth as a woman blows and laughs in water, puffing off waves or spray with a laugh, turning aside her head. It was a gesture half annoyance, half humor. He continued to kiss her while she moved her head and face about under the kisses as if they were small attacking waves.

And so began what, when he looked back on it afterward, was the most embarrassing experience of his life. Even at the time he was appalled, hating her for his ineptitude. For he held her there for what must have been nearly half an hour. She was much shorter than he; he had to bend, and his neck ached. He held her rigid, his thighs on either side of hers, her arms clamped to her side in a bear's hug. She was unable to move, except for her head. When his mouth ground hers open and his tongue moved and writhed inside it, she still remained passive. And he could not stop himself. While with his intelligence he watched this ridiculous scene, he was determined to go on, because sooner or later her body must soften in wanting his. And he could not stop because he could not face the horror of the moment when he set her free and she looked at him. And he hated her more, every moment. Catching glimpses of her great green eyes, open and dismal beneath his, he knew he had never disliked anything more than those "jewelled" eyes. They were repulsive to him. It occurred to him at last that, even if by now she wanted him, he wouldn't know it, because she was not able to move at all. He cautiously loosened his hold so that she had an inch or so leeway. She remained quite passive. As if, he thought derisively, she had read or been told that the way to incite men maddened by lust was to fight them. He found he was thinking: stupid cow, so you imagine I find you attractive, do you? You've got the conceit to think that!

The sheer, raving insanity of this thought hit him, opened his arms, his thighs, and lifted his tongue out of her mouth. She stepped back, wiping her mouth with the back of her hand, and stood dazed with incredulity. The embarrassment that lay in wait for him nearly engulfed him, but he let anger postpone it. She said, positively apologetic, even, at this moment, humorous: "You're crazy, Graham. What's the matter, are you drunk? You don't seem drunk. You don't even find me attractive."

The blood of hatred went to his head and he gripped her again. Now she had got her face firmly twisted away so that he could not reach her mouth, and she repeated steadily as he kissed the parts of her cheeks and neck that were available to him: "Graham, let me go, do let me go, Graham." She went on saying this; he went on squeezing, grinding, kissing, and licking. It might go on all night: it was a sheer contest of wills, nothing else. He thought: it's only a really masculine woman who wouldn't have given in by now out of sheer decency of the flesh! One thing he knew, however: that she would be in that bed, in his arms, and very soon. He let her go, but said: "I'm going to sleep with you tonight. You know that, don't you?"

She leaned with one hand on the mantelpiece to steady herself. Her face was colorless, since he had licked all the makeup off. She seemed quite different: small and defenseless with her large mouth pale now, her smudged green eyes fringed with gold. For the first time, he felt what she must have supposed he had felt hours ago. Seeing the damp flesh of her small face, he felt kinship, intimacy with her; he felt intimacy of the flesh, the affection and good humor of sensuality. He felt she was flesh of his flesh, his sister in the flesh. He felt desire for her, instead of the will to have her; and because of this was ashamed of the farce he had been playing. Now he desired simply to take her into bed in the affection of his senses.

She said: "What on earth am I supposed to do? Telephone for the police, or what?" He was hurt that she still addressed the man who had ground her into sulky apathy; she was not addressing him at all.

She said: "Or scream for the neighbors, is that what you want?"

The gold-fringed eyes were almost black, because of the depth of the shadow of boredom over them. She was bored and weary to the point of falling to the floor; he could see that.

He said: "I'm going to sleep with you."

"But how can you possibly want to?"—a reasonable, a civilized demand addressed to a man who (he could see) she believed would respond to it. She said: "You know I don't want to, and I know you don't really give a damn one way or the other."

He was stung back into being the boor because she had not the intelligence to see that the boor no longer existed, because she could not see that this was a man who wanted her in a way which she must respond to.

There she stood, supporting herself with one hand, looking small and white and exhausted, and utterly incredulous. She was going to turn and walk off out of simple incredulity. "Do you think I don't mean it?" he demanded. She made a movement—she was on the point of going away. His hand shot out on its own volition and grasped her wrist. She frowned. His other hand grasped her other wrist. His body hove up against hers to start the pressure of a new embrace. Before it could, she said: "Oh Lord, no, I'm not going through all that again. Right, then."

"What do you mean, right, then?" he demanded.

She said: "You're going to sleep with me. Okay. Anything rather than go through that again. Shall we get it over with?"

He grinned, saying in silence: no, darling; oh, no, you don't. I don't care what words you use; I'm going to have you now and that's all there is to it.

She shrugged. The contempt, the weariness of it, had no effect on him, because he was now again hating her so much that wanting her was like needing to kill something or someone.

She took her clothes off as if she were going to bed by herself: her jacket, skirt, petticoat. She stood in white bra and panties, a rather solid girl, brown-skinned still from the summer. He felt a flash of affection for the brown girl with her loose yellow hair as she stood naked. She got into bed and lay there, while the green eyes looked at him in civilized appeal: are you really going through with this? Do you have to? Yes, his eyes said back: I do have to. She shifted her gaze aside, to the wall, saying silently: well, if you want to take me without any desire at all on my part, then go ahead, if you're not ashamed. He was not ashamed because he was maintaining the flame of hate for her which he knew quite well was all that stood between him and shame. He took off his clothes and got into bed beside her. As he did so, knowing he was putting himself in the position of raping a woman who was making it elaborately clear she bored him, his flesh subsided completely, sad, and full of reproach because a few moments ago it was reaching out for his sister whom he could have made happy. He lay on his side by her, secretly at work on himself, while he supported himself across her body on his elbow, using the free hand to manipulate her breasts. He saw that she gritted her teeth against his touch. At least she could not know that after all this fuss he was not potent.

In order to incite himself, he clasped her again. She felt his smallness, writhed free of him, sat up and said: "Lie down."

She seemed to have switched on, with the determination to *get it all over with*, a sensual good humor, a patience. He lay down. She squatted beside him, the light from the ceiling blooming on her brown shoulders, her flat fair hair falling over her face. But she would not look at his face. Like a bored, skilled wife she was; or like a prostitute. She administered to him; she was setting herself to please him. Yes, he thought, she's sensual, or she could be. Meanwhile she was succeeding in defeating the reluctance of his flesh, which was the tender token of a possible desire for her, by using a cold skill that was the result of her contempt for him. Just as he decided, Right, it's enough, now I shall have her properly, she made him come. It was not a trick, to hurry or cheat him; what defeated him was her transparent thought: yes, that's what he's worth.

Then, having succeeded, and waited for a moment or two, she stood up, naked, her body speaking to him a language quite different from that of her green, bored eyes. He watched the slight movement of her shoulders: a just-checked shrug. She went out of the room: then came the sound of running water.

Soon she returned in a white dressing-gown, carrying a yellow towel. She handed him the towel, looking away in politeness as he used it. "Are you going home now?" she inquired hopefully.

"No, I'm not." He believed that he would have to start fighting her again, but she lay down beside him, not touching him (he could feel the distaste of her flesh for his). He thought: very well, my dear, but there's a lot of the night left yet. He said aloud: "I'm going to have you properly tonight." She said nothing, lay silent, yawned. Then she remarked consolingly, and he could have laughed outright from sheer surprise: "Those were hardly conducive circumstances for making love." She was consoling him. He hated her for it. A proper little slut: I force her into bed, she doesn't want me, but she still has to make me feel good, like a prostitute. But even while he hated her he responded in kind, from the habit of sexual generosity. "It's because of my admiration for you, because...After all, I was holding in my arms one of the thousand women."

A pause. "The thousand?" she asked, carefully.

"The thousand special women."

"In Britain or in the world? You choose them for their brains, their beauty—what?"

"Whatever it is that makes them outstanding," he said, offering her a compliment.

"Well," she remarked at last, inciting him to be amused again, "I hoped that at least there's a short list you can say I'm on, for politeness' sake."

He did not reply, for he was suddenly aware of being sleepy. He was still telling himself that he must stay awake when he was slowly waking and it was morning. It was about 8:00. Barbara was not there. He thought: my God! What on earth shall I tell my wife? Where was Barbara? He remembered the ridiculous scenes of last night and nearly succumbed to shame. Then he thought, reviving anger: if she didn't sleep beside me here I'll never forgive her...He sat up quietly, determined to go through the house until he found her and, having found her, possessed her. Then the door opened and she came in. She was fully dressed in a green suit, her hair done, her eyes made up. She carried a tray of coffee which she set down beside the bed.

He was conscious of his big loose hairy body, half uncovered. He said to himself that he was not going to lie in bed, naked, while she was dressed. He said: "Have you got a gown of some kind?" She handed him, without speaking, a towel. "The bathroom's second on the left." She went out. He followed, the towel around him. Everything in this house was gay, intimate—not at all like her efficient working room. He wanted to find out where she had slept, and opened the first door. It was the kitchen, and she was in it, putting a brown earthenware dish into the oven. "The next door," said Barbara. He went hastily past the second door, and opened (he hoped quietly) the third. It was a cupboard full of linen. "This door," said Barbara, behind him.

"So all right then, where did you sleep?"

"What's it to do with you? Upstairs, in my own bed. Now, if you have everything, I'll say good-bye, I want to get to the theatre."

"I'll take you," he said at once. He saw again the movement of her eyes, the dark swallowing the light in deadly boredom. "I'll take you," he insisted.

"I'd prefer to go by myself." Then she smiled. "However, you'll take me. Then you'll make a point of coming right in, so that James and everyone can see. That's what you want to take me for, isn't it?"

He hated her, finally, and quite simply, for her intelligence; that not once had he got away with anything, that she had been watching, since they had met yesterday, every movement of his campaign for her. However, some fate or inner urge over which he had no control made him say sentimentally: "My dear, you must see that I'd like at least to take you to your work."

"Not at all: have it on me," she said, giving him the lie direct. She went past him to the room he had slept in. "I shall be leaving in ten minutes," she said.

He took a shower, fast. When he returned, the workroom was already tidied, the bed made, all signs of the night gone. Also, there were no signs of the coffee she had brought in for him. He did not like to ask for it for fear of an outright refusal. Besides, she was ready, her coat on, her handbag under her arm. He went, without a word, to the front door, and she came after him, silent.

He could see that every fiber of her body signalled a simple message: oh God, for the moment when I can be rid of this boor! She was nothing but a slut, he thought.

A taxi came. In it she sat as far away from him as she could. He thought of what he should say to his wife.

Outside the theatre she remarked: "You could drop me here, if you liked." It was not a plea; she was too proud for that. "I'll take you in," he said, and saw her thinking: very well, I'll go through with it to shame him. He was determined to take her in and hand her over to her colleagues, and he was afraid she would give him the slip. But, far from playing it down, she seemed determined to play it his way. At the stage door, she said to the door-man: "This is Mr. Spence, Tom—do you remember? Mr. Spence from last night." "Good morning, Babs," said the man, examining Graham politely, as he had been ordered to do.

Barbara walked on to the door to the stage, opened it, held it open for him. He went in first, then held the door for her. Together they entered the cavernous, littered, badly lighted place. She called out: "James, James!" A man's voice answered from the front of the house: "Here, Babs. Why are you so late?"

The auditorium opened before them, darkish, silent, except for an early morning busyness of charwomen. A vacuum cleaner roared, smally, some-where close. A couple of stagehands were looking up at a drop which had a design of blue and green spirals. James stood with his back to the auditorium, smoking. "You're late, Babs," he said again. He saw Graham behind her and nodded. Barbara and James kissed. Barbara said, giving allowance to every syllable: "You remember Mr. Spence from last night?" James nodded a greet-ing. Barbara stood beside him, and they looked together up at the blue-and-green backdrop. Then Barbara looked again at Graham, asking silently: all right, now, isn't that enough? He could see her eyes, convulsed with boredom.

He said: "'Bye, Babs. 'Bye, James. I'll ring you, Babs." She ignored him. He walked off slowly, listening for what might be said. For instance: "Babs, for God's sake, what are you doing with him?" Or she might say: "Are you wondering about Graham Spence? Let me explain."

Graham passed the stagehands who, he could have sworn, didn't recog-nize him. Then at last he heard James's voice to Barbara: "It's no good, Babs. I know you're enamored of that particular shade of blue, but do have another look at it, there's a good girl." Graham left the stage, walked past the office where the doorman sat reading a newspaper. The man looked up, nodded, went back to his paper. Graham went to find a taxi, reminding himself to think up something convincing before telephoning his wife.

Luckily, he had an excuse not to be at home that day, for this evening he had to interview a young man for television about his new novel.

E.L. Doctorow

E.L. Doctorow was born in New York City in 1931. Doctorow attended the Bronx High School of Science and received a B.A. with honors in 1952 from Kenyon College, studying under *The Kenyon Review*–founder John Crowe Ransom. He continued his education at Columbia University, but was drafted into the army and spent two years in Germany (1953–55). After spending time as a senior editor for New American Library from 1959–64, he assumed the role of editor in chief at Dial Press. By this time his first novel, *Welcome to Hard Times,* had appeared. After five years as an editor, Doctorow was appointed writer in residence at the University of California-Irvine and went on to hold teaching positions at Sarah Lawrence, Princeton, and the Yale School of Drama, and currently holds the Glucksman Chair in American Letters at New York University. It was during the 1970s that Doctorow distinguished himself as a major presence in American fiction, with the publication *The Book of Daniel* in 1971 and *Ragtime* in 1975, which earned him his first National Book Critics Circle Award. He has gone on to publish such novels as *Loon Lake, World's Fair* (winner of the National Book Award)*, Billy Bathgate* (winner of the National Book Critics Circle Award), and *Waterworks*. *Ragtime* and *Billy Bathgate* were both turned into successful motion pictures. Doctorow currently serves on the Advisory Board for *The Kenyon Review*. This story from *Loon Lake* first appeared in *The Kenyon Review* in 1979.

Loon Lake *(1979)*

by E.L. Doctorow
translated by Clementine Rabassa

If you listen the small splash is beaver.
As beaver swim their fur lays back and their heads elongate
and a true imperial cruelty shines from their eyes.
They're rodents after all
Beaver otter weasel mink and rat
rodent species of the Adirondacks
and they redistrict the world.
They go after the young trees and bring them down—
whole hillsides collapse in the lake when they're through.
They make their lodges of skinned poles, mud and boughs
like igloos of dark wet wood
and they enter and exit under water and build shelves
out of the water for the babies.
And when the mahogany speedboat goes by trimmed
    with silver horns
in Loon Lake, in the Adirondacks
the waves of the lake inside the beaver lodge lap gently
against the children's feet in the darkness.

Loon Lake
was once the destination of private railroad cars
rocking on a single track
through forests of pine and spruce and hemlock
branches and fronds brushing the windows of cut glass
while inside incandescent bulbs flickered
in frosted glass chimneys over double beds
and liquor bottles trembled in their recessed cabinet fittings
above card tables of green baize
in rooms entered through narrow doors with brass latches.

If you step on a twig in a soft bed of pine needles
under an ancient stand of this wilderness
you will make no sound
all due respect to the Indians of Loon Lake

the Adirondack nations, with all due respect.
What a clear cold life it must have been.
Everyone knew where they stood
chiefs or children or malcontents
and every village had its lovers whom no one wanted
who sometimes lay down because of that
with a last self pitying look at Loon Lake
before intoning their death prayers
and beginning the difficult business of dying by will
on the dry hummocks of pine needles.
The loons they heard were the loons we hear today
cries to distract the dying
loons diving into the cold black lake
and diving back out again in a whorl of clinging water
clinging like importuning spirits
fingers shattering in spray
feeling up the wing along the rounded body of the
thrillingly exerting loon
beaking a fish
rising to the moon streamlined
its loon eyes round and red.
A doomed Indian would hear them at night in their diving
and hear their cry not as triumph or as rage
or the insane compatibility with the earth
attributed to birds of prey
but in protest against falling
of having to fall into that black water
and struggle up from it again and again
the water kissing and pawing and whispering
the most horrible promises
the awful presumptuousness of the water
squeezing the eyes out of the head
floating the lungs out on the beak which clamps on them
like wriggling fish
extruding all organs and waste matter
turning the bird inside out
which the Indian sees is what death is
the environment exchanging itself for the being.
And there are stars where that happens too in space

in the black space some railroad journeys above the Adirondacks.
Well anyway in the summer of 1937
a chilling summer high in the eastern mountains
a group of people arrived at a rich man's camp
in his private railway car
the men in fedoras and dark double breasted suits
and the women in silver fox and cloche hats
sheer stockings of Japanese silk
and dresses that clung to them in the mountain air.
They shivered from the station to the camp
in an open carriage drawn by two horses.
It was the clearest night in the heavens
and the silhouettes of the jagged pines on the mountaintop
in the moonlight looked like arrowheads
looked like the graves of heroic Indians.

The old man who was their host
an industrialist of enormous wealth
over the years had welcomed to his camp
financiers politicians screen stars
european princes boxing champions and
conductors of major orchestras
all of whom were honored to sign the guest book.
Occasionally for complicated reasons
he received persons strangely undistinguished.
His camp was a long log building of two stories
on a hill overlooking Loon Lake.
There was a great rustic entrance hall
with a wide staircase of halved logs
and a balustrade made of scraped saplings
a living room as large as a hotel lobby
with walls papered in birch bark
and hung with the mounted heads of deer and elk
and with modern leather sofas with rounded corners
and a great warming fireplace of native stone
big enough to roast an ox.
It was a fine manor house lacking nothing
with suites of bedrooms each with its own shade porch
and the most discreet staff of cooks and maids and porters

but designated a camp because its decor was rough hewn.
And this party of visitors were romantic gangsters
thieves, extortionists and murderers of the lower class
and their women who might or might not be whores.
The old man welcomed them warmly
enjoying their responses to his camp
admiring the women in their tight dresses and red lips
relishing the having of them there so out of place
at Loon Lake.
The first morning of their visit
he led everyone down the hill
to give them rides in his biggest speedboat
a long mahogany chriscraft with a powerful inboard
that resonantly shook the water as she idled.
He handed them each a woolen poncho with a hood
and told them the ride was fast and cold
but still they were not prepared when underway
he opened up the throttle
and the boat reared in the water like Buck Jones's horse.
The women shrieked and gripped the gangsters' arms
and spray stinging like ice coated their faces
while the small flag at the stern snapped like a machine gun.
And one of the men lipping an unlit cigarette
felt it whipped away by the wind.
He turned and saw it sail over the wake
where a loon appeared from nowhere
beaked it before it hit the water
and rose back into the sky above the mountain.

The old man rode them around Loon Lake, its islands
through channels where beaver had built their lodges
and everything they saw the trees the mountains
the water and even the land they couldn't see under the water
was what he owned.
And then he brought them in throttling down
and the boat was awash in a rush of foam
like the outspread wings of a waterbird coming to rest
and slowly sedately gliding into the boathouse

a log building extending over the lake.
Two other mahogany boats of different lengths
were tied there each in its berth
and racks of canoes and guide boats upside down
and on walls paddles hanging from brackets
and fishing rods and showshoes for some strange reason.
And not a gangster there did not reflect
how this dark boathouse with its canals
and hollow sounding deck floors
was bigger than the home his family lived in
when he was a kid, as big as the orphans' home in fact.
But one gangster wanted to know about the lake
and its connecting lakes, the distance one could travel on them
as if he was planning a fast getaway.

Just disappearing around the corner out of sight
was the boathouse attendant.
And everyone walked up the hill for drinks and lunch.
Drinks were at twelve thirty and lunch at one thirty
after which, returning to their rooms
the guests found riding outfits laid across their beds
and boots in their right sizes all new.
At three they met each other at the stables
laughing at each other and being laughed at
and the stableman fitted them out with horses
what seemed to be dangerously high horses
and the sensation was particularly giddy when the horses
began to move without warning ignoring them up there in
    the saddles
threatening to launch with each bounce like a paddle ball.
And so each day the best gangster among them realized
there would be something to do they could not do well.

The unchecked walking horses made for the woods
no one was in the lead, the old man was not there
they were alone on these horses who took this wide trail
they seemed to know.
And the gangsters looked around for guidance

but there was none not even from the best gangster among them
and nobody laughed
they were busy maintaining themselves on the tops of these horses
stepping with their plodding footfall through the soft earth
of the wide trail.
By and by proceeding gently downhill they came
to another shore of the lake, of Loon Lake,
and the trees were cut down here and the cold sun shone.
They found themselves before an airplane hangar
with a concrete ramp sloping into the water.
As the horses stood there the hangar doors slid open
a man was pushing back each of the steel doors
although they saw only his arm and hand and shoetops.
And then from a grey cloud over the mountain
beyond the far end of the lake an airplane appeared
and made its descent in front of the mountain
growing larger as it came toward them
a green and white seaplane with a cowled engine and
    overhead wing.
It landed in the water with barely a splash
taxiing smartly with a feathery sound.
The horses nickered and stirred everyone held on
and the lead gangster said whoa boy, whoa boy
and the goddamn plane came right out of the water
up the ramp, water falling from its pontoons
the wheels in the pontoons leaving a wet track on the concrete
and nosed up to the open hangar
blowing up a cloud of dirt and noise.
The engine was cut and the cabin door opened
and putting her hands on the wing struts a woman jumped down
a small woman in trousers and a leather jacket and a silk scarf
and a leather helmet which she removed showing grey
    hair cut close
and she looked at them and nodded without smiling
and that was the old man's wife.

She strode off down the trail toward the big house
and they were not to see her again that day

neither at drinks which were at six thirty
nor dinner at seven thirty.
But her husband was a gracious host
attentive to the women particularly.
He revealed that she was a famous aviatrix
and some of them recognized her name from the newspapers.
He spoke proudly of her accomplishments
the races she won flying measured courses
marked by towers with checkered windsocks
and her endurance flights some of which
were still the record for a woman.
After dinner he talked vaguely of his life
his regret that so much of it was business.
He talked about the unrest in the country
and the peculiar mood of the workers
and he solicited the gangsters' views over brandy
of the likelihood of revolution.
And now he said rising I'm going to retire.
But you're still young said one of the gangsters
for the night the old man said with a smile
I mean I'm going to bed. Good night.

And when he went up the stairs of halved tree trunks
they all looked at each other and had nothing to say.
They were standing where the old man had left them
in their tux and black ties.
They had stood when he stood the women had stood when he
stood and quietly as they could they all went to their rooms
where the bedcovers had been turned back and the reading
    lamps lighted.
And in the room of the best gangster there
a slim and swarthy man with dark eyes, a short man
very well put together
there were doors leading to a screened porch
and he opened them and stood on the dark porch
and heard the night life of the forest and the lake
and the splash of the fish terrifyingly removed from Loon Lake.
He had long since run out of words

for his sickening recognition of real class
nervously insisting how swell it was.
He turned back into the room.
His girl was fingering the hand embroidered initials
in the center of the blanket.
They were the same initials on the bath towels
and on the cigarette box filled with fresh Luckies
and on the matchbooks and on the breastpockets of the pajamas
of every size stocked in the drawers
the same initials, the logo.

The gangster's girl was eighteen
and had had an abortion he knew nothing about.
She found something to criticize, one thing,
the single beds, and as she undressed
raising her knees, slipping off her shoes
unhooking her stockings from her garters
she spoke of the bloodlessness of the rich not believing it
while the gangster lay between the sheets in the initialled pajamas
arranging himself under the covers so that they were neat and tight
as if trying to take as little possession of the bed as possible
not wanting to appear to himself to threaten anything.
He locked his hands behind his head and ignored the girl
and lay in the dark not even smoking.
But at three that morning
there was a terrible howl
from the pack of wild dogs that ran in the mountains—
not wolves but dogs that had reverted
when their owners couldn't feed them any longer.
The old man had warned them this might happen
but the girl crept into the bed of the gangster
and he put his arm around her and held her
so that she would not slip off the edge
and they listened to the howling
and then the sound nearer to the house
of running dogs, of terrifying exertion
and then something gushing
in the gardens below the windows.

And they heard the soft separation
together with grunts and snorts and yelps
of flesh as it is fanged and lifted from a body.
Jesus, the girl said
and the gangster felt her breath on his collar bone
and smelled the jell in her hair, the sweetness of it
and felt the gathered dice of her shoulders
and her shivering and her cold hand on his stomach
underneath the waistband.

In the morning they joined the old man
on the sun terrace outside the dining room.
Halfway down the hill a handyman pushing a wheelbarrow
was just disappearing around a bend in the path.
I hope you weren't frightened the old man said they took a deer
and he turned surprisingly young blue eyes on the best
    gangster's girl.
Later that morning she saw on the hills in the sun
all around Lake Loon
patches of color where the trees were turning
and she went for a walk alone and in the woods she saw
in the orange and yellowing leaves of deciduous trees
the coming winter
imagining in these high mountains
snow falling like some astronomical disaster
and Loon Lake as the white hole of a monstrous meteor
and every branch of the evergreens all around
described with snow, each twig each needle
balancing a tiny snowfall precisely imitative of itself.

And at dinner she wore her white satin gown
with nothing underneath to ruin the lines
and the old man's wife came to dinner this night
clearly younger than her husband, trim and neat
with small beautifully groomed hands and still young shoulders and neck
but brackets at the corners of her mouth.
She talked to them politely with no condescension
and showed them in glass cases in the game room

trophies of air races she had won
small silver women pilots
silver cups and silver planes on pedestals.
Then still early in the evening she said goodnight
and that she had enjoyed meeting them.
They watched her go.
And after the old man retired
and all the gangsters and their women stood around
in their black ties and tux and long gowns
the best gangster's girl saw a large Victrola in the corner
of the big living room with its leather couches and
grand fireplace
the servants spirited away the coffee service
and the gangster's girl put on a record and commanded
everyone to dance.
And they danced to the Victrola music
they felt better they did the fox trot
and went to the liquor cabinet and broke open some scotch
and gin and they danced and smoked
the old man's cigarettes from the boxes on the tables
and the only light came from the big fire
and the women danced with one arm dangling holding
    empty glasses
and the gangsters nuzzled their shoulders
and their new shoes made slow sibilant rhythms
on the polished floors
as they danced in their tuxes and gowns of satin at Loon Lake
at Loon Lake
in the rich man's camp
in the mountains of the Adirondacks.

Julio Cortázar

Julio Cortázar was born in Brussels of Argentine parents in 1914. After World War I his family returned to Argentina, where he received a literature degree from the teachers college in Buenos Aires in 1935. For the next decade, Cortázar taught in secondary schools in several Argentine towns, eventually leaving teaching to become a literary translator for Argentine publishing houses, most significantly translating the complete prose works of Edgar Allan Poe. Always politically active, he refused a chair at the University of Buenos Aires because of his opposition to the Perón regime. In 1951, he moved to France, where he lived until his death, dividing his time between Paris and the provençal town of Saignon. Cortázar's routine for most of his years in France consisted of working for four months as a translator from French and English into Spanish for UNESCO and devoting the rest of the year to his writing and other loves such as the jazz trumpet. Heavily influenced by the surrealist movement, he published poems and plays in the thirties and forties but achieved his first major success with a book of stories, *Bestiario*, in 1951. His novel *Rayuela* (translated by Gregory Rabassa as *Hopscotch*) was widely praised and won Cortázar an enthusiastic international following. He went on to publish such books as *The Winners, All Fires the Fire,* and *Save Twilight* before his death in 1984. Cortázar's short story "Summer" appeared in the first issue of the new series of *The Kenyon Review* in 1979.

Summer *(1979)*

by Julio Cortázar

translated by Clementine Rabassa

In the late afternoon Florencio went down to the cabin with his little girl taking the back road full of holes and loose stones that only Mariano and Zulma were up to following in their jeep. Zulma opened the door for them, and Florencio thought that her eyes looked as if she had been peeling onions. Mariano appeared from the other room, he told them to come in, but Florencio only wanted to ask them to take care of the little girl until the next morning because he had to go to the coast on an urgent matter and there was nobody in the village he could ask to do him this favor. Of course, said Zulma, leave her, don't worry, we'll set up a bed for her here downstairs. Come on in and have a drink, Mariano insisted, it'll only take five minutes, but Florencio had left his car in the village square, he had to take off right away; he thanked them, kissed his little girl who had already spotted the stack of magazines on the bench. When the door closed, Zulma and Mariano looked at each other almost questioningly, as if everything had happened too fast. Mariano shrugged his shoulders and returned to his workshop where he was gluing an old chair; Zulma asked the little girl if she was hungry, she suggested she play with the magazines, in the closet there was a ball and a net for catching butterflies; the little girl said thank you and began to look at the magazines; Zulma watched her a moment while she prepared the artichokes for dinner that evening and thought she could let her play by herself.

Dusk fell early in the south now, they barely had a month left before returning to the capital and getting into that other life during the winter which, in any case, was only a continuation of this one, distantly together, amicably friends, respecting and performing the many trivial, delicate, conventional ceremonies of a couple, as now, when Mariano needed one of the burners to heat the glue jar and Zulma took the pot of potatoes off saying she'd finish cooking them later, and Mariano said thanks because the chair was almost ready and it would be better to do all the gluing in one application, but he had to heat the jar first, of course. The little girl was leafing through the magazines at the end of the large room that was used both as a kitchen and as a living room, Mariano looked in the pantry for some candy to give her; it was time to go out into the garden to have a drink as they watched night fall upon the hills. There was never anybody on the road, the first house in the village could barely be seen at the highest point; in front of them the slope kept on descending to the bottom of the valley which was already in the shadows. Go ahead and pour, I'll be right there, said Zulma. Everything was done in cyclical fashion, each thing in its time and a time for each thing, except for the little girl who had suddenly disturbed the pattern just a bit; a stool and a glass of milk for her, a stroke of her hair, and praise for how well she was behaving. The cigarettes, the swallows clustering above the cabin; everything went along repeating itself, fitting into the right slot, the chair must be almost dry by now, stuck together like that new day which had nothing new about it. The insignificant difference was the little girl that afternoon, as sometimes the mailman would draw them out of their solitude for a moment at midday with a letter for Mariano or Zulma that the addressee would receive and put away without saying a word. One more month of foreseeable repetitions, like rehearsals, and the jeep loaded to the top would take them back to the apartment in the capital, to the life that was only different in form, Zulma's group or Mariano's artist friends, afternoons in the stores for her and evenings in the cafes for Mariano, a coming-and-going separately although they always got together to perform the linking ceremonies, the morning kiss, the neutral programs in common, as now when Mariano offered her another drink and Zulma accepted with her eyes lost in the most distant hills that were tinted already in deep violet.

What would you like to have for supper, little one? Me? Anything you say, ma'am. She probably doesn't like artichokes, said Mariano. Yes, I like them, said the little girl, with oil and vinegar, but only a little salt because it burns. They laughed, they would make a special vinaigrette dressing for her. And boiled eggs, how do you like them? With a teaspoon, said the little girl. And only a little salt, because it burns, teased Mariano. Salt burns a lot, said the little girl, I give my doll her mashed potatoes without salt, today I didn't bring her because my daddy was in a hurry and wouldn't let me. It's going to be a lovely night, thought Zulma out loud, see how clear the air is towards the north. Yes, it won't be too hot, said Mariano bringing the chairs into the downstairs room and turning on the lamps next to the picture window that faced the valley. Automatically he also turned on the radio. Nixon is going to Peking, how about that, said Mariano. There's nothing sacred, said Zulma, and they both laughed at the same time. The little girl was into the magazines and marking the comic strip pages as though she planned to reread them.

Night arrived in between the insecticide Mariano was spraying in the bedroom upstairs and the perfume of an onion that Zulma cut while humming along with a pop tune on the radio. Midway through supper the little girl began to doze over the boiled egg; they joked with her, they prodded her to finish; Mariano had already prepared the cot for her with an inflatable mattress in the farthest corner of the kitchen so they wouldn't bother her if they stayed awhile in the room downstairs listening to records or reading. The little girl ate her peach and admitted she was sleepy. Go to bed, sweetie, said Zulma, don't forget if you have to tinkle, you only have to go upstairs, we'll leave the stairway light on. The little girl half asleep gave them a kiss on the cheek, but before she lay down she selected a magazine and placed it under the pillow. They're unbelievable, said Mariano, such an unattainable world and to think it once was ours, everybody's. Perhaps it's not so different, said Zulma, clearing the table, you too have your compulsions, the bottle of cologne on the left and the razor on the right, and as for me, forget it. But they weren't compulsions, thought Mariano, rather a response to death and nothingness, fixing things and times, establishing rituals and passages in opposition to chaos which was full of holes and smudges. Only now he no longer said it aloud, more and more there seemed to be less of a need to talk to Zulma, and Zulma didn't say anything either that might prompt an exchange of ideas. Take the coffee pot, I've already set the cups on the stool by the chimney. Check to see if there's any sugar left in the bowl, there's a new package in the pantry. I can't find the corkscrew, this bottle of rum has a good color, don't you think? Yes, a lovely color. Since you're going up, bring the cigarettes I left on the dresser. This rum is really good stuff. It's hot, don't you think so? Yes, it's stifling, we'd better not open the windows, the place will fill up with moths and mosquitoes.

When Zulma heard the first sound, Mariano was looking among the stack of records for a Beethoven sonata which he hadn't listened to that summer. He stood still with his hand in the air, he looked at Zulma. A noise as if on the stone steps of the garden, but nobody came to the cabin at that hour, nobody ever came at night. From the kitchen he switched on the lamp that illuminated the nearest part of the garden, saw no one and turned it off. Probably a dog looking around for something to eat, said Zulma. It sounded strange, almost like a snort, said Mariano. An enormous white blur lashed against the window. Zulma muffled a scream, Mariano, with his back towards her, turned around too late, the pane reflected only the pictures and furniture in the room. He had no time to ask anything, the snort resounded near the north wall; a whinny that was smothered just like Zulma's scream, her hands up to her mouth and pressing against the back wall, staring at the window. It's a horse, said Mariano, I hear his hooves, he's galloping through the garden. His mane, his lips, almost as if they were bleeding, an enormous white head was grazing the window; the horse barely looked at them, the white blotch was erased on the right, they heard his hooves again, an abrupt silence coming from the side of the stone steps, the neighing, the flight. But there are no horses in these parts, said Mariano, who had grabbed the bottle of rum by the neck before realizing it and putting it back again on the stool. He wants to come in, said Zulma, glued to the rear wall. Of course not, what a foolish idea, he probably escaped from some herd in the valley and headed for the light. I tell you, he wants to come in, he's rabid and wants to get inside. Horses don't get rabies, as far as I know, said Mariano, I think he's gone, I'll take a look from the upstairs window. No, please, stay here, I can still hear him, he's on the terrace steps, he's stomping on the plants, he'll be back, and what if he breaks the window and gets in? Don't be silly, what do you mean he'll break the window, said Mariano weakly, maybe if we turn off the lights he'll go away. I don't know, I don't know, said Zulma, sliding down until she was sitting on the stool, I heard how he whinnied, he's there upstairs. They heard the hooves coming down the steps, the irritated heavy snort against the door, Mariano thought he felt something like pressure on the door, a repeated rubbing, and Zulma ran to him screaming hysterically. He cast her off, not violently, extended his hand towards the light switch; in the dark (the only light still on was in the kitchen where the little girl was sleeping), the neighing and the hooves became louder, but the horse was no longer in front of the door; he could be heard back and forth in the garden. Mariano ran to turn out the kitchen light without even looking towards the corner where they had put the little girl to bed; he returned to put his arms around Zulma who was sobbing. He caressed her hair and face, asking her to be quiet so he could listen better. In the window the horse rubbed his head against the large pane, not too forcefully, the white blotch appeared transparent in the darkness; they sensed the horse looking inside, as though searching for something, but he could not see them any longer, and yet there he still was, whinnying and puffing, bolting abruptly from side to side.

Zulma's body slipped through Mariano's arms and he helped her sit on the stool again, propping her up against the wall. Don't move, don't say anything, he's leaving now, you'll see. He wants to come in, Zulma said feebly, I know he wants to come in, and what if he breaks the window, what's going to happen if he kicks it in? Sh, said Mariano, please shut up. He's going to come in, muttered Zulma. And I don't even have a shotgun, said Mariano, I'd blast five shots into his head, the son of a bitch. He's not there anymore, said Zulma, rising suddenly, I hear him above, if he sees the terrace door he might come in. It's shut tight, don't be afraid, remember in the dark he's not about to enter a house where he couldn't even move around, he's not that dumb. Oh yes, said Zulma, he wants to come in, he'll crush us against the walls, I know he wants to come in. Sh, repeated Mariano, who also was thinking about it, and could do nothing but wait with his back soaked in cold perspiration. Once again the hooves echoed upon the flagstone steps, and suddenly silence, the distant crickets, a bird high in a walnut tree.

Without turning on the light, now that the window let the night's vague clarity enter, Mariano filled a glass with rum and held it against Zulma's lips, forcing her to drink even though her teeth hit the glass, and the liquor spilled on her blouse; then holding the bottle by the neck he took a long swig and went to the kitchen to check on the little girl. With her hand under the pillow as if clutching the precious magazine, incredibly she was asleep and had heard nothing, she hardly seemed to be there while in the big room Zulma's sobbing broke every so often into a smothered hiccough, almost a shout. It's all over, it's over, said Mariano, sitting up against her and shaking her gently, it was nothing but a scare. He'll be back, said Zulma, her eyes nailed to the window. No, he's probably far off by now, no doubt he escaped from some herd down below. No horse does that, said Zulma, no horse tries to enter a house like that. It's strange, I'll grant you that, said Mariano, maybe we'd better take a look outside, I have the lantern right here. But Zulma had pressed herself against the wall, the idea of opening the door, of going out towards the white shadow that might be near, waiting under the trees, ready to charge. Look, if we don't check to see if he's gone, nobody will sleep tonight, said Mariano. Let's give him a little more time; meanwhile you go to bed, and I'll give you a tranquilizer; an extra dose, poor kid, you've certainly earned it.

Zulma ended up by accepting passively; without turning on the lights, they went towards the stairs and with his hand Mariano motioned towards the little girl asleep, but Zulma scarcely looked at her, she was climbing the stairs reeling, Mariano had to hold her as they entered the bedroom because she was about to bump into the doorframe. From the window that faced the eaves they looked at the stone steps, the highest terrace of the garden. You see, he's gone, said Mariano, fixing Zulma's pillow, watching her undress with mechanical gestures, staring at the window. He made her drink the drops, dabbed cologne on her neck and hands, gently lifted the sheet up to Zulma's shoulders as she closed her eyes and trembled. He wiped her cheeks, waited a moment and went downstairs to look for the lantern; carrying it unlit in one hand and an ax in the other, little by little he opened the door of the large room and went out to the lower terrace where he could get full view of the entire side of the house facing eastward; the night was identical to so many other summer nights, the crickets chirped in the distance, a frog let fall two alternating drops of sound. Not needing the lantern, Mariano saw the trampled lilac bush, the huge prints in the pansy bed, the flowerpot overturned at the bottom of the steps; so it wasn't an hallucination, and, of course, it was better that it not be; in the morning he would go with Florencio to check on the herds in the valley, they weren't going to get the upper hand so easily. Before going in he set the flowerpot straight, went up to the front trees and listened for a long while to the crickets and the frog; when he looked towards the house, Zulma was standing at the bedroom window, naked, motionless.

The little girl had not moved; Mariano went upstairs without making any noise and began to smoke next to Zulma. You see, he's gone, now we can sleep in peace, tomorrow we'll see. Little by little he led her towards the bed, undressed, stretched out on his back still smoking. Go to sleep, everything is all right, it was only an absurd fright. He stroked her hair, his fingers slid down to her shoulder, grazing her breasts lightly. Zulma turned on her side, her back towards him, not speaking; this too was like so many other summer nights.

Getting to sleep should have been difficult, but no sooner had Mariano put out his cigarette than he dropped off suddenly; the window was still open and no doubt mosquitoes would enter, but sleep came first, with no dreams, total nothingness from which he emerged at some moment driven by an indescribable panic, the pressure of Zulma's fingers on one shoulder, the panting. Almost without realizing it, he was now listening to the night, the perfect silence punctuated by the crickets. Go to sleep, Zulma, it's nothing, you must have been dreaming. Insisting she agree with him, that she lie down again, turning her back on him now that she had suddenly withdrawn her hand and was sitting up rigid, looking towards the closed door. He got up at the same time as Zulma, helpless to stop her from opening the door and going to the top of the stairs, clinging to her and asking himself vaguely if it wouldn't be better to slap her, to bring her back to bed by force, to break such petrified remoteness. In the middle of the staircase Zulma stopped, taking hold of the bannister. You know why the little girl is there? With a voice that must have still belonged to the nightmare. The little girl? Two more steps, now almost in the bend that led to the kitchen. Zulma, please. And her voice cracking, almost in falsetto: she's there to let him in, I tell you she's going to let him in. Zulma, don't make me do something I'll regret. And her voice, almost triumphant, still rising in tone, look, just look if you don't believe me; the bed's empty, the magazine on the floor. With a start Mariano headed for Zulma, he sprang towards the light switch. The little girl looked at them, her pink pyjamas against the door that faced the large room, her face drowsy. What are you doing up at this hour, said Mariano wrapping a dish towel around his waist. The little girl looked at Zulma nude, somewhere between being asleep and embarrassed she looked at her as if wanting to go back to bed, on the brink of tears. I got up to tinkle, she said. And you went out to the garden when we had told you to go upstairs to the bathroom. The little girl began to pout, her hands comically lost in the pockets of her pyjamas. It's ok, go to bed, said Mariano, stroking her hair. He covered her, and placed the magazine under the pillow for her; the little girl turned towards the wall, a finger in her mouth as if to console herself. Go ahead up, said Mariano, you see there's nothing wrong, don't stand there like a sleepwalker. He saw her take a couple of steps towards the door of the large room, he blocked her path; everything was fine now, damn it. But don't you realize she's opened the door for him, said Zulma with that voice which wasn't hers. Stop the nonsense, Zulma. Go see if it's not so, or let me go. Mariano's hand closed around her trembling forearm. Get upstairs right now, pushing her 'til he had led her to the foot of the steps, looking as he went by at the little girl who hadn't moved, she must be asleep by now. On the first step Zulma screamed and tried to escape, but the stairway was narrow and Mariano kept shoving her with his whole body; the towel unfastened and fell to the bottom of the stairs. Holding onto her by the shoulders and hurling her upwards to the landing, he flung her toward the bedroom, shutting the door behind him. She's going to let him in, Zulma repeated, the door is open and he'll get in. Lie down, said Mariano. I'm telling you the door is open. It doesn't matter if he comes in or not, let him come in if he wants to, I don't give a damn now whether he comes in or not. He caught Zulma's hands as they tried to repel him, from behind he pushed against the bed, they fell together, Zulma sobbing and begging, helpless to move under the weight of a body that girded her more and more, that bent her to a will murmured mouth to mouth, wildly amidst tears and obscenities. I don't want to, I don't want to, I don't want to ever again, I don't want to, but it was too late now, her strength and pride yielding to that leveling weight, returning her to an impossible past, to the summers without letters and without horses. At some moment—it was beginning to get light—Mariano dressed in silence and went down to the kitchen; the little girl was sleeping with her finger in her mouth, the door of the big room was open. Zulma had been right, the little girl had opened the door but the horse hadn't entered the house. Unless, he thought about it, lighting his first cigarette and looking at the blue ridge of the hills, unless Zulma had been right about that too and the horse had entered the house, but how could they prove it if they had not heard him, if everything was in order, if the clock would continue to measure the morning and later Florencio would come to get the little girl, probably around twelve the mailman would arrive whistling from afar, leaving for them on the garden table the letters that he or Zulma would pick up without saying anything, shortly before deciding by mutual consent what was best to prepare for lunch.

Robert Hass

Robert Hass was born in San Francisco in 1941. As a teenager, Hass became heavily influenced by the San Francisco beat poetry scene in the 1950s, particularly their focus on East Asian literary traditions. Hass attended St. Mary's College in Moraga, California, and married Earlene Leif before graduating in 1963. Hass went on to earn his M.A. and Ph.D. at Stanford University and held teaching positions at the State University of New York at Buffalo and his alma mater St. Mary's College (1971–89) before settling at the University of California-Berkeley, where he currently teaches. His first collection of poetry, *Field Guide,* won the Yale Series of Younger Poets Award in 1971. He went on to publish *Praise, Human Wishes, Sun Under Wood* (winner of the 1996 National Book Critics Circle Award in poetry), and *Twentieth Century Pleasures: Prose on Poetry*, which earned him the 1984 National Book Critics Circle Award in criticism. Hass is a well-known spokesman for literacy, poetry, and ecological awareness, having served two terms as U.S. Poet Laureate. He is also an accomplished translator; his translations of Nobel-laureate Czeslaw Milosz's poems appeared in *The Kenyon Review's* special Nobel issue (Spring 2001). Hass currently lives in Berkeley, California, with his second wife, poet Brenda Hillman, whom he married in 1995. The poems included here appeared in *The Kenyon Review* in 1979.

Santa Lucia *(1979)*
by Robert Hass

I

Art & Love: he camps outside my door,
innocent, carnivorous. As if desire
were actually a flute, as if the little song
transcend, transcend could get you anywhere.
He brings me wine; he believes in the arts
and uses them for beauty. He brings me
vinegar in small earthen pots, postcards
of the hillsides by Cézanne desire has left
alone, empty farms in August and the vague
tall chestnut trees at Jas de Bouffan, fetal
sandstone rifted with mica from the beach.
He brings his body, wolfish, frail,
all brown for summer like croissant crusts
at La Seine in the Marina, the bellies
of pelicans I watched among white dunes
under Pico Blanco on the Big Sur coast.
It sickens me, this glut & desperation.

II

Walking the Five Springs trail, I tried to think.
Dead-nettle, thimbleberry. The fog heaved in
between the pines, violet sparrows made curves
like bodies in the ruined air. *All women
are masochists.* I was so young, believing
every word they said. *Durer is second-rate.*
Durer's Eve feeds her apple to the snake;
snaky tresses, cat at her feet, at Adam's foot
a mouse. Male fear, male eyes and art. The art
of love, the eyes I use to see myself
in love. Ingres, pillows. I think the erotic
is not sexual, only when you're lucky.
That's where the path forks. It's not the riddle
of desire that interests me; it is the riddle
of good hands, chervil in the windowbox,

the white pages of a book, someone says
I'm tired, someone turning on the light.

III

Streaked in the window, the city wavers
but the sky is empty, clean. Emptiness
is strict; that pleases me. I do cry out.
Like everyone else, I thrash, am splayed.
Oh, oh, oh, oh. Eyes full of wonder.
Guernica. Ulysses on the beach. I see
my body is his prayer. I see my body.
Walking in the galleries at the Louvre,
I was, each moment, naked & possessed.
Tourists gorged on goosenecked Florentine girls
by Pollaiuolo. He sees me like a painter.
I hear his words for me: white, gold.
I'd rather walk the city in the rain.
Dog shit, traffic accidents. Whatever god
there is dismembered in his Chevie.
A different order of religious awe:
agony & meat, everything plain afterwards.

IV

Santa Lucia: eyes jellied on a plate.
The thrust of serpentine was almost green
all through the mountains where the rock cropped out.
I liked sundowns, dusks smelling of madrone,
the wildflowers, which were not beautiful,
fierce little wills rooting in the yellow
grass year after year, thirst in the roots,
mineral. They have intelligence
of hunger. Poppies lean to the morning sun,
lupine grows thick in the rockface, self-heal
at creekside. He wants to fuck. Sweet word.
All suction. I want less. Not that I fear
the huge dark of sex, the sharp sweet light,
light if it were water ravelling, rancor,
tenderness like rain. What I want happens

not when the deer freezes in the shade
and looks at you and you hold very still
and meet her gaze, but in the moment after
when she flicks her ears & starts to feed again.

To a Reader *(1979)*
by Robert Hass

I've watched memory wound you.
I felt nothing but envy.
Having slept in wet meadows,
I was not through desiring.
Imagine January and the beach,
a bleached sky, gulls. And
look seaward: what is not there
is there, isn't it, the huge
bird of the first light
arched above first waters
beyond our touching or intention
or the reasonable shore.

Not Going to New York: A Letter *(1979)*
by Robert Hass

Dear Dan—
    This is a letter of apology, unrhymed.
Rhyme belongs to the dazzling couplets of arrival.
Survival is the art around here. It rhymes by accident
with the rhythm of days which arrive like crows in a field
of stubble corn in upstate New York in February.
In upstate New York in February thaws hardened the heart
against the wish for spring. There was not one thing
in the barren meadows not muddy and raw-fleshed.
At night I dreamed of small black snakes with orange markings

disappearing down their holes, of being lost in the hemlocks
and coming to a clearing of wild strawberry, sunlight,
abandoned apple trees. At night it was mild noon in a clearing.
Nothing arrived. This was a place left to flower
in the plain cruelty of light. Mornings the sky was opal.
The windows faced east and a furred snow reassumed the pines
but arrived only mottled in the fields so that its flesh
was my grandmother's in the kitchen of the house
on Jackson Street, and she was crying. I was a good boy.
She held me so tight when she said that, smelling like sleep
rotting if sleep rots, that I always knew how death would come
to get me and the soft folds of her quivery white neck
were what I saw, so that sometimes on an airplane I look down
to snow covering the arroyos on the east side of the Sierra
and it's grandmother's flesh and I look away. In the house
on Jackson Street, I am the figure against the wall
in Bonnard's *The Breakfast Room.* The light is terrible. It is
wishes that are fat dogs, already sated, snuffling
at the heart in dreams. The table linen is so crisp
it puts an end to fantasies of rectitude, clean hands, high art
and the blue beside the white in the striping is the color
of the river Loire when you read about it in old books
and dreamed of provincial breakfasts, the sun the color
of bread crust and the fruit icy cold and there was no
terrified figure dwarf-like and correct, disappearing
off the edge of Bonnard's *The Breakfast Room.* It was not
grandmother weeping in the breakfast room or the first thaw
dream of beautiful small snakes slithering down holes.
In this life that is not dreams but my life
the clouds above the bay are massing toward December
and gulls hover in the storm-pearled air and the last
of last season's cedar spits and kindles on the fire.
Summer dries us out with golden light, so winter
is a kind of spring here—wet trees, a reptile odor
in the earth, mild greening—and the seasonal myths
lie across one another in the quick darkening of days.
Kristin and Luke are bent to a puzzle, some allegory
of the quattrocento cut in a thousand small uneven pieces

which, on the floor, they recompose with rapt,
leisurely attention. Kristin asks, searching
for a piece round at one end, fluted at the other,
"Do you know what a shepherd is?" and Luke, looking for
a square edge with a sprig of Italian olive in it,
makes a guess, "Somebody who hurts sheep."
My grandmother was not so old. She was my mother's mother;
I think, the night before, my father must have told her
we were going to move. She held me weeping, probably,
because she felt she was about to lose her daughter.
We only buried her this year. In the genteel hotel
on Leavenworth that looked across a mile of human misery
to the bay, she smoked regally, complained about her teeth.
Luke watched her wide-eyed, with a mingled look of wonder
and religious dread she seemed so old. And once,
when he reached up involuntarily to touch her withered cheek,
she looked at him awhile and patted his cheek back and winked
and said to me, askance: "Old age ain't for sissies."
This has nothing to do with the odd terror in my memory.
It only explains it—the way this early winter weather
makes life seem more commonplace and—at a certain angle—
more intense. It is not poetry where decay and a created
radiance lie hidden inside words the way that memory
folds them into living. "O Westmoreland thou art a summer bird
that ever in the haunch of winter sings the lifting up of day."
Pasternak translated those lines. I imagine Russian summer,
the smell of jasmine drifting toward the porch. I would like
to get on a plane, but I would also like to sit on the porch
and watch one shrink to the hovering of gulls and glint
in the distance, circle east toward snow and disappear.
He would have noticed the articles as a native speaker wouldn't:
a bird, *the* haunch; and understood little what persists
when, eyes half-closed, lattice-shadow on his face,
he murmured the phrase in the dark vowels of his mother tongue.

Picking Blackberries with a Friend
Who Has Been Reading Jacques Lacan *(1979)*

by Robert Hass

August is dust here. Drought
stuns the road,
but juice gathers in the berries.

We pick them in the hot
slow-motion of midmorning.
Charlie is exclaiming:

for him it is twenty years ago
and raspberries and Vermont.
We have stopped talking

about *L'Histoire de la vérité*,
about subject and object
and the mediation of desire.

Our ears are stoppered
in the bee-hum. And Charlie,
laughing wonderfully,

beard stained purple
by the word *juice*,
goes to get a bigger pot.

Vladimir Nabokov

Vladimir Nabokov was born in St. Petersburg, Russia, in 1899. At the onset of the Russian Revolution, his family emigrated to Berlin, and Nabokov entered Trinity College, Cambridge, from where he graduated three years later in 1923. The year before his graduation, Nabokov's father was murdered by a Russian fascist in Berlin. Nabokov lived in Berlin for the next fifteen years, producing nine novels during this time, including *King, Queen, Knave; Laughter in the Dark;* and *The Gift.* In 1937, Nabokov moved to Paris with his wife and son, where they lived for three years. After receiving a loan from the composer Rachmaninoff, Nabokov moved his family to America, teaching at Wellesley College and Cornell University. He began to write in English instead of his native Russian, penning such novels as *The Real Life of Sebastian Knight* (1941), *Bend Sinister* (1947), and *Lolita* (1955), which brought him international acclaim. His fame was furthered when *Lolita* was made into a highly controversial motion picture directed by Stanley Kubrick in 1962. In 1959, Nabokov moved to Switzerland, the same year his first book of poetry, *Poems,* was released. He continued to write both fiction and poetry, publishing later works like *Transparent Things* and *Look at the Harlequins!* Nabokov was also an avid student of entomology, even having a species of butterfly named for him. He died in 1977 at the age of seventy-eight. His poem "Demon" appeared posthumously in *The Kenyon Review* in 1979.

Demon *(1979)*

by Vladimir Nabokov

translated by Joseph Brodsky

Where have you flown here from? What kind of grief d'you carry?
Tell, flier, why your lips do lack
a tint of life, and why the sea smells in your wings?

And Demon answers me: "You're young and hungry,
but sounds won't satiate you. So don't pluck
your tightly drawn discordant strings.

No music's higher than the silence. You were born
for strict, austere silence. Learn
its stamp on stones, on love, on stars above your ground."

He vanished. Darkness fades. God ordered me to sound.

Samuel Beckett

Samuel Beckett claimed he was born in Foxrock, Dublin, on Good Friday, April 13, 1906, but his birth certificate puts the date a month later. After graduating from Trinity College, Beckett moved to Paris, befriended James Joyce, and in 1930 published his first poem "Whoroscope." After the war, Beckett began to do all of his writing in French. He became one of the most influential writers of the twentieth century, penning dramatic masterpieces such as *Waiting for Godot*, *Happy Days*, and *Endgame*. His minimalist approach (using simple dialogue, often repetitiously) is well exemplified in his brief play "Ohio Impromptu," written for, and first performed at, a Beckett symposium at the Ohio State University in 1981. *The Kenyon Review* recently reprinted his poem "Antipepsis" in an issue celebrating the 100th anniversary of the Nobel Prizes, which Beckett was awarded in 1969 (which his wife, Suzanne Deschevaux-Dumesnil, referred to as "a catastrophe"). Beckett died in Paris in 1989 at the age of eighty-three.

A Piece of Monologue *(1979)*
by Samuel Beckett

Curtain.
Faint diffuse light.
Speaker stands well off centre downstage audience left.
White hair, white nightgown, white socks.
Two metres to his left, same level, same height, standard lamp,
   skull-sized white globe, faintly lit.
Just visible extreme right, same level, white foot of pallet bed.
Ten seconds before speech begins.
Thirty seconds before end of speech lamplight begins to fail.
Lamp out. Silence. Speaker, globe, foot of pallet, barely visible in
   diffuse light.
Ten seconds.
Curtain.

Speaker. Birth was the death of him. Again. Words are few. Dying too. Birth was the death of him. Ghastly grinning ever since. Up at the lid to come. In cradle and crib. At suck first fiasco. With the first totters. From mammy to nanny and back. All the way. Bandied back and forth. So ghastly grinning on. From funeral to funeral. To now. This night. Two and a half billion seconds. Again. Two and a half billion seconds. Hard to believe so few. From funeral to funeral. Funerals of...he all but said of loved ones. Thirty thousand nights. Hard to believe so few. Born dead of night. Sun long sunk behind the larches. New needles turning green. In the room dark gaining. 'Til faint light from standard lamp. Wick turned low. And now. This night. Up at nightfall. Every nightfall. Faint light in room. Whence unknown. None from window. No. Next to none. No such thing as none. Gropes to window and stares out. Stands there staring out. Stock still staring out. Nothing stirring in that black vast. Gropes back in the end to where the lamp is standing. Was standing. When last went out. Loose matches in right-hand pocket. Strikes one on his buttock the way his father taught him. Takes off the milkwhite globe and sets it down. Match goes out. Strikes a second as before. Takes off chimney. Smoke-clouded. Holds it in left hand. Match goes out. Strikes a third as before and sets it to wick. Puts back chimney. Match goes out. Puts back globe. Turns wick low. Backs away to edge of light and turns to face east. Blank wall. So nightly. Up. Socks. Nightgown. Window. Lamp. Backs away to edge of light and stands facing blank wall. Covered with pictures once. Pictures of...he all but said of loved ones. Unframed. Unglazed. Pinned to wall with drawing-pins. All shapes and sizes. Down one after another. Gone. Torn to shreds and scattered. Strewn all over the floor. Not at one sweep. No sudden fit of...no word. Ripped from the wall and torn to shreds one by one. Over the years. Years of night. Nothing on the wall now but the pins. Not all. Some out with the wrench. Some still pinning a shred. So stands there facing blank wall. Dying on. No more no less. No. Less. Less to die. Ever less. Like light at nightfall. Stands there facing east. Blank pinpocked surface once white in shadow. Could once name them all. There was father. That grey void. There mother. That other. There together. Smiling. Wedding day. There all three. That grey blot. There alone. He alone. Not now. Forgotten. All gone so long. Gone. Ripped off and torn to shreds. Scattered all over the floor. Swept out of the way under the bed and left. Thousand shreds under the bed with the dust and spiders. All the...he all but said the loved ones. Stands there facing the wall staring beyond. Nothing there either. Nothing stirring there either. Nothing stirring anywhere. Nothing to be seen anywhere. Nothing to be heard anywhere. Room once full of sounds. Faint sounds. Whence unknown. Fewer and fainter as time wore on. Nights wore on. None now. No. No such thing as none. Rain some nights still slant against the panes. Or dropping gentle on the place beneath. Even now. Lamp smoking though wick turned low. Strange. Faint smoke issuing through vent in globe. Low ceiling stained by night after night of this. Dark shapeless blot on surface elsewhere white. Once white. Stands facing wall after the various motions described. That is up at nightfall and into gown and socks. No. In them already. In them all night. All day. All day and night. Up at nightfall in gown and socks and after a moment to get his bearings gropes to window. Faint light in room. Unutterably faint. Whence unknown. Stands stock still staring out. Into black vast. Nothing there. Nothing stirring. That he can see. Hear. Dwells thus as if unable to move again. Or no will left to move again. Not enough will left to move again. Turns in the end and gropes to where he knows the lamp is standing. Thinks he knows. Was last standing. When last went out. Match one as described for globe. Two for chimney. Three for wick. Chimney and globe back on. Turns wick low. Backs away to edge of light and turns to face wall. East. Still as the lamp by his side. Gown and socks white to take faint light. Once white. Hair white to take faint light. Foot of pallet just visible edge of frame. Once white to take faint light. Stands there staring beyond. Nothing. Empty dark. 'Til first word always the same. Night after night the same. Birth. Then slow fade up of a faint form. Out of the dark. A window. Looking west. Sun long sunk behind the larches. Light dying. Soon none left to die. No. No such thing as no light. Starless moonless heaven. Dies on to dawn and never dies. There in the dark that window. Night slowly falling. Eyes to the small pane gaze at that first night. Turn from it in the end to face the darkened room. There in the end slowly a faint hand. Holding aloft a lighted spill. In light of spill faintly the hand and milkwhite globe. Then second hand. In light of spill. Takes off globe and disappears. Reappears empty. Takes off chimney. Two hands and chimney in light of spill. Spill to wick. Chimney back on. Hand with spill disappears. Second hand disappears. Chimney alone in gloom. Hand reappears with globe. Globe back on. Turns wick low. Pale globe alone in gloom. Glimmer of brass bedrail. Fade. Birth the death of him. That nevoid smile. Thirty thousand nights. Stands at edge of lamplight staring beyond. Into dark whole again. Window gone. Hands gone. Light gone. Gone. Again and again. Again and again gone. 'Til dark slowly parts again. Grey light. Rain pelting. Umbrellas round a grave. Seen from above. Streaming black canopies. Black ditch beneath. Rain bubbling in the black mud. Empty for the moment. That place beneath. Which…he all but said which loved one? Thirty seconds. To add to the two and a half billion odd. Then fade. Dark whole again. Blest dark. No. No such thing as whole. Stands staring beyond half hearing what he's saying. He? The words falling from his mouth. Making do with his mouth. Lights lamp as described. Backs away to edge of light and turns to face wall. Stares beyond into dark. Waits for first word always the same. It gathers in his mouth. Parts lips and thrusts tongue forward. Birth. Parts the dark. Slowly the window. That first night. The room. The spill. The hands. The lamp. The gleam of brass. Fade. Gone. Again and again gone. Mouth agape. A cry. Stifled by nasal. Dark parts. Grey light. Rain pelting. Streaming umbrellas. Ditch. Bubbling black mud. Coffin out of frame. Whose? Fade. Gone. Move on to other matters. Try to move on. To other matters. How far from wall? Head almost touching. As at window. Eyes glued to pane staring out. Nothing stirring. Black vast. Stands there stock still staring out as if unable to move again. Or gone the will to move again. Gone. Faint cry in his ear. Mouth agape. Closed with hiss of breath. Lips joined. Feel soft touch of lip on lip. Lip lipping lip. Then parted by cry as before. Where is he now? Back at window staring out. Eyes glued to pane. As if looking his last. Turns away at last and gropes through faint unaccountable light to unseen lamp. White gown moving through that gloom.

Once white. Lights and moves to face wall as described. Head almost touching. Stands there staring beyond waiting for first word. It gathers in his mouth. Parts lips and thrusts tongue between them. Tip of tongue. Feel soft touch of tongue on lips. Of lips on tongue. Stare beyond through rift in dark to other dark. Further dark. Sun long sunk behind the larches. Nothing stirring. Nothing faintly stirring. Stock still eyes glued to pane. As if looking his last. At that first night. Of thirty thousand odd. Where soon to be. This night to be. Spill. Hands. Lamp. Gleam of brass. Pale globe alone in gloom. Brass bedrail catching light. Thirty seconds. To swell the two and a half billion odd. Fade. Gone. Cry. Snuffed with breath of nostrils. Again and again. Again and again gone. 'Til whose grave? Which…he all but said which loved one's? He? Black ditch in pelting rain. Way out through the grey rift in dark. Seen from on high. Streaming canopies. Bubbling black mud. Coffin on its way. Loved one…he all but said loved one on his way. Her way. Thirty seconds. Fade. Gone. Stands there staring beyond. Into dark whole again. No. No such thing as whole. Head almost touching wall. White hair catching light. White gown. White socks. White foot of pallet edge of frame stage left. Once white. Least…give and head rests on wall. But no. Stock still head haught staring beyond. Nothing stirring. Faintly stirring. Thirty thousand nights of ghosts beyond. Beyond that black beyond. Ghost light. Ghost nights. Ghost rooms. Ghost graves. Ghost…he all but said ghost loved ones. Waiting on the rip word. Stands there staring beyond at that black veil lips quivering to half-heard words. Treating of other matters. Trying to treat of other matters. 'Til half hears there are no other matters. Never were other matters. Never two matters. Never but the one matter. The dead and gone. The dying and the going. From the word go. The word begone. Such as the light going now. Beginning to go. In the room. Where else? Unnoticed by him staring beyond. The globe alone. Not the other. The unaccountable. From nowhere. On all sides nowhere. The globe alone. Alone gone.

Lewis Hyde

Lewis Hyde was born in Boston, Massachusetts, in 1945. Educated at the Universities of Minnesota (B.A) and Iowa (M.A.), Hyde has held many positions in his life, including carpenter, electrician, alcoholism counselor, professor of creative writing at Harvard (six years), and, since 1989, professor at Kenyon College. Hyde is a renowned editor, translator, and author of such books as *This Error Is the Sign of Love, Alcohol and Poetry: John Berryman and the Booze Talking, On the Work of Allen Ginsberg,* and the highly acclaimed *The Gift: Imagination and the Erotic Life of Property.* His most recent book, *Trickster Makes This World,* examines the figure of the trickster in mythology as it relates to today's increasingly complex art and living. A leading expert on the arts and culture, he is the recipient of grants from the National Endowment for the Arts, the National Endowment for the Humanities, and, in 1991, the prestigious MacArthur Foundation. He most recently edited *The Essays of Henry D. Thoreau,* which appeared in May 2002. Hyde splits his time between Gambier, Ohio, and Cambridge, Massachusetts, and currently serves on the advisory board for *The Kenyon Review.* "Some Food We Could Not Eat" appeared in *The Kenyon Review* in 1979.

Some Food We Could Not Eat:
Gift Exchange and the Imagination *(1979)*

by Lewis Hyde

I would like to write an economy of the imagination. I assume any "property system" expresses our own spirit—or rather, one of our spirits, for there are many ways to be human and many economies. As we all know, capitalism brings to life and rewards its own particular spirits (aggression, frugality, independence, and so on). My question is, what would be the form of an economy that took the imagination as its model, that was an emanation of the creative spirit?

The approach I have taken to this question might best be introduced by telling how I came to it in the first place. Some years ago I sat in a coffee-house listening to someone read an exceptionally boring poem. In trying to imagine how or why the poem had come into existence, the phrase "commodity poem" came to mind—as if I had heard the language equivalent to a new Chevrolet. Even at that early point I meant "commodity" as opposed to "gift," for my own experience of poetry (both of reading and of writing) had been in the nature of a gift: something had come to me unbidden, had altered my life, and left me with a sense of gratitude—a form of "exchange," if you will, clearly unlike what happens to most of us in the marketplace.

I am obviously speaking of gifts in a spiritual sense at this point, but I do not mean to exclude material gifts. For spirits take on bodies and it is in that mixture that we find human liveliness and attraction. Both economic and erotic life bring with them a mixture of excitement, frustration, fascination, and confusion because they must occur where body and spirit mingle, and it is in that union we discover the fullness of the world, or find it missing.

I should add that on a more mundane level my topic has found a source of energy in the situation of my own life. For some years now I have tried to make my way as a poet and a sort of "scholar without institution." Inevitably the money question comes up. You have to pay the rent. All artists, once they have passed their thirtieth birthday, begin to wonder how it is that a man or woman who wishes to live by his gifts is to survive in a land where everything is bought and sold.

These beginnings—the money question for myself and a sense of art as an "exchange" different from the market—became focused for me only after some friends had introduced me to the work that has been done in anthropology on gift exchange as a form of property.[1] In many tribal groups a large portion of the material wealth circulates as gift and, not surprisingly, such exchange is attended by certain "fruits": people live differently who treat a portion of their wealth as gift. As I read through the ethnography I realized that in describing gift exchange as an economy I might be able to develop the language I needed in order to address the situation of the artist living in a land where market value is *the* value. At about the same time I began to read all the fairy tales I could find with gifts in them, because the image of what a gift is and does is the same in these tales as it is in the ethnography, but fairy tales tell of gifts in a manner closer to my final concern, the fate of the imagination.

I will not be able to fully describe what I mean by "gift" in the space of one essay. I want, therefore, to remark on two or three characteristics of a gift which shall not be addressed here.

One is that gifts mark or act as agents of individual transformation. Gift exchange institutions cluster around times of change: birth, puberty, marriage, sickness, parting, arrival, and death. Sometimes the gift itself actually brings about the change, as if it could pass through a person's body and leave it altered. The best examples are true teachings—times when some person changes our life either directly or through the power of example. Such teachings are not like schoolbook lessons; they move the soul and we feel gratitude. I think of gratitude as a labor the soul undertakes to effect the transformation after a gift has been received. We work, sometimes for years, until the gift has truly ripened inside of us and can be passed along. (Note that gratitude is not the "obligation" we feel when we accept a gift we don't really want.)

Second, when you give someone a gift, a feeling-bond is set up between the two of you. The sale of commodities leaves no necessary link. Walking into a hardware store and buying a pound of nails doesn't connect you to the clerk in any way—you don't even need to talk to him if you don't want to (which is why commodities are associated with both freedom and alienation). But a gift makes a connection. With many gift exchange situations, the bond is clearly the point—with marriage gifts and with gifts used as peace overtures, for example.

Finally it must be said that gift exchange has its negative aspects. Given their bonding power, "poisonous" gifts and gifts from evil people must be

---

1) The classic work is Marcel Mauss's 1924 "Essai sur le don," now published in English as *The Gift*, trans Ian Cunnison (New York: Norton, 1967).

refused. In a fairy tale, the hero is in trouble if he eats the meal given to him by a witch. More generally, anyone who is supposed to stay "detached" (a judge, for example) shouldn't accept gifts. It is also true that the bonds set up by gift exchange limit our freedom of motion. If a young person wants to leave his or her parents, it's best to stop accepting their gifts because they will only maintain the parent-child connection. As gifts are associated with being connected to a community, so commodities are associated with both freedom and rootlessness.

In part because of these restrictions, I do not feel that gift exchange is, in the end, the exclusive "economy of the imagination." But it is a necessary part of that economy; the imagination will never come to its full power until we are at home with the gifts of both the inner and the outer world. An elaboration of the nature of gift exchange must, therefore, precede any more precise qualifying remarks, and it is this elaboration which I begin here.

I

When the Puritans first landed in Massachusetts they discovered an Indian custom so curious they felt called upon to find a name for it. In 1767, when Thomas Hutchinson wrote his history of the colony, the term was already an old saying: "An Indian gift," he told his readers, "is a proverbial expression signifying a present for which an equivalent return is expected."[2] We still use this, of course, and in an even broader sense. If I am so uncivilized as to ask for the return of a gift I have given, they call me an "Indian giver."

Imagine a scene. The Englishman comes into the Indian lodge. He falls to admiring a clay pipe with feathers tied to the stem. The tribe passes this pipe around among themselves as a ritual gift. It stays with a family for awhile, but sooner or later it is always given away again. So the Indian, as is only polite among his people, responds to the white man's interest by saying, "That's just some stuff we don't need. Please take it. It's a gift." The Englishman is tickled pink. What a nice thing to send back to the British Museum! He takes the pipe home and sets it on the mantelpiece. The next day another Indian happens to visit him and sees the gift which was due to come into his lodge soon. He too is delighted. "Ah!" he says, "the gift!" and he sticks it in his pouch. In consternation the Englishman invents the phrase "Indian giver" to describe these people with such a low

---

2) Thomas Hutchinson, *The History of the Colony of Massachusetts-Bay, vol 1.* Boston: Thomas & John Fleet, 1764; reprint ed New York: Arno Press, 1972), p 469.

sense of private property. The opposite of this term would be something like "white-man-keeper," or, as we say nowadays, "capitalist," that is, a person whose first reaction to property is to take it out of circulation, to put it in a warehouse or museum, or—more to the point for capitalism— to lay it aside to be used for production.

The Indian giver (the original ones, at any rate) understood a cardinal property of the gift: whatever we are given should be given away again, not kept. Or, if it is kept, something of similar value should move on in its stead, the way a billiard ball may stop when it sends another scurrying across the felt, the momentum transferred. You may hold on to a Christmas gift, but it will cease to be a gift in the true sense unless you have given something else away. When it is passed along, the gift may be given back to the original donor, but this is not essential. In fact, it is better if the gift is not returned, but is given instead to some new, third party. The only essential is this: *the gift must always move.* There are other forms of property that stand still, that mark the place or hold back water, but the gift keeps going. Like a bird that rests on the rising air near cliffs, or water at the lip of the falls, standing still is its restlessness and the ease of the gift is in its motion.

Tribal peoples usually distinguish between two sorts of property, gifts and capital. Commonly they have a law which repeats the sensibility implicit in the idea of an Indian Gift. "One man's gift," they say, "must not be another man's capital." Wendy James, a British social anthropologist, tells us that among the Uduk in northeast Africa, "any wealth transferred from one sub-clan to another, whether animals, grain, or money, is in the nature of a gift, and should be consumed, and not invested for growth. If such transferred wealth is added to the subclan's capital [cattle in this case] and kept for growth and investment, the subclan is regarded as being in an immoral rela-tion of debt to the donors of the original gift."[3] If a pair of goats received as a gift from another subclan is kept to breed or to buy cattle, "there will be general complaint that the so-and-so's are getting rich at someone else's expense, behaving immorally by hoarding and investing gifts, and therefore being in a state of severe debt. It will be expected that they will soon suffer storm damage…"

The goats in this example move from one clan to another just as the pipe moved from person to person in my fantasy. And what happens then? If the

---

3) Wendy R. James, "Why the Uduk Won't Pay Bridewealth," *Sudan Notes and Records*, vol 51 (1970), pp 75–84.

object is a gift, it keeps moving, which, in this case, means that the man who received the goats throws a big party and everyone gets fed. The goats needn't be given back but they surely can't be set aside to produce milk or more goats. And a new note has been added: the feeling that if a gift were not treated as such, if one form of property were to be converted to another, something horrible might happen. In folk tales the person who tries to hold on to a gift usually dies; in this anecdote the risk is "storm damage." (What happens in fact to most tribal groups is worse than storm damage—whenever foreigners show up and convert gift to capital, universally the tribal group is destroyed as a group.)

If we turn now to a folk tale we will be able to see all of this from a different angle. Folk tales are like the soul's morality plays—they address the gift as an image in the psyche. They are told at the boundary between our inner feelings about property and the ways in which we handle it in fact. The first tale I have chosen comes from Scotland. It may seem a bit long so early in our discourse, but almost everything in it will be of use. The tale is called "The Girl and the Dead Man."[4] I have put a few obscurities into modern speech, but other than that, this is how the story was told by a Scottish woman in the mid-nineteenth century:

> There was before now a poor woman, and she had a leash of daughters. Said the eldest one of them to her mother, "I had better go and seek for fortune." "I had better," said the mother, "bake a loaf of bread for thee." When the bread was done, her mother said to her, "Which wouldst thou like best, a little bit and my blessing or the big bit and my curse?" "I would rather," said she, "the big bit and thy curse."
>
> She went on her way and when the night was wreathing around her she sat at the foot of a wall to eat the bread. There gathered the ground quail and her twelve puppies, and the little birds of the air about her, for a part of the bread. "Wilt thou give us a part of the bread?" said they. "I won't give it, you ugly brutes; I have not much for myself." "My curse will be thine, and the curse of my twelve birds; and thy mother's curse is the worst of all." She rose and went away, and the bit of bread had not been half enough.
>
> She saw a little house a long way from her; and if a long way from her, she was not long reaching it. She knocked at the door. "Who's

---

4) John Francis Campbell, "The Girl and the Dead Man," in *Popular Tales of the West Highlands, vol 1* (Paisley: Alexander Gardner, 1890: reprint ed Detroit: The Singing Tree Press, 1969), pp 220–25.

there?" "A good maid seeking a master." "We want that," said they, and they let her in.

Her task was to stay awake every night and watch a dead man, the brother of the housewife, whose corpse was restless. She was to have a peck of gold and a peck of silver. Besides this she had, of nuts as she broke, of needles as she lost, of thimbles as she pierced, of thread as she used, of candles as she burned, a bed of green silk over her, a bed of green silk under her, sleeping by day and watching by night. The first night when she was watching she fell asleep; the mistress came in, struck her with a magic club and she fell down dead. She threw her out back in the garbage heap.

Said the middle daughter to her mother, "I had better go seek fortune and follow my sister." Her mother baked her a loaf of bread; and she chose the big half and her mother's curse, as her elder sister did, and it happened to her as it happened to her sister.

Said the youngest daughter to her mother, "I had better go myself and seek fortune too, and follow my sisters." "I had better bake a loaf of bread," said her mother. "Which wouldst thou rather, a little bit and my blessing or the big bit and my curse?" "I would rather the little bit and your blessing."

She went on her way and when the night was wreathing round her she sat at the foot of a wall to eat the bread. There gathered the ground quail and her twelve puppies, and the little birds of the air about her. "Wilt thou give us some of that?" "I will give, you pretty creatures, if you will keep me company." She gave them some of the bread; they ate and they had plenty, and she had enough. They clapped their wings about her 'til she was snug with the warmth.

She went, she saw a little house a long way from her...[here the task and the wages are repeated].

She sat to watch the dead man, and she was sewing; in the middle of the night he rose up and screwed up a grin. "If thou dost not lie down properly, I will give thee the one leathering with a stick." He lay down. After a while he rose on one elbow and screwed up a grin; and a third time he rose up and screwed up a grin.

When he rose the third time she walloped him with the stick. The stick stuck to the dead man and her hand stuck to the stick and off they went! They went forward 'til they were going through a wood; when it was low for her it was high for him; and when it was high for him it was low for her. The nuts were knocking their eyes out and the wild plums taking their ears off, 'til they got through the wood. Then they returned home.

   She got a peck of gold and a peck of silver and the vessel of cordial. She rubbed the vessel of cordial on her two sisters and brought them alive. They left me sitting here, and if they were well, 'tis well; and if they were not, let them be.

There are at least four gifts in this story. The first, of course, is the bread which the mother gives to her daughters as a going-away present. This becomes the second gift when the youngest daughter shares her bread with the birds. She keeps the gift in motion, the moral point of the tale. Several things, in addition to her survival, come to her as a result of treating the gift correctly. These are the fruits of the gift. First, she and the birds are relieved of their hunger. Second, the birds befriend her. And third, she's able to stay awake all night and get the job done. (As we shall see by the end of the essay, these are not accidental results, they are typical fruits of the gift.)

   In the morning the third gift appears, the vessel of cordial. It is a healing liquid, not unlike the "water of life" that appears in folk tales from all over the world. It has power: with it she is able to bring her sisters back to life. This liquid is thrown in as a gift for her successful completion of the task. It's a bonus, nowhere mentioned in the wonderful litany of wages offered to each daughter. We will leave for later the question of where it comes from; for now we are looking at what happens to the gift after it is given, and again we find that this girl is no dummy—she moves it right along, giving it to her sisters to bring them back to life. That is the fourth and last gift in the tale.[5]

---

5) This story illustrates almost all the main characteristics of a gift and so I shall be referring back to it throughout the essay. As an aside, therefore, I want to take a stab at its meaning. It says, I think, that if a girl without a father is going to get along in the world, she'd better have a good connection to her mother. The birds are the mother's spirit, what we'd now call the girl's psychological mother. The girl who gives the gift back to the spirit-mother has, as a result, her mother-wits about her for the rest of the tale.

   Nothing in the tale links the dead man with the girls' father, but the mother seems to be a widow or at any rate the absence of a father at the start of the story is a hint that the problem may have to do with men. It's not clear, but when the first man the daughters meet is not only dead but hard to deal with we are permitted to raise our eyebrows.

   The man is dead, but not dead enough. When she hits him with the stick we see that she is in fact attached to him. So here's the issue: when a fatherless woman leaves home she'll have to deal with the fact that she's stuck on a dead man. It's a risky situation—the two elder daughters end up dead.

   Not much happens in the wild run through the forest, except that everyone gets bruised. The girl

This story also gives us a chance to see what happens if the gift is not allowed to move on. Just as milk will sour in the jug, a gift that is kept still will lose its gift properties. The traditional belief in Wales is that when the fairies give gifts of bread to the poor, the loaves must be eaten that same day or they will turn into toadstools.[6] Some things go rotten when they are no longer treated as a gift.

We may think of the gift as a river and the girl in the tale who treats it correctly does so by allowing herself to be a channel for its current. If we try to dam up the river, one of two things will happen: it will either fill us until we burst or it will seek out another path and stop flowing through us. In this folk tale it is not just the mother's curse that gets the first two girls. The night birds give them a second chance and one imagines they would not have repeated the curse had they met with generosity. But instead the girls try to dam up the flow, thinking that what counts is ownership and size. The effect is clear: by keeping the gift they get no more. They are no longer vehicles for the stream and they no longer enjoy its fruits, one of which seems to be their own lives, for they end up dead. Their mother's bread has turned to toadstools inside of them.

Another way to describe the motion of the gift is to say that a gift must always be used up, consumed, and eaten. *The gift is property that perishes.* Food is one of the most common images for the gift because it is so clear that it is consumed. Even when the gift is not food, when it is something we would think of as durable goods, it is often referred to as a thing to be eaten. Shell necklaces and armbands are the ritual gifts in the Trobriand Islands and, when they are passed from one group to the next, protocol demands that the man who gives them away toss them on the ground and say, "Here, some food we could not eat." Or, again, a man in a different tribe that Wendy James has studied speaks of the money he was given at the marriage of his daughter saying that he will pass it on rather than spend it on himself. Only he puts it this way: "…If I receive money for the children God has given me, I cannot eat it. I must give it to others."[7]

---

manages to stay awake the whole time, however. This is a power she probably got from the birds, for they are night birds. The connection to the mother cannot spare her the ordeal, but it allows her to survive. When it's all over she's unstuck and we may assume that the problem won't come up again.

Though the dilemma of the story is not related to gift, all the psychological work is accomplished through gift exchange.

6) Wirt Sikes, *British Goblins* (London; Sampson Low et al, 1880), p 119.

7) Wendy R James, "Sister-Exchange Marriage," *Scientific American, vol 233,* no 6 (December 1975), pp 84–94.

To say that the gift is used up, consumed, and eaten sometimes means that it is truly destroyed as with food, but more simply and accurately it means that the gift perishes *for the person who gives it away*. In gift exchange the transaction itself consumes the object. This is why durable goods are given in a manner that emphasizes their loss (the Trobriand Islander throws the shells on the ground). A perishable good is a special case and a surer gift because it is sure to be lost.

Now it is true that something often comes back when a gift is given, but if this were made an explicit condition of the exchange it wouldn't be a gift. If the girl in our story had offered to sell the bread to the birds the whole tone would have been different. Instead she sacrifices it—her mother's gift is dead and gone when it leaves her hand. She no longer controls it, nor has she any contract about repayment. For her, the gift has perished. This then is how I use "consume" to speak of a gift—a gift is consumed when it moves from one hand to another with no assurance of anything in return. There is little difference, therefore, between its consumption and its motion. A market exchange has an equilibrium, or stasis: you pay in order to balance the scale. But when you give a gift there is momentum and the weight shifts from body to body.

I must add one more word on what it is to "consume" because the Western industrial world is known for its "consumer goods" and they are not at all what I mean. Again, the difference is in the form of the exchange, a thing we can feel most concretely in the form of the goods themselves. I remember the time I went to my first rare book fair and saw how the first editions of Thoreau and Whitman and Crane had been carefully packaged in heat-shrunk plastic with the price tags on the inside. Somehow the simple addition of air-tight plastic sacs had transformed the books from vehicles of liveliness into commodities, like bread made with chemicals to keep it from perishing. In commodity exchange it's as if the buyer and the seller are both in plastic bags; there's none of the contact of a gift exchange. There is neither motion nor emotion because the whole point is to keep the balance, to make sure the exchange itself doesn't consume anything or involve one person with another. "Consumer goods" are a privatized consuming, not a banquet.

The desire to consume is a kind of lust. We long to have the world flow through us like air or food. We are thirsty and hungry for something that can only be carried inside of bodies. We need it. We want it. But "consumer goods" just bait this lust, they do not satisfy it. They can never, as the gift can, raise lust into a kind of love, an emotional discourse. Love may always grow from lust, but not in the stillness of commodity exchange. The consumer of commodities is invited to a meal without passion, a consumption with neither satiation nor fire. Like a guest seduced into feeding on the drippings of someone else's capital without benefit of its inner nourishment, he is always hungry at the end of the meal, depressed, and weary as we all feel when lust has dragged us from the house and led us to nothing.

Gift exchange has many fruits and to the degree that the fruits of the gift can satisfy our needs there will always be pressure for property to be treated as a gift. This pressure, in a sense, is what keeps the gift in motion. When the Udak warn that a storm will ruin the crops if someone tries to stop the gift from moving, it is really their desire for its motion that will bring the storm. A restless hunger springs up when the gift is not being eaten. The Grimm brothers found a short tale they called "The Ungrateful Son":[8]

Once a man and his wife were sitting outside the front door with a roast chicken before them which they were going to eat between them. Then the man saw his old father coming along and quickly took the chicken and hid it, for he begrudged him any of it. The old man came, had a drink, and went away.

Now, the son was about to put the roast chicken back on the table, but when he reached for it, it had turned into a big toad that jumped in his face and stayed there and didn't go away again.

And if anybody tried to take it away, it would give them a poisonous look, as if about to jump in their faces, so that no one dared touch it. And the ungrateful son had to feed the toad every day, otherwise it would eat part of his face. And thus he went ceaselessly hither and yon about in the world.

This toad is the hunger that appears when the gift stops moving, whenever one man's gift becomes another man's capital. To the degree that we desire the fruits of the gift, teeth will appear when it is hidden away. When property is hoarded, thieves and beggars begin to be born to rich men's wives. A story like this says that there is a force seeking to keep the gift in motion. Some property must perish, its preservation is beyond us. We have no choice, or rather, our choice is whether to keep the gift moving or to be eaten

8) In *The Grimms' German Folk Tales,* Francis P Magoun, Jr and Alexander H Krappe, trans. Copyright © 1960 by Southern Illinois University Press. Reprinted by permission of the Southern Illinois University Press.

with it. We choose between the toad's dumb-lust and that other, graceful perishing in which the gift is eaten with a passion not unlike love.

II

"The gift is to the giver, and comes back most to him—it cannot fail..."
—Walt Whitman, *A Song of the Rolling Earth*

A bit of a mystery still remains in the Scottish tale "The Girl and the Dead Man": where did the "vessel of cordial" come from? My guess is that it comes from the mother, or from her spirit, at least. The gift not only moves, it moves in a circle. In this tale it circles through the mother and her daughter. The mother gives the bread and the girl gives it in return to the birds whom I place in the realm of the mother, not only because it is a mother bird who addresses her but also because there is a verbal link (the mother has a "leash of daughters," the mother bird has her "puppies"). The vessel of cordial is in the realm of the mother as well (the original Gaelic word means "teat of ichor" or "teat of health": it is a fluid that comes from the breast). The level changes, to be sure—it is a different sort of mother whose breasts hold the blood of the gods—but it is still in the maternal sphere. Structurally, then, the gift moves mother → daughter → mother → daughter. In circling twice in this way the gift itself increases from bread to the water of life, from carnal food to a spiritual food. At that point the circle expands as the girl gives the gift to her sisters to bring them back to life.

The figure of the circle in which the gift moves can be seen more clearly if we turn to a story from ethnography. Gift institutions seem to have been universal among tribal peoples; the few we know the most about are the ones that Western ethnographers [studied] around the turn of the century. One of these is the Kula, the ceremonial gift exchange [of] the Massim tribes, peoples who occupy the South Sea Islands off the eastern tip of New Guinea.[9]

There are a dozen or more groups of islands in the Kula archipelago. They are quite far apart—a circle enclosing the whole group would have a diameter of almost three hundred miles. The Kula is (or was sixty years ago) a highly developed gift system conducted throughout the islands. At its heart lies the exchange of two ceremonial gifts, armshells and necklaces. These are passed from household to household, staying with each for a time. So long as

---

9) Bronislaw Malinowski lived on these islands during the first world war. Most of my material on Kula comes from his book, *Argonauts of the Western Pacific* (London: George Routledge and Sons, Ltd, 1922; reprint ed New York: E P Dutton, 1961) chapter 3, pp 81–104.

one of the gifts is residing in a man's house, Bronislaw Malinowski tells us, the man is able "to draw a great deal of renown, to exhibit this article, to tell how he obtained it, and to plan to whom he is going to give it. And all this forms one of the favourite subjects of tribal conversation and gossip…" Armshells and necklaces are talked about, touched, and used to ward off disease. Like heirlooms, they are pools where feeling and power and history have collected. They are brought out and palavered over just as we might do if we had, say, some fine old carpenter's tools that had been used by our own grandfather, or a pocket watch brought from the old country.

Malinowski calls the Kula articles "ceremonial gifts" because their social use far exceeds their practical use. A friend of mine tells me that the gang he ran with in college continually passed around a deflated basketball. The joke was to get it mysteriously deposited in someone else's room. It seems that the clear uselessness of such objects makes it easier for them to be vehicles for the spirit of a group. My father says that when he was a boy his parents and some good friends passed back and forth, again as a joke, a huge open-ended wrench that had apparently been custom cast to repair a steam shovel. The two families found it one day on a picnic and for years thereafter it showed up in first one house and then the other, under the Christmas tree or in the umbrella stand, appearing one year fully bronzed and gift-wrapped. If you have not yourself been a part of such an exchange you will easily turn up a story like this by asking around, for these spontaneous exchanges of "useless" gifts are fairly common, though hardly ever developed to the depth and elegance that Malinowski found among the Massim.

The Kula gifts, the armshells and necklaces, move continually around a wide ring of islands in the archipelago. Each travels in a circle, the red shell necklaces moving clockwise and the armshells moving counterclockwise.

A man who participates in the Kula has gift partners in neighboring tribes. If we imagine him facing the center of the circle with partners on his left and right, he will always be receiving armshells from his partner to the left and giving them to the man on his right. The necklaces flow the other way. Of course these things are not actually passed hand over hand; they are carried by canoe from island to island in journeys that require great preparation and cover hundreds of miles.

The two Kula gifts are exchanged for each other. If a man brings me a necklace, I will give him in return some armshells of equivalent value. I may do this right away or I may wait as long as a year (though if I wait that long I will give him a few smaller gifts in the interim to show my good faith).

When I have received a gift, I can keep it for a time before I pass it on and initiate a new exchange. As a rule it takes between two and ten years for each article in the Kula to make a full round of the islands.

Because these gifts are exchanged for each other it seems we have already broken the rule against equilibrium that I set out in the first section. But let us look more closely. We should first note that the Kula articles are kept in motion, though this does not necessarily mean there is no equilibrium. Each gift stays with a man for awhile, but if he keeps it too long he will begin to have a reputation for being "slow" and "hard" in the Kula. The gifts "never stop," writes Malinowski. "It seems almost incredible at first…but it is the fact, nevertheless, that no one ever keeps any of the Kula valuables for any length of time…'Ownership,' therefore, in Kula, is quite a special economic relation. A man who is in the Kula never keeps any article for longer than, say, a year or two." The Trobriand Islanders know what it is to own property, but their sense of possession is wholly different from the European. The "social code…lays down that to possess is to be great, and that wealth is the indispensable appanage of social rank and attribute of personal virtue. But the important point is that with them *to possess is to give* [my emphasis]— and here the natives differ from us notably. A man who owns a thing is naturally expected to share it, to distribute it, to be its trustee and dispenser."

The motion of the Kula gifts does not by itself assure that there will be no equilibrium, for, as we have seen, they move but they are also exchanged. Two ethics, however, govern this exchange and both of them insure that, while there may be a macroscopic equilibrium, at the level of each man there will be the sense of imbalance, of shifting weight, that always marks a gift exchange. The first of these ethics prohibits discussion: "…the Kula," writes Malinowski, "consists in the bestowing of a ceremonial gift, which has to be repaid by an equivalent counter-gift after a lapse of time…But [and this is the point], it can never be exchanged from hand to hand, with the equivalence between the two objects discussed, bargained about, and computed." A man may wonder what will come in return for his gift, but he is not supposed to bring it up. In barter you talk and talk until you strike a bargain, but the gift is given in silence.

A second important ethic, Malinowski goes on, "is that the equivalence of the counter-gift is left to the giver, and it cannot be enforced by any kind of coercion." If a man gives some crummy necklace in return for a fine set of armshells, people may talk, but there's nothing you can do about it. When we barter we make deals and when someone defaults we go after him, but the gift must be a gift. It is as if you give a part of your substance to your gift partner and then wait in silence until he gives you a part of his. You put yourself in his hands. These rules—and they are typical of gift institutions— preserve the sense of motion despite the exchange involved. There is a trade, but these are not commodities.

We commonly think of gifts as being exchanged between two people and of gratitude as being directed back to the actual donor. "Reciprocity," the standard social science term for the return gift, has this sense of going to and fro between people (the roots are *re* and *pro*, back and forth, like a reciprocating engine). The gift in the Scottish tale is given reciprocally, going back and forth between the mother and her daughter (until the very end).

Reciprocal giving is a form of gift exchange, but it is the simplest. The gift moves in a circle and two people don't make much of a circle. Two points establish a line but a circle has to be drawn on a plane and a plane needs at least three points. This is why most stories of gift exchange have a minimum of three people. I have introduced the Kula circuit here because it is such a fine example. For the Kula gifts to move, each man must have at least two gift partners. In this case the circle is larger than that, of course, but three is its lower limit.

Circular giving differs from reciprocal giving in several ways. The most obvious is this: when the gift moves in a circle no one ever receives it from the same person he gives it to. I continually give armshells to my partner to the west but, unlike a two-person give and take, he never gives me armshells in return. The whole mood is different. The circle is the structural equivalent of the prohibition on discussion. When I give to someone from whom I do not receive (and yet I do receive elsewhere) it is as if the gift goes around a corner before it comes back. I have to give blindly. And I will feel a sort of blind gratitude, as well. The smaller the circle is—and particularly if it is just two people—the more you can keep your eye on things and the more likely it is you'll start to think like a salesman. But so long as the gift passes out of sight it cannot be manipulated by one man or one pair of gift partners. When the gift moves in a circle its motion is beyond the control of the personal ego and so each bearer must be a part of the group and each donation is an act of social faith.

What size is the circle? In addressing this question I have come to think of the circle, the container in which the gift moves, as its "body" or "ego." Some psychologists speak of the ego as a "complex" like any other: the

Mother, the Father, the Me—all of these are important places in the field of the psyche where images and energy cluster as we grow, like stars in a constellation. The ego complex takes on shape and size as the Me, that part of the psyche which takes everything personally, retains our private history, how others have treated us, how we look and feel and so on.

I find it useful to think of the ego complex as a thing which keeps expanding, not as something to be overcome or done away with. An ego has formed and hardened by the time most of us reach adolescence, but it is small, an ego-of-one. Then, if we fall in love, for example, the constellation of identity expands and the ego-of-one becomes an ego-of-two. The young lover, often to his own amazement, finds himself saying "we" instead of "me." Each of us identifies with a wider and wider community as we mature. We come to think and act with a group-ego (or, in most of these gift stories, a tribal-ego), which speaks with the "we" of kings and wise old people. Of course the larger it becomes the less it feels like what we usually mean by ego. Not entirely, though: whether an adolescent is thinking of himself or a nation of itself, it still feels like egotism to anyone on the outside. There is still a boundary.

If the ego were to widen still farther, however, it really would change its nature and become something we would no longer call ego. There is a consciousness in which we act as part of things larger even than the race. When I picture this I always think of the end of "Song of Myself" where Whitman dissolves into the air:

I effuse my flesh in eddies, and drift it in lacy jags.
I bequeath myself to the dirt and grow from the grass I love,
If you want me again look for me under your boot-soles.

Now the part that says "me" is scattered. There is no boundary to be outside of, unless the universe itself is bounded.

In all of this we could substitute "body" for "ego." Aborigines commonly refer to their own clan as "my body," just as our marriage ceremony speaks of becoming "one flesh." Again, the body in this sense enlarges beyond our own skin and in its final expansion there is no body at all. We love to feel the body open outward when we are in the spirit of the gift. The ego's firmness has its virtues, but in the end we seek the slow dilation, to use another of Whitman's words, in which the self enjoys a widening give-and-take with the world and is finally lost in ripeness.

The gift can circulate at every level of the ego. In the ego-of-one we speak of self-gratification and, whether it's forced or chosen, a virtue or a vice, the mark of self-gratification is its isolation. Reciprocal giving, the ego-of-two, is a little more social. We think mostly of lovers. Each of these circles is exhilarating as it expands and the little gifts that pass between lovers touch us because each is stepping into a larger circuit. But when it goes on and on to the exclusion of others it stops expanding and goes stale. D H Lawrence spoke of the "egoisme à deux" of so many married couples, people who get just so far in the expansion of the self and then close down for a lifetime, opening up for neither children nor the gods. A folk tale from Kashmir tells of two Brahmin women who tried to dispense with their alms-giving duties by simply giving alms back and forth to each other.[10] They didn't quite have the spirit of the thing. When they died they returned to the earth as two wells so poisoned that no one could take water from them. No one else can drink from the ego-of-two. It has its time in our maturation, but it is an infant form of the gift circle and does not endure.

In the Kula we have already seen a fine example of the larger circle. The Maori, the native tribes of New Zealand, provide another, similar in some ways to the Kula, but offering new detail and a hint of how gift exchange feels if the circle expands beyond the body of the tribe.[11] The Maori have a word *hau* which translates as "spirit," particularly the spirit of the gift and the spirit of the forest which gives food. In these tribes when hunters return from the forest with birds they have killed they give a portion of the kill to the priests who, in turn, cook them at a sacred fire. The priests eat a few of the birds and then prepare a sort of talisman, the *mauri,* which is the physical embodiment of the forest *hau.* This *mauri* is a gift that the priests give back to the forest where it causes the birds to be abundant so that they may again be slain and taken by hunters.

There are three gifts in this hunting ritual; the forest gives to the hunters, the hunters to the priests, and the priests to the forest. At the end, the gift moves from the third party back to the first. The ceremony that the priests perform is called *whangai hau* which means "nourishing *hau,"* that is, feeding the spirit. To give such a name to the priests' activity says that the addition of the third party keeps the gift in motion, keeps it lively. Put conversely,

10) W Norman Brown, "Tawi Tales" (Unpublished manuscript in the Indiana University Library).

11) Elsdon Best, "Maori Forest Lore…, Part III," in *Transactions of the New Zealand Institute* 42 (1909), pp 433–81, especially p 439. From Marshall Sahlins, *Stone Age Economics* (New York: Aldine-Atherton, Inc., 1972), pp 152 and 158.

without the priests there is a danger that the motion of the gift will be lost. It seems to be too much to ask of the hunters to both kill the game and return a gift to the forest. As we said in speaking of the Kula, gift exchange is more likely to turn into barter when it falls into the ego-of-two. With a simple give-and-take, the hunters may begin to think of the forest as a place to turn a profit. But with the priests present, the gift must leave the hunters' sight before it returns to the woods. The priests take on or incarnate the position of the third thing to avoid the binary relation of the hunters and forest which by itself would not be abundant. The priests, by their presence alone, feed the spirit.

Every gift calls for a return gift, and so, by placing the gift back in the forest, the priests treat the birds as a gift of nature. We now understand that this is ecological. Ecology as a science began toward the end of the nineteenth century, an offshoot of all the interest in evolution. It was originally the study of how animals live in their environments and one of its first lessons was that, beneath all the change in nature, there are steady states characterized by cycles. Every participant in the cycle literally lives off of the others with only the energy source, the sun, being transcendent. Widening this study to include man meant to look at ourselves as a part of nature again, not its Lord. When we see that we are actors in natural cycles then we understand that what nature gives to us is influenced by what we give to nature. So the circle is a sign of ecological wisdom as much as of gift. We come to feel ourselves as one part of a large self-regulating system. The return gift, the "nourishing *hau*," is literally feedback, as they say in cybernetics. Without it, that is to say, with any greed or arrogance of will, the whole cycle gets out of whack. We all know that it isn't "really" the *mauri* placed in the forest that "causes" the birds to be abundant, and yet now we see that on a different level it is: the circle of gifts replicates and harmonizes with the cycles of nature and in so doing manages not to interrupt them and not to put man on the outside. The forest's abundance is in fact a consequence of our treating its wealth as a gift. We shall see as we go along that there is always this link between gift and abundance, as there is always a link between commodities and scarcity.[12]

---

12) When things run in a self-regulating cycle, we speak of time and cause and value in a different way. Time is not linear (it's either "momentary" or "eternal") and one event doesn't "cause" another, they are all of a piece. In addition, one part is no more valuable than another. When we speak of value we assume we can set things side by side and weigh them and compare. But in a self-regulating cycle no part can be taken out; they are all one. Which is more valuable to you, your heart or your brain? The value, like the time, is not comparative, it is either "priceless" or "worthless."

We say these things about gifts as well. It's almost a matter of definition, of course, that gifts

The Maori hunting ritual enlarges the circle within which the gift moves in two ways. First, it includes nature. Second and more importantly, it includes the gods. The priests act out a gift relationship with the deities, giving thanks and sacrificing gifts to them in return for what they give the tribe. A story from the Old Testament shows us the same thing in a tradition with which we are more familiar. The structure is identical.

In the Pentateuch the first fruits always belong to the Lord. In Exodus the Lord tells Moses: "Consecrate to me all the first-born; whatever is the first to open the womb among the people of Israel, both of man and of beast, is mine." The Lord gives the tribe its wealth and the germ of that wealth is then given back to the Lord. Fertility is a gift from God and in order for it to continue, its first fruits must be returned to Him as gift. In pagan times this had included sacrificing the first-born son. The Israelites had early been allowed to substitute an animal for the first-born son, as in the story of Abraham and Isaac. Likewise a lamb was substituted for the first-born of any unclean animal. The Lord says to Moses:

All that opens the womb is mine, all your male cattle, the firstlings of cow and sheep. The firstling of an ass you shall redeem with a lamb, or if you will not redeem it you shall break its neck. All the first-born of your sons you shall redeem.

In a different chapter the Lord explains to Aaron what is to be done with the first-borns. Aaron and his sons are responsible for the priesthood and they minister at the altar. The lambs, calves, and kids are to be sacrificed: "You shall sprinkle their blood upon the altar, and shall burn their fat as an offering by fire, a pleasing odor to the Lord; but their flesh shall be yours…" As in the Maori story, the priests eat a portion of the gift. But its essence is burned and returned to the Lord in smoke.

This gift cycle has three stations and more—the flocks, the tribe, the priests, and the Lord. The inclusion of the Lord in the circle—and this is the point I began to make above—changes the ego in which the gift moves in a way unlike any other addition. It is enlarged beyond the tribal ego and beyond

---

cannot be sold, but here we see their pricelessness as a characteristic that goes with the circle. Likewise gifts have no cause. One doesn't say "I got this gift because I gave him one." Or rather, one can, but if he does he's out of the circle looking in, that is to say, he's begun to barter. In barter the sale causes the return; but gifts just move, that's all. When a wheel spins we don't say that the top of it "causes" the bottom to move around. That's silly. We just say, "the wheel spins," as we say, "the gift moves in a circle." Likewise, the sense of time is different. In exchange trade we know when the debt is due. In gift we do not speak, we turn back to our own labor in silence.

nature. Now, as I said when I first introduced the image, we would no longer call it "ego" at all. The gift leaves all boundary and circles into mystery.

The passage into mystery always refreshes. We lie on the grass and stare at the stars in their blackness and our heaviness falls away. If, when we work, we can look on the face of mystery just once a day, then all our labor satisfies, and if we cannot we become willful and topheavy. We are lightened when our gifts rise from pools we cannot fathom. Then they are not all ego and then they are inexhaustible. Anything that is contained contains as well its own exhaustion. The most perfectly balanced gyroscope slowly wears down. But we are enlivened when the gift passes into the heart of light or of darkness and then returns. This is as true of property as it is of those gifts we cannot touch. It is when the world of objects burns a bit in our peripheral vision that it gives us jubilation and not depression. We stand before a bonfire or even a burning house and feel the odd release it brings. It is as if the trees were able to give the sun return for what enters them through the leaf. Objects pull us down into their bones unless their fat is singed occasionally. When all property is held still then the Pharaoh himself is plagued with hungry toads. When we cannot be moved to move the gift then a sword appears to seek out the first-born sons. But that Pharaoh was dead long before his first-born was taken, for we are only alive to the degree that we can feel the call for motion. In the living body that call is no stranger, it is a part of the soul. When the gift circles into mystery then the liveliness stays and the mood is the same as in those lines of Whitman. It is "a pleasing odor to the Lord" when the first fruits are effused in eddies and drifted in lacy jags above the flame.

We described the motion of the gift earlier in this essay by saying that gifts are always used, consumed, or eaten. Now that we have seen the figure of the circle we can understand what seems at first to be a paradox of gift exchange: when the gift is used it is not used up. Quite the opposite in fact: the gift that is not used is lost while the one that is passed along remains abundant. In the Scottish tale the girls who hoard their bread are fed only while they eat. The meal finishes in hunger though they took the larger piece. The girl who shares her bread is satisfied. What is given away feeds again and again while what is kept feeds only once and leaves us hungry.

The tale is a parable, but in the Kula ring we saw the same as a social fact. The necklaces and armshells are not diminished by their use, but satisfy faithfully. It is only when a foreigner intervenes to buy a few for the museum that they are "used up" by a transaction. The Maori hunting tale showed us that not just food in parables but food in nature remains abundant when it is treated as gift, when we participate in the moving circle and do not stand aside as hunter or exploiter. Gifts form a class of property whose value is only in their use and which literally cease to exist if they are not constantly consumed.[13] When gifts are sold they change their nature as much as water changes when it freezes and no rationalist telling of the constant elemental structure can replace the feeling that is lost.

In E M Forster's novel *A Passage to India,* Dr Aziz, the Moslem, and Fielding, the Englishman, have a brief dialogue, a typical debate between gift and commodity.[14] Fielding says:

"Your emotions never seem in proportion to their objects, Aziz."

"Is emotion a sack of potatoes, so much to the pound, to be measured out? Am I a machine? I shall be told I can use up my emotions by using them, next."

"I should have thought you would. It sounds common sense. You can't eat your cake and have it, even in the world of the spirit."

"If you are right, there is no point in any friendship; it all comes down to give and take, or give and return, which is disgusting, and we had better all leap over this parapet and kill ourselves."

In the world of gift, as in the Scottish tale, you not only can have your cake and eat it too, you can't have your cake *unless* you eat it. It is the same with feeling. Our emotions are not used up in use. They may rise and fall, certainly, but they become strong and sure as we use them and only die away when we try to keep the lid on.

Gift and feeling are alike in this regard. Though once that is said we must qualify it, for the gift does not imitate all emotion, it imitates the emotions of relationship. As I mentioned in my introductory remarks, the gift joins people together. It doesn't just carry feeling, it carries attachment or love. The gift is an emanation of Eros. The forms of gift exchange spring from erotic life and gifts are its vehicles. In speaking of "use," then, we see that the gift displays a natural fact: libido is not lost when it is given away. Eros never wastes his lovers. When we give ourselves to that god he does not leave off his attentions; it is only when we fall to calculation that he remains

---

13) They call this "use-value" in economics. I am not fond of the term. It usually shows up at the bottom line, a passing admission that at the boundary of exchange calculus there are folks who really use property to live.

14) E M Forster, *A Passage to India* (New York: Harcourt Brace and World, Inc., 1924), pp 160 and 254.

hidden and no body will satisfy. Satisfaction comes not merely from being filled but from being filled with a current that will not cease. With the gift, as in love, our satisfaction sets us at ease because we know that somehow its use at once assures its plenty.

Scarcity and abundance have more to do with the form of exchange than with how much stuff is at hand. Scarcity appears when wealth cannot flow. Elsewhere in *A Passage to India,* Dr Aziz says, "If money goes, money comes. If money stays, death comes. Did you ever hear that useful Urdu proverb?" and Fielding replies, "My proverbs are: a penny saved is a penny earned; A stitch in time saves nine; Look before you leap; and the British Empire rests on them." He's right. An empire does need its clerks with their ledgers and their clocks, saving pennies in time. The problem is that wealth ceases to move freely when all things are counted and carry a price. It may accumulate in great heaps but fewer and fewer people can afford to enjoy it. After the war in Bangladesh, thousands of tons of donated rice rotted in warehouses because the market was the only known mode of distribution and the poor, naturally, couldn't afford to buy. Marshall Sahlins, an anthropologist who has done some of the best work on gift exchange, begins a comment on modern scarcity with the paradoxical contention that hunters and gatherers "have affluent economies, their absolute poverty notwithstanding."[15] He writes:

> Modern capitalist societies, however richly endowed, dedicate themselves to the proposition of scarcity. [Both Samuelson and Friedman begin their economies with "The Law of Scarcity"; it's all over by the end of chapter one.] Inadequacy of economic means is the first principle of the world's wealthiest peoples. The apparent material status of the economy seems to be no clue to its accomplishments; something has to be said for the mode of economic organization.
>
> The market-industrial system institutes scarcity, in a manner completely unparalleled and to a degree nowhere else approximated. Where production and distribution are arranged through the behavior of prices, and all livelihoods depend on getting and spending, insufficiency of material means becomes the explicit, calculable starting point of all economic activity. The entrepreneur is confronted with alternative investments of a finite capital, the worker (hopefully) with

15) Sahlins, *Stone Age Economics*, pp 3–4.

alternative choices of remunerative employ....Consumption is a double tragedy: what begins in inadequacy will end in deprivation. Bringing together an international division of labor, the market makes available a dazzling array of products: all these Good Things within a man's reach—but never all within his grasp. Worse, in this game of consumer free choice, every acquisition is simultaneously a deprivation, for every purchase of something is a foregoing of something else, in general only marginally less desirable...

Scarcity appears when there is a boundary. If there is plenty of blood in the system but something blocks its passage to the brain, the brain does well to complain of scarcity. The assumptions of market exchange may not necessarily lead to the emergence of boundaries, but they do in practice. When trade is "clean" and leaves people unconnected, when the merchant is free to sell when and where he will, when the market moves mostly for profit and the dominant myth is not "to possess is to give" but "the fittest survive," then wealth will lose its motion and gather in isolated pools. Under the assumptions of trade, property is plagued by entropy and wealth becomes scarce even as it increases.

A commodity is *truly* "used up" when it is sold because nothing about the exchange assures its return. A visiting sea captain may pay handsomely for some Kula necklaces, but because their sale removes them from the circle it wastes them, no matter the price. Gifts that remain gifts can support an affluence of satisfaction, even without numerical abundance. The mythology of the rich in the over-producing nations that the poor are in on some secret about satisfaction—black "soul," gypsy *duende,* the noble savage, the simple farmer, the virile gamekeeper—obscures the harshness of modern capitalist poverty, but it does have a basis, for people who live in voluntary poverty or who are not capital-intensive do have more ready access to "erotic" forms of exchange that are neither exhausting nor exhaustible and whose use assures their plenty.

If the commodity moves to turn a profit, where does the gift move? The gift in all its realms, from the soul to the kitchen, moves toward the empty place. As it turns in its circle it always comes to him who has been empty-handed the longest, and if someone appears elsewhere whose need is greater it will leave its old channel and move to him. Our generosity may leave us empty, but our emptiness then pulls gently at the whole until the thing in motion returns to fill us up again. Social nature abhors a vacuum. The gift finds us attractive when we stand with a bowl that is unowned and empty. As Meister Eckhart says, "Let us borrow empty vessels."

The begging bowl of the Buddha, Thomas Merton has said, "represents the ultimate theological root of the belief, not just in a right to beg, but in openness to the gifts of all beings as an expression of the interdependence of all beings...When the monk begs from the layman and receives a gift from the layman, it is not as a selfish person getting something from somebody else. He is simply opening himself in this interdependence..."[16] The wandering mendicant takes it as his task to carry what is empty from door to door. There is no profit; he merely stays alive if the gift moves toward him. He makes its spirit visible to us. His well-being, then, is a sign of its well-being, as his starvation would be a sign of its withdrawal. Our English word "beggar" comes from the Beghards, a brotherhood of mendicant friars that grew up in the thirteenth century in Flanders. There are still some places in the East, I gather, where wandering mendicants live from the begging bowl. In Europe they died out at the close of the Middle Ages.

As the bearer of the empty place the holy mendicant has an active duty beyond his supplication. He is the vehicle of that fluidity which is abundance. The wealth of the group touches his bowl at all sides, as if it were the center of a wheel where the spokes meet. The gift gathers there and the mendicant gives it away again when he meets someone who is empty. In European folk tales the beggar often turns out to be Wotan, the true "owner" of the land, who asks for charity though it is his own wealth he moves within and who then responds to neediness by filling it with gift. He is godfather to the poor.

Folk tales commonly open with a beggar motif. In a tale from Bengal, the king has two queens, both of whom are childless.[17] A faquir, a wandering mendicant, comes to the palace gate to ask for alms. One of the queens walks down to give him a handful of rice. When he finds that she is childless, however, he says that he cannot accept the rice but has a gift for her instead, a potion that will remove her barrenness. If she drinks his nostrum with the juice of the pomegranate flower, he tells her, in due time she will bear a son whom she should then call the Pomegranate Boy. All this comes to pass and the tale proceeds.

Such stories say that the gift always moves in its circle from plenty to emptiness. The gift seeks the barren and the arid and the stuck and the

---

16) N Burton et al, ed, *The Asian Journal of Thomas Merton* (New York: New Directions, 1973), pp 341–42.

17) L B Day (Lalavihari De), "Life's Secret," in *Folk-Tales of Bengal* (London: Macmillan, 1883).

poor.[18] A commodity stays where it is and says "I am," but the gift says "I am not" and longs to be consumed. A guest in my home, it has no home of its own but moves on, leaving early in the morning before the rest of us have risen. The Lord says "all that opens the womb is mine" for it is He who filled the empty womb, having earlier stood as a beggar by the sacrificial fire or at the gates of the palace.

III

The gift the beggar gives to the queen in this last folk tale brings the queen her fertility and she bears a child. Fertility and growth are common fruits of gift exchange. Think back on all we have seen so far—the Gaelic tale, the Kula ring, the rites of the first-born, feeding the forest *hau*, and so on— fertility is often a concern and invariably either the bearers of the gift or the gift itself grows as a result of its circulation.

If the gift is alive, like a bird or a cornstalk, then it really grows, of course. But even inert gifts, such as the Kula articles, are *felt* to increase in worth as they move from hand to hand. The distinction—alive/inert—is not finally very useful, therefore, because if the gift is not alive it is nonetheless treated as if it were and whatever we treat as living begins to take on life. Moreover, gifts that take on life will in turn bestow life. The final gift in the Gaelic tale is used to revive the dead sisters. Even if such miracles are rare, it is still a fact of the soul that depression—or any heavy, dead feeling—will lift away when a gift comes toward us. Gifts not only move us, they enliven us.

The gift is a servant to forces which pull things together and lift them up. There are other forces in the world that break things down into smaller and smaller bits, that find the fissures in stones and split them apart or enter a marriage and leave it lifeless at the core. In living organisms, the atomizing forces are associated with decay and death, while the cohering forces, the ones that wrap the morning-glory around a fence post or cover the ashy slopes of a new volcano with little pine trees, these are associated with life. Gift property serves an upward force. On one level it reflects and carries the form of organic growth, but above that, at the level of society and spirit, the gift carries our own liveliness. We spiral upward with the gift, or at least it holds us upright against the forces that split us apart and pull us down.

To speak in this manner risks confusing biological "life" with cultural and spiritual "life"—a confusion I would like to avoid for the two are not

18) Folk tales are the only "proof" I can offer here. The point is more spiritual than social: in the spirit world, new life comes to us when we "give up."

always the same. They are linked, but there is also a gap. In addressing the question of increase let us therefore take a gift at the level of culture—something inorganic and inedible in fact—and see how far we can go toward explaining its *felt* increase without recourse to the natural analogy.

The North Pacific tribes of the American Indians (the Kwakiutl, Tlingit, Haida, and others) exchanged as ceremonial gifts large decorated copper plaques.[19] These coppers were always associated with the property given away at a potlatch—a ceremony that marked important events such as a marriage or, more commonly, the assumption of rank by a member of a tribe. The word *potlatch* means simply "giving."[20]

Coppers increased in worth as they circulated. At the time when Franz Boas witnessed the exchange of a copper in the 1890s, their worth was reckoned in terms of woolen Hudson Bay Company trade blankets. To tell the story briefly and in terms of the increase involved, one of the tribes in Boas's report has a copper to give away; they invite a neighboring tribe to a feast and offer them the gift.[21] The second tribe accepts, putting themselves under the obligation to make a return gift. The transaction takes place the next day on a beach. The first tribe brings the copper and the leader of the second tribe lays down 1,000 trade blankets as a return gift.

Then things get interesting. The chiefs who are giving the copper away don't accept the return gift. Instead they slowly replay the entire history of this copper's previous passages, first one man saying that just two hundred more blankets will be fine and then another saying that really an additional eight hundred will be needed to make everyone feel right, while the recipient of the copper responds saying either "What you say is good, it pleases my heart," or else begging for mercy as he brings out more and more blankets. Five times the chiefs ask for more blankets and five times they are brought out until 3,700 are stacked up in a long row on the beach.

When the copper's entire history has been acted out, the talk stops. Now comes the true return gift, these formalities having merely raised the

---

19) Philip Drucker, *Cultures of the North Pacific* (Scranton, Pa: Chandler Publishing Co, 1965).

20) I cannot here tell the story of potlatch in its full detail, but I should note that two of its better known characteristics in the popular literature—the usurious nature of loans and the rivalry or "fighting with property"—while based on traceable aboriginal motifs, are really post-European elaborations. The tribes had known a century of European trade before Boas arrived. When Marcel Mauss read through Boas's material he declared potlatch "the monster child of the gift system." So it was. As first studied, potlatch was the progeny of a "civilized" commodity trade mated to an aboriginal gift economy; some of the results were freakish.

21) Franz Boas, "The Social Organization and the Secret Societies of the Kwakiutl Indians," *U S National Museum, Annual Report, 1894–1895* (Washington, 1897), pp 311–738. Part 3 of this work is on the potlatch, pp 341–58.

exchange into the general area of this copper's worth. Now the receiving chief, on his own, announces he would like to "adorn" his guests. He brings out two hundred more blankets and gives them individually to the visitors. Then he adds still another two hundred, saying, "you must think poorly of me," and telling about his forefathers.

These four hundred blankets are given without any of the dialogue that marked the first part of the ceremony. It is here that the recipient of the copper shows his generosity and it is here that the copper increases in worth. The next time it is given away, people will remember how it grew by four hundred blankets in its last passage.

To return to the question of increase at the level of culture, there is a particular kind of investment in the exchange of copper. Each time the copper passes from one group to another, more blankets are heaped into it, so to speak. The source of increase is clear: each man really adds to its worth as the copper comes toward him. But it is important to remember that the investment is itself a gift, so the increase is both concrete (blankets) and emotional (the spirit of generosity). At each transaction the concrete increase (the "adornment") is a witness to the increase in feeling. In this way, though people may remember it in terms of blankets, the copper becomes enriched with feeling. And not all feelings, either, but those of generosity, liberality, good will—feelings that draw people together.

Coppers make a good example here because there is concrete increase to manifest the feeling, but that is not necessary. The mere passage of the gift, the act of donation, contains the feeling and therefore the passage alone is the investment. The gift is a pool or reservoir in which the sentiments of its exchange accumulate so that the more often it is given away the more feeling it carries, like an heirloom that has been passed down for generations. The gift gets steeped in the fluids of its own passage. In folk tales the gift is often something seemingly worthless—ashes or coals or leaves or straw— but when the puzzled recipient carries it to his doorstep he finds it turned to gold. In such tales the mere motion of the gift across the boundary from the world of the donor (usually a spirit) to the doorsill of the recipient is sufficient to transmute it from dross to gold.[22]

---

22) Here is a typical tale from Russia: a woman walking in the woods found a baby wood-demon "lying naked on the ground and crying bitterly. So she covered it up with her cloak, and after a time came her mother, a female wood-demon, and rewarded the woman with a potful of burning coals, which afterwards turned into bright golden ducats."

The woman doesn't cover the baby because she wants to get paid, she does it because she's moved to; then the gift comes to her. It increases solely by its passage from the realm of wood-demons to her cottage.

Typically the increase inheres in the gift only so long as it is treated as such—as soon as the happy mortal starts to count it or grabs his wheelbarrow and heads back for more, the gold reverts to straw. The growth is in the sentiment and cannot be put on the scale.

The potlatch can rightly be spoken of as a good-will ceremony. One of the men giving the feast in the potlatch Boas witnessed says as the meal begins: "This food here is the good will of our forefathers. It is all given away." The act of donation is an affirmation of good will. When someone in one of these tribes is mistakenly insulted, his response, rather than turning to a libel lawyer, is to give a gift to the man who insulted him, and if indeed the insult was mistaken, the man gives a gift in return, adding a little extra to demonstrate his good will, a sequence which has the same structure (back and forth with increase) as the potlatch itself. When a gift passes from hand to hand in this spirit—and here we have come back to the question of increase—it becomes the binder of many wills. What gathers in it is not only the sentiment of generosity but the affirmation of individual good will, making of those separate parts a *spiritus mundi,* a unanimous heart, a band whose wills are focused through the lens of the gift. In this way, the gift is an agent of social cohesion and this banding function again leads to the feeling that a gift grows through its circulation. The whole really is greater than the sum of its parts. If it brings the group together, the gift increases in worth immediately upon its first circulation, and then, like a faithful lover, continues to grow through constancy.

I do not mean to imply that gifts such as these coppers are felt to grow merely because the group projects its own life onto them, for that would imply that the group's liveliness can be separated from the gift, and it can't. If the copper is taken away, so is the life. When a song moves us we don't say we've projected our feelings onto the melody, nor do we say a woman projects the other sex onto her lover. Equally the gift and the group are two separate things and there is nothing to be withdrawn. We could say, however, that a copper is an image for the life of the group, for a true image has a life of its own. All mystery needs its image. It needs these two, the ear and the song, the he and the she, the soul and the word. The tribe and its gift are separate but they are also the same—there is a little gap between them so they may breathe into each other, and yet there is no gap at all for they share one breath, one meal for the two of them. People with a sense of the gift not only speak of it as food to eat, they also feed it (as the Maori ceremony "feeds" the forest *hau*). The nourishment flows both ways. When we have fed the gift with our labor and generosity, it grows and feeds us in return. The gift and its bearers share a spirit which is kept alive by its motion among them and from that the life emerges, willy-nilly. Still, the spirit of the gift is alive only when the gift is being passed from hand to hand. When Black Elk, an Oglala Sioux holy man, told the history of the Sioux "sacred pipe" to Joseph Epes Brown, he explained that at the time the pipe had first been given to him, his elders had told him that its history must always be passed down, "for as long as it is known, and for as long as the pipe is used, [the] people will live; but as soon as it has been forgotten, the people will be without a center and they will perish."[23]

The increase is the core of the gift, the kernel. In this essay I use the term "gift" for both the object and its increase, but at times it seems more accurate to speak of the increase alone as the gift and to treat the object involved more modestly as its vehicle or vessel. Certainly it makes sense to say that the increase is the real gift in those cases where the gift-object is sacrificed, for the increase continues despite (even because of) that loss; it is the constant in the cycle, not consumed in use. A Maori elder who told of the forest *hau* distinguished in this way between object and increase, the *mauri* set in the forest and its *hau* which causes the game to abound. In that cycle the *hau* is nourished and passed along while the gift-objects (birds, *mauri*) disappear.

Marshall Sahlins, when he commented on the Maori gift stories, asked that we "observe just where the term *hau* enters into the discussion. Not with the initial transfer from the first to the second party, as well it could if the *hau* were the spirit in the gift, but upon the exchange between the second and third parties, as logically it would if [the *hau*] were the yield on the gift. The term profit is economically and historically inappropriate to the Maori, but it would have been a better translation than 'spirit' for the *hau* in question."

Sahlins's gloss highlights something which has been implicit in our discussion, though not yet stated directly—the increase comes to a gift as it moves from second to third party, not in the simpler passage from first to second. It begins when the gift has passed through someone, when the circle appears. But, as Sahlins senses, "profit" is not the right word. Capital earns profit and the sale of a commodity turns a profit, but gifts that remain gifts do not *earn* profit, they *give* increase. The distinction lies in what we might call the vector of the increase: in gift exchange it stays in motion and follows the object, while in commodity exchange it stays behind (as profit).

---

23) Joseph Epes Brown, *The Sacred Pipe* (Norman: The University of Oklahoma Press, 1953), p xii.

With this in mind, we may return to a dictum laid out early in the essay: one man's gift must not be another man's capital. A corollary may now be developed, saying: the increase which comes of gift exchange must remain a gift and not be converted to capital. St. Ambrose of Milan states it directly in a commentary on Deuteronomy: "God has excluded in general all increase of capital."[24] This is an ethic in a gift society. Just as one may choose to treat the gift as gift or to take it out of circulation, so the increase may either be passed along or laid aside as capital.

I have chosen not to allow this essay to wander very far into the labyrinths of capitalism, so I shall only sketch this choice in its broadest terms. Capital is wealth taken out of circulation and laid aside to produce more wealth. Cattle devoured at a feast are gift, but cattle set aside to produce calves or milk are capital. All peoples have both and need both. A question arises, however, whenever there's a surplus. If you have more than you need, what do you do with it? What happens to the gravy? Capitalism as an ideology addresses itself to this choice and at every turn applauds the move away from gift and calls that sensible ("a penny saved...").[25]

Here it becomes necessary to differentiate two forms of growth, for the growth of capital is not the increase of the gift. Nor are their fruits the same. The gift grows more lively but capital grows in a lump—more cows, more factories...When all surplus is turned to capital, the stock increases but not the liveliness, and there is busyness without elevation, increase without feeling, a growth more sedimentary than organic, the conglomeration of stones rather than the flourishing of trees.

The accumulation of capital has its own benefits—security and material comfort being the most obvious and appealing—but the point here is that whatever those benefits, if they flow from the conversion of gifts to capital then the fruits of the gift are lost. At that point property becomes correctly associated with the suppression of liveliness, fertility, and emotion. To recall our earlier tales, when a goat given from one tribe to another is not treated as a gift, or when any gift is hoarded and counted and kept for the self, then death appears, or a hungry toad, or storm damage. Capitalism as a system has the same problems on a larger scale. Somewhere property must be truly

---

24) St. Ambrose (S Ambrossi), *De Tobias,* a commentary, trans Lois M Zucker (Washington, D. C.: The Catholic University of America, 1933), p 67.

25) To move away from capitalism is not to change the form of ownership from the few to the many, though that may be a necessary step, but to cease turning so much surplus into capital, that is, to treat most increase (even if it comes from labor) as a gift. It is quite possible to have the state own everything and still convert all gifts to capital, as Stalin demonstrated. When he decided in favor of the "production mode" he acted as a capitalist, the locus of ownership having nothing to do with it.

consumed. The capitalist, busy turning all his homemade gravy back to capital, must seek out foreigners to consume the goods (though as before they get only the dumb consumption of commodities). And what was a toad in the psyche or storm damage in the tribe now becomes alienation at home or war and exploitation abroad, those shades who follow capital whenever it feeds on the gift.

The gift remains a gift only so long as its increase remains a gift. Those people, therefore, who prohibit "in general all increase on capital," as St. Ambrose has it, those who insist that any conversion of property from one form to another must be in the direction of the gift, who love the increase more than its vehicles and feel their worth in liveliness, for such people the increase of gifts is not lost and the circle in which they move becomes an upward spiral.

Galway Kinnell

Galway Kinnell was born in Providence, Rhode Island, in 1927. He studied at Princeton University (where he roomed with fellow future Pulitzer Prize–winner W.S. Merwin) and the University of Rochester. During WWII Kinnell served in the U.S. Navy and went on to live in Paris as a Fulbright Scholar. During the 1950s, Kinnell began teaching at schools as geographically varied as the University of Nice, the University of Iran, and the University of Chicago. His first book, *What a Kingdom It Was*, was published in 1960. Throughout the 1960s and '70s, Kinnell became one of the premier American poets, gaining popularity with critics and readers alike with such titles as *Body Rags*, *The Book of Nightmares*, and *Walking Down the Stairs*, a collection of interviews. In 1983, he received both the Pulitzer Prize and the National Book Award for his *Selected Poems* (which includes "Goodbye," originally printed in *The Kenyon Review* in 1979). Kinnell's poems often attempt to explore the self and the transience of life by meditating on objects in the natural world. Recent works include *A New Selected Poems*, *Imperfect Thirst,* and *When One Has Lived a Long Time Alone.* A former state poet of Vermont, Kinnell currently teaches creative writing at New York University.

Goodbye *(1979)*
by Galway Kinnell

1

My mother, poor woman, lies tonight
in her last bed. It's snowing, for her, in her darkness.
I swallow down the goodbyes I won't get to use,
tasteless, with wretched mouth-water.
Whatever we are, she and I, we're nearly cured.

The night years ago when I walked away
from that final class of junior high school students
in Pittsburgh, the youngest of them ran after me
down the dark street. "Goodbye!" she called,
snow swirling across her face, tears falling.

2

Tears have kept on falling. History
has lent them its slanted understanding
of the human face. After each last embrace the dying give
the snow lets fall faster its disintegrating curtain.
The mind shreds the present, once the past is over.

In the Derry graveyard where only her longings sleep
and armfuls of flowers go out in the drizzle
the bodies not yet risen must lie nearly forever…
"Sprouting good Irish grass," the graveskeeper blarneys,
he can't help it, "a sprig of shamrock, if they were young."

3

In Pittsburgh tonight, those who were young
will be less young, those who were old, more old, or more likely
no more; and the street where Syllest,
fleetest of my darlings, caught up with me
and hugged me and said goodbye, will be empty. Well,

one day the streets all over the world will be empty—
already, in heaven, listen, the golden cobblestones have fallen still—

everyone's arms will be empty, everyone's mouth, the Derry earth.
It is written in our hearts, the emptiness is all.
That is how we have learned, the embrace is all.

Derek Walcott

Derek Walcott was born in Saint Lucia, the West Indies, in 1930. He graduated from the University of the West Indies and in 1953 moved to Trinidad,
where he worked as a teacher on several Caribbean islands and, in 1959,
founded the Trinidad Theatre Workshop, which produced many of his early
plays. His breakthrough as a poet came in 1962, with the collection of
poems *In a Green Night*. He remained director of the Trinidad Theatre
Workshop until 1976, publishing many important volumes during this
period, including *The Castaway and Other Poems*, *The Gulf and Other
Poems*, and *Another Life*. Walcott directed his attention increasingly to the
United States, taking a position at the University of Boston in 1981. In 1992,
Walcott was given the Nobel Prize for Literature "for a poetic oeuvre of
great luminosity, sustained by a historical vision, the outcome of a multi-
cultural commitment," citing such works as *Omeros*, *The Arkansas
Testament, Collected Poems: 1948–1984,* and *Dream on Monkey Mountain
and Other Plays*. Walcott continues to hold his position at Boston
University, teaching in the fall and spending the rest of the year in Saint
Lucia. In a recent issue of *The Kenyon Review* celebrating the 100th anniversary of the Nobel Prizes, a previously unpublished conversation between
Walcott and fellow Nobel laureate and poet Joseph Brodsky appeared, in
which Walcott says, "A poem engages immortality…If print were suddenly
removed from the world, there would be a vessel carrying six or seven
poems in his head, and that would be enough to give the race a chance to
begin again."

Piano Practice *(1980)*

by Derek Walcott

April, in another fortnight, metropolitan April.
Light rain-gauze across the museum's entrance,
like their eyes when they leave you, equivocating Spring!
The sun dries the avenue's pumice façade
delicately as a girl tamps tissues on her cheek;
this is my spring piece, can you hear me, Laforgue?
The asphalt shines like sealskin,
like the drizzle trying to bring sadness in,
as furrows part their lips to the spring rain.
But here, in mock Belle Epoque Manhattan,
its avenues hazy as Impressionist clichés,
its gargoyle cornices,
its concrete flowers on chipped pediments,
its subway stops in Byzantine mosaic—
the soul sneezes and one tries to compile
the collage of a lost vocabulary,
the epistolary pathos, the old Laforguian ache.

Deserted piazzas swept by gusts of remorse,
rain-polished cobbles where a curtained carriage
trotted around a corner of Europe for the last time,
the ending that began with Saravejo,
when the canals were folded like accordions.

Now yellow fever flares in the trouble spots of the globe,
rain drizzles on the white iron chairs in the gardens.
Today is Thursday, Vallejo is dying,
but come, girl, get your raincoat, let's look for life
in some café behind tear-streaked windows,
let's give in to the rain, even if I catch
that touch of a fatal chill called Europe.
Perhaps the *fin-de-siècle* isn't really finished,
maybe there's a piano playing it somewhere,
or else they have brought the evening on too early
as the lights go on in the heart of the afternoon.

I called the Muse, she pleaded a headache,
but maybe she was just shy at being seen
with someone who has only one climate,
who knows only Manhattan's mock-malaise,
so I passed the flowers in stone, the sylvan pediments,
alone. It wasn't I who shot the archduke,
I excuse myself of all crimes of that ilk,
I accept the subway's obscene graffiti,
and I could offer her nothing but the predictable
pale head-scarf of the twilight's lurid silk.

Well, goodbye then, I'm sorry I've never gone
to the great city that gave Vallejo fever,
I can offer her nothing but the bracelet of the sun,
I know that I can never
rhyme my exile with the damp fields of Dijon,
but the place I can offer is still yours—
the north coast of an island with wind-bleached grass,
with the one season, with no history,
with stones like white sheep in its pastures
by a silver-circletted sea.

Woody Allen

Woody Allen was born Allan Stewart Konigsberg, in 1935, in Flatbush, Brooklyn. Allen, who adopted the name in 1952, attended New York University after high school, but never graduated (failing the class "Motion Picture Production"). He earned a living in the late 1950s writing for television, earning an Emmy nomination. By the 1960s, Allen had made a name for himself as a stand-up comedian and began writing short stories. After early success in film with movies such as *What's Up, Tiger Lily?*, Allen launched into a career as a film director that has earned him countless accolades, including Academy Awards for his work on such films as *Annie Hall* and *Hannah and Her Sisters*. Allen's publishing career began in 1971 with the release of his book *Getting Even*, a collection of humorous essays, many of which originally appeared in *The New Yorker*. Allen, also an accomplished playwright, went on to write two more books, *Without Feathers* and *Side Effects*. In 1978, his short story "The Kugelmass Episode" won the O. Henry Award First Prize. His story "Retribution" appeared in *The Kenyon Review* in the summer of 1980. *Complete Prose* was released in 1992, with commercial and critical success. He is currently living in New York and making films. In his spare time he plays jazz clarinet with the *New Orleans Funeral and Ragtime Orchestra* at Michael's Pub in Manhattan on Monday nights.

Retribution *(1980)*

by Woody Allen

That Connie Chasen returned my fatal attraction toward her at first sight was a miracle unparalleled in the history of Central Park West. Tall, blond, high cheekboned, an actress, a scholar, a charmer, irrevocably alienated, with a hostile and perceptive wit only challenged in its power to attract by the lewd, humid eroticism her every curve suggested, she was the unrivaled desideratum of each young man at the party. That she would settle on me, Harold Cohen, scrawny, long-nosed, twenty-four-year-old, budding dramatist and whiner, was a *non sequitur* on a par with octuplets. True, I have a facile way with a one-liner and seem able to keep a conversation going on a wide range of topics, and yet I was taken by surprise that this superbly scaled apparition could zero in on my meager gifts so rapidly and completely.

"You're adorable," she told me, after an hour's energetic exchange while we leaned against a bookcase, throwing back Valpollacello and finger foods. "I hope you're going to call me."

"Call you? I'd like to go home with you right now."

"Well great," she said, smiling coquettishly. "The truth is, I didn't really think I was impressing you."

I affected a casual air while blood pounded through my arteries to predictable destinations. I blushed, an old habit.

"I think you're dynamite," I said, causing her to glow even more incandescently. Actually I was quite unprepared for such immediate acceptance. My grape-fueled cockiness was an attempt to lay groundwork for the future, so that when I would indeed suggest the boudoir, let's say, one discreet date later, it would not come as a total surprise and violate some tragically established Platonic bond. Yet, cautious, guilt-ridden, worrier-victim that I am, this night was to be mine. Connie Chasen and I had taken to each other in a way that would not be denied and one brief hour later were thrashing balletically through the percales, executing with total emotional commitment the absurd choreography of human passion. To me, it was the most erotic and satisfying night of sex I had ever had, and as she lay in my arms afterward, relaxed and fulfilled, I wondered exactly how Fate was going to extract its inevitable dues. Would I soon go blind? Or become a paraplegic? What hideous vigorish would Harold Cohen be forced to pony up so the cosmos might continue in its harmonious rounds? But this would all come later.

The following four weeks burst no bubbles. Connie and I explored one another and delighted in each new discovery. I found her quick, exciting, and responsive; her imagination was fertile and her references erudite and varied. She could discuss Novalis and quote from the Rig-Veda. The verse of every song by Cole Porter, she knew by heart. In bed she was uninhibited and experimental, a true child of the future. On the minus side one had to be niggling to find fault. True she could be a tad temperamental. She inevitably changed her food order in a restaurant and always long after it was decent to do so. Invariably she got angry when I pointed out this was not exactly fair to waiter or chef. Also she switched diets every other day, committing with whole heart to one and then disregarding it in favor of some new, fashionable theory on weight loss. Not that she was remotely overweight. Quite the opposite. Her shape would have been the envy of a Vogue model, and yet an inferiority complex rivaling Franz Kafka's led her to painful bouts of self-criticism. To hear her tell it, she was a dumpy little nonentity, who had no business trying to be an actress, much less attempting Chekhov. My assurances were moderately encouraging and I kept them flowing, though I felt that if her desirability was not apparent from my obsessional glee over her brain and body, no amount of talk would be convincing.

Along about the sixth week of a wonderful romance, her insecurity emerged full blown one day. Her parents were having a barbecue in Connecticut and I was at last going to meet her family.

"Dad's great," she said worshipfully, "and great looking. And Mom's beautiful. Are yours?"

"I wouldn't say beautiful," I confessed. Actually, I had a rather dim view of my family's physical appearance, likening the relatives on my mother's side to something usually cultured in a petri dish. I was very hard on my family and we all constantly teased each other and fought, but were close. Indeed, a compliment had not passed through the lips of any member during my lifetime and I suspect not since God made his covenant with Abraham.

"My folks never fight," she said. "They drink, but they're real polite. And Danny's nice." Her brother. "I mean he's strange but sweet. He writes music."

"I'm looking forward to meeting them all."

"I hope you don't fall for my kid sister, Lindsay."

"Oh sure."

"She's two years younger than me and so bright and sexy. Everyone goes nuts over her."

"Sounds impressive," I said. Connie stroked my face.

"I hope you don't like her better than me," she said in half-serious tones that enabled her to voice this fear gracefully.

"I wouldn't worry," I assured her.

"No? Promise?"

"Are you two competitive?"

"No. We love each other. But she's got an angel's face and a sexy, round body. She takes after Mom. And she's got this real high IQ and great sense of humor."

"You're beautiful," I said and kissed her. But I must admit, for the rest of that day, fantasies of twenty-one-year-old Lindsay Chasen did not leave my mind. Good Lord, I thought, what if she is this *Wunderkind*? What if she is indeed as irresistible as Connie paints her? Might I not be smitten? Weakling that I am, might not the sweet body scent and tinkling laugh of a stunning Connecticut WASP named Lindsay—Lindsay yet!—turn this fascinated, though unpledged, head from Connie toward fresh mischief? After all, I had only known Connie six weeks and, while having a wonderful time with the woman, was not yet actually in love with her beyond all reason. Still, Lindsay would have to be pretty damn fabulous to cause a ripple in the giddy tempest of chuckles and lust that made these past three fortnights such a spree.

That evening I made love with Connie, but when I slept it was Lindsay who trespassed my dreams. Sweet little Lindsay, the adorable Phi Beta Kappa with the face of a movie star and the charm of a princess. I tossed and turned and woke in the middle of the night with a strange feeling of excitement and foreboding.

In the morning my fantasies subsided, and after breakfast Connie and I set off for Connecticut bearing wine and flowers. We drove through the fall countryside listening to Vivaldi on FM and exchanging our observations on that day's *Arts and Leisure* section. Then, moments before we passed through the front gate of the Chasens' Lyme acreage, I once again wondered if I was about to be stupefied by this formidable kid sister.

"Will Lindsay's boyfriend be here?" I asked in a probing, guilt-strangled falsetto.

"They're finished," Connie explained. "Lindsay runs through one a month. She's a heartbreaker." Hmm, I thought, in addition to all else, the young woman is available. Might she really be more exciting than Connie? I found it hard to believe, and yet I tried to prepare myself for any eventuality. Any, of course, except the one that occurred that crisp, clear, Sunday afternoon.

Connie and I joined the barbecue, where there was much revelry and drinking. I met the family, one by one, scattered as they were amidst their fashionable, attractive cohorts and though sister Lindsay was indeed all Connie had described—comely, flirtatious, and fun to talk to—I did not prefer her to Connie. Of the two, I still felt much more taken with the older sister than the twenty-one-year-old Vassar grad. No, the one I hopelessly lost my heart to that day was none other than Connie's fabulous mother, Emily.

Emily Chasen, fifty-five, buxom, tanned, a ravishing pioneer face with pulled-back greying hair and round, succulent curves that expressed themselves in flawless arcs like a Brancusi. Sexy Emily, whose huge, white smile and chesty, big laugh combined to create an irresistible warmth and seductiveness.

What protoplasm in this family, I thought! What award-winning genes! Consistent genes too, as Emily Chasen seemed to be as at ease with me as her daughter was. Clearly she enjoyed talking with me as I monopolized her time, mindless of the demands of the other afternoon guests. We discussed photography (her hobby) and books. She was currently reading, with great delight, a book of Joseph Heller's. She found it hilarious and laughing fetchingly as she filled my glass said, "God, you Jews are truly exotic." Exotic? She should only know the Greenblatts. Or Mr. and Mrs. Milton Sharpstein, my father's friends. Or for that matter, my cousin Tovah. Exotic? I mean, they're nice but hardly exotic with their endless bickering over the best way to combat indigestion or how far back to sit from the television set.

Emily and I talked for hours of movies, and we discussed my hopes for the theatre and her new interest in making collages. Obviously this woman had many creative and intellectual demands that for one reason or another remained pent up within her. Yet clearly she was not unhappy with her life as she and her husband, John Chasen, an older version of the man you'd like to have piloting your plane, hugged and drank in lovey-dovey fashion. Indeed, in comparison to my own folks, who had been married inexplicably for forty years (out of spite it seemed), Emily and John seemed like the Lunts. My folks, naturally, could not discuss even the weather without accusations and recriminations just short of gunfire.

When it came time to go home I was quite sorry and left with dreams of Emily in complete command of my thoughts.

"They're sweet, aren't they?" Connie asked as we sped toward Manhattan.

"Very," I concurred.

"Isn't Dad a knockout? He's really fun."

"Umm." The truth was I had hardly exchanged ten sentences with Connie's dad.

"And Mom looked great today. Better than in a longtime. She's been ill with the flu, too."

"She's quite something," I said.

"Her photography and collages are very good," Connie said. "I wish Dad encouraged her more instead of being so old-fashioned. He's just not fascinated by creativity in the arts. Never was."

"Too bad," I said. "I hope it hasn't been too frustrating for your mother over the years."

"It has," Connie said. "And Lindsay? Are you in love with her?"

"She's lovely—but not in your class. At least as far as I'm concerned."

"I'm relieved," Connie said laughingly and pecked me on the cheek. Abysmal vermin that I am, I couldn't, of course, tell her that it was her incredible mother that I wanted to see again. Yet even as I drove, my mind clicked and blinked like a computer in hopes of concocting some scheme to filch more time with this overpowering and wonderful woman. If you had asked me where I expected it to lead, I really couldn't have said. I knew only as I drove through the cold, night, autumn air that somewhere Freud, Sophocles, and Eugene O'Neill were laughing.

During the next several months I managed to see Emily Chasen many times. Usually it was in an innocent threesome with Connie, both of us meeting her in the city and taking her to a museum or concert. Once or twice I did something with Emily alone if Connie was busy. This delighted Connie—that her mother and lover should be such good friends. Once or twice I contrived to be where Emily was "by accident" and wound up having an apparently impromptu walk or drink with her. It was obvious she enjoyed my company as I listened sympathetically to her artistic aspirations and laughed engagingly at her jokes. Together we discussed music and literature and life, my observations consistently entertaining her. It was also obvious the idea of regarding me as anything more than just a new friend was not remotely on her mind. Or if it was, she certainly never let on. Yet what could I expect? I was living with her daughter. Cohabiting honorably in a civilized society where certain taboos are observed. After all, who did I imagine this woman was anyhow? Some amoral vamp out of German films who would seduce her own child's lover? In truth, I'm sure I would have lost all respect for her if she did confess feelings for me or behave in any other way than untouchable. And yet I had a terrible crush on her. It amounted to genuine longing, and despite all logic I prayed for some tiny hint that her marriage was not as perfect as it seemed or that, resist as she might, she had grown fatally fond of me. There were times that I flirted with the notion of making some tepidly aggressive move myself, but banner headlines in the yellow press formed in my mind and I shrank from any action.

I wanted so badly, in my anguish, to explain these confused feelings to Connie in an above-board way and enlist her aid in making sense out of the painful tangle, but I felt to do so invited certain carnage. In fact, instead of this manly honesty, I nosed around like a ferret for bits and clues regarding Emily's feelings toward me.

"I took your mother to the Matisse exhibit," I said to Connie one day.

"I know," she said. "She had a great time."

"She's a lucky woman. Seems to be happy. Fine marriage."

"Yes." Pause.

"So, er—did she say anything to you?"

"She said you two had a wonderful talk afterwards. About her photography."

"Right." Pause. "Anything else? About me? I mean, I felt maybe I get overbearing."

"Oh God, no. She adores you."

"Yes?"

"With Danny spending more and more time with Dad, she thinks of you kind of like a son."

"Her son!?" I said, shattered.

"I think she would have liked a son who is as interested in her work as you are. A genuine companion. More intellectually inclined than Danny. Sensitive to her artistic needs a little. I think you fulfill that role for her."

That night I was in a foul mood and, as I sat home with Connie watching television, my body again ached to be pressed in passionate tenderness against this woman who apparently thought of me as nothing more dangerous than her boy. Or did she? Was this not just a casual surmise of Connie's? Might Emily not be thrilled to find out that a man, much younger than herself, found her beautiful and sexy and fascinating and longed to have an affair with her quite unlike anything remotely filial? Wasn't it possible a woman of that age, particularly one whose husband was not overly responsive to her deepest feelings, would welcome the attention of a passionate admirer? And though it seemed absurd on the surface, might I not, mired in my own middle-class background, actually be making too much of the fact that I was living with her daughter? After all, stranger things happen. Certainly amongst temperaments gifted with profounder artistic intensity. I had to resolve matters and finally put an end to these feelings which had assumed the proportions of a mad obsession. The situation was taking too heavy a toll on me, and it was time I either acted on it or put it out of my mind. I decided to act.

Past successful campaigns suggested instantly the proper route to take. I would steer her to Trader Vic's, that dimly lit, foolproof Polynesian den of delights where dark, promising corners abounded and deceptively mild rum drinks quickly unchained the fiery libido from its dungeon. A pair of Mai Tai's and it would be anybody's ball game. A hand on the knee. A sudden uninhibited kiss. Fingers intertwined. The miraculous booze would work its dependable magic. It had never failed me in the past. Even when the unsuspecting victim pulled back with eyebrows arched, one could back out gracefully by imputing all to the effects of the island brew.

"Forgive me," I could alibi, "I'm just so zonked by this drink. I don't know what I'm doing."

Yes, the time for polite chitchat was over, I thought. I am in love with two women, a not terribly uncommon problem. That they happen to be mother and child? All the more challenging! I was becoming hysterical. Yet drunk with confidence as I was at that point, I must admit that things did not finally come off quite as planned. True, we did make it to Trader Vic's one cold February afternoon. We did also look in each other's eyes and waxed poetic about life while knocking back tall, foamy, white beverages that held minuscule wooden parasols lanced into floating pineapple squares—but there it ended. And it did so because, despite the unblocking of my baser urges, I felt that it would completely destroy Connie. In the end it was my own guilty conscience—or, more accurately, my return to sanity—that prevented me from placing the predictable hand on Emily Chasen's leg and pursuing my dark desires. That sudden realization that I was only a mad fantasizer who, in fact, loved Connie and must never risk hurting her in any way did me in. Yes, Harold Cohen was a more conventional type than he would have us believe. And more in love with his girlfriend than he cared to admit. This crush on Emily Chasen would have to be filed and forgotten. Painful as it might be to control my impulses toward Connie's mom, rationality and decent consideration would prevail.

After a wonderful afternoon, the crowning moment of which would have been the ferocious kissing of Emily's large, inviting lips, I got the check and called it a day. We exited laughingly into the lightly blowing snow and, after walking her to her car, I watched her take off for Lyme while I returned home to her daughter with a new, deeper feeling of warmth for this woman who nightly shared my bed. Life is truly chaos, I thought. Feelings are so unpredictable. How does anyone ever stay married for forty years? This, it seems, is more of a miracle than the parting of the Red Sea, though my father, in his naïveté, holds the latter to be a greater achievement. I kissed Connie and confessed the depth of my affection. She reciprocated. We made love.

Dissolve, as they say in the movies, to a few months later. Connie can no longer have intercourse with me. And why? I brought it on myself like the tragic protagonist of a Greek play. Our sex began falling off insidiously weeks ago.

"What's wrong?" I'd ask. "Have I done something?"

"God no, it's not your fault. Oh hell."

"What? Tell me."

"I'm just not up to it," she'd say. "Must we *every* night?" The every night she referred to was in actuality only a few nights a week and soon less than that.

"I can't," she'd say guiltily when I'd attempt to instigate sex. "You know I'm going through a bad time."

"What bad time?" I asked incredulously. "Are you seeing someone else?"

"Of course not."

"Do you love me?"

"Yes. I wish I didn't."

"So what? Why the turnoff? And it's not getting better, it's getting worse."

"I can't do it with you," she confessed one night. "You remind me of my brother."

"What?"

"You remind me of Danny. Don't ask me why."

"Your brother? You must be joking!"

"No."

"But he's a twenty-three-year-old, blond WASP who works in your father's law practice, and I remind you of him?"

"It's like going to bed with my brother," she wept.

"OK, OK, don't cry. We'll be all right. I have to take some aspirin and lie down. I don't feel well." I pressed my throbbing temples and pretended to be bewildered, but it was, of course, obvious that my strong relationship with her mother had in some way cast me in a fraternal role as far as Connie was concerned. Fate was getting even. I was to be tortured like Tantalus, inches from the svelte, tanned body of Connie Chasen, yet unable to lay a hand on her without, at least for the time being, eliciting the classical expletive, "Yuck." In the irrational assigning of parts that occurs in all of our emotional dramas, I had suddenly become a sibling.

Various stages of anguish marked the next months. First the pain of being rejected in bed. Next, telling ourselves the condition was temporary. This was accompanied by an attempt by me to be understanding, to be patient. I recalled not being able to perform with a sexy date in college once precisely because some vague twist of her head reminded me of my Aunt Rifka. This girl was far prettier than the squirrel-faced aunt of my boyhood, but the notion of making love with my mother's sister wrecked the moment irreparably. I knew what Connie was going through, and yet sexual frustration mounted and compounded itself. After a time, my self-control sought expression in sarcastic remarks and later in an urge to burn down the house. Still, I kept trying not to be rash, trying to ride out the storm of unreason and preserve what in all other ways was a good relationship with Connie. My suggestion for her to see a psychoanalyst fell on deaf ears, as nothing was more alien to her Connecticut upbringing than the Jewish science from Vienna.

"Sleep with other women. What else can I say?" she offered.

"I don't want to sleep with other women. I love you."

"And I love you. You know that. But I can't go to bed with you." Indeed I was not the type who slept around, for despite my fantasy episode with Connie's mother, I had never cheated on Connie. True, I had experienced normal daydreams over random females—this actress, that stewardess, some wide-eyed college girl—yet never would I have been unfaithful toward my lover. And not because I couldn't have. Certain women I had come in contact with had been quite aggressive, even predatory, but my loyalty had remained with Connie; doubly so, during this trying time of her impotence. It occurred to me, of course, to hit on Emily again, whom I still saw with and without Connie in innocent, companionable fashion, but felt that to stoke up embers I had labored so successfully to dampen would only lead to everybody's misery.

This is not to say that Connie was faithful. No, the sad truth was, on at least several occasions, she had succumbed to alien wiles, bedding surreptitiously with actors and authors alike.

"What do you want me to say?" she wept one three A.M. when I had caught her in a tangle of contradicting alibis. "I only do it to assure myself I'm not some sort of a freak. That I still am able to have sex."

"You can have sex with anyone but me," I said, furious with feelings of injustice.

"Yes. You remind me of my brother."

"I don't want to hear that nonsense."

"I told you to sleep with other women."

"I've tried not to, but it looks as if I'm going to have to."

"Please. Do it. It's a curse," she sobbed.

It was truly a curse. For when two people love each other and are forced to separate because of an almost comical aberration, what else could it be? That I brought it on myself by developing a close relationship with her mother was undeniable. Perhaps it was my comeuppance for thinking I could entice and bed Emily Chasen, having already made whoopee with her offspring.

The sin of hubris, maybe. Me, Harold Cohen, guilty of hubris. A man who has never thought of himself in an order higher than rodent, nailed for hubris? Too hard to swallow. And yet we did separate. Painfully, we remained friends and went our individual ways. True, only ten city blocks lay between our residences and we spoke every other day, but the relationship was over. It was then, and only then, that I began to realize how much I had really adored Connie. Inevitable bouts of melancholy and anxiety accentuated my Proustian haze of pain. I recalled all our fine moments together, our exceptional love-making, and in the solitude of my large apartment, I wept. I attempted to go out on dates, but again, inevitably, everything seemed flat. All the little groupies and secretaries that paraded through the bedroom left me empty; even worse than an evening alone with a good book. The world seemed truly stale and unprofitable; quite a dreary, awful place, until one day I got the stunning news that Connie's mother had left her husband and they were getting a divorce. Imagine that, I thought, as my heart beat faster than normal speed for the first time in ages. My parents fight like the Montagues and Capulets and stay together their whole lives. Connie's folks sip martinis and hug with true civility and, bingo, they're divorcing.

My course of action was now obvious. Trader Vic's. Now there could be no crippling obstacles in our path. Though it would be somewhat awkward as I had been Connie's lover, it held none of the overwhelming difficulties of the past. We were now two free agents. My dormant feelings for Emily

Chasen, always smoldering, ignited once again. Perhaps a cruel twist of fate ruined my relationship with Connie, but nothing would stand in the way of my conquering her mother.

Riding the crest of the large economy-size hubris, I phoned Emily and made a date. Three days later we sat huddled in the dark of my favorite Polynesian restaurant, and loose from three Bahias, she poured out her heart about the demise of her marriage. When she got to the part about looking for a new life with less restraint and more creative possibilities, I kissed her. Yes, she was taken aback but she did not scream. She acted surprised, but I confessed my feelings toward her and kissed her again. She seemed confused but did not bolt from the table, outraged. By the third kiss I knew she would succumb. She shared my feelings. I took her to my apartment and we made love. The following morning, when the effects of the rum had worn off, she still looked magnificent to me and we made love again.

"I want you to marry me," I said, my eyes glazed over with adoration.

"Not really," she said.

"Yes," I said. "I'll settle for nothing less." We kissed and had breakfast, laughing and making plans. That day I broke the news to Connie, braced for a blow that never came. I had anticipated any number of reactions ranging from derisive laughter to outright fury, but the truth was Connie took it in charming stride. She herself was leading an active social life, going out with several attractive men, and had experienced great concern over her mother's future when the woman had gotten divorced. Suddenly a young knight had emerged to care for the lovely lady. A knight who still had a fine, friendly relationship with Connie. It was a stroke of good fortune all around. Connie's guilt over putting me through hell would be removed. Emily would be happy. I would be happy. Yes, Connie took it all in casual, good humored stride, natural to her upbringing.

My parents, on the other hand, proceeded directly to the window of their tenth-story apartment and competed for leaping space.

"I never heard of such a thing," my mother wailed, rending her robe and gnashing her teeth.

"He's crazy. You idiot. You're crazy," my father said, looking pale and stricken.

"A fifty-five-year-old *shiksa!?*" my Aunt Rose shrieked, lifting the letter opener and bringing it to her eyes.

"I love her," I protested.

"She's more than twice your age," Uncle Louie yelled.

"So?"

"So it's not done," my father yelled, invoking the Torah.

"His girlfriend's mother he's marrying?" Aunt Tillie yelped as she slid to the floor unconscious.

"Fifty-five and a *shiksa*," my mother screamed, searching now for a cyanide capsule she had reserved for just such occasions.

"What are they, Moonies?" Uncle Louie asked. "Do they have him hypnotized!?"

"Idiot! Imbecile," Dad screamed. Aunt Tillie regained consciousness, focused on me, remembered where she was, and passed out again. In the far corner, Aunt Rose was down on her knees intoning Sh'ma Yisroel.

"God will punish you, Harold," my father yelled. "God will cleave your tongue to the roof of your mouth and all your cattle and kine shall die and a tenth of all thy crops shall wither and…"

But I married Emily and there were no suicides. Emily's three children attended and a dozen or so friends. It was held in Connie's apartment and champagne flowed. My folks could not make it, a previous commitment to sacrifice a lamb taking precedence. We all danced and joked and the evening went well. At one point, I found myself in the bedroom with Connie alone. We kidded and reminisced about our relationship, its ups and downs, and how sexually attracted I had been to her.

"It was flattering," she said warmly.

"Well, I couldn't swing it with the daughter, so I carried off the mother." The next thing I knew, Connie's tongue was in my mouth. "What the hell are you doing?" I said, pulling back. "Are you drunk?"

"You turn me on like you can't believe," she said, dragging me down on the bed.

"What's gotten into you? Are you a nymphomaniac?" I said, rising, yet undeniably excited by her sudden aggressiveness.

"I have to sleep with you. If not now, then soon," she said.

"Me? Harold Cohen? The guy who lived with you? And loved you? Who couldn't get near you with a ten-foot pole because I became a version of Danny? Me you're hot for? Your brother symbol?"

"It's a whole new ball game," she said, pressing close to me. "Marrying Mom has made you my father." She kissed me again and just before returning to the festivities said, "Don't worry, Dad, there'll be plenty of opportunities."

I sat on the bed and stared out the window into infinite space. I thought of my parents and wondered if I should abandon the theatre and return to rabbinical school. Through the half-open door I saw Connie and also Emily, both laughing and chatting with guests, and all I could mutter to myself as I remained a limp, hunched figure was an age-old line of my grandfather's which goes, "Oy vey."

Rita Dove

Rita Dove was born in Akron, Ohio, in 1952. She attended Miami University in Oxford, Ohio, graduating with a B.A. in English in 1973. Dove spent the next two years in Germany as a Fulbright Scholar at Universität Tübingen. She entered the University of Iowa Writers' Workshop, earning her M.F.A. in 1977. While at Iowa, she met German writer Fred Viebahn, whom she would marry in 1979. The following year her first collection of poetry, *The Yellow House on the Corner,* was published. It was followed by *Museum* (1983) and *Thomas and Beulah* (1986), which earned Dove the Pulitzer Prize. In 1981, she began teaching at Arizona State University, a position she would hold until 1989, when she took a position at the University of Virginia, where she is currently Commonwealth Professor of English. Dove continues to be widely read and praised for such books as *Grace Notes*, *Mother Love*, and *On the Bus with Rosa Parks*, which won the National Book Critics Circle Award in 2000. Dove, who is also an accomplished fiction writer and playwright, has acted as an important national ambassador of poetry, serving as Poet Laureate from 1993 to 1995, and contributing texts for such events as the opening weekend of the Centennial Olympic Summer Games in July 1996 and the White House's Millennium New Year's Eve celebration. She has even appeared with Big Bird on *Sesame Street*. Dove currently lives in Charlottesville, Virginia. Her poem "Grape Sherbet" appeared in *The Kenyon Review* in 1982.

Grape Sherbert *(1982)*

by Rita Dove

The day? Memorial.
After the grill
Dad appears with his masterpiece—
swirled snow, gelled light.
We cheer. The recipe's
a secret and he fights
a smile, his cap turned up
so the bib resembles a duck.

That morning we galloped
through the grassed-over mounds
and named each stone
for a lost milk tooth. Each dollop
of sherbet, later,
is a miracle,
like salt on a melon that makes it sweeter.

Everyone agrees—its wonderful!
It's just how we imagined lavender
would taste. The diabetic grandmother
stares from the porch,
a torch
of pure refusal.

We thought no one was lying
there under our feet,
we thought it
was a joke. I've been trying
to remember the taste,
but it doesn't exist.
Now I see why
you bothered,
father.

Italo Calvino

Italo Calvino was born in Santiago de las Vegas, Cuba, in 1923. Calvino left Cuba for Italy in his youth. He joined the Italian Resistance during World War II and after the war settled in Turin, obtaining his degree in literature. Calvino's early fiction was inspired by his participation in the Italian Resistance, including his first novel, *The Path to the Nest of Spiders* (1947), which took him twenty days to complete. In the 1950s, his work turned decisively toward fantasy and allegory, while still remaining politically oriented. He produced three successful novels: *The Cloven Viscount* (1952), *The Nonexistent Knight* (1959), and the most critically acclaimed *The Baron in the Trees* (1957), a whimsical tale of a nineteenth-century nobleman who one day decides to climb into the trees, and who never sets foot on the ground again. In the following decades, Calvino lived in New York, Cuba, and mainly Paris, among other places. On his frequent travels, he once said, "Everything can change, but not the language that we carry inside us, like a world more exclusive and final than one's mother's womb." He continued to write (including his story "Autumn," originally appearing in *The Kenyon Review* in 1983) until his death in 1985 in Siena, Italy. He is considered one of the most important Italian writers of the twentieth century.

Autumn: The Rain and the Leaves *(1983)*

by Italo Calvino

At his job, among his various other responsibilities, Marcovaldo had to water every morning the potted plant in the entrance hall. It was one of those green houseplants with an erect, thin stalk from which, on both sides, broad, long-stemmed, shiny leaves stick out: in other words, one of those plants that are so plant-shaped, with leaves so leaf-shaped, that they don't seem real. But still it was a plant, and as such it suffered, because staying there, between the curtain and the umbrella stand, it lacked light, air, and dew. Every morning Marcovaldo discovered some nasty sign: the stem of one leaf drooped as if it could no longer support the weight, another leaf was becoming spotted like the cheek of a child with measles, the tip of a third leaf was turning yellow; until, one or the other, plop!, was found on the floor. Meanwhile (what most wrung his heart), the plant's stalk grew taller, taller, no longer making orderly fronds, but naked as a pole, with a clump at the top that made it resemble a palm tree.

Marcovaldo cleared away the fallen leaves, dusted the healthy ones, poured at the foot of the plant (slowly, so the pot wouldn't spill over and dirty the tiles) half a watering can of water, immediately absorbed by the earth in the pot. And to these simple actions he devoted an attention he gave no other task of his, almost like the compassion felt for the troubles of a relative. And he sighed, whether for the plant or himself: because in that lanky, yellowing bush within the company walls he recognized a companion in misfortune.

The plant (this was how it was called, simply, as if any more specific name were useless in a setting where it alone had to represent the vegetable kingdom) had become such a part of Marcovaldo's life that it dominated his thoughts at every hour of the day and night. When he examined the gathering clouds in the sky, his gaze now was no longer that of a city dweller, wondering whether or not he should wear his raincoat, but that of a farmer expecting from day to day the end of a drought. And the moment when he raised his head from his work and saw, against the light, beyond the little window of the warehouse, the curtain of rain that had begun to fall, thick and silent, he would drop everything, run to the plant, take the pot in his arms, and set it outside in the courtyard.

The plant, feeling the water run over its leaves, seemed to expand, to offer the greatest possible surface to the drops, and in its joy it seemed to don its most brilliant green: or at least so Marcovaldo thought, as he lingered to observe it, forgetting to take shelter.

They stayed there in the courtyard, man and plant, facing each other, the man almost feeling plant sensations under the rain, the plant—no longer accustomed to the open air and to the phenomena of nature—amazed, much like a man who finds himself suddenly drenched from head to foot, his clothes soaked. Marcovaldo, his nose in the air, sniffed the smell of the rain, a smell—for him—already of woods and fields, and he pursued with his mind some vague memories. But among these memories there surfaced, clearer and closer, that of the rheumatic aches that afflicted him every year; and then, hastily, he went back inside.

When working hours were over, the place had to be locked up. Marcovaldo asked the warehouse foreman: "Can I leave the plant outside there, in the courtyard?"

The foreman, Signor Viligelmo, was the kind of man who avoided burdensome responsibilities: "Are you crazy? What if somebody steals it? Who'll answer for that?"

But Marcovaldo, seeing how much good the rain did the plant, couldn't bring himself to put it back inside: it would mean wasting that gift of heaven. "I could keep it until tomorrow morning…" he suggested. "I'll load it on the rack of my bike and take it home…that way it'll get as much rain as possible."

Signor Viligelmo thought it over a moment, then concluded: "Then you're taking the responsibility." And he gave his consent.

Under the pouring rain, Marcovaldo crossed the city, bent over the handlebars of his motorbike, bundled up in a rainproof windbreaker. Behind him, on the rack, he had tied the pot, and bike, man, and plant seemed a sole thing; indeed the hunched and bundled man disappeared, and you saw only a plant on a bicycle. Every now and then, from beneath his hood, Marcovaldo looked around until he could see a dripping leaf flapping behind him: and every time it seemed to him that the plant had become taller and more leafy.

At home, a garret with its windowsill on the roof, the moment Marcovaldo arrived with the pot in his arms, the children started dancing around it.

"The Christmas tree! The Christmas tree!"

"No, no. What are you talking about? Christmas is a long way off yet!" Marcovaldo protested. "Watch out for those leaves; they're delicate!"

"We're already like sardines in a can, in this house," Domitilla grumbled. "If you bring a tree in, too, we'll have to move out..."

"It's only a plant! I'll put it on the windowsill..."

The shadowy form of the plant on the sill could be seen from the room. Marcovaldo, at supper, didn't look at his plate, but beyond the window panes.

Ever since they had left the half-basement for the garret, the life of Marcovaldo and family had greatly improved. However, living up under the roof also had its drawbacks: the ceiling, for example, leaked a little. The drops fell in four or five distinct places, at regular intervals; and Marcovaldo put basins under them, or pots. On rainy nights when all of them were in bed, they could hear the tic-toc-tuc of the various drips, which made him shudder as if at a premonition of rheumatism. That night, on the contrary, every time Marcovaldo woke from his restless sleep and pricked up his ear, the tic-toc-tuc seemed cheery music to him: it told him the rain was continuing, mild and steady, and was nourishing the plant, driving the sap up along its delicate stalks, unfolding the leaves like sails. Tomorrow, when I look out, I'll find it has grown! he thought.

But even though he had thought about this, when he opened the window in the morning, he couldn't believe his eyes: the plant now filled half the window, the leaves had at least doubled in number, and no longer drooped under their own weight, but were erect and sharp as swords. He climbed down the steps, with the pot clutched to him, tied it to the rack, and rushed to work.

The rain had stopped, but the weather was still uncertain. Marcovaldo hadn't even climbed out of his seat when a few drops started falling again. "Since the rain does it so much good, I'll leave it in the courtyard again," he thought.

In the warehouse, every now and then he went to peek out of the window onto the courtyard. His distraction from work did not please the foreman. "Well, what's wrong with you this morning? Always looking out of the window."

"It's growing! Come and see for yourself, Signor Viligelmo!" And Marcovaldo motioned to him, speaking almost in a whisper, as if the plant were not to overhear. "Look how it's growing! It really has grown, hasn't it?"

"Yes, it's grown quite a bit," the boss conceded, and for Marcovaldo this was one of those satisfactions that life on the job rarely grants the personnel.

It was Saturday. Work ended at one and they were all off until Monday. Marcovaldo would have liked to take the plant home with him again, but now, since it was no longer raining, he couldn't think of any pretext. The sky, however, was not clear: black cumulus clouds were scattered here and there. He went to the foreman, a meteorology enthusiast, who kept a barometer hanging over his desk. "What's the forecast, Signor Viligelmo?"

"Bad, still bad," he said. "For that matter, though it's not raining here, it is in the neighborhood where I live. I just telephoned my wife."

"In that case," Marcovaldo quickly proposed, "I'll take the plant on a little trip where it's raining," and, no sooner said than done, he fixed the pot again on the rack of his bike.

Saturday afternoon and Sunday Marcovaldo spent in this fashion: bouncing on the seat of his motorbike, the plant behind him, he studied the sky, seeking a cloud that seemed in the right mood, then he would race through the streets until he encountered rain. From time to time, turning around, he saw the plant a bit taller: high as the taxis, as the delivery trucks, as the trams! And with broader and broader leaves, from which the rain slid onto his rainproof hood like a shower.

By now it was a tree on two wheels, speeding through the city, bewildering traffic cops, drivers, pedestrians. And the clouds, at the same time, sped along the paths of the wind, spattering a neighborhood with rain, then abandoning it: and the passers-by, one after another, stuck out their hands and closed their umbrellas: and along streets and avenues and squares, Marcovaldo chased his cloud, bent over his handlebars, bundled in his hood from which only his nose protruded, his little motor putt-putting along at full tilt, as he kept the plant in the trajectory of the drops, as if the trail of rain that the cloud drew after itself had got caught in the leaves and thus all rushed ahead, drawn by the same power: wind, cloud, rain, plant, wheels.

On Monday Marcovaldo presented himself, empty-handed, to Signor Viligelmo.

"Where's the plant?" the foreman asked at once.

"Outside. Come."

"Where?" Viligelmo said. "I don't see it."

"It's that one over there. It's grown a bit..." and he pointed to a tree that reached the third floor. It was no longer planted in its old pot but in a kind of barrel, and instead of using his bike Marcovaldo had had to borrow a little motor truck.

"Now what?" The boss was infuriated. "How can we get it into the entrance hall? It won't go through the doors any more!"

Marcovaldo shrugged.

"The only thing," Viligelmo said, "is to give it back to the nursery, in exchange for a plant of the right size!"

Marcovaldo climbed onto the truck again, "I'll go."

He resumed his dash through the city. The tree filled the center of the streets with green. The cops, concerned about traffic, stopped him at every intersection: then—when Marcovaldo explained that he was taking the plant back to the nursery, to get rid of it—they let him go on. But, taking first this street then that, Marcovaldo couldn't bring himself to turn into the one to the nursery. He hadn't the heart to give up his creature, now that he had raised it with such success: nothing in his whole life, it seemed to him, had given him the satisfaction he had received from that plant.

And so he went on, to and fro among the streets and squares and embankments and bridges. And foliage worthy of a tropical forest spread out until it covered his head, back, arms, until he had disappeared into the green. And all these leaves and stems of leaves and the stalk, too (which had remained very slim), swayed and swayed as if in a constant trembling, whether a downpour of rain were striking them, or whether the drops became rarer or stopped altogether.

The rain ceased. It was the hour towards sunset. At the end of the street, in the space between the houses, a light mixed with rainbow settled. The plant, after that impetuous effort of growth that had involved it as long as the rain lasted, was virtually exhausted. Continuing his aimless race, Marcovaldo didn't notice that, behind him, the intense green of the leaves, one by one, was turning to yellow, a golden yellow.

For quite a while now, a procession of motorbikes and cars and bicycles and children had been following the tree that was moving about the city, without Marcovaldo's being aware of them, and the were shouting: "The baobab! The bsaobab!" and with great "Ooooh's!" of wonder they watched the yellowing of the leaves. When one leaf dropped and flew off, many hands were raised to catch it in flight.

A wind sprang up: the golden leaves, in gusts, darted off in midair, spinning. Marcovaldo still thought that, behind him, he had the green, thick tree, when all of a sudden—perhaps feeling himself unsheltered in the wind—he looked back. The tree was gone: there was only a thin stick, from which extended a monstrance of bare stems, and one last yellow leaf at the top still. In the light of the rainbow everything else seemed black: the people on the sidewalks, the façades of the houses that served as backdrop: and over this black, in midair, the golden leaves twirled, shining, hundreds of them: and hundreds of hands, red and pink, rose from the darkness to grab them: and the wind lifted the golden leaves toward the rainbow there at the end of the street, and the hands, and the shouts: and it detached even the last leaf, which turned from yellow to orange, then red, violet, blue, green, then yellow again, then vanished.

Louise Erdrich

Louise Erdrich was born in 1954 in Little Falls, Minnesota. The daughter of a French-Ojibwe mother and a German-American father, and raised mainly in North Dakota, Erdrich is a member of the Turtle Mountain Band of Chippewa. She entered the first coeducational class at Dartmouth College in 1972 through the Native American Studies program, where she met her future husband, Michael Dorris, with whom she would collaborate on many literary projects. Erdrich then worked at a variety of jobs, including teaching poetry and writing through a position at the State Arts Council of North Dakota. Erdrich earned an M.A in creative writing at Johns Hopkins University in 1979 and married Dorris in 1981. Erdrich published a book of poetry, *Jacklight,* and an extremely well received novel, *Love Medicine*, both in 1984 (the same year her story "Lulu's Boys" appeared in *The Kenyon Review*). *Love Medicine* earned Erdrich the National Book Critics Circle Award. She went on to write such novels as *The Beet Queen, Tracks, The Bingo Palace,* and *Tales of Burning Love.* In July of 2000, Erdrich opened her own bookstore, BirchBark Books, a store specializing in Native American literature and crafts, in Minneapolis, where she currently resides.

Lulu's Boys *(1984)*
by Louise Erdrich

On the last day that Lulu Lamartine spent as Henry's widow, her boys were outside drinking beers and shooting plastic jugs. Her deceased husband's brother, Beverly, was sitting across from her at the kitchen table. Having a name some people thought of as feminine had turned Beverly Lamartine to building up his muscles in his youth and they still bulged, hard as ingots in some places, now lost in others. His plush belly strained open the bottom buttons of his black shirt, and Lulu saw his warm skin peeking through. She also saw how the tattoos he and Henry had acquired on their arms, and which Lulu had always admired, were now deep black and so fuzzy around the edges that she could hardly tell what they were.

Beverly saw her looking at the old tattoos and pushed his sleeves up over his biceps. "Get an eyeful," he grinned. As of old, he stretched his arms across the table and she gazed at the figures commemorating the two brothers' drunken travels outside her life.

There was a doll, a skull with a knife stuck in it, an eagle, a swallow, and Beverly's name, rank, and serial number. Looking at the arm made Lulu remember her husband's tattoos. Henry's arms had been imprinted with a banner bearing some other woman's name, a rose with a bleeding thorn, two lizards, and (like his brother's) his name, rank, and serial number.

Sometimes Lulu could not help it. She thought of everything so hard that her mind felt warped and sodden as a door that swells up in spring. It would not close properly to keep the troublesome thoughts out.

Right now she thought of those two lizards on either one of Henry's arms. She imagined them clenching together when he put his arms around her. Then she thought of them coupling the same way she and Henry did. She thought of this while looking at Beverly's lone swallow, a bird with outstretched wings deep as ink and bleeding into his flesh. She remembered Beverly's trick: the wings were carefully tattooed on certain muscles, so that when he flexed his arm, the bird almost seemed to hover in a dive or swoop.

Lulu hadn't seen her husband's brother since the funeral in 1950 with the casket closed because of how badly Henry had suffered in the car wreck. Drunk, he had started driving the old Northern Pacific tracks and either fallen asleep or passed out with his car straddling the rails. Everyone who had been in the bar on the night he died remembered his parting words.

"She comes barreling through, you'll never see me again."

At first they had thought he was talking about Lulu. But even at the time they knew she didn't lose her temper over drinking. It was the train Henry had been talking about. They realized that later when the news came and his casket was sealed.

Beverly Lamartine had shown up from the Twin Cities one hour before his brother's service was held. He had brought along the trophy flag, a black swastika on torn red cloth, that he had captured to revenge the oldest Lamartine, a quiet boy hardly spoken of now, who was killed early on, while still in boot camp.

When the men from the veterans' post lowered Henry's casket into the grave on ropes, there was a U.S. flag draped across it already. Beverly had shaken out the trophy flag. He let it go in the air and the wind seemed to suck it down, the black arms of the insignia whirling like a spider.

Watching it, Lulu had gone faint. The sudden spokes of the black wheel flashed before her eyes and she toppled dizzily, then stumbled over the edge of the grave.

The men were still lowering Henry on ropes. Lulu plunged heavily down with the trophy flag, and the ropes burned out of the pallbearer's hands. The box hit bottom. People screamed, and there was a great deal of commotion, during which Beverly jumped down to revive Lulu. All together, the pallbearers tugged and hoisted her out. The black garments seemed to make her even denser than she was. Her round face and chubby hands were a pale dough color, cold and wet with shock. For hours afterward she trembled, uttered senseless vowels, jumped at sounds and touches. Some people, assuming that she had jumped in the grave to be buried along with Henry, thought much better of her for a while.

But most of her life Lulu had been known as a flirt. And that was putting it mildly. Tongues less kind had more indicting things to say.

For instance, besides the fact of Lulu Lamartine's first husband, why did each of the boys currently shooting milk jugs out front of Henry's house look so different? There were eight of them. Some of them even had her maiden name. The two oldest were Nanapushes. The next oldest were Hansons, and then there were assorted younger Lamartines who didn't look like one another either. Red hair and blond abounded; there was some brown. The black hair on the seven-year-old at least matched his mother's. This boy was named Henry Junior, and he had been born approximately nine months after Henry Senior's death.

Give or take a week, Beverly thought, looking from Henry Junior out the window back to the woman across the table. Beverly was quite certain that he, and not his brother, was the father of that boy. In fact, Beverly had come back to the reservation with a hidden purpose.

Beverly Lamartine wanted to claim Henry junior and take him home.

In the Twin Cities there were great relocation opportunities for Indians with a certain amount of natural stick-to-it-iveness and pride. That's how Beverly saw it. He was darker than most, but his parents had always called themselves French or Black Irish and considered those who thought of themselves as Indians quite backward. They had put the need to get ahead in Beverly. He worked devilishly hard.

Door-to-door, he'd sold children's after-school home workbooks for the past eighteen years. The wonder of it was that he had sold any workbook sets at all, for he was not an educated man and if the customers had, as they might naturally do, considered him an example of his product's efficiency they might not have entrusted their own children to those pages of sums and reading exercises. But they did buy the workbook sets regularly, for Bev's ploy was to use his humble appearance and faulty grammar to ease into conversation with his hardworking get-ahead customers. They looked forward to seeing the higher qualities they could not afford inculcated in their own children. Beverly's territory was a small-town world of earnest dreamers. Part of Bev's pitch, and the one that usually sold the books, was to show the wife or husband a wallet-sized school photo of his son.

That was Henry Junior. The back of the photo was inscribed "To Uncle Bev," but the customer never saw that since the precious relic was encased in a cardboard-backed sheet of clear plastic. This covering preserved it from thousands of mill-toughened thumbs in the working class sections of Minneapolis and small towns within its one-hundred-mile radius. Every year or so Beverly wrote to Lulu, requesting another picture. It was sent to him in perfect good will. With every picture, Beverly grew more familiar with his son and more inspired in the invention of tales he embroidered, day after day, on front porches which were to him the innocent stages for his routine.

His son played baseball in a sparkling white uniform stained across the knees with grass. He pitched no-hitters every few weeks. Teachers loved the boy for getting so far ahead of the other students on his own initiative. They sent him on to various higher grades, and he was invited to the parties of children in the wealthy suburb of Edina. Henry Junior cleared the hurdles of class and intellect with an ease astonishing to Beverly, who noted to his wistful customers how swiftly the young surpass the older generation.

"Give them wings!" he would urge, flipping softly through the cheap pulp-flecked pages. The sound of the ruffled paper was like the panic of fledglings before they learn how to glide. People usually bought, and only later, when they found themselves rolling up a work skills book to slaughter a fly or scribbling phone numbers down on the back of Math Enrichment, would they realize that their children had absolutely no interest in taking the world by storm through self-enlightenment.

Some days, after many hours of stories, the son became so real in Bev's mind that when he came home to the apartment, he half-expected the boy to pounce on him before he put his key in the door. But, when the lock turned, his son vanished, for Elsa would be there, and she was not particularly interested in children, real or not. She was a typist who changed jobs incessantly. Groomed with exquisite tawdriness, she'd fashioned for Bev the image of a modern woman living the ideal career life. Her salary only fluctuated by pennies from firm to firm, but her importance and value as a knower-of-ropes swelled. She believed herself indispensable, but she heartlessly left employers hanging in their times of worst need to go on to something better.

Beverly adored her.

She was a natural blond with birdlike legs and true, no chin, but great blue snapping eyes. She smoked exotically, rolling smoke off her tongue. Often she told Bev that two weeks from now he might not be seeing her again. Then she would soften toward him. The possibilities she gave up to be with him impressed Bev so much, every time, that it ceased to bother him that Elsa showed him off to her family in Saint Cloud only at the height of summer, when they admired his perfect tan.

The boy, though, who was everywhere in his life and yet nowhere, fit less easily into Bev's fantasy of how he lived. The boy made him ache in hidden surprising places, sometimes at night when he lay next to Elsa, his knuckles resting lightly against her emphatic spine. That was the limit of touching she would tolerate in slumber. She even took her sleeping breath with a certain rigid meanness, holding it stubbornly and releasing it with small explosive sighs. Bev hardly noticed, though, for beside her his mind raced through the ceilings and walls.

One night he saw himself traveling. He was driving his sober green car westward, past the boundaries of his salesman's territory, then over the state line and on across to the casual and lonely fields, the rich dry violet hills of the reservation. Then he was home where his son really lived. Lulu came to the door. He habitually blotted away her face and body so that in his thoughts she was a doll of floursacking with a curly black mop on her head. She was simply glad that he had come at last to take the son she had such trouble providing for off her hands. She was glad Henry Junior would be wafted into a new and better metropolitan existence.

This scenario became so real through the quiet hours he lay beside Elsa that Bev even convinced himself that his wife would take to Henry Junior, in spite of the way she shuddered at children in the streets and whispered "Monkeys!" And then, by the time the next workday was half over, he'd arranged for a vacation and made an appointment to have a once-over done on his car.

Of course, Lulu was not made of floursacking and yarn. Beverly had realized that in the immediacy of her arms. She grabbed him for a hug when he got out of his car and, tired by the long trip, his head whirled for a moment in a haze of yellow spots. When she released him, the boys sauntered up, pokerfaced and mildly suspicious, to stand in a group around him and await their introductions. There seemed to be so many that at first he was speechless. Each of them was Henry Junior in a different daydream, at a different age, and so alike were their flat expressions he couldn't even pick out the one whose picture sold the record number of home workbooks in the Upper Midwestern Regional Division.

Henry Junior, of course, was perfectly recognizable after Lulu introduced him. After all, he did look exactly like the picture in Bev's wallet. He put his hand out and shook manfully like his older brothers, which pleased Bev although he had trouble containing a moment of confusion at the utter indifference in the boy's eyes. He had to remember the boy was meeting him for the first time. In a child's world strange grown-ups are as indistinguishable as trees in a forest. Even the writing on the back of those photographs was probably, now that he thought of it, Lulu's.

They went away, started shooting their guns, and then Bev was left with the unexpected problem of the mother of his son, the woman he would just as soon forget. During a moment of adjustment, however, he decided manfully to go through whatever set of manipulations were necessary. He wanted to handle the situation in the ideal, firm but diplomatic, manner. And then, after he'd recovered from the strength of her hug, he had absolutely no doubt that things would go on according to his plan.

"My my my," he said to Lulu now. She was buttering a piece of bread, soft as the plump undersides of her arms. "Lot of water under the dam."

She agreed, taking alert nips of her perfectly covered slice. She had sprinkled a teaspoon of sugar over it, carefully distributing the grains. That was how she was. Even with eight boys her house was neat as a pin. The candy bowl on the table sat precisely on its doily. All her furniture was brushed and straightened. Her coffee table held a neat stack of *Fate* and *True Adventure* magazines. On her walls she'd hung matching framed portraits of poodles, kittens, and an elaborate embroidered portrait of Chief Joseph. Her windowsills were decorated with pincushions in the shapes of plump little hats and shoes.

"I make these." She cupped a tiny blue sequined pump in her hand. "You have a girlfriend? I'll give it to you. Here."

She pushed the little shoe across the table. It skittered over the edge, fell into his lap, and Beverly retrieved it quickly for he saw that her hand was following. He set the blue slipper between them without addressing her implicit question on his status—girlfriend, married, or just looking around. He was intent on bringing up the subject of Henry Junior.

"Remember that time…" he started. Then he didn't know what he was going to say. What did come out surprised him. "You and me and Henry was playing cards before you got married and the boys was asleep?"

He could have kicked himself for having blurted that out. Even after all these years he couldn't touch on the memory without running a hand across his face or whistling tunelessly to drive it from his mind. It didn't seem to have bothered her all these years though. She picked up the story smoothly and went on.

"Oh, you men," she laughed chidingly. Her face was so little like Beverly's floursacking doll he wondered how he had stood imagining it that way all these years. Her mouth was small, mobile, like a puckering flower, and her teeth were unusually tiny and white. He remembered having the urge to lick their smoothness once. But now she was talking.

"I suppose you thought you could take advantage of a poor young woman. I don't know who it was, you or Henry, that suggested after several too many beers that we change our penny ante poker game to strip. Well, I still have to laugh. I had you men right down to your boxer shorts in no time flat, and I was sitting there warm and cozy as you please. I was still in my dress with my shoes on my feet."

"You had them beads on, clip earrings, bangle bracelets, silk stockings," Beverly pouted.

"Garters and other numerous foundation garments. Of course I did. I am a woman of detachable parts. You should know by now. You simply wasn't playing in your league with strip poker."

She had the grace to put a hand to her lips as they uncurved, hiding the little gap-toothed smile he'd doted over at the time of that game.

"Want to know something I never told before?" she said. "It was after I won your shorts with my pair of deuces and Henry's with my eights, and you were naked, that I decided which one to marry."

Beverly was shocked at this statement, bold even for Lulu. His wind felt knocked out of him for a moment because her words called up the old times so clearly, the way he felt when she decided to marry his brother. He'd buried the feelings eventually in the knowledge that she wasn't right for him, man of the world that he was becoming. He congratulated himself for years after on getting free of her slack, ambitionless, but mindlessly powerful female clutches. Right now his reasoning had ripped wide open, however, and jealousy kicked him in the stomach.

Lulu cooed. Her voice was like a wind chime rattling—cheap, sweet, maddening. "Some men react in that situation, and some don't," she told him. "It was reaction I looked for, if you know what I mean."

Beverly was silent.

Lulu winked at him with her bold, gleaming, blackberry eyes. She had smooth tight skin, wrinkled only where she laughed, always fragrantly powdered. At the time her hair was still dark and thickly curled. Later she would burn it off when her house caught fire, and it would never grow back. Because her face was soft and yet alert, vigilant as some small cat's, plump and tame but with a wildness in its breast, Beverly had always felt exposed, preyed on, undressed around her even before the game in which she'd stripped him naked and now, as he found, appraised him in his shame.

"You got your reaction when you needed it," he wanted to say.

Yet, even in his mounting exasperation, he did not lose control and stoop to discussing what had happened after Henry's wake when they both went outside to get some air. He rolled his sleeves down and fished a soft pack of Marlboros from her side of the table. She watched his hand as he struck the match and her eyes narrowed. They were so black the iris sometimes showed within like blue flames. Suddenly, he thought her heartless and wondered if she even remembered what had happened in the shed behind the house. But there was no good way he could think of to ask without getting back down to her level.

Henry Junior came to the window, hungry, and Lulu made a sandwich for him with baloney and hot dog relish. The boy was seven years old, sturdy, with Lulu's delicate skin and the almost Asian looking eyes of all the Lamartines. Beverly watched the boy with electrified attention. He couldn't really say if anything about the child reminded him of himself, unless it was the gaze. Beverly had tried to train his gaze like a hawk to use in barroom staredowns during his tour of duty. It came in handy as well when he made a sale, although civilian life had long ago taken the edge off his intensity, as it had his muscles, his hero's stubborn sagging flesh that he could still muster in a crisis. There was a crisis now. The boy seemed to have acquired the staredown technique naturally. Beverly was the first to look away.

"Uncle Bev," Henry Junior said. "I always heard about the bird on your arm. Could you make it fly?"

So Beverly rolled his shirt sleeve once more and forced his blood up. He flexed powerfully, over and over, until the boy, bored and satisfied, fled back to his brothers. Beverly let his arm down carefully. It was numb. The sound of the .22 reports came thick and fast for a while; then all the boys paused to reload and set the jugs in a line against the fence and argue over whose shot went where.

"They're teaching him to shoot," explained Lulu. "We had two bucks brought down last fall. And pheasants? Those boys will always put meat on my table."

She rambled on about them all, and Bev listened with relief, gathering his strength to pull the conversation back his way again.

One of the oldest boys was going down to Haskell Junior College, while another, Gerry, was testing the limits of the Mission school system, at twelve. Lulu pointed Gerry out among the others. Bev could see Lulu most clearly in this boy. He laughed at everything, or seemed barely to be keeping amusement in. His eyes were black, sly, snapping with sparks. He led the rest in play without a hint of effort, just like Lulu whose gestures worked as subtle magnets. He was a big boy, a born leader, light on his feet and powerful. His mind seemed quick. It would not surprise Bev to hear, many years later, that Gerry had grown up to be both a natural criminal and a hero whose face appeared on the six o'clock news.

Lulu managed to make the younger boys obey perfectly, Bev noticed, while the older ones adored her to the point that they did not tolerate anything less from anyone else. As her voice swirled on, Bev thought of some Tarzan book he had read. In that book there was a queen protected by bloodthirsty warriors who smoothly dispatched all of her enemies. Lulu's boys had grown into a kind of pack. They always hung together. When a shot went true, their gangling legs, encased alike in faded denim, shifted as if a ripple went through them collectively, in a dance step too intricate for the noninitiated eye to imitate or understand. Clearly they were of one soul. Handsome, rangy, wildly various, they were bound in total loyalty, not by oath but by the simple, unquestioning belongingness of parts of one organism.

Lulu had gone silent, suddenly, to fetch something from her icebox. In that quiet moment, something about the boys outside struck Beverly as almost dangerous.

He watched them close around Henry Junior in an impenetrable mass of black and white sneakers, sweatshirts, baseball hats, and butts of Marlin rifles. Through the chinks between their bodies Beverly saw Gerry, dark and electric as his mother, kneel behind Henry Junior and, arm over arm, instruct him how to cradle, aim, and squeeze-fire the .22. When Henry Junior stumbled, kicked backward by the recoil, missing the jug, the boys dusted him clean and set him back behind the rifle again. Slowly, as he watched, Beverly's uneasy sense of menace gave way to some sweet apprehension of their kinship. He was remembering the way he and Henry and Slick, the oldest, used to put themselves on the line for each other in high school. People used to say you couldn't drive a knife edge between the Lamartines. Nothing ever came between them. Nothing ever did or would.

Even while he was thinking that, Beverly knew it wasn't true.

What had come between them was a who, and she was standing across from him now at the kitchen counter. Lulu licked some unseen sweetness from her fingers, having finished her sugared bread. Her tongue was small, flat, and pale as a little cat's. Her eyes had shut in mystery. He wondered if she knew his thoughts.

She padded easily toward him, and he stood up in an odd panic as she approached. He felt his heart knock, urgently as a stranger in trouble, and then she touched him through his pants. He was helpless. His mouth fell on hers and kept traveling, through the walls and ceilings, down the levels, through the broad, warm reaches of the years.

The boys came back very late in the afternoon. By then, Beverly had drastically revised his plans for Henry Junior to the point where he had no plans at all. In a dazed, immediate, unhappy bewilderment he sat on the doily bedecked couch opening and closing his hands in his lap. Lulu was bustling about the kitchen in a calm, automatic frenzy. She seemed to fill pots with food by pointing at them and take things from the oven that she'd never put in. The table jumped to set itself. The pop foamed into glasses, and the milk sighed to the lip. The youngest boy, Lyman, crushed in a high chair, watched eagerly while things placed themselves around him. Everyone sat down. Then the boys began to stuff themselves with a savage and astonishing efficiency. Before Bev had cleaned his plate once, they'd had thirds, and by the time he looked up from dessert, they had melted through the walls. The youngest had levitated from his high chair and was sleeping out of sight. The room was empty, except for Lulu and himself.

He looked at her. She turned to the sinkful of dishes and disappeared in a cloud of steam. Only the round rear of her blue flowered housedress was visible, so he watched that. It was too late now. He had fallen. He could not help but remember their one night together seven years ago.

They had gone into the old shed while the earth was still damp and the cut flowers in their foam balls still exuded scent over Henry's grave. Beverly had kissed the small cries back onto Lulu's lips. He remembered. Then passion overtook them. She hung on to him like they were riding the tossing ground, her teeth grinding in his ear. He wasn't man or woman. None of that mattered. Yet he was more of a man than he'd ever been. The grief of loss for the beloved made their tiny flames of life so sad and precious that it hardly mattered who was what. The flesh was only given so that the flame could touch in a union, however less than perfect. Afterward they lay together, breathing the dark in and out. He had wept the one other time in his life besides post combat, and after a while he came into her again, tasting his own miraculous continuance.

Lulu left him sitting on the couch and went back into the sacred domain of her femininity, the bedroom with the locking door that she left just a crack open. She pulled down the blue-and-white checked bedspread, put the pillows aside, and lay down carefully with her hands folded on her stomach. She closed her eyes and breathed deep. She went into herself, sinking through her body as if on a raft of darkness, until she reached the very bottom of her soul where there was nothing to do but wait.

Things had gotten by Beverly. Night came down. His sad dazzlement abated and he tried to avoid thinking of Elsa. But she was there, filing her orange nails whichever way he ducked. And then there was the way he was proud of living his life. He wanted to go back and sell word enrichment books. No one on the reservation would buy them, he knew, and the thought panicked him. He realized the depth and danger of his situation were great if he had forgotten that basic fact. The moon went black. The bushes seemed to close around the house.

"Retrench," he told himself as the boys turned heavily and mumbled in their invisible cots and all along the floors around him. "Retreat if you have to and forget about Henry Junior." He finally faced surrender; he knew it was the only thing he could possibly have the strength for.

He planned to get into his car while it was still dark, before dawn, and drive back to Minneapolis without Henry Junior. He would simply have to bolt without saying good-bye to Lulu. But when he rose from the couch, he walked down the hall to her bedroom door. He didn't pause but walked right through. It was like a routine he'd built up over time in marriage. The close dark was scented with bath lilac. Glowing green spears told the hour in her side-table clock. The bedclothes rustled. He stood holding the lathed wooden post. And then his veins were full of warm ash and his tongue swelled in his throat.

He lay down in her arms. Whirling blackness swept through him and there was nothing else to do. The wings didn't beat as hard as they used to, but the bird still flew.

Gerald Early

Gerald Early was born in Philadelphia, Pennsylvania, in 1952. He graduated from the University of Pennsylvania and moved back to Philadelphia where he was employed by the city government. Early married in 1977 and went on to receive his Ph.D. in English and American literature from Cornell in 1982. The couple had two children by the time Early took his first teaching job as assistant professor of black studies at St. Louis's Washington University in 1982, where he would steadily rise to a full professorship in both the English and the renamed African and Afro-American studies departments by 1990. Early has become one of the leading cultural critics of many areas of African-American life and history, authoring such books as *Tuxedo Junction: Essays on American Culture; My Soul's High Song: The Collected Writings of Countee Cullen; One Nation Under a Groove;* and *The Culture of Bruising: Essays on Prizefighting, Literature, and Modern American Culture*, which earned Early the 1995 National Book Critics Circle Award and in which appeared Early's essay "The Black Intellectual and the Sport of Prizefighting," originally appearing in *The Kenyon Review* in 1988.

The Black Intellectual and the Sport of Prizefighting *(1988)*

by Gerald Early

I

A Theoretical Prelude

Once I saw a prize fighter boxing a yokel. The fighter was swift and amazingly scientific. His body was one violent flow of rapid rhythmic action. He hit the yokel a hundred times while the yokel held up his arms in stunned surprise. But suddenly the yokel, rolling about in the gale of boxing gloves, struck one blow and knocked science, speed, and footwork as cold as a well-digger's posterior. The smart money hit the canvas. The long shot got the nod. The yokel had simply stepped inside of his opponent's sense of time...

This quotation is from Ralph Ellison's *Invisible Man,*[1] a novel that makes a number of allusions and references to prizefighting. This quotation resonates in a number of very crucial ways. It is, of course, the classic dialectic of boxing: the speedy, scientific boxer versus the artless puncher. But it is also the story of the tortoise and the hare, the con man and the homeboy, the country mouse and the city mouse, Brer Fox and Brer Rabbit. Yet all those classical metaphors of innocence and experience collapse into the image of the prizefighter's confrontation with his opposite, his nemesis, the very antithesis of himself. It was Mark Twain who wrote in his 1889 novel, A *Connecticut Yankee in King Arthur's Court,* that the world's best swordsman needn't fear the second-best swordsman in the world; he needs to fear the man who has never held a sword. In this light, the world's best boxer needn't fear the man who is almost his equal but rather the man who could not possibly match his skill. In other words, the Trickster, inasmuch as he is represented by the slick accomplished boxer, does not need to fear another formidable Trickster; rather he needs to fear that which is the negation of the Trickster, for in the brutal pantomime of the prize ring the Trickster's technique masks the fact that he is the personification of anarchy. Thus, his technique is not a virtue but utter decadence, his paradoxical expression of the contempt of both virtue and technique. And his negation is he who through the complete absence of

---

1) Ralph Ellison, *Invisible Man* (New York: Modern Library, 1952), p 7.

technique wishes to rescue technique from the Trickster's laughing and lurid display of it as a stunt.

Technique—and boxing since its inception in the bare-knuckle days of Broughton and Slack in England has been, in part, nothing more than the history of its own rationalization through the obsessive quest for more reified technique and rules—must always fear, not other techniques but the utter void of technique. It is no accident to speak of confidence games in connection with the metaphor raised by the Ellison quotation. Professional prizefighting, from its early brawling days in eighteenth-century England, has been the sport of the gambler, and the gambler's romance—his dream—has always been to have the long shot come through as a sure thing. Variations on the theme of the victory of the yokel as a fixed fight can be found in such sources as David W. Maurer's accounts of various fight store cons in *The American Confidence Man* and the short stories of Charles Emmet Van Loan in *Inside the Ropes* (1913) and *Taking the Count* (1915). In these stories, in that maddening fluidity of identity that has come to characterize the American, long shots disguise themselves as sure things and sure things masquerade as long shots. Other sources include the actual history of American prizefighting itself: the halcyon days of New York's Horton Law, 1896–1900 (a nice historical chunk detailing sordid wheelings and dealings designed to rip off the unsuspecting public), or a fight such as the Billy Fox–Jake LaMotta middleweight bout on November 14, 1947. LaMotta admitted, several years later before a Senate investigating committee, that he threw this fight on orders of members of organized crime so that the long shot—Fox—would win (which he did by a fourth-round knockout). This is only one of many such examples that riddle a sport that has problems with honesty.

The two most powerful, most staying, images of the yokel and the prizefighter can be drawn from two entirely different realms of American culture, and both involve white fighters. The first is Francis Wallace's 1936 novel, *Kid Galahad,* which was made into a film twice: the first, *The Battling Bellhop,* in 1937 (original theater title was *Kid Galahad*), featured Bette Davis; the latter, *Kid Galahad,* in the early sixties, was a star vehicle for Elvis Presley. It has been made into two films nearly thirty years apart and its basic theme—the good, incorruptible middlewestern country boy goes to the city, becomes a crude but effective boxer in order to save the family farm—has been used in a number of other films. This shows how deeply the Galahad myth of male American innocence (for example, Billy Budd, the American Adam) and inadvertent Horatio-Alger-like success (humility and determination as forms of grace from Ben Franklin to Sylvester Stallone's Rocky) is ingrained in our national consciousness. Dubbed in the novel "Galahad" because of his purity of heart, the former bellhop, fresh from the Navy, is always the long shot in his fights and always knocks out his opponents with one punch. His opponents are always better boxers, better stylists in the ring than he is. The films tend to stress Galahad's ineptitude more than the novel does. Wallace, in the end, is ambiguous. The Kid over the course of the book becomes a pretty good boxer/stylist and in his last fight—a grudge match, as these confrontations usually are in novels and films—is actually beaten severely for the first several rounds. His manager, Nick, pressured by the gangsters and affected by his own jealousy of Galahad, gives him the wrong advice and has him slugging instead of boxing. Eventually, Nick changes his mind and the Kid, through sly boxing, wins the fight. Of course, at novel's end, the Kid quits boxing. He is, after all, not a pug, and his mastery of boxing is not a sign of commitment but an indication of disdain. He does not wish to be tainted by boxing; it is simply the avenue by which he can seize the main chance to remain stolidly agrarian, implacably at peace with a series of values that can scarcely be considered conventional. They are gestures of folksy platitudes: he likes to eat, does not drink, likes to work in the open air, is polite to and shy around women, believes in his country, and yearns for the family hearth. The fact that he has become a decent boxer in the end suggests that he might be corrupted by all this and adopt another series of values—dress fancy, go to nightclubs, chase women, and drink liquor. In the Presley film, the necessity of this reactionary male purity is made clearer by, first, never having Galahad achieve any sort of prowess as a fighter and, second, by having his ultimate opponent be a slick, accomplished Hispanic boxer. The element of race is never very distant in the novel, although none of Galahad's opponents is black or Hispanic. The book is the sort of generally racist fare that one might expect from a bad novel written in the early thirties by a white writer. This was, after all, when the radio serialization of *Amos and Andy* began and books such as *Bigger and Blacker* and *Dark Days and Black Knights* by Octavus Roy Cohen and other such comic denigrations of blacks (published just a few years earlier) were still quite popular. And the country was still segregated. The issue is always Galahad's whiteness as inextricably bound to his maleness and to his pious set of provincial American moral bromides. In this sense, Wallace's novel and the films that resulted from it are nothing more than measured refinements of certain boxing novels by white male writers,

both British and American, written during that fifty years preceding the publication of *Galahad:* George Bernard Shaw's *Cashel Byron's Profession*
(1886), Arthur Conan Doyle's *Rodney Stone* (1896), Jack London's *The
Game* (1905), W.R.H. Trowbridge's *The White Hope* (1913), and Robert E.
Howard's *The Iron Man* (1930), the last indicative of the type of pulp material serialized in *Fight Stories* Magazine. These books, by and large, being
metaphorical discourses on the philosophical issue of the universe-of-force,
on the sociopolitical issue of social Darwinism, and on the popular romance
of American capitalism simply highlights their preoccupation with race. As
Ronald E. Martin has argued in his literary study of the social Darwinism
era: "The theme of evolutionary racism is an important one in late-
nineteenth century..."; or "the universe-of-force viewpoint was of a piece
with some of the Western world's most pernicious social practices and theories at the turn of the century. Force-thinking generally rationalized racism,
class superiority, imperialism, the acquisition of wealth, and the veneration
of the 'fittest.'"[2] (Other scholars of this era, notably George M. Fredrickson,
Rayford Logan, and Richard Hofstader have made this point as well.) The
good white fighter in these novels, who is not always inept in the technical
sense, in the end symbolizes the essence of the "white civilization" that
seemed to be standing at the brink of either an endless dawn of imperialistic
dominance or the eternal night of nonwhite domination. It is the central
myth of the key novel of Victorian America: Edgar Rice Burroughs's *Tarzan
of the Apes* (1913), the quintessential blending of athleticism and racism.
The power and popularity of this conjunction is revealed ironically in F.
Scott Fitzgerald's 1925 novel, *The Great Gatsby,* where Tom Buchanan, the
powerful football player, talks about reading Goddard's *The Rise of the
Colored Empires,* and it is also suggested by Gatsby's reading of *Hopalong
Cassidy,* a dime novel adventure from the same tradition of racist adventure
westerns as those of Johnston McCulley, the creator of Zorro. These facts
help explain my belief that *Gatsby* is a reworking of a western; in part, at
least, a reworking of Owen Wister's *The Virginian,* leading to the great
masked avenger, Ben Cameron, in Thomas Dixon's *The Clansman* (1905).
This novel is essentially a little boy's adventure-romance about how white
civilization must be rescued in much the same manner that a princess is rescued from a dragon. It is indeed quite striking how both vigilantism and ter-
rorism, from Zorro to Batman to G.I. Joe, is the theme of male adolescent

---

2) Ronald E. Martin. *American Literature and the Universe of Force* (Durham: Duke University Press,
1981), p 71. p xv.

literature. Sanitized as a reactionary political literature, it simply becomes a little-boy genre for little-boy minds.

An important historic conjunction was taking place between approximately 1870 and 1930: boxing was changing from a bare-knuckle, irrational sport of indeterminate length to a rationalized sport of gloves governed by time; these changes helped to make it more popular. In addition, social Darwinism in particular and popular science in general were now a part of mass culture; ordinary people thought about science in a positive way, and blacks began to achieve notice in boxing and in American popular culture itself, through the image of bruisers. More so than baseball, pedestrianism (race walking), or jockeying, the other three professional sports that had a significant black presence in the late nineteenth century, boxing was the one sport that could produce an intense if vulgar fame, enough so that Corbett, Sullivan, Fitzsimmons, and Jeffries, the important champions before Jack Johnson, had to draw a color line against black challengers during their reigns. In other words, conditions were such that professional boxing was metamorphosed into an American sport, serving a particular and powerful set of collective psychic needs. With the completion of its final stages of development, the recodification of the rules, and the entry of the black, boxing was now ready to become the most metaphorical drama of male neurosis ever imagined in the modern world.

This leads me to discuss the second example or image of the yokel and the boxer, this taken from an actual prizefight. In April 1915, black heavyweight champion Jack Johnson defended his title for the last time against Jess Willard of Kansas in Havana. Johnson, who had won the title on Christmas Eve, 1908, when he defeated Tommy Burns in Australia, had not had an easy time of it during his reign. A conviction for the violation of the Mann Act in 1912 led to his flight from America; in 1915, after he had been abroad for a few years, he was no longer lionized, and was in fact broke and possessor of a title that didn't mean much. It was a strange fight. Johnson has always maintained that he threw the fight—he lost by a knockout in the twenty-sixth round—in a deal to return to the United States and beat the Mann Act rap; yet right before the fight he was confident in his utterances published in black-and-white newspapers and was telling all his black fans including his mother to bet on him. (Of course, black fighters had betrayed black sports in fixed fights before: fifteen years earlier, in December 1900, in Chicago, black lightweight Joe Gans threw a fight to featherweight Terry McGovern and blacks on the South Side took a bath.) Despite his age—

thirty-seven—and lack of conditioning caused by an extensive period of inactivity and lack of strenuous competition, Johnson was favored to win because he was such an outstanding boxer. Willard was not even the most distinguished of a mediocre lot of white hopes, though he was probably the biggest. Johnson had been involved in a fixed championship fight with a white challenger before: on October 16, 1909, in Colma, California, Johnson fought middleweight champion Stanley Ketchel on the condition that he carry him for the distance and not try to knock him out. When Ketchel tried a doublecross and knocked Johnson down in the twelfth round of the battle, Johnson arose and knocked Ketchel unconscious with an uppercut that broke off Ketchel's front teeth at the gum line. Being a black fighter, Johnson knew all about faking fights with white fighters. It was a common practice at this time. Such notable black fighters as Sam Langford, Sam McVey, Denver Ed Martin, Joe Jeanette, and others carried their share of incompetent white fighters.

But the fact of the matter is that Johnson, despite the claim in his autobiography and in the "Confessions" he sold to *Ring* Magazine editor Nat Fleischer, did not throw the fight to Jess Willard. He lost in much the same manner that the slick boxer always loses to the yokel. He could not knock out Willard despite administering substantial punishment. Johnson tired because of his age and lack of condition, and eventually, with the hot sun beating down on him, Willard was able to land the one punch that put him on the floor.

Willard's victory was the beginning of the glorification of the white yokel in boxing (although, admittedly, Willard himself was never very well liked by the white public). Johnson's claim for a fix made the white yokel's claim essentially ambiguous and made the fight between the white yokel and the black boxer a comic encounter. Excepting Jack Dempsey and Gene Tunney, virtually every white champion (despite his style) has been a yokel: Sharkey, Braddock, Schmeling, Baer, Carnera, Marciano, Johansson, Coetzee.

The most notable contests for all of these fighters were against their significant black opponent. Louis fought and defeated the first five mentioned; Walcott, Charles, Louis, and Moore fought Marciano; Patterson became Johansson's alter ego, and Leon Spinks and Greg Page did the same for Coetzee. (One might throw in Jerry Cooney and Jerry Quarry who fit this mold, although they never became champions.) In their fights against black opponents, these fighters were not expected to win by guile or by ability. They were expected to win as Willard had against Johnson: take punishment, then land the ultimate blow.

sure, there have been black fighters who have been known as
s; Sonny Liston comes to mind, as does current heavyweight cham-
pio.. like Tyson, though neither of them, to borrow a phrase from A.J.
Liebling, would be considered nearly as "gauche and inaccurate" as Rocky
Marciano who, along with Dempsey, is the most mythical of the great white
fighters. But the greatest black fighters in the twentieth century, those most
famous and highly regarded by experts, were tricksters of style: Jack
Johnson, Muhammad Ali, Sugar Ray Robinson, and Sugar Ray Leonard:
indeed the title "sugar," given to a fighter in recognition of the refulgences
of his style, has never been given to a white fighter. Even Joe Louis, despite
his reputation as a heavy hitter, was really a stylist, "as elegant as the finest
of ballet dancers," Ralph Ellison said in an interview.

Against black opponents the white yokels were not even really fighters;
they were more like preservers of the white public's need to see Tricksters
pay a price for their disorder. Liebling was right in the end: if the black
fighter as Trickster sees the white yokel as nemesis, then the white yokel
becomes Ahab and the black Trickster the ultimate blackness of the black
whale; the ring itself becomes the place where ideas of order are contested.

II
Black Writers and the Sport of Prizefighting

There has never been a full-length nonfiction treatise on the sport of boxing by a black writer on the order of those by white authors such as A.J.
Liebling's *The Sweet Science* (1982), George Plimpton's *Shadow-Box*
(1977), Joyce Carol Oates's *On Boxing* (1987), Thomas Hauser's *The Black
Lights* (1986), or Norman Mailer's *The Fight* (1975). Exceptions are the
autobiographies of black fighters, the books by blacks such as Art Rust,
Harry Edwards, Oceania Chalk, and A.S. "Doc" Young that may contain a
section on boxing (while discussing blacks in sports generally), former light
heavyweight champion José Torres's fine biography of Muhammad Ali, the
sociological articles by Nathan Hare, a former boxer, and a book such as Al-
Tony Gilmore's *Bad Nigger* (1975) on the trials and tribulations of Jack
Johnson. Indeed, the most complete, though not necessarily the most accurate, history of blacks in the sport was written by the previously mentioned
Jewish editor of *Ring* Magazine, Nat Fleischer; he composed five volumes
published between 1938 and 1947 dealing with that subject called *Black
Dynamite* that extends from Molineaux to Joe Louis *(Black Dynamite: The*

Story of the Negro in the Prize Ring from 1782 to 1938). James Weldon Johnson provided a capsule history of blacks in the sport in his 1930 study *Black Manhattan;* this made him the first black intellectual to consider at any length the cultural importance of prizefighting for Afro-America.[3]

No black mainstream fiction writer has written a novel using a boxing theme in the same manner as Leonard Gardner in *Fat City* (1969), Nelson Algren in *Never Come Morning* (1963), W.C. Heinz in *The Professional* (1958), or Budd Schulberg in *The Harder They Fall* (1947). Boxing has been mentioned in some black novels and has, in fact, figured as an important image in a few, but there has been no black novel on boxing by a major black writer. There is a genre of black novels published by Holloway House in California called "novels of the black experience" generally characterized by potboiler plots and a type of effective, if occasionally pornographic, naturalism. The leading writers of these types of books are Iceberg Slim and the late Donald Goines. One of these may deal with boxing, a likely subject for these books.

It is odd that major works on the sport of prizefighting, either fiction or nonfiction, have not been produced by black writers. Boxing figures prominently in the social and cultural history of blacks in America; indeed, one could argue that the three most important black figures in twentieth-century American culture were prizefighters: Jack Johnson, Joe Louis, and Muhammad Ali. Certainly, there have been no other blacks in the history of this country who have been written about as much and whose actions were scrutinized so closely or reverberated so profoundly. We know from such books as Lawrence Levine's brilliant study, *Black Culture and Black Consciousness* (1977), that black prizefighters were important and celebrated personages in Afro-American folk lore; indeed, these fighters were more celebrated in Afro-American folk lore and life generally than other important black pioneers in sports such as Jackie Robinson, Jesse Owens, or Wilma Rudolph. Furthermore, prizefighting appears in important instances in other facets of Afro-American culture ranging from Adam Clayton Powell, Sr.'s, funeral oration for African boxer Battling Siki, to jazz trumpeter Miles

---

3) Black intellectuals such as Roi Ottley and J. Saunders Reddings have devoted chapters in certain of their nonfiction work to black prizefighters, notably Joe Louis. Indeed, West Indian scholar C.L.R. James mentions both Louis and boxing in his book on cricket, *Beyond Boundary* (London: Hutchinson and Co., 1969). Space does not permit me to comment on them, and as the books are unclassifiable, I have not placed them in the list above. Two other notable essays on this subject by Ishmael Reed are "The Greatest; My Own Story," in *Shrovetide in Old New Orleans* (New York: Doubleday, 1978) and "The Fourth Ali," in *God Made Alaska for the Indians* (New York: Garland Publishing, 1982).

Davis's fascination with presenting himself, in alter ego guise, as a prize-fighter; this obsession culminated artistically with the release in 1971 of his soundtrack album entitled, "Jack Johnson." The subject receives mention in such significant black autobiographies as Maya Angelou's *I Know Why the Caged Bird Sings* (1969) and *The Autobiography of Malcolm X* (1973). It also surfaces in Richard Pryor's routine about Muhammad Ali and Leon Spinks, and rap star L.L. Cool J appears on the back of his latest album punching a heavy bag.

Among the more important works by Afro-American intellectuals and creative writers on the subject of prizefighting are the following: Larry Neal's essay, "Uncle Rufus Raps on the Squared Circle," which originally appeared in the *Partisan Review* (Spring, 1972); Jervis Anderson's "Black Heavies," which appeared in *American Scholar* (Summer, 1978); Eldridge Cleaver's "Lazarus, Come Forth" from his book, *Soul on Ice* (1981); Amiri Baraka's "The Dempsey-Liston Fight" from his book, *Home: Social Essays* (1966); Richard Wright's three journalistic pieces: "Joe Louis Uncovers Dynamite" (October 8, 1935) and "High Tide in Harlem: Joe Louis as a Symbol of Freedom" (July 5, 1938), both published in *New Masses,* and "And Oh—Where Were Hitler's Pagan Gods?" which appeared in the *Daily Worker* (June 24, 1938); and John A. Williams's "Jack Johnson and the Great White Hope" from his book, *Flashbacks* (1973). They are not, taken as a body, the *most* important or impressive interpretative work by a black writer on the sport; the best, aside from Torres's biography of Muhammad Ali, are Ralph Ellison's *Invisible Man* and three essays by former heavyweight champion Floyd Patterson: two 1965 *Sports Illustrated* pieces, "I Want to Destroy Clay" and "Cassius Clay Must Be Beaten," and a later *Esquire* piece entitled "In Defense of Cassius Clay" (August, 1966).

The Baraka essay, written in 1964, and the Cleaver essay, which was published in 1968, deal basically with the same thing: the meaning of the phenomenon of Sonny Liston, Floyd Patterson, and Muhammad Ali as the most powerful black presences in American popular culture of the sixties. Their discussion of the racial obsessions that underlie the design of American masculinity is essentially accurate although they both tend to sound like Baldwin, finally; as one unidentified critic put it, Baldwin seems to think that the secret notion behind the pathology of racism is that all whites madly desire to sleep with any Negro they can find.[4] The discussion about boxing and

---

4) Quoted in Fern Marja Eckman. *The Furious Passage of James Baldwin* (New York: M. Evans & Co., 1966), p 165.

American sport, on the other hand, is quite weak; Cleaver's ultimate summation of American sports as bloodlust and competition is essentially the simplistic polemic of "leftist humanism" that was to characterize later radical writers such as Paul Hoch. It is a criticism that blames the current craze for sports on the commercialization of athletics in bourgeois culture, an assumption that overlooks the popularity of competitive sports in communist countries. There is not a shred of evidence to indicate that sports are any less competitive in communist countries or that having sports run by the State results in a more "humane" or "holistic" concept of sport and play. Allen Guttmann has provided a thorough-going critique of both the Marxist and neo-Marxist analyses of sports in bourgeois culture. Moreover, the political deconstruction of the symbolism of Liston, Patterson, and Ali by Cleaver and Baraka actually seems to be working with the same set of assumptions about the critical reading of fights used by the whites they condemn. Liston, Patterson, and Ali represent the good, the bad, and the ugly in everyone's morality play; it is simply a matter of musical chairs when the time comes to personify the abstraction. In this sense, I assume that Neal's piece, published in 1972, was meant to be a correction, an attempt to escape the previous politically motivated way the black intellectuals read prizefights after the coming of Liston and Ali in the sixties. Neal's article is a strategic plea for reconciliation. Uncle Rap, despite his scientific-mythical jargon, which sounds like nothing so much as Sun Ra in one of his more lucid moments, returns the reading of fights and of blacks in American popular culture to the framework of black folk lore; this, for Neal, is the only trustworthy critical measure of black aesthetic conceptualization. In this way, the fight between Frazier and Ali is not simply dialectical war—the affirming self and the blank twin of its own negation—but rather the confrontation between two classic aspects of Afro-American style and being, a Ruth-Benedict-like assertion of the Apollonian and the Dionysian, a dialectical moralism that implies its own peaceful synthesis through the respectful admission of each for the other's existence as a necessary antithesis.

Williams's essay, originally written in 1968 as a preface for Howard Sackler's hit play, *The Great White Hope*, but which Sackler eventually rejected, is simply a sloppy piece of writing. A paragraph such as the following is really an inexcusable distortion:

Having failed to dethrone Johnson in the ring, white forces, public and private, launched an attack on his personal life that drove his first wife to suicide and sent Johnson to Europe to avoid going to jail on trumped-up charges. He spent about two years in Europe. He went into show business, fought sparingly, avoiding other Negro boxers as often as he could. Tutored by Belmonte and Joselito, he also fought a bull in the Barcelona ring. On the whole his life abroad was bitter.[5]

The death of Johnson's wife was not really the result of any public campaign to get him. Williams fails to note the salient point that Johnson's wife was white and committed suicide primarily because of the difficulty white women faced socially at the "degradation" of being married to a black man. Johnson was also notoriously unfaithful. He was convicted for violating the Mann Act, a trumped-up charge only in the sense that the law might be argued to have been trumped-up. The conviction was valid enough. Largely, Johnson ran into trouble because of his public association with several white women, a fact that Williams neglects to mention. Undoubtedly, it was short-sighted, cruel, and utterly reprehensible for Johnson's society to have condemned him because he desired white women, but it is the height of historical disservice not to state the facts of the case because of a disdain of or distaste for them. "Bitter" is surely an odd word to use in connection with Johnson's life. Johnson probably felt a certain amount of bitterness about his exile, but he seems to have made the best of it. Desperation might be a better word to describe Johnson in some stages of his life, for he was always the hustler looking eagerly for the main chance.

Anderson's 1978 essay on Louis, Ali, and Johnson, largely a historical descriptive piece in the same mode, is much better than the Williams piece. When Anderson speaks of Johnson as full of "confidence (perhaps overconfidence), high self-esteem, a strong belief in his legal rights as a citizen, and a joyous obedience to what was dramatic and colorful in his character,"[6] he is much closer to the truth than Williams ever was. Admittedly, of course, the passage of ten years made writing a piece on Johnson a great deal easier because it was not necessary for it to be so politically charged or self-conscious. But it is Anderson who reaches the more politically meaningful conclusion when he writes: "Yet there were at least two important characteristics that all three men [Ali, Louis, and Johnson] shared: each was superbly gifted as a boxer, and each desired very much to be himself."

---

5) John A. Williams, *Flashbacks: A Twenty-Year Diary of Article Writing* (New York: Doubleday, 1973), p 279.

6) Jervis Anderson, "Black Heavies," *American Scholar* (Summer, 1978), p 390.

Obviously, there isn't really very much a gifted person could want to be but himself, if he wants to be able to exploit his gifts at all; yet the statement compellingly reveals the true political importance of Ali, Louis, and Johnson: for a black public person to be both gifted and true to himself is not automatic or, one should say, axiomatic, and it is bound to be subversive by extending the scope and expressive range of black humanity in mainstream culture.

The Wright essays are an early indication of his preoccupation with the tyrannical blandishments of American popular culture. In his August 1938 piece in *New Masses,* "High Tide in Harlem," he calls both Joe Louis and Max Schmeling "puppets," which implies that not only are they manipulated but also their contrived gyrations are manipulating the public that watches them. He calls the second fight between Schmeling and Louis, probably one of the most famous events in the history of sports, "a colorful puppet show," "one of the greatest dramas of make-believe ever witnessed in America," and "a configuration of social images whose intensity and clarity had been heightened through weeks of skilful and constant agitation" (p. 18). Wright's fascination with popular culture would make itself apparent in such later works as *Native Son* (1966) where Bigger Thomas would live in a world of newspapers, cheap magazines, and movies; he would be literally entrapped by the images of popular culture in the room of the Dalton's former chauffeur, Green, whose walls were covered by pictures of "Jack Johnson, Joe Louis, Jack Dempsey, and Henry Armstrong…Ginger Rogers, Jean Harlow, and Janet Gaynor."[7] Prizefighters and Hollywood actresses, the kings and queens of American popular culture. (One is reminded of the scene in James Weldon Johnson's 1912 novel, *The Autobiography of an Ex-Colored Man,* where the hero enters the room of his "club" to discover pictures "of Peter Jackson, of all the lesser lights of the prizefighting ring, of all the famous jockeys and the stage celebrities…")[8] Bigger, who is not very articulate, never smiles, and seems sullen, brings to mind the young Joe Louis who was described by white sportswriters of the period as being sullen and who was featured in a *New Republic* article entitled, "Joe Louis Never Smiles" (October 9, 1935). And the Louis career of the poor southern boy—living with a stepfather since his real father had been placed in an insane asylum—being brought north to the big city by his family in search of employment

7) Richard Wright, *Native Son* (New York: Harper & Row, 1966), p 60 (original date of publication, 1940).

8) James Weldon Johnson, *The Autobiography of an Ex-Colored Man* in *Three Negro Classics,* ed. John Hope Franklin (New York: Avon Books, 1965), p 450.

and fresh opportunities, was the Bigger Thomas career and the Richard Wright career as well. It was also the career of two of Louis's biggest fans in pugilistic circles: Floyd Patterson and Sonny Liston. Incidentally, Thomas was the last name of Joe Louis's character in the 1937 film *Spirit of Youth,* which starred Louis. Wright, a frequent movie goer and admirer of Louis during the 1930s, may have seen this film. He wrote the lyrics to "King Joe," a song honoring Joe Louis. Count Basie wrote the music and Paul Robeson supplied the voice. It may have been, as Ralph Ellison pointed out, an unfortunate collaboration in an aesthetic sense, but it reveals the power of Louis's attraction for Wright. In his autobiography, *Black Boy* (1945), Wright's critique of popular culture continues in the depiction of his growth from reading material like Zane Grey's *Riders of the Purple Sage* (1912) to essays by H.L. Mencken. His conversation with the African boy who wishes to be a detective in *Black Power* (1954), the depiction of the black woman desperately straightening her hair in *The Color Curtain* (1956), the inescapable radio in *Lawd Today* (1963), and the magazines read by the white women cafeteria workers in *American Hunger* (1944) all show how the machinations of popular culture are emotionally crippling, self-destructive escapism. The three Wright boxing pieces taken together reveal an essential ambivalence: Joe Louis is a product of American popular culture, a creation of it, in effect, and therefore is nothing more than the convenient bread-and-circus invention of white American capitalists; Joe Louis, however, is a hero of the black masses, a potential source of political mobilization because he can so deeply excite so many blacks. Wright's pieces are absorbed by this idea: how Louis affects large numbers of blacks. Each of his pieces is, in fact, more about how blacks in Harlem respond after a Louis victory than about Louis himself. Wright's ambivalence is not so much that of the Marxist trying to find an ideological way to tap an unreconstructed political resource as it is that of the black trying to find a psycho-historical way to tap the complexity of his own injured consciousness.

But it is Ellison in *Invisible Man* who fully elaborates upon the ambiguity of the black in boxing that Wright only suggests in his Joe Louis pieces. The battle royal scene at the beginning of Ellison's novel, one of the most famous fictional boxing depictions in American literature, is meant to conjure up images of turn-of-the-century black fighters who received their training in the sport as youths in just this way. Nat Fleischer in his multivolume history of blacks in the prizefights describes black battle royals as commonplace. But the black fighter that Ellison particularly wants to suggest is Jack Johnson who, as biographers Finis Farr, Al-Tony Gilmore, and Randy Roberts have made clear, was a frequent participant in the battle royal in his youth. In this way, Ellison alludes to the three most important black figures of early twentieth century America: Booker T. Washington—the Invisible Man's graduation speech is in fact Washington's Atlanta Cotton Exposition Speech of 1895; W.E.B. DuBois—the Invisible Man is the tenth boy in the battle royal, a reference to DuBois's concept of the Talented Tenth to which the Invisible Man would naturally feel he belongs (according to Fleischer, normally nine youths participated in a battle royal but, of course, any number could participate); and Jack Johnson—by the battle royal itself. One might imagine that Johnson was much like Tatlock, the tough winner of the encounter. There has been much discussion about the scene showing how white men used both sex—the white woman dancer with the flag tatooed near her genitals—and money—which is what, finally, the boys are fighting for—to manipulate blacks and to keep them divided. Therefore, the scene works, in part, in much the same way as Wright's fight scene with another black boy near the end of *Black Boy;* this fight was instigated, created by white men who wanted to be entertained by seeing two black youths fight. The scene in Wright's book operates as an ironical comment on the event which foreshadows the conclusion of Frederick Douglass's 1845 *Narrative,* his classic confrontation as a teenaged boy with the white slave-breaker, Covey. Like Douglass, Wright is the troubled black boy who cannot live under the system and who ultimately flees. Unlike Douglass, though, Wright, through his fight scene, asserts the utter impossibility of finding his manhood through any sort of direct confrontation with white men. That impossibility is symbolized by Wright's being forced to leave the optical company after being trapped between two benches by a white man at either end. This probably explains why Wright, like many other blacks, was so deeply affected by Louis: Louis had the devoutly-wished-for opportunity that Douglass had—to confront a white man squarely with his fist.

But the most telling part of the Ellison scene occurs when the Invisible Man suggests to Tatlock: "Fake like I knocked you out, you can have the prize." "I'll break your behind," he whispered hoarsely. "For *them?*" "For *me,* sonofabitch!"[9] Louis was heroic, in part, through the accident that he was permitted to fight white men in fights that resonated with meaning for both blacks and whites. But it was not Louis who determined his opponents or

---

9) Ellison. *Invisible Man.* p 20.

defined the meaning of his fights. Presumably, since Louis wanted to be a fighter, he would have fought anyone, black or white. In the days when the color line was drawn in boxing, black fighters did get a chance to fight white fighters on occasion, but very often these fights were fixed so that the white fighter would win. In most instances, great black fighters at the turn of the century spent much of their careers fighting each other; these tended to be their most vicious fights as there was little reason for one black fighter to throw a fight to another black. When the Invisible Man suggests that *he* should win the fake fight, he is putting himself in the position of the white fighter in the integrated fight. Naturally, Tatlock rejects this. Moreover, Tatlock wants to win because, freed from the fakery of the racially integrated fight, he can display completely his abilities as an athlete; he asserts that he does this not for the *audience,* but for *himself.* The ambiguity here which I think is a crucial issue for the black intellectual and prevents him from celebrating boxing in the way the white intellectual can is that boxing, finally, for the black fighter is an apolitical, amoral experience of individualistic esteem which the black fighter purchases at both the expense of his rival's health (and often his own) and his own dignity. For the black intellectual, boxing becomes both a dreaded spectacle and a spectacle of dread. The black fighter is truly heroic for the black masses and the black intellectual only when he is fighting a white fighter, or someone who has been defined as representing white interests; the battle then becomes the classic struggle between the black and the white over the nature of reality. When the black fighter fights another black, how does he differ from Stagolee, the legendary black badman who preyed on his own, or Brer Rabbit, the Trickster, whose victories are limited and short-term and whose motives are often selfish and shallow? Moreover, the black fighter's heroic moment is never one in which he is in control but simply his own desperate effort not to be swallowed in a sea of black anonymity. In this regard, it is interesting to note that virtually every heavyweight champion before Louis drew the color line and would not fight black fighters for the championship. This included Jack Johnson, who fought only one black fighter during his eight-year reign as champion. Louis was the first true democratic champion of boxing who fought all corners. In a sense he had to, but nonetheless he established a tradition in the very breadth of his daring and excellence that has produced a certain anxiety-of-influence in the black champions who have come after him.

And this brings us to Patterson's essays on boxing; it was Patterson, oddly enough, who continued the democratic impulse of Louis, not by the example of his career, which was pretty selective, but by the example of one fight. He fought Sonny Liston, giving the ex-con a crack at the title when neither blacks nor whites wanted him to have it. Patterson thought such an opportunity would change Liston, make him respectable and anxiety-ridden. It didn't. But it probably changed Patterson forever. That is, it made him even more insufferably insane about respectability and more anxiety-ridden than anyone has a right to be. Patterson must rank along with José Torres as one of the most thoughtful men ever to enter the boxing ring. Perhaps his constant reflection impaired his ability as a fighter, but it is difficult to say. He was small for a heavyweight and this meant, all other factors being equal, that he stood little chance against either Sonny Liston or Muhammad Ali, his two archrivals, who, through the sheer grandeur of their size, ushered in a new era in boxing. Patterson was fascinated with the man he called Cassius Clay, or rather the man he refused to call Muhammad Ali. Perhaps he saw Ali as an alter ego. Perhaps Ali was the fighter that he, Patterson, always aspired to be. He expresses in the two *Sports Illustrated* articles previously mentioned the belief that if he had fought Liston the way Ali did, boxing and moving, he would have won. He probably wouldn't have, but isn't it pretty, for Patterson, to think so? These articles were probably condemned by most black intellectuals of the time as the ravings of a particularly pathetic Uncle Tom. To be sure, Patterson did show a certain insipid naïveté and even wrongheadedness in his condemnation of Ali and the black Muslims, expressing feelings akin to the outraged middle-class black who finds that his lower-class cousin has gone balmy over some sort of storefront charlatanism. But his basic instincts about the inadequacy of the Muslim response to American racism proved to be generally correct. The importance of these essays is not, however, what Patterson has to say about Ali, a man he hardly knows and is even less capable of understanding, but what they say about Patterson himself. And it is the subject of Patterson that most concerns Patterson. Despite his claims of loving the sport of boxing, Patterson complains that the sport has alienated him from his wife and children, has made him vicious against his opponents (a viciousness he finds he must have if he is to win and to counter the complaint expressed by Ingemar Johansson that Patterson "is too nice"), and has forced him to act out other people's hatred vicariously and publicly for money. Despite this, Patterson feels deeply that being heavyweight champion of the world means a great deal. As he eloquently puts it:

You've got to go on. You owe it to yourself, to the tradition of the title, to the public that sees the champion as somebody special, to every-thing that must become sacred to you the first time you put gloves on your hands. You've got to believe in what you're doing or else nobody can believe that anything is worthwhile.[10]

Or in another passage he reveals his own sense of peculiar burden by virtue of having been champion:

...I do feel partially responsible for the title having fallen into the wrong hands because of my own mistakes. I want to redeem myself in my own eyes and in the mind of the public. I owe so much to box-ing—everything I have, the security of my family, my ability to express myself, the places I've been, the people I've met. A man has got to pay his debts or he can't live with himself comfortably.[11]

In the end, he condemns Ali for not recognizing that any black champion must fight out of the Joe Louis tradition: he must be responsible, and he must acknowledge the larger white society whom he is forced to represent by virtue of his position. Patterson virtually admits that boxing is ugly but that it is the duty of the champion, the black champion, to transcend the ugli-ness of the sport for his society; in this sense he reminds one of Gene Tunney, the last American heavyweight champion who seemed unsuited temperamentally to be a boxer and obsessed with elevating the status of the sport. It is the black champion's burden and his honor. In this instance, of course, he reminds us of Louis. It is no coincidence, then, that he was cham-pion during the late fifties, the era of the Negro proving himself worthy of integration, the era of Sidney Poitier, who was the personification of black honor on the screen: the sort of honor that received, at one time, the dubious recognition from whites that here (in their opinion) was a black who was white inside. Whether Patterson was neurotically fishing for a compliment of that sort, the kind which dogged the great black heavyweight contender of the 1880s, Peter Jackson, is not nearly as important as the fact that honor so painfully bedeviled him, probably because being black and living in the modern world makes it so difficult to find frameworks for the display of it. If Patterson was so disliked by the black intellectuals of the day, it is most

10) Floyd Patterson. "I Want to Destroy Cassius Clay." *Sports Illustrated* (October 19, 1964), p 61.
11) Patterson. "I Want to Destroy Cassius Clay," p 44.

likely because his position, as he defined it in the sport of prizefighting, is so similar to their own: part of a tradition which they are unable to denounce but unable to embrace completely, torn by doubts not only about the nature of their ability but also about the meaning of what they do in a society where their position is so precarious; shackled by a seemingly ignoble past that can only be lived down by the pretensions of an inhuman nobility. What Patterson hated about both Ali and Liston was that they both thought they could, through flights of escapism, avoid a dilemma that Patterson thought was ineluctable and, unfortunately, character-building; it was not simply a quest for moral order but for redemptive piety. Liston, through his defeats at the hands of Ali, simply acquiesced in being what whites said he was. In essence and in fact, Liston quit. Liston accepted the blackness of blackness. Ali, by becoming a black Muslim, decided he wished to change the terms, to escape the blackness of blackness by redefining the terms in his own way. Liston accepted defeat as his lot; Ali denied its possibility. Patterson felt that the black champion, like the black intellectual, could do neither. For Patterson one could neither accept the terms nor redefine them; one must heroically struggle *with* them, constantly defending one's rights to participate in the discourse. Although there may be several books about prizefighting in the future written by black intellectuals, it is easy to understand why there have been so few thus far. The ambiguities of boxing, so accurately defined and symbolized by Patterson, seem, in some respects, impossible to overcome or to feel comfortable with, as black people, in the final analysis, were never comfortable with Patterson. After all, Patterson lost twice to Liston (1962, 1963) and twice to Ali as well (1965, 1972). Patterson was never able to convince his children that his training headquarters was not his home. It is doubtful he ever convinced himself (and certain he convinced no one else) that his edifice of Negro rectitude is, at last, the house black people wish to live in.

Reginald McKnight

Reginald McKnight was born in 1956 in Fürstenfeldbruck, Germany, and grew up in New York, California, Colorado, Texas, Alabama, and Louisiana. McKnight joined the Marine Corps and after his honorable discharge, he earned an Associate's Degree in anthropology in 1978. He received his B.A. in African Studies and African Literature at Colorado College in 1981 and, in 1987, his M.A. at Denver University. His first book, a collection of stories entitled *Moustapha's Eclipse*, was published in 1988. McKnight then published his first novel, *I Get on the Bus* in 1990 and, two years later, his second book of stories, *The Kind of Light That Shines on Texas*. The title story of that collection, which originally appeared in *The Kenyon Review* in 1989, received both an O. Henry Award and the Kenyon Review Award for Literary Achievement. He has since published another collection of stories, *White Boys,* and another novel, *He Sleeps*, as well as won a Pushcart Prize, along with another Kenyon Review Award for Literary Achievement. McKnight has a distinguished teaching career, holding positions at the University of Pittsburgh, Carnegie Mellon University, University of Maryland, and, currently, at the University of Michigan. McKnight has many ties to *The Kenyon Review*, serving on the advisory board and participating in the summer writing programs sponsored by *The Kenyon Review* for adults and high school students.

The Kind of Light That Shines on Texas *(1989)*

by Reginald McKnight

I never liked Marvin Pruitt. Never liked him, never knew him, even though there were only three of us in the class. Three black kids. In our school there were fourteen classrooms of thirty-odd white kids (in '66, they considered Chicanos provisionally white) and three or four black kids. Primary school in primary colors. Neat division. Alphabetized. They didn't stick us in the back, or arrange us by degrees of hue, apartheidlike. This was real integration, a ten-to-one ratio as tidy as upper-class landscaping. If it all worked, you could have ten white kids all to yourself. They could talk to you, get the feel of you, scrutinize you bone deep if they wanted to. They seldom wanted to, and that was fine with me for two reasons. The first was that their scrutiny was irritating. How do you comb your hair—why do you comb your hair—may I please touch your hair—were the kinds of questions they asked. This is no way to feel at home. The second reason was Marvin. He embarrassed me. He smelled bad, was at least two grades behind, was hostile, dark skinned, homely, closemouthed. I feared him for his size, pitied him for his dress, watched him all the time. Marveled at him, mystified, astonished, uneasy.

He had the habit of spitting on his right arm, juicing it down 'til it would glisten. He would start in immediately after taking his seat when we'd finished with the Pledge of Allegiance, "The Yellow Rose of Texas," "The Eyes of Texas Are upon You," and "Mistress Shady." Marvin would rub his spit-flecked arm with his left hand, rub and roll as if polishing an ebony pool cue. Then he would rest his head in the crook of his arm, sniffing, huffing deep like blackjacket boys huff bagsful of acrylics. After ten minutes or so, his eyes would close, heavy. He would sleep 'til recess. Mrs. Wickham would let him.

There was one other black kid in our class, a girl they called Ah-so. I never learned what she did to earn this name. There was nothing Asian about this big-shouldered girl. She was the tallest, heaviest kid in school. She was quiet, but I don't think any one of us was subtle or sophisticated enough to nickname our classmates according to any but physical attributes. Fat kids were called Porky or Butterball; skinny ones were called Stick or Ichabod. Ah-so was big, thick, and African. She would impassively sit, sullen, silent as Marvin. She wore the same dark blue pleated skirt every day, the same ruffled white blouse every day. Her skin always shone as if worked by

Marvin's palms and fingers. I never spoke one word to her, nor she to me.

Of the three of us, Mrs. Wickham called only on Ah-so and me. Ah-so never answered one question, correctly or incorrectly, so far as I can recall. She wasn't stupid. When asked to read aloud she read well, seldom stumbling over long words, reading with humor and expression. But when Wickham asked her about Farmer Brown and how many cows, or the capital of Vermont, or the date of this war or that, Ah-so never spoke. Not one word. But you always felt she could have answered those questions if she'd wanted to. I sensed no tension, embarrassment, or anger in Ah-so's reticence. She simply refused to speak. There was something unshakable about her, some core so impenetrably solid, you got the feeling that if you stood too close to her she could eat your thoughts like a black star eats light. I didn't despise Ah-so as I despised Marvin. There was nothing malevolent about her. She sat like a great icon in the back of the classroom, tranquil, guarded, sealed up, watchful. She was close to sixteen, and it was my guess she'd given up on school. Perhaps she was just obliging the wishes of her family, sticking it out 'til the law could no longer reach her.

There were at least half a dozen older kids in our class. Besides Marvin and Ah-so there was Oakley, who sat behind me, whispering threats into my ear; Varna Willard with the large breasts; Eddie Limon, who played bass for a high school rock band; and Lawrence Ridderbeck, whom everyone said had a kid and a wife. You couldn't expect me to know anything about Texan educational practices of the 1960s, so I never knew why there were so many older kids in my sixth-grade class. After all, I was just a boy and had transferred into the school around midyear. My father, an air force sergeant, had been sent to Viet Nam. The air force sent my mother, my sister Claire, and me to Connolly Air Force Base, which during the war housed "unaccompanied wives." I'd been to so many different schools in my short life that I ceased wondering about their differences. All I knew about the Texas schools is that they weren't afraid to flunk you.

Yet though I was only twelve then, I had a good idea why Wickham never once called on Marvin, why she let him snooze in the crook of his polished arm. I knew why she would press her lips together, and narrow her eyes at me whenever I correctly answered a question, rare as that was. I knew why she badgered Ah-so with questions everyone knew Ah-so would never even consider answering. Wickham didn't like us. She wasn't gross about it, but it was clear she didn't want us around. She would prove her dislike day after day with little stories and jokes. "I just want to share with you all," she would say, "a little riddle my daughter told me at the supper table th'other day. Now, where do you go when you injure your knee?" Then one, two, or all three of her pets would say for the rest of us, "We don't know, Miz Wickham," in that skin-chilling way suckasses speak, "where?" "Why, to Africa," Wickham would say, "where the knee grows."

The thirty-odd white kids would laugh, and I would look across the room at Marvin. He'd be asleep. I would glance back at Ah-so. She'd be sitting still as a projected image, staring down at her desk. I, myself, would smile at Wickham's stupid jokes, sometimes fake a laugh. I tried to show her that at least one of us was alive and alert, even though her jokes hurt. I sucked ass, too, I suppose. But I wanted her to understand more than anything that I was not like her other nigra children, that I was worthy of more than the non-attention and the negative attention she paid Marvin and Ah-so. I hated her, but never showed it. No one could safely contradict that woman. She knew all kinds of tricks to demean, control, and punish you. And she could swing her two-foot paddle as fluidly as a big league slugger swings a bat. You didn't speak in Wickham's class unless she spoke to you first. You didn't chew gum, or wear "hood" hair. You didn't drag your feet, curse, pass notes, hold hands with the opposite sex. Most especially, you didn't say anything bad about the Aggies, Governor Connolly, LBJ, Sam Houston, or Waco. You did the forbidden and she would get you. It was that simple.

She never got me, though. Never gave her reason to. But she could have invented reasons. She did a lot of that. I can't be sure, but I used to think she pitied me because my father was in Viet Nam and my uncle A.J. had recently died there. Whenever she would tell one of her racist jokes, she would always glance at me, preface the joke with, "Now don't you nigra children take offense. This is all in fun, you know. I just want to share with you all something Coach Gilchrest told me th'other day." She would tell her joke, and glance at me again. I'd giggle, feeling a little queasy. "I'm half Irish," she would chuckle, "and you should hear some of those Irish jokes." She never told any, and I never really expected her to. I just did my Tom-thing. I kept my shoes shined, my desk neat, answered her questions as best I could, never brought gum to school, never cursed, never slept in class. I wanted to show her we were not all the same.

I tried to show them all, all thirty-odd, that I was different. It worked to some degree, but not very well. When some article was stolen from some-one's locker or desk, Marvin, not I, was the first accused. I'd be second. Neither Marvin nor Ah-so nor I were ever chosen for certain classroom honors—"Pledge leader," "flag holder," "noise monitor," "paper passer outer," but Mrs. Wickham once let me be "eraser duster." I was proud. I didn't even care about the cracks my fellow students made about my finally having turned the right color. I had done something that Marvin, in the deeps of his never-ending sleep, couldn't even dream of doing. Jack Preston, a kid who sat in front of me, asked me one day at recess whether I was embarrassed about Marvin. "Can you believe that guy?" I said. "He's like a pig or something. Makes me sick."

"Does it make you ashamed to be colored?"

"No," I said, but I meant yes. Yes, if you insist on thinking us all the same. Yes, if his faults are mine, his weaknesses inherent in me.

"I'd be," said Jack.

I made no reply. I was ashamed. Ashamed for not defending Marvin and ashamed that Marvin even existed. But if it had occurred to me, I would have asked Jack whether he was ashamed of being white because of Oakley. Oakley, "Oak Tree," Kelvin "Oak Tree" Oakley. He was sixteen and proud of it. He made it clear to everyone, including Wickham, that his life's ambition was to stay in school one more year, 'til he'd be old enough to enlist in the army. "Them slopes got my brother," he would say. "I'mna sign up and git me a few slopes. Gonna kill them bastards deader'n shit." Oakley, so far as anyone knew, was and always had been the oldest kid in his family. But no one contradicted him. He would, as anyone would tell you, "snap yer neck jest as soon as look at you." Not a boy in class, excepting Marvin and myself, had been able to avoid Oakley's pink bellies, Texas titty twisters, moon pie punches, or worse. He didn't bother Marvin, I suppose, because Marvin was closer to his size and age, and because Marvin spent five-sixths of the school day asleep. Marvin probably never crossed Oakley's mind. And to say that Oakley hadn't bothered me is not to say he had no intention of ever doing so. In fact, this haphazard sketch of hairy fingers, slash of eyebrow, explosion of acne, elbows, and crooked teeth, swore almost daily that he'd like to kill me.

Naturally, I feared him. Though we were about the same height, he outweighed me by no less than forty pounds. He talked, stood, smoked, and swore like a man. No one, except for Mrs. Wickham, the principal, and the coach, ever laid a finger on him. And even Wickham knew that the hot lines she laid on him merely amused him. He would smile out at the classroom, goofy and bashful, as she laid down the two, five, or maximum ten strokes on him. Often he would wink, or surreptitiously flash us the thumb as

Wickham worked on him. When she was finished, Oakley would walk so cool back to his seat you'd think he was on wheels. He'd slide into his chair, sniff the air, and say, "Somethin's burnin. Do y'all smell smoke? I swanee, I smell smoke and fahr back here." If he had made these cracks and never threatened me, I might have grown to admire Oakley, even liked him a little. But he hated me and took every opportunity during the six-hour school day to make me aware of this. "Some Sambo's gittin his ass broke open one of these days," he'd mumble. "I wanna fight somebody. Need to keep in shape 'til I git to Nam."

I never said anything to him for the longest time. I pretended not to hear him, pretended not to notice his sour breath on my neck and ear. "Yep," he'd whisper. "Coonies keep ya in good shape for slope killin." Day in, day out, that's the kind of thing I'd pretend not to hear. But one day when the rain dropped down like lead balls, and the cold air made your skin look plucked, Oakley whispered to me, "My brother tells me it rains like this in Nam. Maybe I oughta go out at recess and break your ass open today. Nice and cool so you don't sweat. Nice and wet to clean up the blood." I said nothing for at least half a minute, then I turned half right and said, "Thought you said your brother was dead." Oakley, silent himself, for a time, poked me in the back with his pencil and hissed, "Yer dead." Wickham cut her eyes our way, and it was over.

It was hardest avoiding him in gym class. Especially when we played murderball. Oakley always aimed his throws at me. He threw with unblinking intensity, his teeth gritting, his neck veining, his face flushing, his black hair sweeping over one eye. He could throw hard, but the balls were squishy and harmless. In fact, I found his misses more intimidating than his hits. The balls would whizz by, thunder against the folded bleachers. They rattled as though a locomotive were passing through them. I would duck, dodge, leap as if he were throwing grenades. But he always hit me, sooner or later. And after a while I noticed that the other boys would avoid throwing at me, as if I belonged to Oakley.

One day, however, I was surprised to see that Oakley was throwing at everyone else but me. He was uncommonly accurate, too; kids were falling like tin cans. Since no one was throwing at me, I spent most of the game watching Oakley cut this one and that one down. Finally, he and I were the only ones left on the court. Try as he would, he couldn't hit me, nor I him. Coach Gilchrest blew his whistle and told Oakley and me to bring the red rubber balls to the equipment locker. I was relieved I'd escaped Oakley's stinging throws for once. I was feeling triumphant, full of myself. As Oakley and I approached Gilchrest, I thought about saying something friendly to Oakley: good game, Oak Tree, I would say. Before I could speak, though, Gilchrest said, "All right boys, there's five minutes left in the period. Y'all are so good, looks like you're gonna have to play like men. No boundaries, no catch outs, and you gotta hit your opponent three times in order to win. Got me?"

We nodded.

"And you're gonna use these," said Gilchrest, pointing to three volleyballs at his feet. "And you better believe they're pumped full. Oates, you start at that end of the court. Oak Tree, you're at th'other end. Just like usual, I'll set the balls at mid-court, and when I blow my whistle I want y'all to haul your cheeks to the middle and th'ow for all you're worth. Got me?" Gilchrest nodded at our nods, then added, "Remember, no boundaries, right?"

I at my end, Oakley at his, Gilchrest blew his whistle. I was faster than Oakley and scooped up a ball before he'd covered three quarters of his side. I aimed, threw, and popped him right on the knee. "One-zip!" I heard Gilchrest shout. The ball bounced off his knee and shot right back into my hands. I hurried my throw and missed. Oakley bent down, clutched the two remaining balls. I remember being amazed that he could palm each ball, run full out, and throw left-handed or right-handed without a shade of awkwardness. I spun, ran, but one of Oakley's throws glanced off the back of my head. "One-one!" hollered Gilchrest. I fell and spun on my ass as the other ball came sailing at me. I caught it. "He's out!" I yelled. Gilchrest's voice boomed, "No catch outs. Three hits. Three hits." I leapt to my feet as Oakley scrambled across the floor for another ball. I chased him down, leapt, and heaved the ball hard as he drew himself erect. The ball hit him dead in the face, and he went down flat. He rolled around, cupping his hands over his nose. Gilchrest sped to his side, helped him to his feet, asked him whether he was OK. Blood flowed from Oakley's nose, dripped in startlingly bright spots on the floor, his shoes, Gilchrest's shirt. The coach removed Oakley's T-shirt and pressed it against the big kid's nose to stanch the bleeding. As they walked past me toward the office I mumbled an apology to Oakley, but couldn't catch his reply. "You watch your filthy mouth, boy," said Gilchrest to Oakley.

The locker room was unnaturally quiet as I stepped into its steamy atmosphere. Eyes clicked in my direction, looked away. After I was out of my shorts, had my towel wrapped around me, my shower kit in hand, Jack Preston and Brian Nailor approached me. Preston's hair was combed slick and plastic looking. Nailor's stood up like frozen flames. Nailor smiled at me with his big teeth and pale eyes. He poked my arm with a finger. "You fucked up," he said.

"I tried to apologize."

"Won't do you no good," said Preston.

"I swanee," said Nailor.

"It's part of the game," I said. "It was an accident. Wasn't my idea to use volleyballs."

"Don't matter," Preston said. "He's jest lookin for an excuse to fight you."

"I never done nothing to him."

"Don't matter," said Nailor. "He don't like you."

"Brian's right, Clint. He'd jest as soon kill you as look at you."

"I never done nothing to him."

"Look," said Preston, "I know him pretty good. And jest between you and me, it's cause you're a city boy—"

"Whadda you mean? I've never—"

"He don't like your clothes—"

"And he don't like the fancy way you talk in class."

"What fancy—"

"I'm tellin him, if you don't mind, Brian."

"Tell him then."

"He don't like the way you say 'tennis shoes' instead of sneakers. He don't like coloreds. A whole bunch a things, really."

"I never done nothing to him. He's got no reason—"

"And," said Nailor, grinning, *"and,* he says you're a stuck-up rich kid." Nailor's eyes had crow's-feet, bags beneath them. They were a man's eyes.

"My dad's a sergeant," I said.

"You chicken to fight him?" said Nailor.

"Yeah, Clint, don't be chicken. Jest go on and git it over with. He's whupped pert near ever'body else in the class. It ain't so bad."

"Might as well, Oates."

"Yeah, yer pretty skinny, but yer jest about his height. Jest git im in a headlock and don't let go."

"Goddamn," I said, "he's got no reason to—"

Their eyes shot right and I looked over my shoulder. Oakley stood at his locker, turning its tumblers. From where I stood I could see that a piece of cotton was wedged up one of his nostrils, and he already had the makings of a good shiner. His acne burned red like a fresh abrasion. He snapped the locker open and kicked his shoes off without sitting. Then he pulled off his shorts, revealing two paddle stripes on his ass. They were fresh red bars speckled with white, the white speckles being the reverse impression of the paddle's suction holes. He must not have watched his filthy mouth while in Gilchrest's presence. Behind me, I heard Preston and Nailor pad to their lockers.

Oakley spoke without turning around. "Somebody's gonna git his skinny black ass kicked, right today, right after school." He said it softly. He slipped his jock off, turned around. I looked away. Out the corner of my eye I saw him stride off, his hairy nakedness a weapon clearing the younger boys from his path. Just before he rounded the corner of the shower stalls, I threw my toilet kit to the floor and stammered, "I—I never did nothing to you, Oakley." He stopped, turned, stepped closer to me, wrapping his towel around himself. Sweat streamed down my rib cage. It felt like ice water. "You wanna go at it right now, boy?"

"I never did nothing to you." I felt tears in my eyes. I couldn't stop them even though I was blinking like mad. "Never."

He laughed. "You busted my nose, asshole."

"What about before? What'd I ever do to you?"

"See you after school, Coonie." Then he turned away, flashing his acne-spotted back like a semaphore. "Why?" I shouted. "Why you wanna fight *me*?" Oakley stopped and turned, folded his arms, leaned against a toilet stall. "Why you wanna fight *me,* Oakley?" I stepped over the bench. "What'd I do? Why me?" And then unconsciously, as if scratching, as if breathing, I walked toward Marvin, who stood a few feet from Oakley, combing his hair at the mirror. "Why not him?" I said. "How come you're after *me* and not *him*?" The room froze. Froze for a moment that was both evanescent and eternal, somewhere between an eye blink and a week in hell. No one moved, nothing happened; there was no sound at all. And then it was as if all of us at the same moment looked at Marvin. He just stood there, combing away, the only body in motion, I think. He combed his hair and combed it, as if seeing only his image, hearing only his comb scraping his scalp. I knew he'd heard me. There's no way he could not have heard me. But all he did was slide the comb into his pocket and walk out the door.

"I got no quarrel with Marvin," I heard Oakley say. I turned toward his voice, but he was already in the shower.

I was able to avoid Oakley at the end of the school day. I made my escape by asking Mrs. Wickham if I could go to the restroom.

"Restroom,'" Oakley mumbled. "It's a damn toilet, sissy."

"Clinton," said Mrs. Wickham. "Can you not wait 'til the bell rings? It's almost three o'clock."

"No ma'am," I said. "I won't make it."

"Well, I should make you wait just to teach you to be more mindful about…hygiene…uh things." She sucked in her cheeks, squinted. "But I'm feeling charitable today. You may go." I immediately left the building, and got on the bus. "Ain't you a little early?" said the bus driver, swinging the door shut. "Just left the office," I said. The driver nodded, apparently not giving me a second thought. I had no idea why I'd told her I'd come from the office, or why she found it a satisfactory answer. Two minutes later the bus filled, rolled, and shook its way to Connolly Air Base.

When I got home, my mother was sitting in the living room, smoking her Slims, watching her soap opera. She absently asked me how my day had gone and I told her fine. "Hear from Dad?" I said.

"No, but I'm sure he's fine." She always said that when we hadn't heard from him in a while. I suppose she thought I was worried about him, or that I felt vulnerable without him. It was neither. I just wanted to discuss something with my mother that we both cared about. If I spoke with her about things that happened at school, or on my weekends, she'd listen with half an ear, say something like, "Is that so?" or "You don't say?" I couldn't stand that sort of thing. But when I mentioned my father, she treated me a bit more like an adult, or at least someone who was worth listening to. I didn't want to feel like a boy that afternoon. As I turned from my mother and walked down the hall I thought about the day my father left for Viet Nam. Sharp in his uniform, sure behind his aviator specs, he slipped a cigar from his pocket and stuck it in mine. "Not 'til I get back," he said. "We'll have us one when we go fishing. Just you and me, out on the lake all day, smoking and casting and sitting. Don't let Mamma see it. Put it in y' back pocket." He hugged me, shook my hand, and told me I was the man of the house now. He told me he was depending on me to take good care of my mother and sister. "Don't you let me down, now, hear?" And he tapped his thick finger on my chest. "You almost as big as me. Boy, you something else." I believed him when he told me those things. My heart swelled big enough to swallow my father, my mother, Claire. I loved, feared, and respected myself, my manhood. That day I could have put all of Waco, Texas, in my heart. And it wasn't 'til about three months later that I discovered I really wasn't the man of the house, that my mother and sister, as they always had, were taking care of me.

For a brief moment I considered telling my mother about what had happened at school that day, but for one thing, she was deep down in the halls of *General Hospital,* and never paid you much mind 'til it was over. For another thing, I just wasn't the kind of person—I'm still not, really—to discuss my problems with anyone. Like my father I kept things to myself, talked about my problems only in retrospect. Since my father wasn't around, I consciously wanted to be like him, doubly like him, I could say. I wanted to be the man of the house in some respect, even if it had to be in an inward way. I went to my room, changed my clothes, and laid out my homework. I couldn't focus on it. I thought about Marvin, what I'd said about him or done to him—I couldn't tell which. I'd done something to him, said something about him; said something about and done something to myself. *How come you're after* me *and not* him? I kept trying to tell myself I hadn't meant it that way. *That* way. I thought about approaching Marvin, telling him what I really meant was that he was more Oakley's age and weight than I. I would tell him I meant I was no match for Oakley. *See, Marvin, what I meant was that he wants to fight a colored guy, but is afraid to fight you cause you could beat him.* But try as I did, I couldn't for a moment convince myself that Marvin would believe me. I meant it *that* way and no other. Everybody heard. Everybody knew. That afternoon I forced myself to confront the notion that tomorrow I would probably have to fight both Oakley and Marvin. I'd have to be two men.

I rose from my desk and walked to the window. The light made my skin look orange, and I started thinking about what Wickham had told us once about light. She said that oranges and apples, leaves and flowers, the whole multi-colored world, was not what it appeared to be. The colors we see, she said, look like they do only because of the light or ray that shines on them. "The color of the thing isn't what you see, but the light that's reflected off it." Then she shut out the lights and shone a white light lamp on a prism. We watched the pale splay of colors on the projector screen; some people ooohed and aaahed. Suddenly, she switched on a black light and the color of everything changed. The prism colors vanished, Wickham's arms were purple, the buttons of her dress were as orange as hot coals, rather than the blue they had been only seconds before. We were all very quiet. "Nothing," she said after a while, "is really what it appears to be." I didn't really understand then. But as I stood at the window, gazing at my orange skin, I wondered what kind of light I could shine on Marvin, Oakley, and me that would reveal us as the same.

I sat down and stared at my arms. They were dark brown again. I worked up a bit of saliva under my tongue and spat on my left arm. I spat again, then rubbed the spittle into it, polishing, working 'til my arm grew warm. As I spat, and rubbed, I wondered why Marvin did this weird, nasty thing to himself, day after day. Was he trying to rub away the black, or deepen it, doll it up? And if he did this weird nasty thing for a hundred years, would he spitshine himself invisible, rolling away the eggplant skin, revealing the scarlet muscle, blue vein, pink and yellow tendon, white bone? Then disappear? Seen through, all colors, no colors. Spitting and rubbing. Is this the way you do it? I leaned forward, sniffed the arm. It smelled vaguely of mayonnaise. After an hour or so, I fell asleep.

I saw Oakley the second I stepped off the bus the next morning. He stood outside the gym in his usual black penny loafers, white socks, high water jeans, T-shirt, and black jacket. Nailor stood with him, his big teeth spread across his bottom lip like playing cards. If there was anyone I felt like fighting, that day, it was Nailor. But I wanted to put off fighting for as long as I could. I stepped toward the gymnasium, thinking that I shouldn't run, but if I hurried I could beat Oakley to the door and secure myself near Gilchrest's office. But the moment I stepped into the gym, I felt Oakley's broad palm clap down on my shoulder. "Might as well stay out here, Coonie," he said. "I need me a little target practice." I turned to face him and he slapped me, one-two, with the back, then the palm of his hand, as I'd seen Bogart do to Peter Lorre in *The Maltese Falcon*. My heart went wild. I could scarcely breathe. I couldn't swallow.

"Call me a nigger," I said. I have no idea what made me say this. All I know is that it kept me from crying. "Call me a nigger, Oakley."

"Fuck you, ya black ass slope." He slapped me again, scratching my eye. "I don't do what coonies tell me."

"Call me a nigger."

"Outside, Coonie."

"Call me one. Go ahead."

He lifted his hand to slap me again, but before his arm could swing my way, Marvin Pruitt came from behind me and calmly pushed me aside. "Git out my way, boy," he said. And he slugged Oakley on the side of his head. Oakley stumbled back, stiff-legged. His eyes were big. Marvin hit him twice more, once again to the side of the head, once to the nose. Oakley went down and stayed down. Though blood was drawn, whistles blowing, fingers pointing, kids hollering, Marvin just stood there, staring at me with cool eyes. He spat on the ground, licked his lips, and just stared at me, 'til Coach Gilchrest and Mr. Calderon tackled him and violently carried him away. He never struggled, never took his eyes off me.

Nailor and Mrs. Wickham helped Oakley to his feet. His already fattened nose bled and swelled so that I had to look away. He looked around, bemused, wall-eyed, maybe scared. It was apparent he had no idea how bad he was hurt. He didn't even touch his nose. He didn't look like he knew much of anything. He looked at me, looked me dead in the eye in fact, but didn't seem to recognize me.

That morning, like all other mornings, we said the Pledge of Allegiance, sang "The Yellow Rose of Texas," "The Eyes of Texas Are upon You," and "Mistress Shady." The room stood strangely empty without Oakley, and without Marvin, but at the same time you could feel their presence more intensely somehow. I felt like I did when I'd walk into my mother's room and could smell my father's cigars, or cologne. He was more palpable, in certain respects, than when there in actual flesh. For some reason, I turned to look at Ah-so, and just this once I let my eyes linger on her face. She had a very gentle-looking face, really. That surprised me. She must have felt my eyes on her because she glanced up at me for a second and smiled, white teeth, downcast eyes. Such a pretty smile. That surprised me too. She held it for a few seconds, then let it fade. She looked down at her desk, and sat still as a photograph.

Philip Levine

Philip Levine was born in Detroit, Michigan, in 1928. He attended Wayne State University, taking classes at night while working days at one of Detroit's automobile manufacturing plants. Levine moved around the country for several years, marrying and starting a family. After discovering his son had a childhood form of asthma, Levine moved from Iowa, where he attended graduate school, to the drier climate of California, settling in Fresno. In 1958, he took a teaching position at Fresno State University, where he would remain until his retirement. In 1963, Levine's first book, *On the Edge,* was published. Two years later, Levine spent time in Spain, which would prove to be the subject of many of his finest poems. His second book, *Not This Pig,* appeared in 1968, establishing him as a prominent young poet, one of the first to articulate the experiences of the working class. He has gone on to become one of America's most celebrated poets, winning the Pulitzer Prize, the National Book Award, and two National Book Critics Circle Awards with such books as *Years From Somewhere, Ashes: Poems New and Old, What Work Is, The Simple Truth,* and, most recently, *The Mercy*. He has taught at many universities including Princeton, Brown, Tufts, Columbia, and New York University. He currently splits his time between Fresno and New York. His poem "Agnus Dei" appeared in *The Kenyon Review* in 1989.

Agnus Dei *(1989)*
by Philip Levine

My little sister created the Lamb of God.
She made him out of used-up dust mops
and coat hangers. She left him whitewashed
at the entrance to the Calvin Coolidge branch
of the public library, so as to scare
the lady librarian who'd clucked at each of us,
"Why do you want to read a grown-up book?"
The lamb sagged against the oaken doors,
high and dark in the deep vault of morning,
and said nothing as we scampered off
across the dew-wet lawns, our shoes darkening.
The rest of our adventure made the *Times,*
how Officer German took in the lamb and made
a morning meal of milk and mucilage
and wrapped him warmly in out-of-town papers.
How he slept unnoticed for hours and wakening
rose in a shower of golden dust, bellowing
in rage, and sent Miss Greenglass running
to the Ladies Restroom where she fainted
and, waking, changed her life. Books scattered.
There was weeping and gnashing. The lamb escaped
through an expensive, leaded windowpane
and entered the late afternoon flying low
over the houses of the middle class
until clouds obscured the world, and it was done.
My brother Leopold read this all out loud
on Sunday morning while our parents slept
above us in a high dark room we never entered,
and the cellar moaned and rumbled, warming
us the best it could. A fresh wind rapped
at the front windows, and we stared in silence
as, bloodred and wrinkled, the new elm unleaved
in public, shuddering with the ache of its growing.

Yusef Komunyakaa

Yusef Komunyakaa was born in Bogalusa, Louisiana, in 1947. When he was eighteen he entered the Vietnam War as a correspondent with the military newspaper *The Southern Cross*, for which he received the Bronze Star. Educated at the University of Colorado, Colorado State University, and the University of California at Irvine, he currently teaches at Princeton. Among a multitude of awards, including the Pulitzer Prize (1994) and the Kingsley Tufts Poetry Award, Komunyakaa won the Kenyon Review Award for Literary Achievement in 1991. His latest publications include *Talking Dirty to the Gods* and *Pleasure Dome: New and Collected Poems, 1975–1999*. In an interview with William Baer that appeared in *The Kenyon Review*, Spring 1998, Komunyakaa said, "Poetry, I believe, has to be informed by a need. Otherwise, it becomes a kind of artificial apparatus that the poet straps on, and it becomes more of a burden than a kind of telling moment—a poem is a moment of both confrontation and celebration." "History Lessons" appeared in *The Kenyon Review* in 1991.

History Lessons *(1991)*

by Yusef Komunyakaa

1

Squinting up at leafy sunlight, I stepped back
& shaded my eyes, but couldn't see what she pointed to.
The courthouse lawn where the lone poplar stood
Was almost smooth as a pool table. Twenty-five
Years earlier it had been a stage for half the town:
Cain & poor white trash. A picnic on saint augustine
Grass. A few guitars & voices from hell.
No, I couldn't see the piece of blonde rope.
I stepped closer to her, to where we were almost
In each other's arms, & then saw the flayed
Tassel of wind-whipped hemp knotted around a limb
Like a hank of hair, a weather-whitened bloom
In hungry light. That was where they prodded him
Up into the flatbed of a pickup.

2

We had coffee & chicory with lots of milk,
Hoecakes, bacon, & gooseberry jam. She told me
How a white woman in The Terrace
Said that she shot a man who tried to rape her.
How their car lights crawled sage fields
Midnight to daybreak, how a young black boxer
Was running & punching the air at sunrise.
How they tarred & feathered him & dragged the corpse
Behind a Model T through the Mill Quarters,
How they dumped the prizefighter on his mother's doorstep,
How two days later three boys
Found a white man dead under the trestle
In blackface, with the woman's bullet
In his chest, his head on a clump of sedge.

3

When I stepped out on the back porch
The pick-up man from Bogalusa Dry Cleaners

Leaned against his van, with an armload
Of her Sunday dresses, telling her
Emmitt Till had begged for it
With his damn wolf whistle.
She was looking at the lye-scoured floor,
White as his face. The hot words
Swarmed out of my mouth like African bees
& my fists were cocked,
Hammers in the air. He popped
The clutch when he turned the corner,
As she pulled me into her arms
& whispered, *Son, you ain't gonna live long.*

Richard Howard

Richard Howard was born in Cleveland, Ohio, in 1929. He received a B.A. (1951) and M.A. (1952) from Columbia University, afterwards spending two years in Paris studying at the Sorbonne. After returning to the United States, Howard supported himself first as a lexicographer and then as a translator of French. Since 1958, he has translated more than 150 books and is considered one of the leading authorities of French literature. Howard also quickly cemented his reputation as one of the nation's most talented crafts-men of poetry with the publication of such early books as *Quantities*, *The Damages*, and *Untitled Subjects*, which earned him the Pulitzer Prize in 1970. Howard has held teaching positions at many universities, including the University of Cincinnati, the University of Houston, and, currently, Columbia University. He is also a renowned editor, currently serving as poetry editor for the *Paris Review* and the *Western Humanities Review*. Howard, whose recent books include *Like Most Revelations*, *Trappings,* and a new translation of Antoine De Saint-Exupery's *The Little Prince,* currently lives in New York. His poem "Occupations" appeared in *The Kenyon Review* in 1992.

Occupations *(1992)*
by Richard Howard

Of course we're still using the old stationery—who can find paper these days?—but as you see, the lettering outside has already been changed, and to all intents and purposes this is now the Galerie Millon (I was Mathilde Millon before the late M. Bernheim married me). And I believe the Reichsmarschall will find that nothing shown him is on the list of Proscribed Artists. May I call your attention to these—no, not the very recent things: anything begun since 1942 I find a bit too stiff (no doubt the rigidity of an intimated end), but a choice among the later canvases, my dear Reichsmarschall...After all, the man is well into his seventies, and we may call anything done in the last decade a late work, wouldn't you say? Though the gallery has represented Bonnard since...oh goodness, since before my marriage, these paintings have just reached us. The old fellow keeps them ever so long in his studio, done there at Le Cannet, endlessly reworking what I feel to be the lessons he has learned—you see, here? and over here, par- ticularly —from his friend Matisse.

8 January
42. Le Cannet.

Dear Matisse, I have sad news:
Marthe has died—of what she called
her "immortal disease"...First the lungs
were attacked, then the digestive tract,
yet she managed to survive each new onset
for all the pain she must have been suffering,
until at last, just six days ago,
the heart gave out. We laid her to rest
in the graveyard I can see
from upstairs at Le Bosquet:
a comfort to me,
knowing she is there...

I think you recall
the strange delusion:
unclean! Marthe unclean!—which kept
her so many hours immersed

in the bath. We had made it a joke
between us—very nearly a joke,
enough of one for me to paint her there,
how many times? A modern Naiad, or as
Monet would have said, a nenuphar!
Our little ceremony for Marthe
brought back the time, can it be
twenty years? when Vuillard and I
and old Clemenceau
laid Monet to rest...
So much of life is
buried already!

Just consider this delightful view of a mimosa tree from the studio window,
for example: it was begun in 1939, along with other momentous enterprises,
if I may say so, and not finished (though what works by this painter can ever
be called finished?)—not released, then, until only a few weeks ago, when the
old fellow himself had the canvas sent to me directly. We may sell it along
with these others—thank goodness he is exempt from the Doctrinal Tests,
though like Matisse and Dufy not considered "meritorious"...

All the same I still believe
in reality, the way
Cézanne believed in it—I believe
in repetition, that is, and I am
at work on some new views of the Bay...They must
be new, because every day I see different
things, or I see things differently:
the sky, the fields, the water beyond,
it all keeps changing, you could
drown in the differences.
Yet that is just what
keeps us alive, no?
Despite our bad skies,
how the spring responds!
Daily on my walks, some new
species of flower appears—
as if each one were having its turn!
this morning the first almond blossoms,

like proclamations attached to the bare trees
(a kind of bravery, I can't help thinking)
   and soon the mimosas will begin
   to set yellow pennons in the woods,
      as if it was a signal!
   Of course everything begins
      on the ground and moves
      up, but I see things
         best against the light…

I can let you have such work in lots, at a most attractive rate for the whole group here in the gallery…Amusing, by the way, that barely perceptible woman's face down there on the left, yes, at the very bottom, almost drowned out by the light. She is looking up the stairs toward the painter, not out the window at all, where the mimosa suffuses the whole picture wih gold, filling the window so that it has something of the appearance of stained glass.

      the horizon lies
    much lower in my landscapes
    than it ever did before…
You know, at our age, we tend—except
for P, of course, who is hardly one of us—
to be more interested in objects than in
    the construction of the universe.
   These encroachments, these occupations—
      by disease, by sorrow, by
      the Germans—come in great waves,
        you know what I mean:
        that thing old Rodin
           always used to say,
           about how it takes
     an exceptional array
     of circumstances to grant
   a man seventy years of life and
   the luck to keep doing what he loves.
Oh, the waves come, they keep coming over us,
and though we may be nearly drowned, they leave us
    just where we were, and we know that if
    they are strong, we are even stronger,

for they pass, and we remain…
"Old Rodin": what insolence,
   my calling him that!
   we're both much older
      than he lived to be,
     pontificating
in front of the Gates of Hell
—remember those afternoons
in the Rue de Varennes, lecturing
overdressed women in his garden…
Did you ever believe we would be that old?

Such a pleasure, my dear Reichsmarschall, indeed a privilege, to be able to offer these canvases for actual purchase. Only last May, you know—we were obliged to destroy—in the courtyard of the Louvre!—some five hundred pictures by Masson, Leger, poor old Kisling, even Picasso, really horrors—all canvases entirely unfit for sale. The fire went on all day, and the smoke covered the sky, even the next morning…

     27 February.
     Dear Matisse,
It is not easy, keeping abreast
of events, nor have I any great
   longing to know what may be
   happening in the world, I
     almost said the real
     world. Don't believe that.
      A few days ago
      I learned about Joss—
not how he died, just his death.
All that *l'Eclaireur de Nice*
reports is that he had been "ailing"…
Over forty years since Bernheim-Heune
took me on, you must have come to the gallery
soon after—about nineteen hundred and nine?
  What a long time Joss did the one thing!
  Most people are not conscious enough
    to exult in monotony,
    but perhaps God is—perhaps

God says each morning
to the moon: "Encore!"
I know that is what
Joss would say to me
whenever a show came down.
And today, inside black borders,
Mathilde Bernheim writes to say she is
asking "his" painters to testify—
you must have had the same letter—to what Joss
has accomplished for "Independent French Art."
She thinks this will save her family
from the persecutions…I was glad
to write, as you must have been,
and Dufy, Rouault, Derain…
But to tell the truth
none of this will do
the least bit of good.

I am so happy to know that this lot is passing to such appreciative hands, and eyes, of course. Is it not charming, the woman at her toilette, seen as if by accident through the doorway? Wonderful, that in these dark times the painter could find so much light to celebrate, such depths to plumb so brilliantly!

Dear Matisse, you know
as well as I: the Germans
acknowledge a single name
among "French" painters. Our conquerors
recognize only our conqueror,
if I may put it that way—perhaps you see
Monsieur Picasso as no such thing, Matisse,
but I have textual evidence
as to how that Spaniard has seen me.
"I like him best, your Bonnard,"
he once wrote Joss (who of course
passed on this good news)
"when he is not thinking
of being a painter,
when his canvases

are full of literature"
—this is really what he said—
"rotten with anecdotes." Did that suffice?
Not for our Pablo. Kahnweiler was
kind enough to send the latest bulletin,
and I am compelled to copy it out here
for your edification—one way
to exorcise the curse of the thing,
or so I hope: "What he does
is not painting—he never
goes beyond his own
sensibility.
He doesn't know how
to choose. Take his sky—
first he paints blue, more or less
the way it looks. Then he looks
a while longer and sees mauve in it,
so he adds a touch or two of mauve,
just to be sure. Then he assumes there may be
a little pink there too—why not add some pink?
If he looks long enough he'll wind up
adding a little yellow, instead
of deciding what color
the sky really ought to be.
Is that painting? No,
that's taking advice
from Nature, asking
her to supply you
with information: Bonnard
obeys Nature! another
decadent, the end of an old idea…"
There you have the words, my dear Matisse,
of a fellow artist, a practitioner
of the *metier* we have shared, all of us
for how many years? Is this the man
I can ask to speak to Herr Abetz
in behalf of Joss Bernheim—
and of Mathilde Bernheim?

If you can do it,
I leave it to you.

Very well, we shall send the entire shipment to your private car at the Gare de l'Est. Two cars? All the better! And the bill to the Einsatzstab Rosenberg. No, no, all these have come to us from the artist himself—not one from other dealers. Graf Metternich was at some pains to stipulate: the stock of Seligmann, Wildenstein, Loeb, e tutti quanti must be transferred to the Embassy as a security for eventual peace negotiations. I understand perfectly.

                    …After yesterday
                I belong, once more,
            to the human race—a trial
            member, but a member still,
        all because they have decided to
        operate: the surgeon has bestowed
    civil status, even a country, on me:
    my country is The Hospital, and I am
            Dr A's patient in Room 14,
        on whom Dr B will operate.
            The corridor where I walk
            and wait and write this to you
                is my realm; no one
                dreams of disputing
                    the territory.
                I see other men,
            and women too, who have been
            operated on, brought back
    on their gurneys, the surgeons, interns
    and nurses clustering around them
    like white flies. Through their doors I can hear the groans
    these patients make, even in their sleep, the same
        groans I shall make, when it is my turn.
        The nurses know me, and I know them:
            one comes for "temperature,"
            one for "blood," and another
                with "pills." The pill nurse
                is pretty, the rest

are young. When I walk
past their glassed-in booth
I always hear them talking
about us, their patients. Theirs.
And for the first time in a long while
I find humanity better than
I had supposed. Now I can more easily
regard my own death, which no longer divides
me from the world. It is possible,
nothing more. It becomes a simple
statistic. In rooms off this
corridor, a percentage
of patients must die,
and this percentage
is what they attempt
to reduce. Each nurse
in this wing will regard my
death as her failure—the one
who looks like Danielle Darrieux's
daughter says that after each "decease"
she won't sleep for a week. My death no longer
exposes me to the living. That is why
I have made my will so easily
and told my notary where to find
the pictures I had hidden
so long. I have forgotten
nothing, for it seems
only fair to meet
with an attentive
precision the same
precision they devote to
my file, from which no X-ray,
blood-analysis, or fever-chart
is missing. I too want to present
the anesthesiologist with a man
according to the rules. But once you obey
the rules, there is nothing left to do
but wait. I wait. And I look for what

it could mean, this death of mine
that seems so near. I admit
I will be nothing
(otherwise death is
not death, and even
one's thoughts about it
are just playing with words). And
without my body, what is
left of me? No reading the paper,
no talk with the doctor making rounds.
No action of any kind. But do I make
these actions I assume I am making now?
It is my newspaper, printed in
an edition of thousands, that puts
pressure on me to read it;
the doctor comes when he feels
like coming, evades
my questions, departs:
there is my freedom.
Which is nothing but
my uncertainty about
what is going to happen
next. Of course, that is my freedom, but
having been introduced into this
vast machinery, I am not even sure
such uncertainty as to my fate is part
and parcel of my life—my death is
not enough to dispel it. No doubt
I am the total of my
memories and nothing else,
that huge collection
gathered by my life
and dispersed by my
death. But so many
of these memories—I see
now they don't belong to me...
What did I do that was mine? I went
to the parish school, served out my term

In the infantry—and I was not alone.
In each photograph I belong to a group,
    and someone must draw a little cross
    over my head if I am to be
        identified. Dear Matisse,
        nothing is there. What remains
           is the almond tree
           I was working on
                the morning I came
                to the hospital.
    Pray God it will be there still
    if I am allowed to go home.

Of course we have carefully weeded out all the identifiable portraits: in the Bonnard lot there were a number of studies of my late husband and his family, his friends. They were obliged to join the others in three requisitioned rooms in the Louvre, where as you know they were slashed to ribbons by members of the Einsatzstab themselves—a regrettable procedure, but apparently a necessary one. You know, my dear Reichsmarschall, we French have an old poem which I always like to recite in times like these:

    I claim the right to act as if
    the War was an old dog sitting
    at the lovely feet of our France...

Eavan Boland

Eavan Boland was born in Dublin in 1944. She lived in Ireland until the age of six, when her family relocated, first to London, then to New York. Boland returned to Ireland as a teenager and attended Trinity College in Dublin. After earning her B.A., she lectured at Trinity, but in 1967 decided to put her academic career on hold and dedicate herself to writing poetry. That same year Boland published her first book, *New Territory*. She married novelist Kevin Casey in 1969 and moved to the Dublin suburb of Dundrum, where she reared her two daughters and continued to write. She published *The War Horse: Poems* before moving to the United States in 1979. Boland taught at a number of universities while penning books such as *In Her Own Image*, *The Journey and Other Poems*, *An Origin Like Water: Collected Poems 1967–1987,* and *Against Love Poems* that have established her as the pre-eminent Irish woman poet of her generation. She currently is a professor of English at Stanford University. Boland has published regularly in *The Kenyon Review*; her poem "What Language Did" originally appeared in its pages in 1994.

What Language Did *(1994)*

by Eavan Boland

The evening was the same as any other.
I came out and stood on the step.
The suburb was closed in the weather

of an early spring and the shallow tips
and washed-out yellows of narcissi
resisted dusk. And crocuses and snowdrops.

I stood there and felt the melancholy
of growing older in such a season,
when all I could be certain of was simply

in this time of fragrance and refrain,
whatever else might flower before the fruit,
and be renewed, I would not. Not again.

A car splashed by in the twilight.
Peat smoke stayed in the windless
air overhead and I might have missed it:

A presence. Suddenly. In the very place
where I would stand in other dusks, and look
to pick out my child from the distance.

was a shepherdess, her smile cracked,
her arm injured from the mantelpieces
and pastorals where she posed with her crook.

Then I turned and saw in the spaces
of the night sky constellations appear,
one by one, over rooftops and houses,

and Cassiopeia trapped: stabbed where
her thigh met her groin and her hand
her glittering wrist, with the pinpoint of a star

And by the road where rain made standing
pools of water underneath cherry trees,
and blossoms swam on their images,

was a mermaid with invented tresses,
her breasts printed with the salt of it and all
the desolation of the North Sea in her face.

I went nearer. They were disappearing.
Dusk had turned to night but in the air—
did I imagine it?—a voice saying:

This is what language did to us. Here
is the wound, the silence, the wretchedness
of tides and hillsides and stars where

we languish in a grammar of sighs,
in the high-minded search for euphony,
in the midnight rhetoric of poesy.

We cannot sweat here. Our skin is icy.
We cannot breed here. Our wombs are empty.
Help us to escape youth and beauty.

Write us out of the poem. Make us human
in cadences of change and mortal pain
and words we can grow old and die in.

Ha Jin

Ha Jin was born in Liaoning, China, in 1956. From the age of fourteen until he was twenty, Jin served in the People's Liberation Army in China. After his service, Jin wanted to enter college, but could not because schools of higher learning remained closed during the Cultural Revolution, which began in 1966 and ended in 1976. He taught himself English working the night shift as a railroad telegrapher. In 1977, colleges reopened and Jin eventually received his B.A. and M.A. from Chinese universities. In 1985, he moved to the United States to pursue graduate work in English at Brandeis University. He decided to remain in the U.S. after the Tiananmen Massacre in 1989, when he "realized it would be impossible to write honestly in China." His first two books of fiction, *Ocean of Words* (1996) and *Under the Red Flag* (1997), appeared after his two acclaimed poetry collections *Between Silences* (1990) and *Facing Shadows* (1996). *Ocean of Words* received the PEN/Hemingway Award. In 1988, he published a novella, *In the Pond,* and in 1994, Jin was awarded the Kenyon Review Award for Literary Achievement in Fiction for his story "Emperor." His novel *Waiting* (1999) received the National Book Award for fiction. He is currently a professor in English at Emory University.

Emperor *(1995)*
by Ha Jin

We were playing horse ride in the afternoon on Main Street, which was a noncombat zone for the boys in Dismount Fort. The fourteen of us were in two groups. Seven were riding on the backs of the others, and we wouldn't switch roles until one rider's feet touched the ground. It was hot, though a breeze came now and then.

"Look at that," our emperor Benli said, pointing to a horse cart coming up the street. The harness bells jingled listlessly while the horses' hooves thudded on the white gravel. The cart was loaded with a mountain of beehives.

"Let's hit him," Bare Hips said. He referred to the cart driver, who looked tipsy and was humming a folk song.

Benli ordered, "Get ready."

We set about collecting stones and clods and hiding ourselves in the ditch along the road. About fifty paces behind us stood five latrine cleaners, resting in the shade of locusts. Ten buckets, filled with night soil, were reeking. Amused, they watched us preparing to ambush the enemy's vehicle.

"Give me that brick, Grandson," Hare Lips said.

"No," Grandson said timidly, hiding the fragment of a brick behind him.

"Got a problem, eh? Refusing your grandpa?" Hare Lips slapped him on the face and grabbed the brick away from him.

Grandson didn't make a peep. He had another nickname, Big Babe, because he looked like a girl with curved brows, round eyes, a soft face, and a pair of plump hands with fleshy pits on the knuckles. He was too timid to fight anybody and every one of us could beat him easily. That was why he became our Grandson.

The cart was coming close, and the driver's voice was clear now:

Square tables I ordered four.
Long benches we have twelve.
Meat and fish course by course.
My brothers, help yourselves—

"Fire!" Benli shouted.

We started throwing stones, bricks, wooden grenades, and clods at the horses and the driver. He sat up with a start and turned his small egg-shaped face to us. Then he swung his long whip to urge the horses on. The lash was cracking like firecrackers while our missiles hit both the man and the horses, which were startled and began galloping. The latrine cleaners laughed noisily behind us.

Suddenly the whiplash touched the top of the load. A beehive tumbled down the other boxes, fell off the cart, and crashed to the ground. Bees gushed out from all the hives. In a few seconds the cart was swathed by a golden cloud ringing madly.

"Oh Mother! Help!" the driver yelled.

The horses sprang up and plunged into the ditch on the other side of the road. The cart careened, turned over, and scattered the hives everywhere. Most of the bees were swarming to the struggling horses and the man; some were flying to us.

"Help! Help!" the driver screamed, but none of us dared move close. Even the latrine cleaners were too scared to go over, though one of them was running away to the Commune Clinic, which was nearby, to get help. Stunned, we dropped our weapons and watched speechlessly.

The three horses disentangled themselves and ran off with long neighing. The black shaft-horse was charging toward us, and we all went behind the thick trees. It dashed by with a loud fart and kicked down two buckets of night soil. The street at once smelled like a compost heap.

"Hel—p," the man groaned in the ditch, his voice very small. We couldn't see him. Over there only the swarm of bees was waving and rolling in the breeze.

Half an hour later most of the bees had flown away, and the medical people rescued the cart driver. He had stopped breathing, though we were told that his heart was still alive. His face was swollen, covered with blood and crushed bees, and his fingers looked like frozen carrots. They carried him on a stretcher, rushing back to the Commune Clinic.

Then Zu Ming, the head of town police, arrived and ordered everyone not to move, including the latrine cleaners. He must have heard that we had thrown things at the cart, for promptly he questioned us about who had started it. If we didn't tell him, he said he would lock us up in the police station for a few days. We were scared.

"You," Zu pointed at Sickle Handle, "you hit a beehive with a stone, didn't you?" Zu's face was dark and long, so long that people called him Donkey Face.

"No, I didn't." Sickle Handle stepped away.

"How about you?" Zu pulled Benli's ear.

"No, not me." Our emperor grimaced, a thread of saliva dribbling from the corner of his mouth. "Oh, let me go, Uncle. It hurts."

"Then tell me who started it." Zu twisted Benli's ear harder.

"Ouch! Not me."

"Tell me who did it." A cigarette bobbed around the tip of Zu's nose as two lines of smoke dangled beneath his nostrils.

"He did it," Benli moaned.

"Who?"

"Grandson."

"Louder, I can't hear you."

"Grandson."

"Who is Grandson?" Zu let Benli go and looked around at us. Our eyes fell on Big Babe.

"No, I just threw one clod," Grandson said, his face turning pale.

"All right, one is enough. You come with me." Zu went up to Grandson, who was about to escape. Grandson had hardly run a step when Zu caught him by the neck. "You piglet, where are you going?" He threw him on his broad shoulder and carried him away to the police station.

"Fuck your mother!" Grandson yelled at Benli.

We all followed them to see what would happen to him, while the latrine cleaners laughed with their heads thrown back, pointing at Grandson who was kicking in the air. Then they shouldered their loads of night soil and set out for Elm Village, where they lived. One of them carried two empty buckets with his pole.

"Stop it!" Zu whacked Grandson on the back, who stopped kicking instantly.

"Fuck all your grandmas!" Grandson shouted at us, wailing and sniffling.

We didn't swear back and followed them silently. The hot sun cast our slant shadows on the whitish road; cicadas were hissing tirelessly in the treetops. We hated Zu Ming, who only dared to bully us children. Two months before he had gone to Dalian City with a truck from the Fertilizer Plant. There they had been caught by the gunfire of the revolutionary rebels. The driver, Squinty's father, was hit by a bullet in the leg, but he managed to drive the truck out of the city. Though nothing touched Zu, he was so frightened he messed his pants. The whole town knew that.

The blue door of the police station closed behind them. Bang, we heard Zu drop the boy on the floor.

"Oh! My arm," Grandson cried.

Immediately we rushed to the windows to watch. "Take this. I'm going to break your legs too." Zu kicked Grandson in the hips and stomach.

"Don't kick me!"

Two policemen came in, and Zu turned to them to explain what had happened. Fearing they might detain Grandson for long and hurt him badly, Benli told Hare Lips, "Go tell his uncle that Big Babe is in trouble here."

Grandson's parents had died seven years before in a famine, so he lived at his uncle's. One reason we would make fun of him was that all his cousins were small girls. We could beat him or do him in without worrying about being caught by a bigger brother.

"Did you overeat, huh? Have too much energy?" Shen Li shouted, clutching Grandson's neck. Shen was a squat young man, like a Japanese soldier, so we called him Water Vat.

"Don't. You're hurting me!" Grandson cried.

"How about this?" A slap landed on his face.

"Oh!"

"Tell us why you did that."

"No, I didn't."

"You still don't admit it. All right, let your grandpa teach you how to be honest." Shen punched him in the flank.

"Ouch!" Grandson dropped to the floor, holding his sides and yelling, "Help! They're killing me."

"Shut up!" Zu ordered, and pulled him to his feet. "Now tell me, did you do it or not?"

Grandson nodded.

"Sign your name here then." Zu took him to a desk and pointed at a sheet of paper.

We were restless outside, having never seen how the police handled a child criminal. We were also anxious to get him out.

Finally Grandson's uncle came, wearing blue work clothes covered with oil stains. We stepped aside to let the tall man go in. A few of us even ventured to enter together with him, but Water Vat pushed us back and shut the door.

We thought Grandson's uncle would be mad at the police, but to our surprise he cursed his nephew instead. "How many times did I tell you not to cause trouble on the streets, huh? Young rabbit, I'd better kill you or starve you to death." He slapped him on the face.

The policemen took both of them into another room. Since we couldn't see them anymore, we left the windowsills, cursing the police and their families. We swore we would whack Zu's oldest daughter once she started her first grade.

A few minutes later, the door opened and Grandson and his uncle came out, the three policemen following behind. "Liu Bao," Zu said aloud, "keep a good eye on your boy. You see, that cart driver could be killed. We don't want the youngster to commit homicide."

"I will, Chief Zu," Grandson's uncle said, then turned around and cursed under his breath, "Son of a bitch!" He gnashed his teeth, his wrinkled face ferocious.

Grandson had black eyes and swollen lips. His yellow T-shirt was stained with the blood from his nose. The red characters, "Revolution to the End," became blurred on his chest. He was too deflated to swear anymore and only looked at us with his dim eyes.

His uncle took off his own straw hat and put it on Grandson's head. With his sinewy arm around his nephew's neck, the man led the boy home.

For a week Grandson didn't show up on the streets. During the day we played games—hitting bottle caps, fanning paper crackers, throwing knives, and waging cricket fights; in the evenings we gathered at the train station to make fun of strangers, calling them names or firing at them with slingshots. They could never catch us in the darkness. If they chased us we could easily throw them off, since they were not familiar with the streets and alleys. If they were women we would follow them and chant, "My little wife, come home with me. There's a warm bed and hot porridge." The women would stop to swear curses, which we always took with laughter. In the meantime, we had a big fight with the boys from Sand Village. They defeated us because they outnumbered us two to one. Also, their emperor Hu Ba was notorious for his ferocity. Most boys in town and its vicinity would slink away at the sight of him. On a victory, he would whip his captives with iron wire and even pee into their mouths. We were lucky, since we got captured and flogged but weren't humiliated further. They didn't catch our emperor, though, because Benli was a fast runner. They pursued him twenty *li* until he reached his aunt's home in Horse Village.

On the following Wednesday Grandson came out. To our amazement, all the bruises had disappeared from his face. He looked calm and was reticent, but his eyes were shining strangely.

That afternoon we did a clod-fight in the backyard of the Middle School, where some sunken vegetable cellars could be used as trenches and strongholds. More clods were available there too, since no stones or any other hard things were allowed in a fight among friends. Emperor Benli divided us fourteen boys into two groups, one of which was to hold the eastern part of the yard while the other the western part. The two groups would attack and counterattack until one side surrendered.

Bare Hips, Big Shrimp, Grandson, Squinty, two smaller boys, and I were to fight Benli, Hare Lips, Sickle Handle, and four other fellows. We collected clods and placed them on the edge of our trench, for we knew Benli's team was always offensive initially. We wanted to consume their ammunition first. Once they ran out of clods, we would fight them back to their trench and rout them there.

The fight started. As we expected, they began charging at us. Missiles were whirring over our heads while we were waiting patiently for them to come close. Our commander Bare Hips raised his hands, his fingers circling his eyes like binoculars, to observe the enemy approaching.

"Ready," he cried.

Every one of us held big clods like apples, preparing to give them the best of it. Bare Hips raised his left hand. "Fire!"

We all threw out clods, which stopped their charging immediately. "Ouch!" One clod exploded on Hare Lip's head. With both hands around his skull, he fled back to their trench.

We jumped out to fight at close quarters. Seeing us fully equipped, they all turned around to escape except Benli, who was still moving toward us. I hit him in the chest with a clod. It didn't stop him. Grandson hurled a big one at him, and it struck his head. "Oh!" Benli collapsed to the ground.

We laughed and ignored him, who had been wiped out. We went on chasing the remnants. Hiding in the trench, they all saw their commander knocked down; since they had no ammunition left, we subdued them easily—one by one they raised their hands to surrender.

"Grandson, you ass ball!" Benli yelled behind us, and rushed over. "Fuck your grandma, you used stones." On his forehead a slant cut was bleeding. Blood trickled down around his left eye.

"So what?" Grandson said calmly. His voice startled us.

"Damn you, you took revenge." Benli moved forward, grabbing for him.

"Yes, I did." Grandson whipped out a dagger and waved it. "You touch me, I'll stab you through."

Benli froze, his hand covering his forehead. We dropped our clods and moved to separate them. Benli turned around to look for a stone while Grandson produced a cake of lead, which looked like a puck and was used in the game of hitting bottle caps. He raised it and declared, "I'm ready, Benli. You come close, I'll crush your skull with this." He looked pale, but his eyes were gleaming. "Come on, Benli," he said. "You have your parents at home. I don't have a mother. Let's kill each other and see who will lose more."

The emperor looked confused. We pushed him away and implored him not to provoke Grandson further, who was simply crazy and would do anything and could hurt anybody. We mustn't fight like this within our own camp.

"Enjoy picking apples at Willow Village, you bastard of a capitalist-backer," Grandson shouted at Benli. This was too much. Our emperor burst into tears. We knew his father had recently been removed from the Commune Administration for being a capitalist-backer and was going down to the countryside to reform himself through labor. The family was moving soon.

"Give me some paper, White Cat," Benli muttered to me. But I didn't have any paper with me.

"Here, here you are." Big Shrimp gave him an unfolded handbill.

Benli wiped the blood and sweat off his face and blew his stuffy nose. He couldn't stop his tears. We had never seen him cry like this before.

"Come on, let's go home," Bare Hips said. He took Benli's arm, and we started moving out of the yard.

Grandson was standing there alone in the scorching sun, as though he were not one of us. He chopped the lead in his hand with the dagger, watching us retreating; he spat to the ground and stamped on his own spittle.

After that fight, Grandson said he hated his nicknames and would threaten to hit whoever happened to call him Grandson with the cake of lead, which he always carried with him. As for the other nickname Big Babe, we already dropped it of our own accord. In school, teachers called him Liu Damin, which was his real name but too formal to us street urchins. Only nicknames were acceptable among us. However, we found a solution to this problem. Benli was busy all the time helping his parents pack up and seldom played with us now, so we called Grandson "Vice-Emperor." And he seemed to like that name. To tell the truth, he wasn't a great fighter, but he was fierce and had more guts than the rest of us. Nobody among us dared challenge

386 • *The Best of The Kenyon Review*

Emperor Benli and only Grandson could do it. Besides, he had been practicing with sandbags at night and had hard fists now. More important, after Benli's leaving we would have to choose a new emperor for our empire—the eastern part of town. Grandson seemed to be a natural candidate.

The day before Benli left we held a small party for him on top of a large haystack behind the Veterinary Station on the northern hill. Sickle Handle had lately stolen ten *yuan* from his father, who was a widower and a master blacksmith in the inn for carters and would get drunk at the end of the day. The old man couldn't keep track of his money, so his son always had a bit of cash in his hands and would share it with us. For the farewell party we bought sodas, boiled periwinkles, Popsicles, moon cakes, toffees, melons, and haw jelly. Benli and Grandson were no longer on hostile terms, though they remained distant toward each other. We ate away, reminiscing about our victories over the enemies from different streets and villages and competing with each other in casting swears. A few golden butterflies and dragonflies were fluttering around us. The afternoon air was warm and clean, and the town below us seemed like a green harbor full of white sails.

Next morning we gathered at Benli's house to help load two horse carts. To our surprise, no adults showed up from the neighborhood, and we small boys could carry only a chair or a basin. Fortunately the two cart drivers were young and strong, so they helped move the big chests, cauldrons, and vegetable vats. Benli's father had seldom come out since he was named a capitalist-backer. We were amazed to find that his hair had turned gray in just two weeks. He looked downcast and his thick shoulders stooped. Throughout the moving he almost didn't say a word. Benli was quiet too, though his small brothers and sisters were noisy and often in our way. Before the carts departed, Benli's mother, a good woman, gave us each a large apple-pear.

After Benli left, the boys in the other parts of town attempted to invade our territory a few times, but we defeated them. To Grandson's credit, it must be said that he was an able emperor, relentless to the enemy and fair and square with his own men. Once we confiscated a pouch of coins from Red Rooster on Eternal Way, and Grandson distributed the money among us without taking a *fen* for himself. Another time we stole a crate of grapes from the army's grocery center; we all ate to our fill and took some home, but Grandson didn't take any back to his uncle's. Yet we couldn't help calling him Grandson occasionally, though nobody dared use that name in his presence. Since he held the throne firmly, the territorial order in town remained the same. No one could enter our streets without risking his skin.

And of course we wouldn't transgress the borderlines either, unless it was necessary.

One afternoon we went shooting birds around the pig farm owned by the army. It was a stuffy day and we felt tired. For more than two hours the seven of us had killed only four sparrows. There weren't many birds to shoot at, so we decided to go and watch the butchers slaughtering pigs for the army's canteens and the officers' families. Then came Squinty, running over and panting hard. "Quick, let's go," he said, waving his hands. "Just now I saw Big Hat in town buying vinegar and soy sauce."

At once our spirit was aroused. Grandson told us to follow him to intercept Big Hat at the crossroads of Main Street and Blacksmith Road; then he ordered Squinty to run home and tell other boys to join us there. We set out running to the crossroads, waving our weapons and shouting, "Kill!"

Big Hat was the emperor of Green Village, whose boys we didn't know very well but fought with whenever we ran into them. He had gotten that nickname because he always wore a marten hat in winter and would brag that the hat made lots of big girls crazy about him. Usually, he would come to town with two or three of his strong bodyguards, but today, according to Squinty's information, he did shopping here by himself. This inspired us to capture him. To subdue those country bandits, we had to catch their ringleader first.

No sooner had we arrived at the crossroads than Big Hat emerged down Blacksmith Road. He was walking stealthily under the eaves on the left-hand side of the street, carrying on his back an empty manure basket and holding, in one hand, a long dung-fork and, in the other, a string bag of bottles. He looked taller than two months before when we had fought under White Stone Bridge near his village. Seeing us standing at the crossroads, he turned around. At this instant, Doggy and Squinty with a group of boys came out of the street corner and cut off Big Hat's retreat. Both units of our troops charged toward him, with sticks and stones in our hands. Knowing his doom, Big Hat stopped, put down the basket and the bottles, and stood with his back against the wall, holding the dung-fork.

"Put down your arms and we'll spare your life," Doggy cried. We surrounded him.

"Doggy," Big Hat said, "you son of a black-hearted rich peasant, don't stand in my way, or else we'll smash your old man's head next time he's paraded through our village." He grinned, and a star-shaped scar was revealed on his stubbly crown.

Doggy lowered his eyes and stopped moving. Indeed several weeks before, his father, a rich peasant in the old days, had been beaten in the marketplace during a denunciation. "Stop bluffing, you son of an ass!" Grandson shouted.

"Grandson," Big Hat said, "let me go just this once. My granduncle is waiting for me at home. We have guests today." He pointed at the squat bottle containing white spirits. "My granduncle is a sworn brother of Chairman Ding of our commune. If you let me go, I'll tell him to help promote your dad."

We all turned to look at Grandson. Apparently Big Hat thought Grandson's uncle was his father.

"Tell your granduncle we all fuck him and your grandaunt too!" Grandson said.

"Come on, your old man will be the head of his workshop if you let me go just this once. My granduncle is also a friend of Director Ma of the Fertilizer Plant."

"Fuck your granduncle!" Grandson plunged forward and hit Big Hat on the forehead with the cake of lead.

Big Hat dropped to the ground without making a noise, and the dung-fork sprang off and knocked down one of the bottles. Blood dripped on the front of his gray shirt. Between his eyebrows was a long, clean cut as if inflicted by a knife. The air smelled of vinegar.

Big Hat was lying beneath the wall, his eyes shut and his mouth vomiting froth. We were scared and thought Grandson must have knocked him dead, but we dared not say a word.

A moment later Big Hat came to and began crying for help. Grandson went over and kicked him in the stomach. "Get up, you bum." He clutched his collar and pulled him up on his knees. "Today you met your grandpas. You must kowtow to everybody here and call us grandpa, or you won't be able to go home tonight."

We were too shocked to do anything. "Grandson," Doggy tried to intervene, "spare his life, Grandson. Let him—"

"Cut it out. Don't call me that," Grandson yelled without looking at Doggy, then turned to Big Hat. "Do you want to call us grandpa or not?"

"No." Tears covered Big Hat's face.

"All right." Grandson stepped away, picked up the fork and smashed all the bottles. Dark soy sauce and colorless liquor splashed on the gravel and began fading away. "All right, if you don't, you must eat one of these." He pointed to the horse droppings a few paces away.

"No!"

"Eat the dung," Grandson ordered, and whacked Big Hat on the back with the fork.

"Oh, help!"

The street was unusually quiet, no grown-ups in sight. "Yes or no?" Grandson asked.

"No!"

"Say it again."

"No!"

"Take this." Grandson stabbed him in the leg with the fork.

"Oh! Save my life!"

One of the prongs pierced Big Hat's calf. He was rolling on the ground, cursing, wailing, and yelling. Strangely enough, no grown-ups ever showed up.

This was too much. Surely we wanted to see that bastard's blood, but we wouldn't kill him and go to jail for that, so a few of us moved to stop Grandson.

"Keep back, all of you." He wielded the fork around as if he would strike any of us. We stood still.

Grandson picked up one of the droppings with the fork and raised it to Big Hat's lips. He threatened, "If you don't take a bite I'll gut you. Open your mouth."

"Oh! You bandit," Big Hat moaned with his eyes closed. His mouth opened a little.

"Open big," Grandson ordered, and thrust the dung into his mouth.

"Ah!" Big Hat spat it out and rubbed his lips with his sleeves. "Fuck your mother!" he yelled, and lay on his side wailing with both hands covering his face.

Grandson threw the fork to the other side of the street; he looked around at us with his crazed eyes, then walked away without a word. His broad hips and short legs swayed as though he were stamping and crushing something.

Without any delay we all ran away, leaving Big Hat to curse and weep alone.

Shortly afterwards Grandson became famous. Boys of the lower grades in our Central Elementary School would tremble at the mere sight of him. With him leading us, we could enter some other areas of town without provoking a fight. Except for us, no one dared play on Main Street any longer—the former noncombat zone was under our control now. Some of the officers' children, a bunch of weaklings though they ate meat and white bread and wore better clothes, even begged us to protect them on their way to school and back home. They would pay us with tickets for the movies shown in the army's theater and with tofu coupons, since Sickle Handle's father, the old blacksmith, had lost all his teeth and liked soft food. For a short while, our territory was expanding, our affairs were prosperous, and our Eastern Empire began to dominate Dismount Fort.

But a month later, Grandson's uncle failed to renew his contract and couldn't find work in town. We were surprised to hear that he hadn't been a permanent, but a temporary worker in the Fertilizer Plant. The Lius decided to return to their home village in Tile County.

Grandson left with the family, and our empire collapsed. Since none of us was suited to be an emperor, the throne remained unoccupied. Now boys from the south even dared to play horse ride in front of our former head-quarters—Benli's house. We were unable to go to the department store at the western end of Main Street or to the marketplace to buy things for our parents and rent picture-story books. Most of us were beaten in school. Once I was caught by Big Hat's men at the millhouse and was forced to meow for them. How we missed our old glorious days!

As time went by, we left, one after another, to serve different emperors.

Joyce Carol Oates

Joyce Carol Oates was born in 1938, in a rural area just outside Lockport, New York. While attending Syracuse University on scholarship, she won the coveted *Mademoiselle* fiction contest and graduated as valedictorian. Oates earned an M.A. in English at the University of Wisconsin where she met and married Raymond J. Smith. They settled in Detroit while she took a teaching position at the University of Windsor in Canada, where she remained from 1968 to 1978. This was a period of tremendous productivity for Oates, seeing two or three books a year, including *Them* (winner of the National Book Award), *Wonderland*, *Do with Me What You Will*, and *The Assassins*. In 1978, Oates began teaching at Princeton, where she remains as professor of creative writing. Her later work has displayed a remarkable diversity, moving away from the psychological realism of her previous work into gothic novels, poetry, even suspense novels published under the pseudonym Rosamond Smith. Twice nominated for the Nobel Prize, Oates continues to prove herself among the finest contemporary fiction writers in America with such recent titles as *Blonde, We Were the Mulvaneys*, and *My Heart Laid Bare*. Oates currently serves on the advisory board for *The Kenyon Review*.

Death Mother *(1995)*

by Joyce Carol Oates

Driving the car fast, then faster. Then braking. Then releasing the brake. And again her foot hard on the gas pedal and the car leapt forward and I wasn't crying, the side of my head striking the door handle but I wasn't crying. It's right for you to die with your mother *she was saying.* I'm your mother, I'm your mother, I'm your mother. *Drinking from the thermos clasped tight between her knees. Radio turned up high. So she'd sing. Talk to herself, and to me, break off singing and begin to laugh, and to sob.* You love me don't you, you're my baby girl, they can't take you from me. I'm your mother *and the car began to shudder, the gas pedal pressed to the floor and my head struck the window and everything went flamey-bright and went out.*

She saw, on the opposite bank, across the gorge, perhaps fifty feet away, an absolutely still, unmoving figure—a woman? in white?—and came to a halt, staring. Her mind was struck blank. She had no thoughts, at all. Someone brushed past her pushing a bicycle, a young man who seemed to know her name, addressed her familiarly, but she didn't hear him, didn't reply. It was all happening swiftly yet with dreamlike slowness yet still she couldn't quite comprehend except to think *But I would sense it: I would know. If she comes back. If that's possible.*

It was 6:50 A.M. The thermometer on the front porch of Jeannette's residence had read five degrees below zero, but here on the open pedestrian bridge, in knifelike gusts of wind, it was even colder. Vapor rose in patches out of the gorge where thirty feet below water spilled noisily from conduits, flowing and steaming in a saw-toothed passage through ice. So Jeannette's view of the figure on the other side of the gorge was obscured.

She was in motion again, crossing the bridge, at about the halfway point now, *no turning back.* It was a familiar route, she took it every day, twice a day, over the deep gorge that wound through the wooded campus, the trick she'd learned at the very start was not to look down, still less to stare down, to slow to a dreamy halt and lean against the railing, stare down at rocks, trickling water. It was hypnotic but not if you didn't look. The footbridge sometimes swayed in the wind, and sometimes it swayed in no discernible wind at all. There were tales of student suicides from the bridge, rumors of other, not quite successful attempts, before Jeannette's time she believed, the tragedies of strangers. She was not thinking of that now, nor of the eerie-humming vibration of the bridge. She was all right. And not alone, she was just one of a number of students on the footbridge, not likely to be singled out. Others passed her with quick, fearless strides, making the bridge sway even harder. The delicious manic energy of dawn: you woke abruptly from sleep already excited, breath shortened, eager for—what? *Not possible. Don't be ridiculous. You know better.* Yet there the woman stood, unmistakably.

In one stiffening arm Jeannette carried her canvas satchel crammed with books and purse, with her free hand she groped for the railing, to steady herself. Below, where she dared not look, were jagged hunks of ice, icicles six feet long, gigantic teeth, thin rapid hissing trickles of water, stunted shrubs growing weirdly sideways, even downward out of rock. Winter had been long, the gorge was filled with snow, unevenly, a look of caprice, the consequence of sudden small avalanches. Above, a gunmetal sky, lightening by slow degrees without warming. *You know better.*

She knew. She'd left home, she'd come to Nautauga College, she was a striking and lively and much-admired young woman here, she was not a person readily identified by those she'd left behind. If the woman on the opposite bank was in fact watching Jeannette she'd be confused, thrown off the scent, seeing how in a clumsy down khaki parka with a hood, in dark wool slacks tucked neatly into boots to conserve body warmth, hauling her satchel, she resembled any student at the college, or nearly.

Somehow, how?—this person I've become.

It was March 1959. She was on her way to Reed Hall, where she worked in the cafeteria. It was an ordinary morning. It would be an ordinary day. If she could force herself to cross the footbridge: to ignore the woman waiting for her. *Not for me. Impossible.*

Yet now—now she'd lost her nerve, that happened sometimes. It was something physical, you felt it in the pit of the belly. Anxiously recalling she'd left her desk lamp on, had she?—in her room. Had she left it on? Getting up so early, before dawn, winter mornings pitch-black as night, yet her pulse already racing, all sleep banished with icy water splashed on her face, in her eyes. Though she'd be late at the cafeteria she couldn't bear the possibility of her lamp burning for hours in the empty room. And maybe she hadn't made up her bed, she couldn't remember. It tore at her nerves like ripped silk to think of such small imperfections. So there was no choice but for her to head back. Already turning, hurrying. Against the flow of others, thickly bundled in winter clothes, breaths steaming, all of them known to Jeannette as she was known to them, their eyes caught curiously at her, they were mildly surprised at the look on her face, but she had no time for them, scarcely heard them, desperate to get off the footbridge, her head lowered, tears on her cheeks like flame swiftly turning to rivulets of frost she brushed at irritably, blindly with her mittened hand.

The last time, seven years ago?—when I was twelve. In the locked ward of the State Psychiatric Hospital at Port Oriskany. A three-year sentence to the women's prison at Red Bank ran concurrently with psychiatric treatment, so-called. Mother?—it's Jeannette. Don't you know me? Mother? *She'd been so drugged, her eyes so puffy, the pupils retracted to pinpricks, I couldn't tell whether she recognized me, or even saw me.*

But then it hadn't ever been clear—whether she'd known me, or my sister Mary. Loving, hugging, kissing us. Pummeling, punching, kicking, yanking at our hair that was wheat-colored, fine, a wan curl in it like hers. Trying to set me afire—an "accident" with a space heater. Trying to kill us all in the car. And Mary, what she'd done to Mary. Never clear whether she saw us, recognized us, at all: her daughters. Not herself.

The second time, no mistaking her.

Late morning, descending the steep granite steps of the Hall of Languages, Jeannette was talking animatedly with friends, talking and laughing when suddenly she saw the figure, the woman: *her.* Not twenty feet away. So calmly, obviously waiting for Jeannette, her daughter. Fixed and unmoving as a stone figure amid a diverging stream of students who scarcely glanced at her, and of whom she was oblivious. An eccentrically dressed woman of no immediately evident age except not young.

One of Jeannette's friends was asking was something wrong, Jeannette who was Jeannie to them, pretty Jeannie Harth, so suddenly still, frightened, staring. But recovering enough to assure them no nothing, nothing wrong, please go on without her.

Moving quickly away before anyone could question her. And calmly too making her way to the woman, the woman who waited for her. Thinking, *She was never so tall before!*

"Mother?—is it you?"

Of course, Mrs. Harth—simply standing there, waiting. How like her if you knew her, or if you didn't. The pale pebble-colored lips drawn back from stained, uneven teeth, a sudden fierce smile—and her eyes deep-set and shadowed and the eyelids puffy, red-rimmed, faded brown eyes how like

Jeannette's own, and Mary's. *We don't laugh, and we don't cry. Nobody knows our secrets.* Jeannette was clutching her mother's hand, Mrs. Harth was clutching Jeannette's, not taking her eyes from Jeannette's face.

For a long moment neither spoke. Then, awkwardly, both at once—"My God, Mother—it *is* you!" and "I—was afraid you wouldn't know me, Jeannette."

So strange, amid the boisterous commotion of young people, in the bright-dazzling sun of noon; on this ordinary weekday, with no warning. Always, Jeannette had thought she'd be notified beforehand, her father at least would have called her, some warning if only a dream, a nightmare of her own. She was saying, trying to speak evenly, "Where have you come from, Mother? Are you—?"

Mrs. Harth continued to stare at her, hungrily. "Am I 'out'? Yes, Jeannette. I'm 'out.'"

She spoke with that air of almost girlish, flirtatious irony, an irony that invited you to laugh though of course you must not laugh, that Jeannette remembered with sudden, sick clarity.

Now we should hug one another, should kiss but Jeannette stood awkward and unmoving, still clutching her mother's hand; as her mother clutched hers, her fingers surprisingly strong. But then she'd always been a strong woman, don't be deceived.

How odd, how eccentric, Mrs. Harth's appearance: on this freezing winter day in upstate New York she wore a cream-colored, somewhat soiled and wrinkled cloth coat in a bygone style, a sash tied and drooping at her waist, like a negligee; her gloves were beige lace; about her head, only partly covering her thin, graying-yellow hair was a gauzy, pink-translucent scarf of the kind a romantically minded woman might wear on a cool summer evening. An odor of dried leaves, like camphor, lifted from her. Mrs. Harth's eyes were slyly quick-darting and alert as if she was aware of others watching yet would not acknowledge these others. Her papery-pale, puckered skin was tightly creased across her forehead, a maze of wrinkles, though she was only—how old?—not old!—forty-two, forty-three? And that face once so beautiful, was it possible?

Jeannette said quickly, fighting the urge to cry, "Let's go somewhere warm, Mother—you must be freezing."

"Me? *I* don't mind the cold, I'm used to it."

A quick comeback reply, like TV. And the ironic smile, the anxious eyes.

And there suddenly Jeannette was leading her mother, arm linked firmly through her mother's arm, in the direction of Nautauga's Main Street, away from the college. She knew of a tearoom patronized by local women shoppers, where students rarely went. Friends called out to her, *Hi Jeannie!* like chattering birds she did not hear. A young man, a tenor in the college choir, who'd taken Jeannette out several times, passed within inches, speaking to her, and Jeannette may have murmured a response but did not look up, staring in confusion at the trampled snow underfoot. Mrs. Harth said brightly, "There's a friend of yours," as if she expected to be introduced, or was teasing Jeannette with this possibility, and quickly Jeannette murmured, "I don't know him well, really," and Mrs. Harth said, "But you have many friends here, Jeannette? Don't you?" her voice low and even and not at all accusing, and Jeannette said, laughing nervously, "Not many! A few," and Mrs. Harth said, emphatically, "You were always selective about your friends. Like me."

They walked on. It could not be happening, yet how simply, it was. Mother and daughter, daughter and mother. Jeannette Harth's mother Mrs. Harth, come to visit. Why was it so unusual, why should it seem to upset Jeannette quite so much? Mrs. Harth was saying, giving Jeannette's arm a little tug, "No one can betray you like a friend—or a *loved one. You* know the expression *loved one?"*

"I...don't know."

"It isn't strangers who break our hearts!"

This was uttered with such smiling vehemence, such a steaming breath and a coquettish toss of the pink-gauzy head, Jeannette stared at her mother, uncomprehending.

Why. Why here. Why now. What do you want of me.

Making their way across the icy quadrangle, through a gauntlet of sorts, Jeannette hearing, not hearing her name called out—that pretty lyric-melodic name that so suited her, in this place: *Jeannie! Jeannie Harth!* Girls from her cottage, girls from the dining hall, a young man from her philosophy class. Jeannette dared not look at them, with Mrs. Harth gripping her arm. Dared not reply beyond a vague mumble of recognition, acknowledgment. For of course Mrs. Harth was staring at them critically. For of course she would judge them, her daughter's friends, what few friends she had. *Is that the best you can do! I call that pitiful.*

Yet how fair-minded how pleasant saying, "It seems very nice here. Nautauga College. Not like Port Oriskany, not like Erie Street, at all. Or your old school? You fit right in here, Jeannette, I can see!" Clearing her throat, a gravelly grating sound, and Jeannette flinched thinking *she will spit, she will spit it out,* but no she did not, must have swallowed it, all the while smiling and glancing about lurching a little, slipping on the sidewalk so that Jeannette had to steady her, practically support her. What ridiculous shoes Mrs. Harth was wearing, Jeannette stared in disbelief: cheap shiny black patent-leather pumps with painfully pinched toes and a thin, near stiletto heel. A ladder-run in one of her beige nylon stockings.

They were standing on the curb waiting for the light to change. Flashing red, warning DON'T WALK DON'T WALK. Jeannette was saying what a surprise, how wonderful to see her mother, hesitantly asking how long would she be visiting, did she think? and Mrs. Harth said "That depends."

"Depends—?"

The light changed to green WALK WALK WALK. Hand in hand, Jeannette and Mrs. Harth crossed Main Street. "Upon circumstances," Mrs. Harth said, clearing her throat. "Upon *you.*"

Jeannette's breath was gone, she could not reply. Mrs. Harth squeezed her hand in girlish excitement, like one sharing a secret just a bit prematurely. She said, "I have all my earthly possessions with me in my car. Did you know I have a car? Did you know I have my license? I'm parked there." Pointing beyond Main Street, matter-of-factly. "There is nowhere else I have to be now that I'm *here,* Jeannette. With you."

She was driving the car fast, then faster. Then she braked. Then released the brake. And again her foot hard on the gas pedal and the car leapt forward and I wasn't crying, the side of my head hit against the door handle but I wasn't crying. I couldn't see where we were going only the tops of trees rushing past. It's right for you to die with your mother *she was saying.* I'm your mother, I'm your mother, I'm your mother. *That smell of her when she hadn't bathed, hadn't washed her hair. The animal smell. Her hair snarled and matted. But she was pretty—Mother. Even with the smeared Noxema on her face, where she'd been picking at herself. Sometimes a trickle of bright blood through the greasy white face cream. From a scab on her face she'd picked. And her fingers, her nails, the nails bright red. The cuticles bloody.* Just you and me, nobody will know where we are, it's right for us to be together. I'm your mother forever and always. Forever and always! *Drinking from the thermos clasped tight between her knees. Drinking then wiping her mouth on the back of her hand. The radio turned up high. So she'd sing. She'd talk to herself, and to me, and she'd sing, and she'd break off singing and begin to laugh, and to sob. Speeding through a red light pressing the palm of her hand against the car horn. The sound of it filled the car, so loud. And her laughing, angry sobbing.* You love me don't you, you're my baby girl, they can't take you away from me. I'm your mother, I'm your mother *as she hit the brakes and the car jumped and skidded and swerved and there was the sound of another car's horn and Mother yelled out the window sobbing and jammed her foot on the gas pedal again and the car leapt forward throwing up gravel where we'd drifted onto the gravel shoulder of the highway. I wasn't crying, my face was wet and my breath coming choked but I wasn't crying, I knew there was no way out, Mother was saying* You love me, I'm your mother and I love you, you're my little girl, it's right for us to die together *and there was a siren coming up fast behind us and the car swerved and shuddered, the red speedometer needle at eighty-five miles an hour, the car wouldn't go any faster and Mother was sobbing and I was thrown against the door, my head hit the window and everything went flamey-bright and then out. I was nine years old. That was November 1949. I hadn't known about Mary. What had happened to Mary. Where Mother had taken her, and left her.*

"I don't know what your father has told you about me, Jeannette. Or any of them. It's in their interests to lie about me."

In the cozy interior of the Village Tea Room, amid a clatter of dishware, cutlery, women's raised voices, amid lavender floral wallpaper and hanging pots of ivy, Mrs. Harth had reluctantly removed her gauzy scarf, her soiled cream-colored coat which was draped over the back of her chair. Yet she'd kept her beige lace gloves on. Her hands shook just slightly as she poured tea for Jeannette and for herself. Her eyes were sunken but bright, alert. Watchful. Her mouth twitched and smiled. *You love me, I'm your mother. I'm mother, mother.* As Mrs. Harth spoke in her low, intense, earnest voice she repeatedly touched Jeannette's arm; and Jeannette shivered at the strangeness of it, the wonder, not simply that after seven years her mother had returned to her, in fact it had been much longer. Many times Mrs. Harth had disappeared from the house and returned and disappeared and returned again, the times confused, bleeding into one another like loose snapshots in an album, and the child Jeannette had once been was not a child she knew or could recall or wished to recall. Not simply that strangeness, but the strangeness too of touch: another living being touching you: flesh and bone, another's secret heartbeat, warm-coursing blood, another's vision of you, knowledge of you, desire. For there were men who had touched Jeannette too, or had wanted to touch her, in desire. And always that immediate response, that panicked shuddering sensation *Don't touch me! Don't hurt me!* yet again *Please touch me, please hold me, I'm so lonely, I love you.*

"Jeannette?" Mrs. Harth's lips pursed, hurt. Creases like bloodless knife cuts bracketed her mouth. "Aren't you listening?"

Jeannette said quickly, "Yes. But I don't remember."

"What don't you remember?"

Jeannette ducked her head, smiled. For the question was really a riddle, wasn't it. *What don't you remember?*

Jeannette said, childlike in earnest, staring at her mother's hand gripping a delicate china cup, the tattered fingertips of the beige lace gloves, "—I don't remember very much about what Dad told me, it was a long time ago and we never talk about it any longer." She paused, still smiling. *We never talk about you any longer. I would not ask, and he would not tell if I did ask.* "And I don't remember much about—what happened."

Mrs. Harth's lips twitched in a smile. Her eyes were steely, resolute. "What happened—when?"

When Mary died. When they took you away.

Carefully, Jeannette said, "When Mary died."

There was a silence. Mrs. Harth touched her hair with beige-lace fingers; her hair that was stiff looking, thin, the hue of stained ivory. Groped for her teacup. At the sound of Mary's name, so soft as to be almost inaudible, Mrs. Harth's subtly ravaged face became impassive, almost peaceful.

Beneath her coat, Jeannette saw, her mother was wearing an oyster-white dress, or was it layers of filmy pale cloth like curtains?—there seemed to be no collar to the costume, no visible buttons. The gauzy material was draped loose across Mrs. Harth's bosom in rumpled layers. Since they'd been seated in the tearoom, a sharp, acrid smell as of something brackish wafted against Jeannette's nostrils amid the warm yeasty smell of baked goods. Her mother's body. Her mother's hair, clothes. Recalling the odor of her mother's body in the days of her mother's sickness which she had believed, as a young child, to be the odor of the very air, very life itself. The rank tallow-like smell of the hair that was so fascinating, the briny stench of the champagne-colored negligee Mrs. Harth wore inside the house, and wore and wore as if it were a loose second skin. The soiled undergarments on the bathroom floor, kicked about, blood-stained panties, Jeannette and Mary crouched staring in fascinated horror, reaching out daringly to touch. *Dirty girls! Both of you! Aren't you ashamed!*

What is there to do with *shame,* where exactly do you hide *shame,* you pretty girl, and "popular," too!

Every morning no matter how freezing the fourth-floor bathroom of the residence, showering, shampooing her hair, vigorously, harshly. The body can't distinguish between *cleansing* and *punishing,* for the body is ignorant, and mute besides.

In high school, back in Port Oriskany: she'd been a different girl, then. Where they know you, you're known. Where you're known, you're *you.* Shrinking in the restrooms dreading what she might overhear, you don't want to eavesdrop, not ever. And after gym class having to strip naked amid the squealing giggles of the other girls so easily naked, pale and slippery as fish, darting through the stinging needles of water, the hot shower first, then warm then cold then the foot rinse, in a paroxysm of shame so her body prickled and her eyes rolled in their sockets. *Don't look! don't look! I'm a freak, I'm not one of you!*

Mrs. Harth was watching her closely, it was possible that Mrs. Harth knew exactly what she was thinking. Saying, "So! You're happy here, Jeannette? So far from home?" Inside the woman's level, uninflected voice, doubt sounded sly as a hinge that needs oiling.

Jeannette said quickly, "I—love it here."

"Hmm?"—Mrs. Harth cupped a hand to her ear.

"I love it here."

There was a pause: a moment for contemplating such a claim.

Mrs. Harth sipped her tea in thin, savorless swallows, like a duty. She did not mean to sound suspicious, of course, but—"How did you happen to come *here,* Jeannette? Of all places?"

"I have a scholarship. A work-scholarship. It pays my full tuition and–"

Mrs. Harth interrupted, *"Only* here? You didn't win any other scholarships, anywhere in the state?"

Jeannette's gaze plummeted to the tabletop. Lavender tablecloth, so attractive, feminine. Just-visible stains, rings from the teapot. Scattered crumbs from the cinnamon toast Mrs. Harth had broken into small pieces, most of which lay on her plate uneaten. *Don't you know I can read your mind. Don't you know I'm your mother, your mother, your mother.*

Jeannette said quietly, stubbornly, "I did. But I wanted to come here, to study music."

"Music! That's new."

"Music education. So that I can teach."

"Teach."

Mrs. Harth took a small sip of tea, swallowed with an expression of disdain. After a pause she said, as if they'd been speaking of this all along, "Your father is a bitter man—I don't wonder, Jeannette, you've come so far to escape him. And *her.*"

Jeannette protested weakly, "But it wasn't for that reason at all, Mother. Really—"

"Yes," said Mrs. Harth grimly, laying a beige-gloved hand on Jeannette's arm, both to comfort and to silence, "—I don't wonder."

It was past one o'clock when Jeannette and Mrs. Harth emerged from the Village Tea Room into the bright, cold, gusty March air, Jeannette had missed her one o'clock lecture not having wanted to hurry her mother, not wanting to be rude. The question in her mind was where would her mother spend the night.

Mr. Harth had remarried, soon after the divorce. The end of that, the beginning of something new. There was a second *Mrs. Harth* in Port Oriskany but the woman was not quite real to Jeannette, a nice woman, a kindly woman, generous and, yes, motherly. So many women of a certain age were motherly.

Never had Jeannette told her father's wife *Don't imagine that I need, or want, another mother: I don't.* But the woman seemed to know, just the same.

Jeannette had a class, her three o'clock music lecture, and somehow it happened that Mrs. Harth was coming with her. "Where else would I go, dear?" she said, smiling, sliding an arm through Jeannette's. "I'm all alone here except for *you.*"

"You might not like the class, Mother. It's—"

"Oh, I'm sure I will! You know I like music."

"But this is—"

"*—love* music. You know I used to sing in the church choir when I was a girl."

No choice, then. Jeannette led the way.

Introduction to Twentieth-Century Music was held in the amphitheater of the Music School, on the far edge of the quad. The lecturer was Professor Hans Reiter, a popular campus figure, burly and good-natured and explosive in his enthusiasms, a bearish dark-bearded man with a boiled-looking skin, thick glinting glasses. He played records and tapes for the class at a deafening volume sometimes, and lectured over the music. Often, in the right mood, he played piano from a standing position as he spoke—rough, impassioned playing, the inner soul of music Jeannette supposed. She loved Professor Reiter and was shy of him. Usually she sat with her friends near the front of the room but this afternoon, Mrs. Harth's arm tight through hers, she avoided even glancing in that direction (were her friends looking for her? looking at her? at her and this woman so obviously her mother?) but sat with her mother at the very rear. The subject of today's lecture was Stravinsky and *The Rite of Spring.* Incantatory chords, breathless leaps of sound, that strident-erotic *beat beat beat* Jeannette tried to hear purely as music, not as pulsations in the blood. She hunched over her notebook taking notes rapidly, eyes downcast. Beside her Mrs. Harth sat stiff, arms folded across her chest. Now, in the amphitheater, she was cold. Would not remove her coat. Not at all charmed by the professor's lecture style, his bouncing about at the front of the room, witty exegesis of the composer's "revolutionary genius" amid the "dense philistine ignorance" of the era. How forced, self-dramatizing, braying Reiter sounded, to Jeannette's ear! She was deeply embarrassed, after the class murmuring an apology to Mrs. Harth as they left the building, quickly as Jeannette could manage; Mrs. Harth laughed a dry mirthless laugh, arm tight through Jeannette's, saying, "So that's what a *college lecture* is. A fat, loudmouth fool like that—*professor*. And that ugly beard. And such silly music, like you'd hear on the radio. Imagine, a man gets *paid* for such nonsense!"

It was the very voice of Jeannette's childhood, raw envious spiteful Port Oriskany, glowering with satisfaction. Jeannette cast her eyes down to the trampled snow, and said nothing.

But Mrs. Harth, stimulated, was speaking animatedly. She was incensed, outraged, yet amused—you just had to laugh, didn't you? What a fancy college education is worth. So much fuss, people putting on airs, and what is it? *She'd* had to quit high school at the age of sixteen to work, to help support her family; oh yes, *she'd* hoped to be a teacher, too. "But nobody ever handed me a *scholarship* on a silver platter." This was the first Jeannette had ever heard of any of this, but she did not question it; only murmuring she was sorry, and Mrs. Harth added, with bitter satisfaction, "*I* had to drop out of school to work, then to marry. Too young for any of it—but it had to be. And babies, too—had to be."

Had to be. Had to be. The words hung in the air like steaming exhaled breaths.

Jeannette heard herself asking, "Where—would you like to go now, Mother? I'm afraid I have library assignments, and I have to work the dinner shift at the cafeteria, and tonight I have a choir rehearsal—" Her voice trailed off weakly. *All I want is a life, a new life for myself that has nothing to do with who I am, or was. All I want is to be free.* Her body was chill and clammy inside her clothes and her heart beat so quickly, Mrs. Harth must sense it.

Mrs. Harth was squinting at her. That dry ironic smile playing about her lips. With the air of speaking to a small or dull child she said, "Jeannette, I'm all alone here in—Nautauga. And anywhere in the world. Except for *you*, dear. How long I visit, where I go depends on *you*."

Laughing, that delicious cascading sound. And her eyes bright, her long nails fluttering the air like shiny crimson butterflies. Get in! Hurry get in, girls! Before it's too late! That humid, hot August day, early evening; Mother had left us to live somewhere else and Dad would never speak of her but suddenly there Mother was—come to pick Mary and me up at Grandma's in this car that was silver on top and aqua on the bottom—so pretty!—so shiny!—Grandma was inside so didn't see, we were playing in the front yard and Mother came laughing to pull us away, her finger to her lips meaning Quiet! quiet! *laughing driving us all the way to the beach to Lake Oriskany and she wasn't the way we remembered her but so pretty now, so happy! a sharp lemony smell in her hair, her hair not greasy but shiny, whipping in the wind like laughing and her mouth bright red like Ava Gardner's on a movie poster.* Hey: you know I love you, your mother's crazy about you, you're my baby girls aren't you!—*at a stoplight hugging and kissing us 'til it hurt, and another time pulling over at the side of the road so cars honked passing us, then at the beach Mother ran up and down the boardwalk pulling us by the hands buying us fizzing Cokes and orangesicles which were her favorite too, sharp-tasting orange ice and vanilla ice cream at the center so delicious!—and Mother's legs were pale and covered in pale brown hairs in the sun where she drew her dress up, past her knees, she was barefoot her toenails bright crimson and there was a man up on the boardwalk leaning on the railing watching us, watching her and he came down to the beach and he and Mother began talking, laughing, Mother said,* These are my little girls Jeannette and Mary, *saying,* Aren't they beautiful! *and the man squatted in the sand beside Mary and me smiling at us, said,* They sure are, yeah they're beautiful *smiling up at Mother*—just like you.

Mother and the man went away, Only for a few minutes *Mother said kissing us* I'll be right back: don't go away! don't go away or the police will come and arrest you! *but they didn't come back and didn't come back and we were crying and a woman asked us who we were, were we alone, two little girls like us?—she took us to the ladies' restroom up on the boardwalk and bought us Cokes and we took them back to the beach because Mother would be so angry if we were gone and after a while a policeman did come by, asked us where we lived and we were crying hard by now, we were afraid to tell him because if he took us away when Mother came back she would be so surprised so hurt so angry she would never take us away in her car again, she would never love us again so it was a long time before we told him, I think it must have been me who told, I was the older of the sisters, I was always the older, I was Jeannette.*

That was why she never wanted to be alone with another girl. Especially a girl she liked, trusted. One of the girls in Briarly Cottage where she roomed. You had to be careful. Might start talking, telling too much. Might start crying. Lose control, say too much, once it's out it can never be retracted. *The worst thing: to give yourself away in exchange for not enough love.*

"Tell me which way to turn, Jeannette!—I've never driven in this city before."

Mrs. Harth spoke gaily and coquettishly yet at the same time in reproach. Jeannette gave directions: left onto Main Street, three blocks to the bridge, left again on Portsmouth to South Street…Strange how, through the filmy windows of Mrs. Harth's lead-colored Dodge, the familiar streets, the red brick "historic" buildings of Nautauga College, even the long sloping campus lawn were altered; how childish, self-absorbed, unattractive Jeannette's fellow students appeared, on the sidewalks, crossing against traffic. The car's windshield was coated with a fine grit that reflected sunshine in a way that made everything bleakly, flatly sepia-stained, as in a fading photograph.

Mrs. Harth's car was one Jeannette had never seen before, of course. A 1954 model Dodge, lead-colored, with rust-stippled fenders and bumpers; riding oddly high off the ground, so you had to step up to climb inside. The smell was brackish, sour. In the back, what appeared at first glance to be random debris was in fact Mrs. Harth's personal possessions: untidy piles of clothes, shoes, a pillow with a stained embroidered pillowcase, cardboard boxes, grocery bags stuffed with items. A soiled gray blanket, taped to the left rear window, had slipped partway. The car windows were rolled up tight and Jeannette's nostrils pinched against the smell her mother seemed not to notice.

Jeannette didn't want to think what such evidence suggested.

Crossing a two-lane bridge over the Nautauga River, which was a narrow but swift-flowing river, now covered in ice, Mrs. Harth overreacted at the approach of a truck, pressed down hard on the gas pedal and swerved toward the railing; Jeannette felt a moment's sick panic—*She will drive us off the bridge, that's her plan!* But Mrs. Harth regained control of the car, driving on.

Jeannette remembered those wild, wild rides, her mother at the wheel. To Lake Oriskany. But the return—back to Erie Street—was vague, undefined; like a dream of profound intensity that nonetheless fades immediately upon waking.

And now they were at Jeannette's residence, the quaintly called "Briarly Cottage," which was an ordinary wood frame dwelling of four floors with a shingled dormer roof like a heavy brow, on a half block of similar drab houses, once private and now partitioned into rooms for students who couldn't afford better housing, nearer campus. Mrs. Harth stared with a look of personal hurt, incredulity. "*This* is it?—your *residence?*"

Jeannette murmured it was fine, fine for her, she'd made good friends here. There were eighteen girls, scholarship students—

"And you so proud of that, your *scholarship,*" Mrs. Harth said, removing the key from the ignition and throwing it, with an emphatic gesture, into her bag. "*I* wouldn't wonder this fancy college put you here on purpose, to insult you."

"Insult me?—why?"

The question hung in the air, unanswered.

With mincing steps, for of course the sidewalk hadn't been shoveled, Jeannette helped her mother ascend the walk to the house. The older woman's arm was tight through hers; their breaths steamed faintly, as if in anticipation. Beneath the dry camphor smell of Mrs. Harth's hair and clothes was a sharper lemony smell, all but indistinguishable. Her skin, maybe. That heat that used to rise from her skin. As Jeannette was about to open the front door, a Negro girl came out, one of Jeannette's friends, big smile, big eyes, a friendly and popular girl named Kitty, and in an instant Kitty glanced from Jeannette to Mrs. Harth to Jeannette again, seeing whatever it was in Mrs. Harth's face, maybe noting how, with an involuntary intake of breath, Mrs. Harth's arm tightened on Jeannette's, and her smile dimmed discreetly, and she only murmured, "H'lo, Jeannie," in that way that signals no reply or animation is expected.

Inside, Mrs. Harth said in a lowered voice, with grim satisfaction, *"What did I tell you?*—there it is! Putting you in a place with one of *them,* that's the insult."

Jeannette protested, "But, Mother—"

"They give you tuition money, oh yes, but they make you beg—*crawl* for it. *I* would never."

"Mother, that's ridiculous. Nautauga College is—"

"'Ridiculous,' am I? Oh? For speaking the truth, miss? Which your father would never, would he? Which you're ashamed to hear." Mrs. Harth sighed, drawing her filmy glamour scarf off her head, as if reluctantly; glancing about, her forehead creasing, nostrils pinching, into the cramped parlor off the front hall. Fortunately, none of Jeannette's housemates were in there. "I call this pitiful," Mrs. Harth said. "A daughter of *mine."*

"I'm happy here," Jeannette said, with childlike stubbornness. "This is my second year and I'm *happy here."*

"Of course, you'd tell yourself that," Mrs. Harth said simply. "That's what people do."

And there were the steep stairs, three flights to Jeannette's fourth-floor room. And there was the antiquated bathroom with its ineradicable odors, door ajar. When Jeannette opened the door to her room she winced at the sight, seeing it through Mrs. Harth's eyes: the ceiling that slanted beneath the eaves, the narrow cot-like bed covered with a cheap chenille spread, a college-issue pinewood chest of drawers, aluminum desk, ugly crooknecked lamp, and shabby swivel chair. On the bare floorboards, a thin machine-woven rug Jeannette had bought for $9.98 at a local discount store, liking its rust-orange gaiety; on the walls cheap glossy prints of nature photographs and works of art—Van Gogh's *Starry Night,* for one. Jeannette's hope had been to make the small room seem spacious by suggesting, as of windows opening out, other dimensions, other worlds. Instead, the reproductions, all of them slightly curling from the radiator heat, gave the room a cluttered, tacky look.

The single window in the room looked out over an expanse of weather-worn roof and snow-smutty yards; in the distance, across the gorge, drained oddly of color and flattened like paper cutouts, the handsome spires and towers of the college.

Mrs. Harth was breathless from the stairs. But entered the room tall, incensed. "So!—*this."*

Jeannette closed the door behind them, trembling with dread.

"These hundreds of miles you've come—such pride in your *scholarship*—imagining yourself so superior to your mother? For *this*?"

Jeannette protested, "Mother, I've never imagined myself—"

"Oh no? Don't lie: not to Mother. *I* can see into your heart."

Mrs. Harth paced about, untying the sash of her flared coat, sniffing and squinting and peering into corners. Here was her old energy, liquid-bright eyes and sharp elbows, that girlish air of conspiracy, angry elation. "It's good I came here! I knew I was wanted! To rescue you! Take you away, yes? I *knew*."

"Take me away, Mother? Where?"

Mrs. Harth put a forefinger to her lips, slyly. Then placed that same forefinger to Jeannette's lips, to seal them.

Yes it was an accident. I always believed so. She loved us, she held us and kissed us and slept sometimes in our bed with us or she would take us into her bed, hers and Dad's, during the day, for a nap. And she would bathe us. There was no difference between her and us. I always believed so. The accident was with Drano. You know what Drano is—liquid Drano. The sharp terrible fumes stinging your eyes, burning your nostrils. Sit! Damn you, sit! *she was screaming. Because we didn't want to, we were trying to get away. Because the enema bag, the tube, was known to us, and we hated it.* Sit! In this tub! You bad girls, you dirty girls, obey your mother! *But I squirmed out of the tub, out of her hands, naked and slippery as a fish.*

"Christus, der ist mein Leben, Sterben ist mein Gewinn...dem tu ich mich ergeben..."

Jeannette was singing as she'd never sung before, an edge of anxiety to her voice, eyes fixed urgently on the young choirmaster's face. Her soprano voice rising, pleading as if it were an impersonal cry through her throat, *"... mit Freud fahr ich dahin."* Bach's exquisite cantata, the music that coursed through her blood, filling her with an almost unbearable yearning; the tension of the long day, dread rising to panic yet to a strange sort of elation, now her mother had returned to her, now the waiting was over. She hadn't realized how long she'd been waiting.

There was a stop, phrases repeated. The choirmaster's name was McBride and he was demanding, sometimes impatient. Short-tempered. Jeannette imagined herself in love with him, he was so distant from her. Yet he'd chosen her to sing one of the solos in the upcoming Easter concert.

Again, now, to the top of the page, and again: Jeannette sang until her lungs ached, her eyes welled with tears. Even if Mrs. Harth would be taking her from Nautauga, even if there would be no Easter concert. Did it matter what the German words meant? *Since Christ is all my Being, Dying is all my gain. To Him my soul is fleeing, nought can her joy regain.*

Jeannette had left her mother back in her room, in her bed, sleeping. Mrs. Harth had been too exhausted even to have dinner. In the morning, she said, they would decide what course of action to take. What was best for Jeannette. What must be done, where they would go. She'd spoken softly, framing Jeannette's face with her cool dry hands. Jeannette had cried a little but Mrs. Harth had not cried for there was no need.

We don't laugh, and we don't cry. Nobody knows our secrets.

Mrs. Harth was not in the amphitheater, yet midway in an ascending phrase *"mit Fried und Freud ich fahr dahin"* Jeannette saw her figure there at the very rear, stiff with disapproval, arms folded across her chest, as she'd sat in that identical seat for Professor Reiter's lecture. Seeing, Jeannette lost the words of the cantata, faltered, and broke. The other singers continued. Sopranos, altos, tenors, basses. It was as if a deer had fallen dead, shot by a hunter, as the herd ran on, oblivious. Jeannette hid her eyes and when she lowered her hands she saw at the shadowy rear of the banked rows of seats nothing more than carelessly slung down coats, parkas.

Of course, Mrs. Harth wasn't there. What need, to follow Jeannette to choir rehearsal?

At this moment sleeping in Jeannette's bed in one of Jeannette's flannel nightgowns.

Later, McBride led Jeannette exactingly through her first recitative which at the start of rehearsals she'd delivered self-consciously, as if distrusting her merely spoken voice; tonight, the words seemed to burst from her throat. *"Nun, falsche Welt! Nun hab ich weiter nichts mit dir zu tun..."* McBride nodded: OK. Then to Jeannette's chorale part, the rapturous evocation of a savior raised miraculously from the dead: *"Valet will ich dir geben, du arge falsche Welt...Da wird Gott ewig lohnen dem, der ihm dient alihier."* It was a spirited, demanding passage, and Jeannette was equal to it. Though her throat was beginning to ache and her eyes felt seared, burnt in their sockets from exhaustion.

McBride was smiling, he *was* impressed.

Rehearsal ended at 10:30 P.M. Jeannette edged away, grabbed her parka, hurried up the aisle to leave before anyone could speak to her; her problem was, at Nautauga, she had too many friends. Too many people who were attracted to her, or believed they were. *They don't know me but what they know, they like.* She was hurrying out of the semi-darkened building except at one of the front doors she paused leaning her forehead against the door, she felt her heart beating quickly yet calmly, what premeditation! what cunning! *It's a fantasy, you're being ridiculous. You know better.*

Still, she'd seen him looking at her, she'd been seeing, and not seeing, for weeks. Since the start of rehearsals, though he'd never seemed explicitly to be favoring her.

Waiting for McBride, who, a few minutes later, as she'd known he would, came whistling by; McBride in his sheepskin jacket and fur hat, a swagger to him, the kind of man who controls by withholding praise until you're weak and ravenous with hunger. Others were with him but he waved them on, he was looking at Jeannette who'd turned her face toward him, baring it like a flame, mute and exposed.

McBride politely asked would Jeannette like a ride home and Jeannette said yes thank you, calling him, as all the undergraduates did, *Dr. McBride.*

They walked to McBride's Volkswagen parked in a nearby lot, their booted feet breaking icy crusts of snow. It was very cold now. But no wind, only a dry crackling air that burnt the nostrils and made the eyes well with tears of hurt and protest. Their breaths steamed like little private pockets of thought, or desire. When Jeannette slipped on a patch of ice, McBride murmured, "Hey!" and deftly caught her elbow, just enough to reposition her; his touch, his gloved fingers against the bulky fabric of the parka, made her feel giddy, faint. He was talking in his brisk animated way about the evening's rehearsal that had gone fairly well, considering the enormous difficulty of Bach's music and the choir's relatively untrained voices. There was a phrase of his he used often, wryly, yet with a kind of brotherly affection for his singers: "We're getting there, eh?"

A windless still night, palely illuminated by a three-quarter's moon, a mad-eye moon, high overhead. Jeannette's eyes ached from just this moonlight as if she'd been crying, for hours, without knowing it.

Wait for you. Don't stay away long. Jeannette?

No, Mother. Where would I go?

This, then: they climbed into McBride's car laughing at their mutual awkwardness, their long legs, and McBride asked Jeannette where she lived for of course he had no idea and Jeannette told him and he asked was that the far side of the gorge and she said yes. He said she would have to direct him, then—he wasn't familiar with that side of campus. He lived on the east side, himself.

Driving then out of the lot and onto a side street and a few blocks to the very bridge, nearly deserted now, which eight hours before Mrs. Harth had driven them across in the lead-colored Dodge. Where they might have had an accident, swerving into the railing and through into the frozen river, but by chance had not. Jeannette's pulse raced now as then and she knew McBride sensed it.

Here too, as out of the gorge, thin drifting columns of mist rose dream-like from the river; the effect was of something delicate as lace, or very breath itself, fading as you stared. McBride said casually, driving the Volkswagen as if it were a clever toy, "Jesus, it's beautiful here, isn't it? Upstate New York. It feels like the Arctic to me. I'm from Brooklyn, you know—this is all new to me."

It was the most Jeannette had ever heard the man utter, and the only personal revelation.

McBride followed Jeannette's soft-murmured directions, turning left, and again left, approaching hilly rutted South Street. At first he wasn't going to take note of Jeannette's crying. For she cried that softly, unobtrusively; you could ignore it if you wished. For she was a well-mannered girl, discreet. She'd had no lovers, nor had ever been close to loving. This, McBride seemed to know, or to sense; he was eleven years her senior, a lifetime.

Finally he said, "Look, Jeannette, what's wrong?—has something happened to you?" and it was that plunge, a blind plunge like stepping through cracking ice, the irremediable shattering. For Jeannette heard herself cry, "I can't go back there! My room! Not yet! I can't—" Already McBride had braked the car, jammed the brake down with the heel of his boot; the car spun on the salt-strewn ice, but held. They sat, side by side, at first motionless and not looking at each other as Jeannette wept now freely helplessly. "All right," McBride said. "You don't have to. You can do something else."

McBride brought Jeannette Harth back to his apartment, where they would spend the night.

And all this unpremeditated, the sheerest chance.

McBride, who'd been married unwisely young, and divorced; who knew better than to involve himself, or even to appear to involve himself, with undergraduate women, many of whom openly adored him—there he was, leading a terrified trembling girl into his darkened apartment, quiet as stealth; himself terrified as if he'd been handed a musical composition he'd never before seen nor even heard played and shoved out on stage before a vast audience and made to perform, playing a musical instrument clumsy in his hands, exposed to public ridicule. Yet: how excited, how happy he was, and how Jeannette laughed, breathless, giddy, as he poured them each a glass of red wine and his hand was perceived as shaking as much as hers, or nearly. Jeannette meant to say, "I've never drunk this before!" but the words came out, "I've never done this before!" Swallowing, she tasted tartness as of overripe fruit; an inky pool spread immediately in her panicked-parched mouth, warming her throat, her chest, even, uncomfortably, her belly. She could not have said if it was delicious, or bitter, or both.

Bravely then Jeannette began to speak, as in a recitative. She was in love with him—Dr. McBride. She'd been in love with him for—a long time. Her voice was so faint, McBride came to sit clumsily beside her, stroking her hands which were chill and inert. "I know I should be ashamed," Jeannette said miserably, "—I know I shouldn't be telling you this." McBride laughed, saying, "Who should you tell, then?"

Eventually they were in McBride's bedroom, and lying in an anguished, delicious tangle on his bed. McBride may have sensed that Jeannette was not telling him *why* exactly she was here, *why* tonight, that there was something withheld; it was all happening too fast for him. Though he was older, should have known better. But there was Jeannette saying, "Please make love to me? You don't have to love me." So childlike in pleading, her voice slurred by wine. McBride kissed her eyelids and told her she was beautiful but did not make love to her precisely, nor would he. Jeannette said, "It's enough for me to love you, you don't have to love me, I promise!" McBride said, "Well, maybe." They were lying together perspiring and short of breath partly undressed on McBride's bed. How dizzy, and how happy! How strange to Jeannette that she should feel, in a stranger's arms, such extraordinary happiness, such buoyant happiness she took to be love. And she might utter his full, remarkable name now: *Michael McBride.*

In this place unknown to her, a room darkened except where moonlight slyly entered an unshaded window.

When Jeannette awoke, wine groggy, it was much later, yet still dark; by the faintly glimmering undersea-green numerals of a bedside clock she saw it was 6:15 A.M. Where was she, and what had she done! She eased herself from the partly undressed heavily sleeping man, crept silently into another room, where a single light still burned—there was her parka, there her mittens, her boots. On a coffee table cluttered with newspapers, magazines, books—two bottles of wine, one empty and one part-filled. *What have I done, what will happen now!*

In a bathroom mirror she examined her flushed, slightly swollen face, her vein-reddened eyes. She filled a basin and lowered her burning face to it, water cold as she could bear.

Leaving his apartment, by stealth leaving the red brick apartment complex she'd known, in fact, was his, though had never before approached. How had she been so reckless! so shameless! *"Weil du vom Tod erstanden bist, werd ich im Grab nicht bleiben"* she was singing under her breath, there was McBride's habit of singing, whistling to himself, even if she never saw him again, never would she forget him, his kindness to her, and the intimacy between them—*"Dein letztes Wort mein Auffahrt ist!"*

And now she was approaching the gorge. Out of which vertical vapor clouds were lifting, of the shape of icicles, dreamlike and silent. No one was in sight, it was just dawn. A somber dawn that more resembled dusk. Jeannette paused before stepping onto the footbridge—was there anyone on the other side, waiting? Through her life after this morning she would recall how, returning to the residence, to her mother, she had no idea of what she would say to the woman, nor even of how she would present herself: a daughter who had committed an unspeakable betrayal against her mother, a daughter who had simply done as she'd pleased, and not an ounce of guilt? She crossed the footbridge without daring to look down, and on the other side began to run, all the way up the hill to South Street and to the gray, shingled wood frame house that was Briarly Cottage, where, with dream-logic, there stood Mrs. Harth in the street by the lead-colored Dodge, seemingly waiting for her. The car's motor was running, poisonous pale smoke billowed from the exhaust. And there, Mrs. Harth in her creamy flared cloth coat with the hastily tied sash, the gauzy scarf tied tight about her head. Waiting for Jeannette, for how long? She must have been sitting in the car, the motor running, and seeing Jeannette approach she'd climbed out, calling to her before she was well within earshot, "Get here! Get in this car! At once! We're leaving!"

Jeannette balked, stopping dead on the walk.

It was now dawn, faint bruised-red cloud strata in the eastern sky, by quick degrees lightening, though very cold. Jeannette saw her mother's mouth working angrily and her breath in steamy puffs that looked angry, too. "Jeannette, come here! Get in this car! How could you! Dirty, filthy girl! Get here, get *in*. I'm taking you *away.*"

Jeannette shook her head. "Mother, no."

Mrs. Harth said contemptuously, "'No'?—how dare you! *I'm* your mother, I say get *in."*

Jeannette had approached, like a cautious child, or a dog, to about ten feet of the Dodge, whose chassis vibrated and shuddered as if in disbelief; she would come no closer, in terror that her mother might rush at her, grab her. How weakly she might yield, as she'd done long ago, if those talon-fingers seized her! Mrs. Harth's sunken eyes glared, her mouth worked. "Get *in!* I'm telling you—get *in!* I'm taking you away!"

Jeannette hid her eyes, banishing the sight. Yet: I *will see her, I will hear her, all my life.*

Had anyone heard her mother's cries, was anyone watching from the windows of the cottage, or from other houses on the block?—would word of this be passed on, among Jeannette Harth's friends, and those who hardly knew her at all? Would *he* hear, eventually?—or would she tell him herself, eventually?

Jeannette stood mute and stubborn, shaking her head *no, no, no,* until finally, Mrs. Harth climbed into the car and slammed the door behind her and in a paroxysm of fury, tires spinning and sliding on the icy street, drove off: downhill on South Street, spewing exhaust, a right turn at the bottom of the hill, past a row of parked cars, within the space of twenty seconds, so quickly!—out of sight.

Thomas Glave

Thomas Glave was born in a predominantly Caribbean and African-American Bronx neighborhood, being raised in Baychester, New York, and in Kingston, Jamaica. He graduated with honors in English and Latin American Studies from Bowdoin College in 1993. Glave went on to receive his M.F.A. from Brown University in 1998. In his second year at Brown, Glave published two stories, "The Final Inning" and "Their Story," in *The Kenyon Review*. "The Final Inning" went on to win a 1997 O. Henry Award, making Glave only the second gay African-American writer to win the award since novelist James Baldwin. He traveled as a Fulbright Scholar in 1998–99 to Jamaica, where he studied Jamaican historiography and Jamaican/Caribbean intellectual and literary traditions and helped found the Jamaica Forum of Lesbians, All-Sexuals, and Gays (J-FLAG). His first collection of fiction, *Whose Song? And Other Stories* came out in 2000 to critical acclaim. Glave has taught at Brown University, Naropa, Cleveland State Universities, and the University of Virginia, and is presently an assistant professor of English and Africana Studies at the State University of New York, Binghamton. "The Final Inning" appeared in *The Kenyon Review* in 1996.

The Final Inning *(1996)*

by Thomas Glave

And whether or not Duane had really made a beautiful or no *fly* corpse or not
with all of his fingernails and fierce teeth intact beneath the lid of that closed
coffin, and why the fuck his mother had just had to wear that shitcolored
crushed-velvet or whatever it was tacky suit (to match her just-as-tacky
crushed-velvet also shitcolored hat with that old cheap-looking Saint
Patrick's–green fake daffodil on it), and if it was true that Uncle Brandon
McCoy had made a goddamned fool out of himself again by crying like a big
old droopingass baby in front of all those people instead of acting like a
grown (old broken-down) man should even in the midst of all that grief for
the fallen brother, and what it was exactly somebody had said to the minister
(Reverend Dr. Smalls, old pompous fire-and-brimstone drunkass) about
going on and eating up all the (greasy-nasty, Cee-Cee had said) fried chicken
so that there wasn't even a decent leg left for nobody, not for *nobody*,
honey—when it was all over and they were all over it and just dying to get
home and take off heels and pantyhose and loosen up bra straps and what not,
those things, they all agreed, weren't even really the issues: by then they just
wanted to leave it all behind (especially what had happened in the church)
and get back to where they were now, which was back in Tamara's house in
that most northeastern (and inaccessible, the black people who lived there
cursed and praised) Bronx neighborhood, Sound Hill; in her living room,
with the heat on because it had gotten even colder, hadn't it, she said, and the
television on too because it always was and like always now was showing
some dumbass sitcom about two high-yellow girls as usual who couldn't even
keep their trashy-looking hair straight, do you believe the shit they were putting on TV these days, Jacquie said, but it couldn't get no worse than that
other show about that black family that was all doctors and what not, Cee-
Cee said, cause I ain't never seen nobody like that acting like all we got is fly
furniture and no problems, did you?—Nicky said; and all of them, even
Jacquie's husband Gregory sitting off real quiet in the corner with two-year-
old Gregory Jr. asleep on his knee and the *Sports Illustrated* open on the side
table in front of him, said they hadn't, and laughed. Laughter out of and into
sound and pulse as sharp or strained as anything else they might be feeling
or making out and maybe even that one-half of one percent better.

The sad occasion had been over, more or less, for a few hours—ever
since they'd all laid Duane away in the hard late-autumn earth of Saint

Raymond's out by Whitestone, beneath the watchful distrusting eyes of the fastidious-when-it-came-to-Negroes groundskeeping Italians (most of whom felt they themselves had pushed *this far* and even farther into the merciful hands of the Virgin in order to escape those colored hands stretched out today in grief and unbelieving fury to the hardedged sky—would the colored people even want heaven, too, now that they'd taken over everything else?). The main after-burial get-together was still going on at Miss Geneva Mack's—in the Valley, near the church used by some Sound Hill people, where the service had taken place—but after a few too many minutes of gossip that didn't interest anybody, kids who *weren't* cute, if only you knew, Ma'am, and just about enough senior citizen smalltalk of Mylanta and bloodclots and how it would come to us all someday and Lord, what a tragedy it was that such a fine young man had met the Savior so early but he sure had gone on up to Him with a beautiful-looking coffin, praise Jesus!—the five of them plus Gregory Jr. had piled easily enough again into Gregory Sr.'s car the same way they had on the way to the church. A little respite was in order now that they had done with the Saint Raymond's part of it that everybody hated but for decency's sake couldn't miss, since all present had wanted to appear duly respectful, you know, the way you should for someone like Duane whom almost everyone had loved in spite of *that* (yes, *that*, but still, you had to have some feeling for the dead, didn't you?). Last regards had been paid at the cemetery to Duane's mother and stepfather (still in a severe state of shock after what had happened); Cee-Cee and Nicky and Tamara had finally been pulled away from chatting with the Reverend, who had proved inconsolable despite his drunkenness: it wasn't none of it his fault, what had happened in church, he shouldn't even worry about it, they'd said, although everyone knew that if the old alcoholic nigger had put the whiskey *behind* his shelf instead of all out front *on* it for a change none of the disgraceful shit today would have happened. Now, back in Sound Hill, they were all tired and cold and disgusted and just flat out, that was all. Tamara had put on the lima beans, Cee-Cee was helping with the rice, and Jacquie was trying to season the meat in that kitchen that was looking more nasty to her today than ever before because (yes, Tamara was her friend, but, well, speak the truth before God, girl, she thought) she had seen not one but two roaches about which she would be sure to tell Gregory later. But then petty shit like that didn't matter so much now after such a sad occasion, with everybody talking and the TV blaring and the 40s of Olde English out on the living-room table and Tamara looking for her house shoes and her husband Kevin still not back with their kids Jaycee and Cassandra from Mrs. Shirley's: watching football with Mrs. Shirley's Harry after the funeral, now wasn't that some shit? she said; all the others except Gregory sucked their teeth and shook their heads. The house was still too damn cold, right down there on the Sound, after all, but the principal shit was Duane and *those others too,* still on everybody's mind after what had happened.

"Cause, girl," Tamara was saying to any one of them except Gregory, popping a halfcooked lima bean into her mouth and spitting out the skin, which she never ate, into the sink, "Lemme tell you. I ain't never think I'd live to see no shit like that. You know—"

"Word. You!" Cee-Cee said, pushing Jacquie out of the way to stand in a corner over the rice. The best corner, in fact, for affecting officiousness while nudging surreptitiously out from her behind the underwear that insisted on catching up in it beneath the folds of that stiff mourning dress she hardly ever wore.

"A damn shame. That's all that was," she said and lifted the lid off the rice pot to stir the water.

"What was?" Jacquie said, swaying to nobody's rhythm. "Why you holding your face over the pot, Cee-Cee? You think we want your makeup all in the rice?"

"Bitch, don't try it. You the one"—she replaced the lid on the pot and managed easily enough to rub her backside against the stove-door handle and there, she was free again—"you the one put on so much damn makeup couldn't nobody see that pimple on your chin you so de*ter*mined to try and hide—"

"Who you calling a bitch? Me and your grandmother."

"Your funky ass. Don't be talking bout my grandmother. She could—"

"Now what y'all fussing about? Tamara, this food is not even ready." Nicky strolled into the kitchen on long legs not quite hidden beneath the most elegant-looking black wool pantsuit all of them had ever seen and would have done more than kill to have. She had already had some of the Olde English, finally had found her cigarettes, and now with the contentment of the smooth dark cat that always lolled somewhere in the marshy fields of her eyes slowly began to pull in sweet soft drags of a Newport.

"I forgot his name already," Jacquie said. "After he got up there and dissed everybody I wouldn't even want to—"

"Dissed? That's what you gone call it? *Dissed?*" Cee-Cee stretched out three fingers toward Nicky's cigarette in a gimme-one gesture. "That shit wasn't even about no dissing. That was just goddamn disrespecting blasphemy, that's all. I wish it hada been me sittin up there with Duane's mother. I woulda knocked the shit outa him first and put a foot in his ass second."

"OK."

"Y'all come on and sit in the living room," Tamara said, wiping her hands on the curtains over the kitchen window. "One thing I can't stand is sittin up in the kitchen talking bout dead people while food be on the stove." And I can't stand Nicky with her nasty self puttin no damn cigarette ashes in my sink neither, she thought but didn't say either as she pulled one more lima bean out of the pot and this time pulled the skin off her tongue before she flicked it off into the sink.

"Y'all still going on about what happened in the church?" Gregory said, looking up from the *Sports Illustrated* and over the head of his sleeping son just long enough to give Jacquie an appreciative glance before he returned to a photograph in the magazine that had caught his eye. The look was returned with another, deeper one, which could have passed between them comfortably enough then as only one edging of that almost unbearable love she possessed not only for the man whose gaze mirrored the silent ponderings and longings of her own (and whose lashes, like those arcing hummingbirds they yearned to become in dreams, nightly fluttered over the comforts her body offered that the dreams did not) but also for their child spread in smallish sleep across her husband's broad thighs. The child did not yet bear Gregory's unmistakably solitary look, which to her eyes had always spoken either of too many winding rivers already walked by the soul or the hands' constant reaching for what the ten fingers could not provide. Any or all of it might have worried or pleased her at the same time; speculations aside, they missed the look she gave him just then. Like so many others who knew them, distinct but distrusted, only occasionally acknowledged other versions of themselves, they rarely looked far enough into those interiors that were both theirs and hers, the here-and-always silty brew and the joy, the source of which none of them (through choice or necessity or the simple desire for safety, however they imagined it) had ever plumbed, had ever wanted to plumb. Their attention for the moment was anyway, as almost always, scattered: between the TV (they turned it off, they wanted music, it would go better with the Olde English) and Cee-Cee's *Don't be mean girl, I gave you five cigarettes last week to Nicky's I know you did cause I gave you six the week before so now I guess you could go out and get you a pack,* but then finally handing one over as the marshes wavered to stillness-accord in her eyes (Cee-Cee didn't never buy no cigarettes but still that was one of her main home girls), and Tamara putting on some Aretha and doing a jerky, rhythmless "white girl" dance to the first song that made them all laugh again, none of them had time to notice the new little things like that distant ticking sound in Gregory's voice when he spoke, or how hard up tighttight his right hand was gripping his little boy's small soft baby-shoulder.

"Lemme take him, Greg," Jacquie said. "I need to put his ass in the bed."

"You could put him right upstairs, girl," Tamara said. "Ooh, I love this song!"

"He all right. I got him," Gregory said, shifting thighs.

"Anyway, like I was saying," Cee-Cee said, exhaling a cloud of smoke and rolling her head back to rest it on the back of the couch where the three of them sat across from Gregory—Tamara was dancing—"I ain't never seen no shit like that neither. All in the church! And you know Duane's mother was through."

"Not just his mother," Jacquie said. "You ain't see Mr. Jackson?"

"I did," Tamara said.

"We *all* did, honey," Cee-Cee said. (The cigarette was sweet, the smoke was floating over her tongue, and *Breathe it in,* she thought, just like:) "—that old man got up and started *screaming,* honey. 'You will not say these things about my son! You will leave this church now! Get out of God's house!' *Honey.. .?"* She raised her head and looked out at them with both arms stretched out along the sofa back—the easy, lazy stance they all associated with her.

"I thought I was gone fall out myself," she said.

"We all was," Tamara said, shaking on to the chorus. "How could you not? I mean, now, that was wrong—"

"Damn right."

"—it was, you know? I mean now how you gone sit up in church at somebody's goddamn funeral and bring out all kindsa shit—"

"That probably ain't even true," Jacquie said.

"Well, I don't know bout all that. But I'm saying how you gone get up there and do that shit when ain't nobody even want your white-lookin ass up there in the first place?"

"He wasn't white," Gregory said. "The dude that got up and spoke? He wasn't no white. But I wish y'all would stop—"

"Looked white to me," Cee-Cee said, chugging.

"Aw, girl, he did not. You gone sit there black as me and tell me you can't tell a—a half-breed when you see one? Come *on,"* Tamara said. She came and sat down on the floor next to Jacquie and looked up briefly at Nicky, who the entire time had remained silent and still behind the marshes, on her second glass.

"Hmmph. Half-breed. Somebody's business." Cee-Cee pronounced the words with particular contempt, as if describing someone who habitually shit on the only good side of his mother's bed. "See…that's why. Breeding, honey. Wouldn't no real black person do some shit like that."

"I don't know," Jacquie said. "A whole bunch of them stood up when he asked everybody to stand."

"Yeah," Tamara said. "The faggots did."

"Well, they was all faggots."

"Like I said," Cee-Cee came in again, "wouldn't no *real* black…"

"On *that* side of the church," Tamara said. "In the back, thank God. All sittin in a group. You see that shit?"

"You know we did," Cee-Cee said, putting out the cigarette.

"Faggots and bulldaggers. Ain't that some shit? With their hair all shaved off and zigzagged and earrings and nose rings—"

"Nasty. Probably all boggered up."

"That's how that shit spreads," Cee-Cee said.

"Girl…"

"—and *car*rying on—"

"Why y'all gotta keep talking about it?" Gregory said, shifting again and fastening his grip on his son and again staring down and out at that something anything not there but there.

"Why not? A goddamn freak show," Cee-Cee said, leaning forward. She snatched another cigarette out of Nicky's pack on the table, lit it that fast, and exhaled two river-colored smoke streams from angry nostrils.

"Why the fuck not?" she asked again, turning to Gregory and then away and over to Tamara stretching her legs out on the rug. Now it was her turn for the Olde English. Aretha was crooning out that very oldie *Who's Zoomin Who?* and Tamara's lips were there with her and her hips too, lacking the grace but filled with the intent.

"It wasn't all that, Cee-Cee. You got a real problem when it comes to…" It was the first time Nicky had spoken since they had left the kitchen. The marshes in her eyes had filled with the afternoon light of that other place quite clearly known only to her: the heavy sunset color of drowned fields descending beneath those lashes, a small space of enclosed time hours, even light-years, beyond the chilly Sound Hill late afternoon.

"It wasn't even all that," she said.

"What you mean?" Cee-Cee said.

"I *mean,* you got a problem."

"What kinda problem?"

All eyes in the room drove toward the marshes and stopped there.

"I mean…like, you…you don't like them."

"Them who?"

"You…well…umh…homos." (But oh no, now, she thought, she could be stronger than that with the Olde English, she thought, braver and maybe even—)

"Gay people," she said.

"Well—" Cee-Cee was facing the marshes directly. They were deeper than they had ever appeared before. They had in fact, without warning or comfort, given way to that untracked country which, even for those who thought (or had dared to think) they had always known the easiest way in— that simple road, the things you said or didn't, the half-smiles and the sliding glances, right?—confounded even the most scrupulous eye on the way back out into the farther brown that signaled both the marshes' end and the deeper waters' beginning.

"Well, no, I guess I don't—" (but it was all getting in her way, all around. Was that why her own voice suddenly sounded so—? And what was there just beyond those marsh-reeds pulling her out into—? The quick chill before that unknown whatever, nothing else and nothing noble, either, hurled her back onto firmer ground) "—like no fucking faggots, girlfriend. Not up in no damn church. Not all up in somebody's goddamn funeral. Not calling nobody out when…—you acting like there's something to like. You gone sit up there in this house in Sound Hill with Duane dead and buried over in Saint Raymond's and his mother and Mr. Jackson over in Co-Op—"

"I know where we at."

"Ooh, yeah, Cee-Cee, Nicky *knows* where she at," Jacquie said and poked Nicky in the ribs, cause why we gotta go into all this now? she thought, feeling suddenly the surge of an unwelcome river rising up around their feet—it might have been the strangeness of panic, or anything else which had the all-knowing eyes of recognition but no comforting or settled-in name. The other woman smiled and slapped away her hand but they all knew that meant nothing. "Y'all know Miss Nicky ain't got just one but *two* men up on Gun Hill Road..."

"You stinking ho," Nicky said, almost laughing. "Liar!"

"—one name Billy and the other this Puerto Rican dude who ain't got shit in his pants to satisfy nobody—you know them Ricans just swear they all that"—they were all laughing easily enough now and the two were half-wrestling where they sat until Nicky let out a scream of half-real enough-now as Jacquie pulled at the weave that had cost eighty-five dollars at Jonay's up on White Plains Road and which, even in play, she wasn't about to have any-body mess up after the rain that afternoon had almost reclaimed it for free.

"Liar. Liar." (Straightening up and straightening out the hair, and Jacquie smiling in a relief wide enough for all: the river had returned to its proper place, wouldn't rise up and...). "You one ho and a half, honey. You gone go and bring in all you *think* you know about my business—"

"You said it wasn't true. Don't want nobody to talk about your business, baby? Don't have none then."

"Like you."

"May-be," Cee-Cee came in again. "But I'ma tell y'all one thing. When I die ain't *nobody*"—she leaned forward suddenly, the lioness in her jaw—"ain't nobody gonna drag my shit all out in the street in no church. You know what I mean?"

"Not like how they did Duane, you mean," Nicky said. "Poor old Duane," she said, more quietly.

"Word! And you know"—Cee-Cee lowered her voice to the confidential tone—"I got to say, when he got up there and started to speak I got scared. I'm telling y'all, I thought I was gonna pee on my dress."

"Wouldn't be the first time," Jacquie said.

"Shut up."

"What you was scared of? That one of em was gone jump up and bite you?" Nicky snorted.

"On the titties, probably," Jacquie said and laughed over in Gregory's direction. He returned a weak smile. "So put on some Luther 'ready, Tamara. I don't want to hear no more 'retha's old fat ass."

"I was just gone do that."

"I knew they wasn't gone *bite* me." Cee-Cee was going on. But I'm say-ing—I'm saying—"

"You thought Duane's mother was gone get up there and smack the shit outa him," Jacquie helped.

"Exactly. You said it!"

"Well, she didn't."

"Nope. Just sat there screaming and crying."

"So did everybody else," Tamara said.

"Why y'all gotta keep going on and on about this damn funeral?" Gregory put in again. "I just can't stand—"

"Aw, shut up. Your own Aunt Hattie almost had a damn heart attack."

"That's cause she ain't used to people talking about—talking about—"

"Faggots," Tamara helped this time. Luther's croons did not quite cover Nicky's and Gregory's flinches.

"Faggots." He heard the word—

(—but it had flown up against his cheek where he sat almost but not quite motionless holding his son: holding him *faggots* and caressing him the word searing his flesh and thinking)

(:—again? thinking but didn't want to now oh no but yes of those places, parks: alleyways: redlit (bloodlit) bars: fuckrooms/darkrooms and those piss-streets too he knew had known and: but no. Hadn't been him there. Had never been him among the ghosts and the searchers and the lonelyones, walking: looking: stroking and sliding, taking in: going in *now give it to me tight tight-tight;—never* him back there but somebody else one of the ghosts: :a spirit: :a dream or someotherbody fucking else in the moment and moments there *lonely and* so he? the someotherbody sucking a pair of thighs or a bootstrap with lace so that he?—had wanted *remember aw shit now* to go down to that part the belly or the *aw yes* and travel it, Jesus: hold it or him the whole thing body and go to the feeling, Jesus: kissing and stroking and holding and take it and *aw fuck Jesus yes* and ***:—*faggots* but naw don't be calling them that now naw but OK *sucker* and *punk* call them that: wandering again on those streets with the the the: *Faggots*. He. Who had been unhappy and. Had wanted to wander, kiss manflesh. Find. Jacquie *but then can't tell Jacquie.*—wandering again and *he'd been so scared!* because yup one time he had kinda sorta without words told Duane about all of it, everything, parks; bathrooms; movies and the: —Duane who had understood kind of, Duane like a brother down homie who wouldn't never say nothing to nobody, DuaneDuane dead now and:—so now? he being Gregory who could? or couldn't go on with this kinda shit much more Jacquie could? or couldn't lie much longer Jacquie or keep on pretending to want to be with her *like that* when no he didn't really want to and honest to God one time thinking about Duane and *notsafe* and at the funeral shit-scared cause maybe one of them would have *known* or thought maybe could tell? he Gregory was a little *that way*, was close to them. Close to them, living as he did up there in Co-Op City nearby Sound Hill and Baychester and Gun Hill with a family but who still no goddamnit fuck it all would not couldn't ever stick up for their faggot asses nor get into it when the homies was beating up on them; would not (couldn't) claim his hidden name among them and the shared desire, anger, simply to be allowed to live and be: not near his family, he thought; not with them, he thought. Holding his little baby boy. Jacquie nearby. Not with them. Never.)

"You see what I mean?" Jacquie was saying. "You could talk to the nigger 'til you dead in the face and he just go right on acting like he don't hear nobody." Her tone was the betty's outer crust firm to the touch but almost all of them knew where the goodfilling sweet lay beneath it.

"He just sad, that's all," Cee-Cee said.

"No, he ain't sad, he sorry. Greg, answer Tamara. Did you know Duane was funny?"

"What?"

"Did you know Duane was a faggot, Greg?" Tamara asked him herself. "Cause—I swear to God, y'all, I ain't know 'til now. To*day*. You hear me?"

"Might not be true," Jacquie said.

"Oh, girl, it's true." Cee-Cee said, "And Tamara, you knew. No, don't open up your face to say nothing, girl! How you gone sit up there and say you ain't know when you living right here and Duane and his mother and Mr. Jackson used to come over here almost every week for Friday dinner—"

"Used to."

"Used to, could've, was gonna—but they did, right?—and you *used to* go with em up to Holy Rosary Church on Sunday and then y'all would come back here and hang out and what not—don't tell me, girl, I know!—and him sittin up in here at your table switching his ass round the house helping you *dec*orate and shit and watching him swing them earrings and carrying on talking bout going down to D.C. for some march and shit and all a that and you gone sit up here and tell me you ain't know? Come *on*, now. You woulda been blind if you didn't."

"Word," Jacquie said. "She got a point, T. Plus—"

"—Or stupid." Cee-Cee was not through. "I know you ain't stupid and you ain't blind neither so how the fuck you gone sit up here and say you ain't know?"

"Well…dag, Cee-Cee. He ain't never *told* me."

"That was one fine-ass nigger, too, girl," Jacquie said, glancing over at Gregory, but that was all right—he was staring out the window. Another light rain had begun to fall. "And had some body on him," she added in a lower voice.

"I know. He ain't never *tell* nobody. But—"

"That's a lie, Cee-Cee. He told me," Nicky broke in.

"Told *you*? When?"

(Yes, he thought, the God's honest truth, he had told her, Nicky, but why? did you have to tell her or anybody up here Duane? why? couldn't you keep it downtown with all them downtown faggots (—:don't call them that:—) that came up to the funeral? why?)

(—But had *had* to, Duane had said: they were all his family and friends, weren't they? Had always loved him (they said), would always care for him (they said), wouldn't they? Hadn't become like whities who dissed their own at the drop of a hat, had they? Ooh but they didn't want nobody to know you had it, Duane. When they heard you had it said Yup serves his ass right cause you *know* he got it from hanging out with them nasty old white boys Village faggots downtown too much and: that's why you was *funny* they said: even now they won't stop talking about it and Nicky was saying)

"Yes, he did. Said he thought his mother mighta said something. Yes, he did. Coupla months ago. Oh yes he did."

"You lying!" Tamara said.

"Girl, you ever see me up in here lying?"

"His *mother*? Ain't that some shit? I ain't even know she knew!"

"Hell yeah she knew." Nicky turned the marshes toward her cigarettes, lit one, and sat back, closing her eyes for a moment. The Olde English had begun to feel reckless in her veins, as it had in everybody's.

"She just didn't want to say nothing, that's all," she said.

"Um-hmm. But see—I'm sorry—I can't blame her," Tamara said.

"I can."

"What you mean?" Cee-Cee said. Luther was still singing.

The marshes opened again and turned—flickered, ever so slightly— toward Gregory. They were black as the night now descending, revealing only the shape of small scurrying things before the moon's glide.

"Because"—(her voice soft as the marsh-darkness he didn't turn his head to see, shimmying out toward him as if seeking a partner for that step-and-feint they might both have recognized on some other night—the most elusive, most interlocking dance of all) "—because, y'all...—they was gone bury him with—with a *lie*. Can you imagine?"

"Imagine what, girl?" Tamara said.

"She buggin," Cee-Cee said—but she was sitting very still.

"Naw, I ain't buggin. I know just what I'm saying. It's like—he lived his whole life—…see, y'all don't know, y'all didn't know Duane the way I knew him."

For the first time Gregory turned toward the marshes and felt their sweep of memory and night-knowledge shawl down over him through the silence. Luther sang no more.

"—the way he used to talk about how hard it was being so—outside the family and everything—"

"What you mean?" The new anxiety in Cee-Cee's voice could have built easily enough to agony someplace else: the simple shame of crucial words unspoken, the fearlatch left undone. He heard with them and knew—or thought he knew.

"What you saying, Nicky?" Cee-Cee went on and was leaning forward, almost on her feet. "He wasn't outside the family. All them people—his mother and Mr. Jackson and his Aunt Gracie and Sheila—that girl that got pregnant with Marcus—"

"She did? Get outa here."

"—they all loved him," Cee-Cee would not stop. "How you gone say he was outside the family when you saw the way everybody was crying and carrying on when they brought him in? Does that sound like somebody outside the family to you? Does it, Tamara?"

Tamara remained silent, a headshake saying neither yes nor no.

"Does it, Greg?"

(—holding his son verytight on his lap, tighttight like back in the church, and sitting; staring; at that very too-shiny coffin; he, sitting there senseless, staring but not believing (no!) that what had been Duane was *in there* ninety pounds lighter than what Duane had used to be: that ain't even you in there, he had thought, O my God: not even no you with all them purple marks on your face (:the coffin had been closed:) and your hands with them purple marks on them and up on your chest too O my God Duane even on your eyes and in your mouth and you skinny like a damn rail with your hair all funny too (chemotherapy, radiation, drugs: had made what had been hair into— *that*?) O my God Duane: remembering and holding still on his lap tighttight his son not even you *wasn't even no you* he had thought

—Jacquie's shoulder pressed tight into him but she wouldn't cry, he'd thought, she wasn't no crying type: knowing he would much later. Yes, God. With his face pressed into that warm hot full space between her breasts, sobbing like a damn baby: that wasn't no Duane, he had half-wept silently at the cemetery into her softwarm body, Duane didn't die he didn't, just like

Duane's mother screaming MY BABY MY BABY in the church and carry-ing on with all them others screaming *No, Jesus* to Jesus who didn't never listen. All of them sitting up and frozen, hands flying up to heaven when it had happened. The faggot...

"—got up outa his place, honey," Tamara was saying.

(—his *place* in the back where all of them had been asked or no, told) to sit and who invited them anyway? Jacquie had asked him later but he couldn't answer that: wondering if the *I don't know* in his eyes behind the grief and the pain and so much else she didn't have no idea about had been good enough for her:—but then it was like the faggot who had been crying with the rest of them had looked dead straight at him Gregory sitting there holding his son on his lap next to that strong-looking serious woman Jacquie his wife and Gregory Jr.'s mother: had been as if the faggot had recognized something or maybe had Duane told him something about the men, Duane, about the blackmen and the brownmen and the whitemen who had done him, Gregory, shared fuckheat and wanting-someone-for-whatever-heat in all them dark places (:holding his son tight, tighttight   Don't hold me so tight, Daddy, Greggie Jr. had cried out over the cries of the women with the sound of that light autumn rain falling over the church:)—had the faggot walking up there to the pulpit seen that in his eyes? the wanting and the searching and the? seen it? and gone on to push aside the minister and in his black leather jacket and jeans and boots wearing goddamn Lord Jesus not one ear-ring but four and looking out at him and everybody past the minister who began to shout Sit down boy this is a funeral where you think you at as he the faggot began to say   )

"'You're killing us! With this silence! You won't stop, you keep on killing us!'" Tamara said, almost laughing, imitating—

(—just like that he thought, seeing it yet again, still holding his son tight-tight: the one they had called a halfbreed, lightskinned, who even talked white like them trying-to-be-white downtown niggers on the West Side and the East Side and in the Village, that one: starting to shout from the pulpit with his back turned to the choir and all eyes looking at him in had it been disbelief disgust? hate? or the rage of *We oughta kill that fucking faggot right now. Kill his motherfucking faggot ass. Outside the church or in it. Right here. Anywhere.* Or had those downturned mouths and pressed lips finally been feeling with the outrage and hatredscorn that more unavoidable discharge of loss: the need to spew out with the screams and shouts what the hands and heart couldn't contain, the eyes not witness and live: that their very same adored Duane Taylor Clayton Ross was laying up there with his hands you couldn't see folded over his chest all hidden beneath the wood and flowers and his mother and stepfather screaming over him and screaming even more when the faggot began to shout and you could see them everybody going from one to the other)

the faggot remember (:don't call him that:)	*the others: everybody*
and my name *(then louder)* my name is JAMES MITCHELL SCROG GINS and no you won't make me SHUT UP cause I'm PROUD to be here today as a GAY friend of DUANE'S and a *(shouting over the rage)* HUMAN BEING GODDAMNIT just like DUANE WAS TOO and now why won't you SAY IT he died of AIDS of AIDS *(Lord God the screaming (remember how their eyes looked everybody shouting* SIT DOWN WHERE YOU THINK YOU AT SIT DOWN) say it AIDS we all KNOW IT because I know some of you know I HAVE THIS DISEASE TOO and I took care of him so I know many of you KNOW ME and what you're doing today is WRONG WRONG Duane wasn't ASHAMED of it either but all of you people YOU'RE KILLING US you won't STOP you keep right on KILLING US like you didn't even want us to come today to SAY GOOD-BYE to our friend our LOVER and then we came but you	They: thinking: everybody yes with hands up in the air over hats and balding heads: hands fluttering to the top of the church and O my God Lord Sweet Jesus what is happening God who is this boy standing up there where's the minister well why don't you stop him what kinda going on is that and (faggot shit: growls: sissy shit: abomination: growls) O Jesus Jesus Jesus! No my son ain't no homosexual no my cousin ain't no faggot no my nephew didn't have no damn AIDS the devil's disease don't you say that in this church and O you you filthy:—and the screaming and the children Mommy who's that man and look: O God Almighty the women the ladies crying and the men their nostrils flaring and saying muttering growling We should kick his motherfucking mulatto-looking ass and getting ready to do it too: but then you could see some people thinking from what you could see in their eyes the way their heads nodded soft and slow and the ladies' dark eyes so dark revealing

made us wait out in the COLD RAIN and then SIT WAY IN THE BACK BACK OF THE CHURCH: how can you KEEP ON DOING THIS: when is it going to STOP: now how can you bury him and say you LOVE HIM and not say one word about how HE LOVED OTHER MEN he loved all of us and WE LOVED HIM Yes he had AIDS it KILLED HIM we us here now we should SAY IT SAY IT you're trying to IN him I'm bringing him OUT again for God's sake please I'm asking you for once won't you just SAY IT SAY IT

The faggot continuing Jesus

:—I want all of you now who were proud of Duane as a proud out open GAY MAN to stand up WITH ME STAND for a moment of silence STAND

He had said
Stand
(the last inning   the inning was over)

that way showing so much so little under those tacky hats their eyes saying only in part You speak the truth up there boy but O God O Jesus but still you speak it all the same because it's all true all of it: under three hats three ladies in particular nodding Yeah we sure do know how he died but ain't nobody saying nothing cept "a long illness" and that boy is right rightright: could even be my grandson my godson or: but something and no it can't keep going on because He the One knows don't He: knows the truth about all of it and if we sitting right here with the dead boy's mama and can't even speak the truth now so damn late in the day when are we ever gone speak it and now just think think about it what in the hell kinda going on is that?

"Yes, he did, honey," Tamara was saying—and every face there was attendant, looking or unwilling to look into that slow yet sudden shock of memory. "Asked us all to stand *up*. In the church. 'Which one a y'all *proud* a him? Stand up!'"

(—and everybody back there in pain, he thought. Crying. Eyes closed. Hurt by the truth. The *truth* truth. Couldn't take it. Not about nobody like you Duane. They all could take the truth about everything else but: about knocked-up teenagers, crackhead sons, numbers-running uncles, raped nieces, drive-by shootings, mixed-race marriages, retarded cousins, rat-filled projects, shitbigoted Koreans, pigfaced skinheads, African famines, Chinese massacres, psycho Jamaicans, right-wing terrorists, sellout nigger judges, even white-trash serial killers: but not about nobody they cared about supposed to be black and strong like you was Duane but with that faggot shit: what to them was whitefolks shit, another sick nasty fuckedup white thing like that nasty old AIDS, just like nasty whitefolks, not for no black man we know and Jesus have mercy Jesus don't want to talk about it never. Not to kiss another man, rock to slow dreams between his hips. Lay across his dusky thighs, smell his dusk, his musky parts in the hands; a palm to those musk-dusky parts moistened by the mouth. Not to love nor touch nor hold nor look him in the face and *see.* Never. Not one of our own. Not in the church. Too many rivers to cross. And specially not one a *them* telling your business about how he *loved* you and how you had *it* and how Jesus Savior he *had it* too. Couldn't take it. *I* couldn't take it, Duane. Can't.)

"I can't neither, Tamara," Jacquie was saying—a hint of that something of outrage or shame clouding into the same storm in all their eyes that was now descending not as cool easing rain but as that same old and loathsome bitter ash, weed: what would linger there long after the storm's eye and the parched brown field always beneath it, always so untended, had gone. It was there, from within those separate and gathered storms and the ash, that they sensed what she, out of that silence, suddenly knew—that he whom she loved, still holding on his broad lap their son, was (but for how long? and why?) in flight heavy with purpose and sadness away from her—from all of them.

(—because the faggot had wanted to show out, that was all, he thought: say No, *This* was Duane who died a *that thing.* That thing he Gregory knew he didn't have. *Did not have it—:)*

"—so then, y'all," Nicky's voice, still soft, full of the evening that had crept down from beneath those lashes, "see, Jimmy went back—"

"Jimmy! Jimmy!" Cee-Cee and Tamara shouted at the same time. "You—you know him?"

"Jimmy. James Mitchell Scroggins. Who got up. Yeah, Jimmy. I know him"—so softly, like music!—and looking straight at him. Penetrating, parting him. His hands on his son. Tighttight.

"How'd *you* know him?" Jacquie asked, moving her feet back. The river was rising again.

The other woman didn't answer. Her eyelids were drooping down. She settled herself back on the sofa. Stretched out her legs again as if the living room had once more become that which it could no longer be—comfortable, that was all, with nothing more than the smell of cooking rice and lima beans drifting in to them from the kitchen.

"I don't think y'all really want to know," she said from the twilight. "Do y'all?"

"Don't play, girl. Say what you got to say."

So alongside or even above their pursuit of something reckless, aloft, she spoke. "He used to be over there all the time," she said, very softly.

"Who? Not—"

"Jimmy. James."

"Over in—"

"Duane's apartment, Jacquie. Right on over there in Co-Op. The same one."

(Hearing the tiredness in her voice, he thought. Thinking as she was of that time of catheters and blood and—)

"He used to go over there, you mean?" It was Cee-Cee again, beginning to grasp the vaguest sense of it except for what was passing in silence between Nicky and the man seated there holding so tighttight his child-son on his lap: understanding even that, maybe, the heavy falls behind the silence cast over what did not fit, what could not ever be imagined to fit, there.

"I guess"—Nicky, sitting up with that startling abruptness they would all later remember; Nicky all at once fierce; the marshes afire, the dry storm ignited, swirled into their midst—"I guess if y'all had gone over there more often y'all woulda seen him. Y'all woulda seen him holding Duane up in his arms like he was a little baby or I don't know what. Kissing up on him even with them purple spots all on his face. Telling him he loved him, he loved him so much and all kindsa shit. Wiping the shit outa his ass—"

(Holding his son. But Jesus don't let her go off on them. Jacquie getting ready to get up and *sit down Jacquie* and Tamara looking like she want to curse somebody out now please Nicky don't say no more girl)

"Nicky." Tamara's voice rang out not-calm-but-calm, crackling the incipient warning ice. "Don't be talking that kinda shit in here, girl. You see we all just come from a funeral and I don't *think—*"

"—and him holding him"—implacable, in the deep river dark now beyond the marshes—"—holding him, Tamara—where you going, Jacquie?"

"You see we got food on the stove, don't you? Kevin and them'll be back soon from—"

"Sit your behind down." More than the hint of a snarl.

"Girl...see, now, I know you must be buggin. This ain't even your damn—"

"Sit down." Leaning forward very far; the eyes very bright; the storm-fire running wild. "Y'all don't want to hear it. We sittin up in here talking bout faggots this and faggots that. Talking shit. Tamara, don't you open up your face to say nothing to me."

"I ain't say shit to you. But I'ma tell you now—"

(Holding him. Verytight. Tighttight).

"You ain't gone tell me nothing. Y'all can't say shit to me cause—word, the whole time Duane was sick I ain't never seen not *one* a y'all up in his house. Not to stop by and visit. Not even to call. So now y'all can sit up in here talking bout faggot so-and-so but when the shit was down y'all couldn't even *visit* the motherfucker. I ain't never seen not *one* a y'all. Not one!"

"Hold on, girl!"

"I don't know who she think she talking to like she crazy. She—"

"You, Cee-Cee." Nicky got up to stand over her. The other woman's angry face didn't turn away from the possible smack it anticipated—if smack were to come, it would be easier to take than that acid-wash of the truth, the little jump-up truths or the greater wordless one, from which it had already turned long ago like the rest of them.

"I'm talking to you. And you, Tamara. And you, Jacquie."

"Don't put me in it."

"In it? You already in it. You don't even know how much you in it." Not looking at him. "You just as bad as everybody else, running your mouth *after* he's dead talking bout his *life*style and carrying on, but word, Jacquie, I ain't never seen your black ass neither when he had to have that old nasty catheter up in his chest. Y'all can talk a whole lotta shit, but what the fuck y'all really know about faggots? You ever kiss one?"

"Nicky!" But too late. Much too late. She had jumped way past what they would have once called their own innocence. It was only then that they saw that, like all those others who inhabited their eyes, she had in fact never been innocent, had never had any use for it, as, differently, they had never been either but did. They couldn't pull her back now, or even—especially—themselves.

"I'm telling y'all now"—swaying over Cee-Cee—"—y'all don't know nothing cause y'all didn't wanna know. I was going up there every day. Oh yes I was. Every damn day and I saw what y'all so busy calling faggots."

Not looking at him. "Taking care a him. Jimmy. Cause didn't nobody else do it. Not even—not even his *mother.*"

"Nicky—"

"Not even that bitch. You know she came by there two days one time and ain't never come back. And Mr. Jackson ain't never come. Guess maybe they couldn't take looking at all them faggots."

"Nicky…"

"Reverend Smalls didn't neither. Miss Cee-Cee, where was you at that whole time?"

(Her power. Fascinating him. Terrifying him. He couldn't speak. Could only stare the way he had stared in church. But now even his face was gone. He had left only a pair of hands to hold on to things, a clenched asshole to relieve the icy lead in his bowels, a pair of legs with which he could run. Runrun away from her voice saying   )

"—so don't say shit, Jacquie, cause I *heard* Duane say—Tamara, don't you walk outa here!"

"I ain't going no place, girl. But you are."

"You damn right. When I get ready. You listen. I heard him say, on his *death*bed, 'Nicky girl, don't let Mama and them tell no lies. They gone try to change it and say I died a something else. I know she gone try cover it up,' he said. And she did. Everybody did, tried to, 'til the one y'all keep calling the faggot, who got a *name,* by the way, in case y'all forgot, his name is Jimmy, James M. Scroggins—"

Tamara had already retrieved Nicky's coat from the hall closet and then that fast (not hardly fast enough, they would say later) was in front of her with it and then—since even that didn't work—thrust it full force into those furious arms and jerked her own head back toward the front door.

"You got five seconds to get outa here," she said.

"Or what? You gone throw me out? Bitch, ain't nobody scared a you. Just cause *your* man fucks every ho up and down the Valley—"

"Get out! Get the fuck out!"—and there would have been a fight then for real if Cee-Cee hadn't sprung up and separated them and with Jacquie's help (who hadn't wanted to go near the crazy bitch, she would say later, but she hadn't been able to stand one more minute of all that goddamned cursing in front of her baby boy and her husband) got her to the front door and out into the dark cold Sound Hill evening with that constant breeze off the Sound more chilly tonight that carried her words down to Noah Harris's and O.K. Griffith's and the Walkers and the Goodmans and God knows even as far away as Pelham Parkway and Baychester: just get that lowclass ugly-mouthed bitch the fuck outa my house, Tamara was screaming, with Gregory Jr. awakened by all the commotion crying Mommy and then Daddy and Jacquie screaming back Shut up at the baby because Nicky had almost punched her in the mouth on the way out, shouting as she went that didn't none of them know what a *real* faggot was or a real man neither since it was what they'd called the faggots who'd kept Duane alive as long as they had, and y'all bunch a bitches was as bad as the worst kinda crackers, and now quiet as y'all wanted to keep it (except there, for so many curious faces had begun to peek out from behind curtains and from over awnings along Sound Hill Avenue) everybody in Sound Hill *and* Baychester *and* the Valley knew Tamara's Kevin had picked up that nasty VD last summer from that old broken-toothed crackhead Jamaican ho up on White Plains Road, and wasn't it true that Cee-Cee's brother Jervis had gotten another one a them Puerto Rican bitches pregnant, cause everybody knew that yellow nigger didn't never date no black girl, and all a that wasn't even the real shit to what she *could* say but she knew at least one person there had loved Duane and anyway she had promised the dead she wouldn't never tell nobody's secret that shouldn't be told—looking back at Gregory once more with a last fire which scorched him to crucible ash on the spot, a moment of fiery intelligence from which he would never, for the rest of his nights and days in and out of that company and others, recover. It was only after they closed the door on all that outrage and pain (and then became aware of their own gliding up the smooth back of their necks, gathering spit at the swallow-point in their throats, bristling on to the ever-so-delicate eyebrow's curve) that they realized that what could serve as distraction-relief and the greatest tragedy of all had actually occurred: the lima beans had burnt black, what had been the rice had scorched, and not two but three enormous roaches had gotten into the meat and ruined it, ruined it, ruined it, Tamara began to cry, her sisters standing all around with their faces hidden within those sudden useless cages of their hands—a flock of fragile birds clustered for safety beneath that lingering storm and every other yet to come, descending.

—Up, upup the stairs. Feeling all the light and shadow in the universe flying about him; holding onto his baby boy who had fallen asleep again on his shoulder at the end of all *that;* nobody wanting to mention Duane's name; nobody wanting to follow up on what had been said; nobody wanting to—; then he had slipped away with his child and begun to climb the stairs, *time to put my baby boy to bed for real* he'd thought and would do now *cause I can do that much and maybe even a whole lot more,* he'd thought, *I got that kinda courage, enough for everybody*—now at the top of the stairs, almost believing his own nervechatter as he thought again too of how that night— fuck yes, that night—he would nuzzle into that space always there between her breasts: always there, warm, dark, rich, deep, for him, he thought; where he could without fail find just enough of himself and know that she would always offer that shared part of the inner life to him without complaint or anger, without inquiry, without demanding too hard what she still thought he, even as far as the sheathed truth stripped naked and lean, could give: once somebody gave up their soul to you, he thought, you could always go back to that part of them where it was safe: that was true, he thought, open- ing the guest bedroom door, feeling his child pressing into him: that space would always be there for that smaller version of himself, he thought, prayed, and was, at least tonight, wasn't it?—smiling that not happy but weary smile as he listened to Jacquie and the others downstairs fussing; thanking something deep within himself for still being able to feel within and without that offered no-questions part of her, as he felt again the rise within of the stranger, the he-without-face or name, placeless, loose, as the grief began to settle over him again: for Duane; grief for whom he had loved, he thought, remembering, grief... For all of them.

Duane who was with him now. Scolding him. Hovering. Admonishing him as he lay the sleeping child down on the star-patterned quilt made by Tamara's Aunt Gannell. His right hand beginning to stroke his baby's sleep- ing cheek as, lowering his face to that other, his left hand folded the broad blue quilt-thickness over the child, who smiled just then as if even from so far away in that dream-forest of tall dandelions through which he was now walking with two tiger-mamas, he felt the long passionate protective kiss his father's mouth and eyes and entire body bestowed upon him. *With him now:* that presence, you, Duane?—that (he couldn't be imagining it, he thought) put a consoling arm about him. *But don't worry,* he mouthed out soundlessly to the darkness, *I ain't gone bring home nothing to make her sick, Duane.* Those deeper eyes watching him in the dark; admonishing, sorrowful. *Aw shit, Duane, you know I just let em suck on me a little no more. Well no the truth like you know sometimes a whole lot more.* Lowering his eyes before the ghost or whatever it was watching, waiting; then bending over his son whom he knew then more than ever he would defend from everything. Everything, Duane. Even you. You the dead and…but now too much to remember, he thought, too many names, faces, things to take in, forget, release…so go on now. Leave. Go on, now, get out!…and then the thing, whatever it was or once had been, sorrowful, longing, mute, and invisible as every other fallen body in that infinite outer and inner world, vanished into the darkness, and with that vanishing he knew it would appear no more.

Jacquie's footsteps on the stairs he thought. Thinking (knowing? more than ever? praying) he didn't need Duane nor nobody to tell him what was right nor how to take care of his own family. How to protect them and himself and everybody. Didn't need no ghost to tell him nor no faggot screaming up in no church neither. I'm the one, he thought, the main one up on it, he thought; sensing Jacquie slip through the door behind him as she came up and squeezed a hand deep into the exhausted sunken field of his left shoulder. Before she sat down next to him on the bed for what he knew would be the beginning of a long something-or-other between them, a meeting of lips and lipstick, he pressed the covering in more tightly around Gregory Jr. and thought with some surprise *He's mine   I made him I ain't never gone let nobody not nobody hurt him.* (She'd begun to massage his neck, he'd begun to give himself over to her, and aw yes, girl, all right, now. Yes.) Not nobody. Not no vicious gossip nor what nobody says. I'ma keep y'all safe from that, he thought. As sure as he knew his name and who he was. (He had always known his name, he thought, who he was.) Keep them very safe from ghosts and secrets and redrooms filled with:—*it wasn't safe,* some other ghost had once hissed into his innermost parts: *notsafe notsafe. Wasn't safe that time,* another had said, *who wants to be safe?*—keep them secure from all that and much more, he thought, lowering the grief-veil in his eyes as he gave what remained of him, the closures and the fells, into her openings: I got it all under control right here, he thought, stroking she who was with him now alive, Jesus, amen, yes: the other hand caressing his child: knowing now for all time in that darkness that this silence and shadow were *it*, where they had always lived, would continue to live: where he would keep them with every power possible, *safesafe*: now there and falling back into the dark above the world where the dead and the ghosts slept and rose, walked, searching: his hands there now clasping them the living and the flesh and the protected hot blood to his chest tight tighttight, for that time and ever after shielded from that outer world of lies, safe from other people's eyes, he thought. Safe from the truth.

Charles Wright

Charles Wright was born in Pickwick Dam, Tennessee, in 1935 and grew up in Kingsport, Tennessee, near Knoxville. He attended Davidson College in North Carolina, where he majored in history. In 1957, Wright entered the army and was sent to Verona, Italy, as a member of a counterintelligence unit. After his army tour, he studied at the University of Rome and attended the Iowa Writers' Workshop. In 1966, he began teaching at the University of California at Irvine, returning to Italy two years later as a Fulbright Scholar. He has since taught at the University of Iowa, Columbia University, Princeton University, and the Universita degli Studi in Florence, Italy. He joined the faculty at the University of Virginia at Charlottesville in 1983, where he is currently Souder Family Professor of English. His first book, *The Grave of the Right Hand* was published in 1970, which was followed by *Hard Freight*, *China Trace*, and *Country Music: Selected Early Poems*, which earned Wright the National Book Award. In the 1990s, Wright was one of America's most honored poets, winning virtually every major award for such books as *The World of the Ten Thousand Things*, *Chickamauga,* and *Black Zodiac*. His latest book, *A Short History of the Shadow,* was released in 2002. His poem "Basic Dialogue" appeared in *The Kenyon Review* in 1997.

Basic Dialogue *(1997)*

by Charles Wright

The transformation of objects in space,

                                        or objects in time,

To objects outside either, but tactile, still precise...

It's always the same problem—

Nothing's more abstract, more unreal,

                                        than what we actually see.

The job is to make it otherwise.

Two dead crepe myrtle bushes,

                                tulips petal-splayed and swan-stemmed,

All blossoms gone from the blossoming trees—the new loss

Is not like old loss,

Winter-kill, a jubilant revelation, an artificial thing

Linked and lifted by pure description into the other world.

Self-oblivion, sacred information, God's nudge—

I think I'll piddle around by the lemon tree, thorns

Sharp as angel's teeth.

                        I think

I'll lie down in the dandelions, the purple and white violets.

I think I'll keep on lying there, one eye cocked toward heaven.

April eats from my fingers,

                                nibble of dogwood, nip of pine.

Now is the time, Lord.

Syllables scatter across the new grass, in search of their words.

Such minor Armageddons.

Beside the waters of disremembering,

                                        I lay me down.

Ruth Stone

Ruth Stone was born in 1915 in Roanoke, Virginia, but moved as a child to Indianapolis, Indiana. At age nineteen, Stone moved to Illinois with her first husband. While there, she met and married the poet and novelist Walter Stone. The couple had three daughters, and the family moved to Vassar College in 1952. Ruth Stone first published poetry in *The Kenyon Review* in 1953. Tragically, while spending time in England in 1959, Walter Stone committed suicide. It was in this same year that Stone's first book of poems, *In an Iridescent Time*, was published. Soon thereafter she was awarded a Kenyon Review Fellowship in Poetry, and with the prize money, Stone bought a house in Vermont, a place she has returned to during the summers between teaching jobs for decades. Stone is famous for her prowess as a teacher of poetry and has taught at a multitude of colleges and universities, including Harvard, Indiana University, the University of California at Davis, New York University, and, most recently, Harpur College. Her poems often deal with death and loss, but point out the humor and beauty that occurs in the midst of tragedy. She is the author of such books as *Cheap, Second-Hand Coat,* and *Who Is the Widow's Muse* and has won numerous awards, including the Delmore Schwartz Award (1983), the Whiting Writer's Award (1986), and the Paterson Poetry Prize (1988). In 2000, she won the National Book Critics Circle Award for her collection *Ordinary Words*. In 2002, at the age of eighty-seven, she was awarded the National Book Award for her eighth collection, *In the Next Galaxy*. Stone retired from teaching as Bartle Professor of English at Harpur College last December. The poems reprinted here span nearly half a century. "Memoir" appeared in *The Kenyon Review* in 1956; "The Word *Though* As a Coupler" and "This Space" appeared in 1999.

The Word *Though* as a Coupler *(1999)*
by Ruth Stone

Though is a thick syllable
a qualifier, a gate slowly opening,
and can be rimmed with replaceable
shark's teeth. Or tongued *although*,
may dance, bursting into esters,
geometric pollen or the chaos
of successful flowers. *Though* as one
and one may lead to love, hate,
or indifference. *Although* can never
quite spit these crucifying nails
and often flutters, exhausted
as snow-pitted vireos; those last
late clutches that survived the up-north
summer; only to be sleeted
on their flyways against the steel
lines of communication towers.

This Space *(1999)*
by Ruth Stone

Rushing past us
faster than this
with a few glitches

everything you love,
like a film
in reverse.

Can this fist
in your skull
hold all that?

Like the leaves of
gloxinia; lobed maps
you cannot read.

their mysterious
patterns; fingerprints
of the universe.

Though you call it
longing, it is
the same need

that clings
in the tidal pool,
that sucks

itself to this rock
within the irresistible vector
of the ocean's pull.

Author Index

About the Editor

David Lynn has been the editor of *The Kenyon Review* since 1994. His novel, *Wrestling with Gabriel*, was released in late 2002. *Fortune Telling*, a collection of stories, appeared in 1998. He is also the author of *The Hero's Tale: Narrators in the Early Modern Novel*, a critical study. His stories and essays have appeared in magazines and journals in America, England, India, and Australia. David Lynn lives in Gambier, Ohio, with his wife, Wendy Singer, and their two children, Aaron and Elizabeth. He is also Professor of English at Kenyon College.